Praise for
THE ROMAN MYSTERIES

'superb detective series set in ancient Rome, where four children from different backgrounds band together to solve mysteries and right wrongs . . . steeped in fantastically interesting and authentic historical detail.'   *Daily Mail*

'instantly accessible adventure . . . which has trans-century appeal'   *Guardian*

'Caroline Lawrence's *The Thieves of Ostia* and its sequel *The Secrets of Vesuvius* are a fresh type of historical novel full of drama and fun . . . This series promises many delights to come.' *The Times*

'*The Secrets of Vesuvius* in the immensely readable Roman Mysteries series by Caroline Lawrence again features a kind of classical famous five . . . An enormous amount of information about the ancient world is conveyed under the guise of a jolly good romp.'   *Times Educational Supplement*

'The wonders of ancient Rome weren't quite so wonderful in my schooldays . . . but this is about to change all that . . . If they liked *Gladiator*, young readers will appreciate this too.'
Belfast Telegraph

To find out more about the Roman Mysteries, visit www.romanmysteries.com

THE ROMAN MYSTERIES
by Caroline Lawrence

THE ROMAN MYSTERIES OMNIBUS

Caroline Lawrence

Orion
Children's Books

This omnibus edition first published in Great Britain in 2005
by Orion Children's Books
a division of the Orion Publishing Group Ltd
Orion House
5 Upper St Martin's Lane
London WC2H 9EA

Originally published as three separate volumes:
The Thieves of Ostia
First published in Great Britain in 2001 by Orion Children's Books
The Secrets of Vesuvius
First published in Great Britain in 2001 by Orion Children's Books
The Pirates of Pompeii
First published in Great Britain in 2001 by Orion Children's Books

Text copyright © Caroline Lawrence 2001
Maps and plans by Richard Russell Lawrence
© Orion Children's Books 2001

1 3 5 7 9 10 8 6 4 2

A catalogue record for this book is
available from the British Library

ISBN 1 84255 503 0

Typeset at The Spartan Press Ltd,
Lymington, Hants

Printed and bound in Great Britain by
Clays Ltd, St Ives plc

www.orionbooks.co.uk

CONTENTS

These stories take place in Ancient Roman times, so a few of the words may look strange.

If you don't know them, 'Aristo's Scroll' at the back of the book will tell you what they mean and how to pronounce them.

THE THIEVES
OF OSTIA

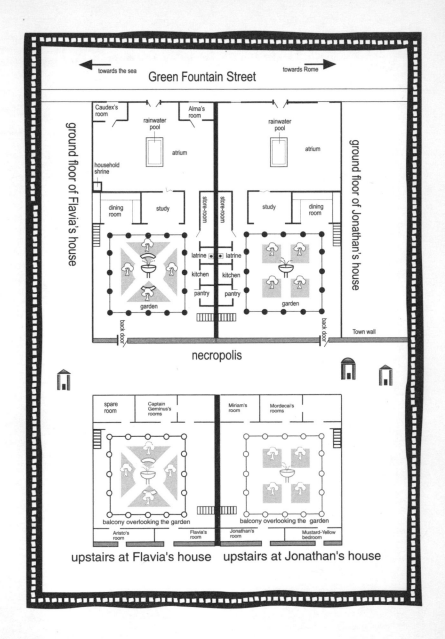

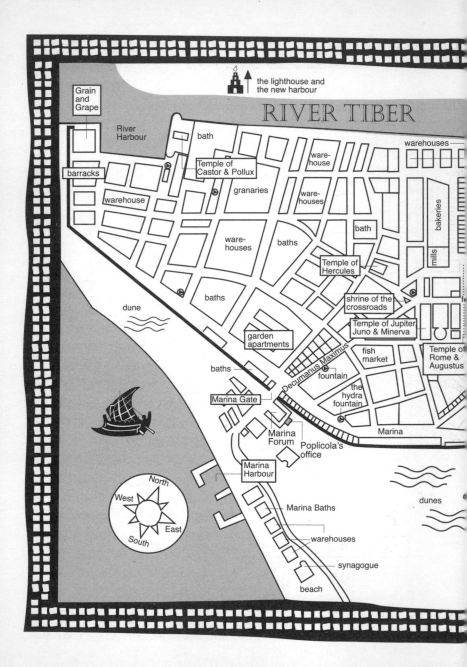

the lighthouse and
the new harbour

RIVER TIBER

Grain
and
Grape

River
Harbour

bath

warehouses

Temple of
Castor & Pollux

ware-
house

warehouses

barracks

granaries

ware-
houses

bakeries

warehouse

bath

mills

ware-
houses

baths

Temple of
Hercules

dune

baths

shrine of the
crossroads

Temple of Jupiter
Juno & Minerva

Temple of
Rome &
Augustus

garden
apartments

fish
market

baths

Decumanus Maximus

fountain

Marina Gate

the
hydra
fountain

Marina
Forum

Marina

Poplicola's
office

North

Marina
Harbour

West

East

South

Marina Baths

dunes

warehouses

synagogue

beach

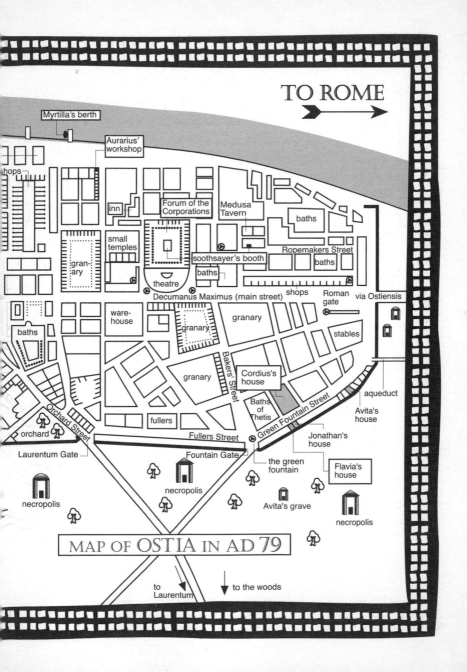

TO ROME

Myrtilla's berth

Aurarius' workshop

shops

inn

Forum of the Corporations

Medusa Tavern

baths

small temples

granary

Ropemakers Street

soothsayer's booth

baths

baths

theatre

Decumanus Maximus (main street)

shops

Roman gate

via Ostiensis

ware-house

granary

granary

baths

stables

granary

Bakers' Street

Cordius's house

aqueduct

fullers

Baths of Thetis

Green Fountain Street

Avita's house

Orchard Street

Fullers Street

Jonathan's house

orchard

Laurentum Gate

Fountain Gate

the green fountain

Flavia's house

necropolis

Avita's grave

necropolis

necropolis

MAP OF OSTIA IN AD 79

to Laurentum

to the woods

To my mother and father,
for all their love and support

SCROLL I

Flavia Gemina solved her first mystery on the Ides of June in the tenth year of the Emperor Vespasian.

She had always had a knack for finding things her father misplaced: his best toga, his quill pen, and once even his ceremonial dagger. But this time there had been a real crime, with a real culprit.

It was a hot, still afternoon, for the sea breeze had not yet risen. Flavia had just settled herself in the garden by the fountain, with a cup of peach juice and her favourite scroll.

'Flavia? Flavia!' Her father's voice came from the study. Flavia took a sip of juice and quickly scanned the scroll to find her place. She would just read one or two lines. After all, the study was so close, just the other side of the fig tree. Her house – like many others in the Roman port of Ostia – had a secret garden at its centre, invisible to anyone on the street. From that inner garden it was only a few steps to the dining room, the kitchen, the storeroom, a small latrine, and the study.

'Flavia!'

She knew that tone of voice.

'Coming, pater!' she called. Hastily, she set down

her cup on the marble bench and placed a pebble on the open scroll to mark her place.

In the study, her father was desperately searching through various scrolls and sheets of parchment on the cedarwood table. Although Marcus Flavius Geminus was extremely competent aboard his own ship, on land he was hopelessly absent-minded.

'Oh pater!' Flavia tried to keep the impatience out of her voice. 'What have you lost now?'

'It isn't lost! It's been stolen!'

'What? What's been stolen?'

'My seal! My amethyst signet-ring! The one your mother gave me!'

'Oh!' She winced. Her mother had died in childbirth several years previously, and they both still missed her desperately.

Flavia touched her father's arm reassuringly. 'Don't worry, pater. I always find things, don't I?'

'Yes. Yes, you do . . .' He smiled down at her, but Flavia could see he was upset.

'Where did you last see it?' she asked.

'Right here on my desk. I was just letting these documents dry before I sealed them.'

Flavia's father planned to sail for Corinth at the end of the week. As a ship owner and captain, it was his responsibility to make sure the paperwork was ready.

'I left the study for just a moment to use the latrine,' he explained. 'When I returned, the ring was gone. Look: the documents are here. The wax is here. The candle is here, still lit. But my ring is gone!'

'It wasn't the wind, there's no hint of a breeze,' Flavia mused, gazing out at the fig tree. 'The slaves are napping in their rooms. Scuto is sleeping under the jasmine bush: he didn't even bark. Yes, it's a mystery.'

'It's one of the few things of hers I have left,' murmured her father. 'And apart from that, I need it to seal these documents.' He ran a hand distractedly through his hair.

Flavia had an idea: 'Pater, do you have another seal?'

'Yes, but I rarely use it. My suppliers might not recognise it . . .'

'But it has Castor and Pollux engraved on it, doesn't it?'

Her father nodded. Castor and Pollux, the mythological twins known as the Gemini, had always been linked to the Geminus family.

'Well then, everyone will know it's yours. Why don't you use that ring to finish sealing the documents, and I'll try to find the stolen one.'

Captain Geminus's face relaxed and he looked at his daughter fondly.

'Thank you, my little owl.' He kissed the top of her head. 'What would I do without you?'

As her father went upstairs to search the chest in his bedroom, Flavia looked around. The study was a small, bright room with red and yellow plaster walls and a cool, marble floor. It was simply furnished with a cedarwood chair, the table which served as a desk, and a bronze standing-lamp. There was also a bust of the Emperor Vespasian on a pink marble column beside the desk.

The study had two doors. One small folding door led into the atrium at the front of the house. On the opposite wall a wide doorway opened directly out onto the inner garden. This could be closed off with a heavy curtain.

Now this curtain was pulled right back, and sunlight from the garden fell directly onto the desk, lighting up the sheets of parchment so that they seemed to glow. A little inkpot blazed silver in the sunshine. It was fixed onto the desk so that it would not go missing. For the same reason, the silver quill pen was attached to the desk by a silver chain. Flavia rolled the chain absently between her thumb and forefinger and observed how it flashed in the direct sunlight.

Suddenly her keen grey eyes noticed something. On one of the sheets of parchment – a list of ships' provisions – was a faint black mark that was neither a letter nor a number. Without touching anything, Flavia moved her face closer, until her nose was inches from the sheet.

No doubt about it. Someone – or something – had touched the ink while it was still tacky and had made this strange V-shaped mark. As she looked closer, Flavia could make out a straight line between the two leaning lines of the V, like the Greek letter *psi*: ᴪ

At that moment, something rustled and flapped in the garden. Flavia glanced up and saw a large black and white bird sitting on a branch of the fig tree: a magpie. The bird turned its head and regarded her with one bright, intelligent eye.

In an instant, Flavia knew she was looking at the thief. She knew magpies loved glittering things. The bird had obviously stepped on the parchment before the ink had dried and then left its footprint.

Now she must discover where its nest was.

Flavia thought quickly. She needed bait; something bright and shiny. Without turning her head or making a sudden movement she surveyed the study. There were various scrolls stored on shelves along the walls, but they were parchment or papyrus, and their dangling labels only leather. The wax tablets on the desk were too big for the bird to carry and the little bronze oil-lamp too heavy.

There was only one thing she could think of to tempt the bird. Slowly she reached up to her throat and undid the clasp of a silver chain. Like every freeborn Roman boy or girl, Flavia wore a special amulet around her neck. One day, when she married, she would dedicate this bulla to the gods of the crossroads.

But for now, the chain it hung on would serve another useful purpose. Slipping the bulla into the coin purse which hung from her belt, she carefully set the chain in a pool of sunlight. It sparkled temptingly.

Slowly, Flavia backed out of the study and squeezed past the folding door into the cool, dim atrium. As soon as she was out of the magpie's sight, she crept along the short corridor which led back to the garden.

Peeping round the corner, she was just in time to see the magpie fly down into the study. Flavia held her breath and prayed her father would not come back and disturb the bird.

A moment later the magpie flew back up onto a branch, the chain dangling from its beak like a glittering worm. It remained there for a moment looking around, then flew away over the red-tiled roof to the south, towards the graveyard.

Flavia ran through the garden and opened the small back door. For an instant she hesitated.

She knew the heavy bolt would fall back into place behind her and she would be locked out. If she went through the doorway she would leave the protection not only of her home, but of Ostia: her house was built into the town wall.

Furthermore, the door led directly into the necropolis, the 'city of the dead', with its many tombs and graves scattered among the trees, and her father had warned her never to go there.

But she had promised to find his ring: the ring her mother had given him.

Flavia took a deep breath and stepped out. The door shut behind her and she heard the bolt fall. There was no going back now.

She was just in time to glimpse a flutter of glossy black and white as the bird flew to a tall umbrella pine. She ran quickly and quietly, keeping the trunk of a large cypress tree between herself and the feathered thief.

The magpie flew off again and Flavia ran to the pine tree. Peeping out from behind it, she saw nothing; no movement anywhere. Her heart sank.

Then she saw it. In an old oak near a large tomb something flashed. Something flashed black and white. It was the magpie. It had popped up from the trunk of the oak like a cork ball in a pond, and its beak was empty!

For a few minutes the magpie preened itself smugly, no doubt pleased at its afternoon's haul. Presently it hopped onto a higher branch, cocked its head for a moment and flew back towards the north, probably to see if there was any treasure left in her house.

Flavia dodged among the tombs and trees and reached the old oak in no time. The bark was rough and scratched her hands but its roughness helped her to get a good grip. She went up it with little difficulty.

When she reached the place where the trunk forked into branches, her eyes opened in amazement: a small treasure trove of bright objects glittered there. Her chain lay on top. And there was her father's signet-ring! With a silent prayer of thanks to Castor and Pollux, she slipped the ring and chain into her drawstring coin purse.

Digging deeper, she found three silver bangles and a gold earring. Flavia put these in her purse as well, but decided to leave an assortment of cheap copper chains and earrings; they had gone green with age. With her fingertip she gingerly pushed aside some glittery shards of Alexandrian glass. Beneath them, right at the bottom, lay another earring, which was still bright and yellow. Heavy, too: it was gold. It had three tiny gold chains with a pearl dangling at the end of each, and it was set with a large emerald. Flavia marvelled at its beauty before slipping this earring into her coin purse, too.

Now she must go quickly, before the big magpie returned. She was just about to ease herself down when a noise made her hesitate. It was an odd, panting sound.

She looked nervously at the large tomb a few yards to her right. It was shaped like a small house, with a little arched roof and door. She reckoned it might hold as many as twenty funeral urns, filled with the ashes of the dead.

But the panting did not come from the tomb. It came from directly below her.

Flavia looked down, and her heart skipped a beat. At the foot of the tree were at least half a dozen wild dogs, all staring hungrily up at her!

SCROLL II

Flavia's knees began to tremble uncontrollably. She held onto the tree so tightly her knuckles went white. She must be calm. She must think. Glancing down at the wild dogs again she decided there was only one rational thing to do.

Flavia Gemina screamed.

Although her hands were shaking, she managed to pull herself back up onto a branch. Below her the dogs whined and growled.

'HELP!' she yelled. 'Help me, someone!'

The only response was the rhythmic chirring of cicadas in the afternoon heat.

'Help me!' she shouted, and then, in case someone heard her but didn't think to look up, 'I'm in a tree!'

Most of the dogs were now sitting at the base of the trunk, panting and gazing up at her. They seemed to be smiling at her predicament. There were seven of them, most of them mangy and thin and yellow. The leader was a huge black hound – a mastiff – with evil red eyes and saliva dripping down his hairy chin.

'Stupid dogs!' Flavia muttered under her breath. The leader growled, almost as if he had understood her thoughts.

Suddenly, one of the yellow dogs yelped and leapt to

his feet, as if stung by a bee. Then the leader snarled and writhed in pain. A stone had struck him! Flavia saw the next stone fly through the air, and then another, striking with amazing accuracy. The dogs whimpered and yelped and slunk off into the woods.

'Quickly!' a voice called from below. 'Come down quickly before they come back!'

Flavia didn't think twice. She closed her eyes and jumped out of the tree.

'Ouch! My ankle!' Flavia started to run, but a stab of pain shot through her leg and almost made her sick. A boy about her own age ran out from behind a tree. He put his arm awkwardly around her waist and pulled her forward.

'Come *on*!' he urged, and she could see that his dark eyes were full of fear. 'Quickly!'

With each step the pain eased a bit, but they were not moving quickly. They had almost reached the umbrella pine when the boy looked back, stopped, and reached towards his belt.

'Hang on to the tree!' he commanded, pushing Flavia forward. He pulled out his sling, and reached into a leather pouch which hung from his belt. Fitting a sharp stone into the sling he moved a few feet away and swung it quickly round his head. Flavia gripped the tree and closed her eyes. She heard the sling buzz like an angry wasp. Then a dog's yelp and a satisfied 'Got him!' from the boy.

'Come on!' he urged. 'The leader's down but I don't think I killed him. They'll probably be after us in a minute!'

Flavia took a deep breath and moved as quickly as she could. Dry thistles scratched her legs and the boy's strong grip hurt her as he half lifted, half pulled her forward.

Suddenly the boy cried out in a language Flavia had never heard before.

They were nearly at her back door. But the boy was leading her away from it, to the right.

'No! My house is there!' she protested.

The boy ignored her and called out again in his harsh language. He was pulling her to the back door of the house next to hers. He glanced back and muttered something in Latin which Flavia understood perfectly. It was not a polite word.

She heard the dogs barking behind her. The boy pulled her more urgently and she could hear him gasping for breath. The door was closer; now she could see its rough surface beneath the peeling green paint. But by the sound of it, the pack was nearly upon them. At any moment she expected to feel sharp teeth sink into her calf.

Suddenly, the green door swung open. A tall, black-robed figure emerged, pointed at the dogs and bellowed something in an unknown language.

For an instant the dogs stopped dead in their tracks. That instant was enough for the tall figure to grab them both, pull them through the open door and slam it in the dogs' startled faces.

Flavia sobbed with relief. Strong arms held her tight and the rough cloth against her nose smelled spicy and comforting.

Abruptly a dog's cold nose pressed into her armpit. Flavia screamed again and jumped back. A pretty white dog with brown eyes grinned up at her, its entire rear end wagging with delight.

'Bobas! Down! Go away! *Bad* dog!' said the man in black sternly. Bobas took no notice and gave Flavia a long, slobbery kiss.

At this Flavia began to giggle through her tears. This was the dog she had heard barking for the past week, since the mysterious family had moved in to old Festus's house. She sniffed and wiped her runny nose with her arm. Then she stepped back to have a good look at her rescuer.

'Allow me to introduce myself,' said the man in a pleasantly accented voice. 'My name is Mordecai ben Ezra and this is my son Jonathan.' He gave a very slight bow. 'Peace be with you.'

Flavia looked at the boy who had saved her life.

Jonathan was bent over, resting his hands on his knees and breathing hard. He had a rather square face and masses of curly hair. He looked up at her, grinned and also nodded, but seemed unable to speak.

'Miriam!' the boy's father called. 'Bring the oil of marjoram quickly!' And almost apologetically to Flavia: 'My son is somewhat asthmatic.'

Jonathan's father had a sharp nose and a short grizzled beard. Two long grey ringlets of hair emerged from a black turban wound around his head. He looked very exotic and even odd, but his heavy-lidded eyes were kind.

A beautiful girl of about thirteen ran up with a tiny

clay jar. She uncorked it and held it under Jonathan's nose.

'This is my daughter Miriam,' said Mordecai proudly. 'Miriam, this is . . .'

They all looked at her.

'Flavia. Flavia Gemina, daughter of Marcus Flavius Geminus, sea captain,' she said, and added: 'Your next door neighbour.'

'Flavia Gemina, will you come into the garden and have a drink and tell us how you came to be pursued by a pack of angry dogs?'

'Yes,' said Flavia, but as she stepped forward, she gasped with pain.

'Your ankle.' Mordecai bent and probed Flavia's swollen right ankle. She winced again, though his fingers were cool and gentle.

'Come. I'm a doctor.' And before she could protest, he had lifted her off her feet and was carrying her in his arms. Jonathan followed, breathing easier now but still holding the oil of marjoram under his nose.

The doctor carried Flavia through a leafy inner garden towards the study. Although the house was laid out exactly like hers, it was a different world. Every surface was covered with multi-coloured carpets and cushions. In the study, instead of a desk and chair, there was a long striped divan going right round the walls. Mordecai set her on this long couch against several embroidered cushions which smelled faintly of some exotic spice: cinnamon, perhaps.

'Miriam, please bring some water, some clean strips of linen and some balm – the Syrian, not the Greek . . .'

'Yes, father,' the girl replied, and then said something in the strange language.

'Please speak Latin in front of our guest,' Mordecai chided gently.

'Yes, father,' she said again, and went out of the room.

'Jonathan,' said the doctor, 'would you prepare some mint tea?'

'Yes, father,' said the boy, breathing easier.

Flavia continued to look round in wonder. There were only three or four shelves of scrolls in her father's study. Here the walls above the divan were covered with them. Nearby, on a carved wooden stand, was the most beautiful open scroll Flavia had ever seen. It was made of creamy, thick parchment and covered with strange black and red letters. Beneath it lay a richly embroidered silk cover of scarlet, blue, gold and black.

Mordecai followed her gaze, then moved over to the scroll.

'We are Jews and this is our holy book,' he said softly. He kissed his fingertips and almost touched the scroll. 'The Torah. I was reading it when I heard my son call.' He rolled it up and reverently slipped it into its silk cover.

Miriam reappeared with a bowl and pitcher, and to Flavia's surprise she began to wash her feet. Jonathan's sister had dark curls like her brother, but her skin was pale and her violet eyes were grave.

While Miriam was drying Flavia's feet, Jonathan came in with four steaming cups on a tray. He handed one to Flavia, who sniffed its minty aroma and gratefully sipped the strong, sweet brew.

Meanwhile, Mordecai applied ointment to her inflamed ankle and began to bind it securely with strips of linen.

'Tell us your story, please,' he said as he worked.

'Well, I was up in the tree when the dogs came and I knew I could never get past them but your son scared them away and . . and I think he saved my life.' Flavia felt as if she were going to cry again so she took a large gulp of mint tea.

'And may I ask what a Roman girl of good birth was doing up a tree in the middle of a graveyard?' asked Mordecai as he tied off the last strip of linen and patted Flavia's ankle.

'I was looking for the magpie's nest. And I found treasure! I found two gold earrings, and three silver bangles, and got my chain back, and of course my father's . . .' Flavia stopped short. 'Oh no! My father will be worried sick! He has probably sent Caudex out to look for me by now! Oh, I must go home straight away!' She set her cup on a low table.

'Of course,' smiled Mordecai. 'Your ankle was only twisted. It should be fine in a day or two. Jonathan, have you recovered sufficiently to escort this young lady next door?'

'Yes, father,' replied Jonathan.

Together they eased Flavia off the couch and helped her hobble through the atrium. Miriam followed behind. At the front door Flavia turned.

'Goodbye! And thank you! I'm sorry I didn't finish the tea. It was delicious!'

'Peace be with you,' said Mordecai and Miriam together. Each gave a little bow as Jonathan helped

Flavia out of the door and along the pavement to her house.

Lifting the familiar bronze knocker of Castor and Pollux, Flavia rapped sharply several times. From deep within she heard Scuto barking and after what seemed like ages the peephole opened and she saw Caudex's bleary eyes staring out. It was a full minute before the sleepy doorkeeper managed to slide the bolt back and pull the door open.

'Pater! *Pater*!' Flavia cried. Jonathan followed curiously as she pushed past Caudex and her bouncing dog. 'Where are you, pater!' she called.

'Here in the study, my dear.' Her father did not sound very worried.

'Pater! I'm here! I've found the ring and I'm safe!' She limped through the folding door, coming up to her father from behind.

Marcus sat bent over the desk, carefully dripping wax on a document.

'And why shouldn't you be safe?' he asked absently, pressing a ring into the hot wax.

'PATER!'

Her father turned round and then jumped to his feet.

'Great Neptune's beard!' he cried. 'What's happened to you? Look at yourself! Your arms are scratched, your hair full of twigs, your tunic torn and dirty, and – and your ankle is bandaged! Whatever happened?'

He peered past her suspiciously.

'And who, may I ask, is this?'

SCROLL III

Ostia, the port of Rome and the town where Flavia lived, was occasionally foggy in the early mornings. And so it was on the morning of Flavia's birthday, three days after she had found the magpie's nest. As a birthday treat, her father had agreed to take her to the goldsmith, to see how much she could get for her little treasure trove.

They left the house shortly after dawn and the mist swirled around them as they walked up Bakers Street towards the river.

'Pater, why can't we go to the town forum? There's a man who buys jewellery there . . .'

'I told you before. You will get a better deal from Aurarius the goldsmith. He is a friend of mine and he will not cheat you, as that perfumed Phoenician in the forum will certainly do. Have you got everything?'

Flavia touched the soft leather coin purse tied to her belt. It contained the objects she had found in the magpie's nest. She was hoping to sell them and buy a set of all twelve scrolls of the *Aeneid*, a book she had always wanted. She had recently seen a set in the forum at the bookseller's stall. It was a beautiful parchment version with illustrations. But the bookseller was asking a vast sum: one hundred sesterces. Flavia hardly dared hope the jewellery in her purse would fetch that amount.

They crossed the Decumanus Maximus carefully. Because it was the town's main street as well as the road to Rome, it was usually covered with horse and donkey dung. There were no handy stepping stones, as in some other Roman towns, but Flavia and her father crossed without mishap. They passed the theatre and the forum of the corporations on their left and stopped to press themselves against the wall of a tavern as a mule-drawn cart rattled down the narrow street.

As they approached the river, the fog grew thicker and damper. The tops of the tall brick warehouses were not even visible as they passed beneath them. Flavia shivered and pulled her woollen cloak closer around her shoulders. Ostia had three harbours: a little marina for Ostia's fishing boats, pleasure craft and smaller merchantmen, a large harbour for the massive grain ships from Egypt, and the river harbour between the two. Here vessels could unload and either have their cargoes towed by barge up to Rome or stored in warehouses. Flavia and her father turned left at the river and walked past these warehouses as they made for Aurarius's workshop.

Above her, unseen gulls wheeled and cried peevishly in the fog, and she heard the creak of timber and clink of ships' tackle to her right. The wooden quay was damp beneath her leather boots.

Figures loomed up out of the mist, terrifying men with broken noses, mangled ears and meaty arms. Some had lost arms or hands or legs. But their ugly faces always broke into grins when they saw her father, and they invariably greeted him politely.

Suddenly, Flavia heard a sound which chilled her blood: the crack of a whip and clink of chains. Out of the mist emerged a pitiful sight: a line of women, naked and chained at the neck. Most of them seemed to be Egyptian or Syrian, but one or two were dark-skinned Africans. Their heads had been shaved and they were terribly thin. Some had open sores.

Flavia could hear their teeth chattering, but otherwise they were totally silent. Apart from their iron collars and chains, they wore nothing but crude wooden tags with prices scrawled on them.

The whip cracked again and out of the mist came the person Flavia feared most in the world: Venalicius, the slave-dealer. There were many rumours about Venalicius, the most recent that he had kidnapped a nine-year-old girl named Sapphira and sold her to a Syrian merchant. This was illegal, but once a child had fallen into Venalicius' hands and his ship had sailed, there was virtually no way of ever finding the child again, or of proving the slave-dealer's guilt.

Venalicius had one blind eye: a horrible, milky orb that sat in its socket like a peeled egg. His teeth were rotten and his nose sprouted tufts of mouldy hair. Worst of all, one ear was missing, bitten off by a slave he had afterwards crucified, if the rumour was true. The wound still seeped a horrible yellow pus. Once, Venalicius had whispered to Flavia when her father wasn't looking: 'I'll make a slave of you, too, my dear, if I ever catch you!'

Flavia shivered again and averted her eyes. But just

as she did, she noticed a figure at the end of the line. It was a dark-skinned girl about her own age. She was not weeping, but her beautiful amber eyes looked blank with despair. Her hands hung limp by her side, not bothering to cover her nakedness. Around her neck – beneath the iron collar – hung a wooden plaque with six C's scrawled crudely upon it.

'Six hundred,' whispered Flavia to herself.

In a moment the girl had disappeared along with the others into the mist, as Venalicius drove them into town.

Flavia and her father moved silently on, both subdued by the sight of the slaves.

'Pater, what will happen to them?' Flavia asked presently.

'You know what happens to slaves,' her father replied quietly. 'Those women don't look terribly healthy and unless they speak Latin they'll end up doing menial work: cleaning, sewing . . . Perhaps some of them will become cooks, if they're lucky.'

'Like Alma?'

'Yes, like your nurse Alma.'

'Pater . . .' Flavia took a deep breath: 'Pater, what will happen to the girl?'

There was such a long pause she thought he would not answer her. Her father guided her carefully around a mound of silver fish spilling from a yellow net. Then:

'She may become a lady's maid. Or a cook's assistant. Or perhaps someone will buy her for a wife,' he said quietly.

'A wife!' cried Flavia in horror. 'But she's my age!'

'Perhaps a bit older. You know that eleven or twelve is not too old for slaves to marry.'

Flavia said nothing more until they reached Aurarius's shop. It was at the end of a row of brick workshops built against one of the large warehouses along the waterfront. Tatters of fog swirled around the shop and the roof of the warehouse above it was swallowed in the mist.

The goldsmith Aurarius – a wizened, slightly cross-eyed man – looked up from his charcoal brazier and greeted them cheerfully. A big watchdog dozed at his feet.

The smith examined the contents of Flavia's pouch with interest.

'Hmmm. The bangles are nice but not worth more than two or three sesterces. This earring is lovely. It's made of electrum. Mixture of gold and silver which can be melted down. I'll give you a hundred and fifty sesterces for it . . .'

He emptied the last object from the purse into his palm and his eyes widened. He glanced up at Flavia's father and then brought the earring almost to the tip of his nose.

'This one with the emerald is really special,' he said. 'Pure gold, maybe Greek manufacture, and one of the finest stones I've ever seen. Too bad you don't have its mate. The pair would be worth eight or nine hundred sesterces. But on its own I could only offer you four hundred . . .'

He looked gravely at Flavia.

'Your father's done me many favours, so tell you

what: I'll give you six hundred sesterces for all four pieces. It's a fair price. You won't get better.'

'I'll take it,' said Flavia immediately, and held out a trembling hand to receive six gold coins, each worth a hundred sesterces. It was an enormous sum.

Flavia's heart was pounding as she slipped the coins into her pouch. She turned to her father.

'Pater, may we go to the forum right away? I know what I want to buy for my birthday.'

The mist cleared as they made their way to the central town forum and the soft blue sky promised a perfect day. Flavia walked quickly through the fish market, past fishmongers boasting loudly about their red mullet, sole and squid. She hurried past the fruit-sellers who were hawking their pomegranates, melons and peaches; past the jewellery stall, the toy stall, the pottery stall and the clothes stall. She did not even glance at the book stall as she passed. As they entered the forum, she walked so fast that her father had to hurry to keep up with her.

By the time Flavia Gemina approached the slave stall she was almost running. She looked around anxiously and then let out her breath.

'Thank goodness, she's still there!'

Wedged between a banker's stall and a public scribe's, in the shadow of the temple of Rome and Augustus, was a slightly raised wooden stage. The slave women she had seen earlier stood on this platform while Venalicius strutted up and down before them, shouting out their virtues. Already a crowd was gathering to look and prod and poke the slaves, who were still completely naked.

'How can they treat them like that? Like animals,' murmured Flavia. Untying her coin purse, she began to move forward.

Her father's firm hand on her shoulder stopped her short.

'Let me handle this,' he warned. 'Venalicius might try to take advantage of you. He can smell a serious buyer from half a mile away. He might raise his price or even double it.'

'He can't *do* that! Can he?'

'He can do whatever he likes until she is sold,' replied her father gravely. 'Keep back. Out of sight.'

Flavia handed the leather purse to her father and stepped back behind one of the marble pillars of the colonnade. Captain Geminus pushed through the crowd and began to walk casually up and down the line. Flavia noticed that the price for the girl was double the price of most of the other women, and she shivered in the morning sunshine.

'Ah, the young sea captain: Marcus Flavius Geminus! Are you a serious buyer, or just looking?' sneered Venalicius. Flavia saw her father's back stiffen, but he moved on quietly.

'How much is this one?' she heard him ask as he stopped in front of a red-eyed young woman in her late teens.

'Three hundred sesterces. Can't you read?' snapped the slave-dealer.

Another man, a soldier, had stopped in front of the girl. Flavia held her breath. She saw the soldier reach out and open the girl's mouth to examine her teeth. Then he bent and peered at the price round her neck.

He stood again and looked at the girl, who stared straight ahead. Flavia's fingernails dug into her palm.

Abruptly, the soldier shook his head and moved on. Flavia slowly let out her breath in a huge sigh of relief. 'Hurry, pater!' she whispered to herself.

As the soldier walked off, her father indicated the girl and said calmly to Venalicius, 'I'll take this one please.'

'Just a moment,' smirked the slave-dealer, 'I'm dealing with another customer.' He made a great pretence of helping a fat merchant in a grubby toga who was examining another woman.

That slave-dealer is torturing me on purpose! thought Flavia to herself. And then: oh please, Castor and Pollux, let me be able to buy her.

After what seemed like ages the fat merchant turned away, making a joke to a friend. The two of them went off laughing. Venalicius turned at last to her father.

'Yes, Captain Geminus?'

'I'd like to buy this girl,' repeated her father.

The slave-dealer raised his ugly head and seemed to look around the crowded marketplace with his horrible blind eye. Flavia ducked back behind the marble column and pressed her cheek against its reassuring solidness.

Then she heard Venalicius say very clearly to her father, 'The African girl costs seven hundred sesterces.'

SCROLL IV

The price-tag around the slave-girl's neck read six hundred, but now Venalicius was asking for seven! Flavia wanted to shout that it wasn't fair. Instead, she bit her lip and swallowed her protest. Tears blurred her vision. She had been so close to saving the girl. So close to having someone her own age to be with. So close to . . .

'Very well,' she heard her father say in a matter-of-fact voice. 'Here you are.'

Flavia did not dare break the spell by looking. She shut her eyes tight and held her breath.

A minute later she heard the slave-dealer call out mockingly: 'I hope she serves you well, Captain!'

Flavia opened her eyes and peeked around the column. Her father was moving through the crowd, and the girl was with him. Flavia ran to meet them.

'Pater! The extra hundred sesterces! The gold in my bag was only worth six hundred!'

'I paid the extra amount.'

'But so much, pater!'

'You are forgetting that today is special. Happy birthday, my dear.'

Flavia threw her arms round her father and hugged him tightly. She wanted to hug the girl, too, and tell her everything was going to be all right now, but something about the slave-girl's empty look stopped her. Instead Flavia slipped off her cloak and gently wrapped it around the girl's naked body.

Then they took her home.

Later that morning, Flavia made an important discovery: the slave-girl she had bought spoke no Latin, and only a little Greek.

The girl had said nothing on the way home, or when Flavia had bathed the sores on her neck with a sea sponge and applied some of Mordecai's soothing aloe balm. But after Flavia had taken her up to her bedroom and dressed her in a soft yellow tunic, the girl had looked up timidly at Flavia and recited in a faltering voice:

'Greetings. My name is Nubia. How may I please you?'

'Hello, Nubia! I'm Flavia Gemina, daughter of Marcus Flavius Geminus, sea captain!'

Nubia looked at her blankly and then repeated: 'Greetings. My name is Nubia. How may I please you?'

Flavia realised the girl didn't understand the words she was reciting. She probably didn't know any Latin at all.

'Flavia,' said Flavia slowly, pointing at herself. 'I am Flavia.'

'Flavia,' repeated Nubia haltingly.

'Yes! Are you hungry, Nubia?'

Nubia looked blank. Flavia opened her mouth and pointed inside. The girl started back with horror.

Flavia pretended to chew something.

Nubia's eyes lit up and she nodded.

'Come on then! Let's go down to the kitchen and see what Alma is cooking!' Flavia quickly reached for Nubia's hand but the girl drew back with a frightened expression.

Flavia remembered that when she first got Scuto he also cringed at any sudden movement. Her father said it was because he had been beaten.

'Don't be afraid! Come!' said Flavia and moved slowly towards the doorway of her bedroom.

Nubia followed hesitantly as they went down the wooden stairs, past the sunny garden, and into the small kitchen.

Alma, Flavia's former nursemaid, had recently taken over kitchen duties. The previous cook, Gusto, had died shopping for leeks in the forum when a donkey kicked him in the head.

Alma had proved to be an excellent cook, and was daily growing plumper from sampling her own recipes. She was tasting something at that very moment, leaning over the glowing ashes on the kitchen hearth with a spoon half poised above a steaming pan. Flavia greeted her and then introduced Nubia.

'Alma, this is Nubia. Nubia, this is Alma: she used to be my nurse.'

'Welcome, Nubia,' beamed the cook. Normally she would have thrown her arms around such a sad-looking creature and given her a warm embrace, but she had been alerted to treat the new slave gently. Even Scuto had been shut away in the storeroom for the time being.

'I'm just cooking your birthday dinner,' said Alma,

'so I can't stop to chat. But I've prepared some fruit and bread. Take it into the garden.' She handed Flavia a platter laid out with various fruits and a flat round loaf of bread.

Nubia pointed to a date and said 'date' very softly in Greek.

'Yes! That's the Greek word for date!' said Flavia. 'Do you understand Greek? Do you want a date?' And then in Greek, 'Take one!'

Nubia looked at her in awe and disbelief. Slowly she reached out her hand and took a date. She closed her eyes as she ate it and a look of pure delight passed over her lovely face.

'Have much.' Flavia's Greek was not very fluent. She had only been studying it for two years. Now she wished she had worked harder at it.

'Have big date!' she tried again. Nubia understood and solemnly took another date.

'Let's go . . . garden,' said Flavia, when she had remembered the Greek word for garden. She led the way to her favourite seat by the fountain.

Nubia stared in amazement at the spout of water shooting up from the copper pipe in the centre of the marble basin. Slowly she put her finger in it, then quickly withdrew it as if she had been burned.

'Water!' she said in Greek, and then, 'I drink?'

'Yes! You can drink it!' cried Flavia in delight. And demonstrated the fact.

Nubia drank, too, for a long time and then turned back to the plate. They sat on the marble bench, and together they named the foods: bread, date, peach, grapes, apples. Then Nubia set down to eating in earnest. She had two pieces of bread, a bunch of grapes, half an apple and a whole peach. Finally she ate up every date on the plate.

'You like dates?' said Flavia.

'Yes like dates,' replied Nubia with her mouth quite full.

'Better stop. Enough,' said Flavia in Greek. And then, reverting to Latin, 'I'm having a birthday dinner party in a few hours and there will be lots of delicious food. Jonathan from next door is coming, and his father Mordecai and his sister Miriam and my father, of course, and you're coming too, so don't eat too much.'

Nubia gazed solemnly at Flavia.

'Lots more later good food,' said Flavia in Greek, with a sigh, and wished again that she had paid more attention during lessons with her tutor Aristo.

Flavia was determined that her birthday dinner party would be a success. Her plan was to have Nubia recline next to Miriam, who seemed so quiet and gentle. She herself would lie on the same couch as Jonathan, and her father and Mordecai would take the third couch.

'No,' said her father firmly, 'I'm afraid it's no good.'

'Why not, pater?'

'First of all, you're not old enough to recline at dinner yet . . .'

Flavia started to protest but he held up his hand and smiled.

'If it were just a family gathering, I would let you recline. But it's not. Furthermore, you told me our next door neighbours are foreigners. From Judaea, was it?'

Flavia nodded.

'Well, they might not feel comfortable reclining. Better to sit, don't you think, my little owl?' He ruffled her hair affectionately.

'Yes, pater,' she sighed.

'Also,' said Captain Geminus, 'did you know that when a mistress invites her slave to recline, it means she is granting that slave her freedom?'

Flavia shook her head.

'At least wait until Nubia has learned enough Latin to find her way around Ostia before you set her free,' he said with a smile.

So Flavia modified her plan and her seating arrangement.

The six of them sat around a large oval table which Caudex and her father had carried in from the atrium. Flavia seated Nubia next to Miriam, and was glad to see Jonathan's sister give the African girl a warm smile.

When her guests were seated, Flavia handed out garlands of ivy and violets which she had made herself. Mordecai balanced his garland on top of his white turban and didn't seem to mind when Jonathan and Flavia giggled at him.

Captain Geminus poured the wine, well-watered for the children, and they all toasted Flavia's health. Nubia wrinkled her pretty nose when she first tasted the wine, but soon took another sip.

After the toast there was an awkward silence. The doctor sat stiffly in a green silk kaftan while her father fiddled with the folds of his toga. Flavia glanced anxiously towards the kitchen, wondering what was keeping Alma. Jonathan whistled a little tune under his breath and then winked at Flavia.

Finally, Alma proudly carried in the first course and set it on the table: sea snails fried in olive oil, garlic and pepper. The snails had been placed back in their shells and Alma handed each diner a special spoon with a small hook at one end to extract the snail.

'Are we permitted to eat these, father?' whispered Jonathan, gazing in dismay at the creatures.

'God has made all things clean,' his father murmured, and politely took a snail.

Flavia showed Jonathan how to extract a snail and then watched as he gingerly picked up one of the shells between finger and thumb and hooked out its contents. He paused to examine it: the snail was small and twisted and rubbery and brown. Jonathan closed his eyes, took a deep breath and put it in his mouth.

He chewed.

He opened his eyes.

He smiled.

'Mmmm!' he beamed, and eagerly finished off the rest. Under the stern gaze of her father, Miriam also made a brave attempt. Nubia, imitating Flavia to see how it was done, ate up every snail on her plate.

Jonathan wiped his hands on his tunic, which already had a dribble of garlic oil down the front. Then he drained his wine cup with a smack of his lips. Nubia, watching him carefully, also wiped her hands on her tunic and smacked as she drained her wine cup.

Flavia smiled.

'For our next course we're having dormice stuffed with chopped sows' udders,' she announced brightly.

Mordecai and his children froze in horror.

Nubia looked blank.

'Flavia . . .' said her father with a warning look.

'Just joking,' giggled Flavia. 'My favourite food is really roast chicken. You do like roast chicken, don't you?'

After that the party perked up nicely. Everyone relaxed and laughed and ate up their roast chicken and told stories about the most revolting food they had ever been offered.

Mordecai had once found a sheep's eyeball in his stew while dining with a camel trader in Judaea. Flavia's father had devoured a delicious fish soup in the port of Massilia and discovered a rotten fish head at the bottom of his bowl. Just last week, Miriam had deeply offended her host by refusing to eat three roast quail whose tiny charred heads dangled woefully. And Flavia swore she knew a baker who added chalk and sand to his flour, in order to cut costs.

But Jonathan's experience beat them all. Once, when chewing a mouthful of meat pie bought from a street vendor in Rome, his tongue had encountered something tough and gristly. Pulling it out of his mouth to inspect it, he had discovered, to his horror, that it was the tip of someone's finger.

Everyone groaned and pushed their plates away. Luckily they had finished the main course. Captain Geminus refilled empty wine cups and presently Alma came in with the dessert course: dates and slices of sugary pink watermelon.

Jonathan, who was becoming slightly tipsy, pretended that two dates were his eyes and a slice of watermelon his grinning mouth. Flavia giggled and Nubia smiled for the first time.

Encouraged by the success of this antic, Jonathan stuck a leftover snail up each nostril. Flavia snorted with laughter, Nubia giggled and Miriam rolled her eyes. Mordecai cleared his throat.

'With your permission, I think it's time for us to take our leave,' he said, with a significant glance at his son.

'But first, happy birthday, Flavia. This is from us all.' He reached under his chair and brought out a fat leather cylinder tied with a scarlet ribbon.

Flavia knew immediately that it was a scroll case. With excited fingers she opened the leather top and pulled out one of the scrolls inside.

'It's not new, I'm afraid,' said Mordecai in his accented voice. 'To tell the truth I have two sets, so I thought I could spare this one.'

Flavia's eyes opened wide with delight as she unrolled the papyrus. 'It's the *Aeneid*. It's the very thing I wanted. And look at the beautiful illustrations!'

Everyone pushed back their chairs and crowded around to look at the scroll and admire the pictures.

'Flavia?' prompted her father. 'What do you say?'

'Oh! Thank you Doctor Mordecai, Jonathan, Miriam. It's such a generous gift. Thank you!' And then: 'Look, Nubia! I can help you learn Latin by reading this story to you.'

But Nubia was not in her chair. She had vanished.

SCROLL V

'Oh no, I knew it would all be too much for her!' cried Flavia. 'She only came off the slave ship this morning!'

'Don't worry,' said Mordecai. 'Perhaps the food was too rich for her. She may be in the latrine.'

But when Flavia reported that Nubia wasn't there, they all began to worry and decided to search the house.

Still wearing their party garlands, Mordecai and Flavia's father looked downstairs, while Jonathan, Miriam and Flavia searched the upstairs bedrooms. The doorkeeper Caudex, dozing in the atrium, swore that no one had gone out. Alma, scrubbing plates in the kitchen, had the back door constantly in her line of sight. She was sure Nubia had not gone near it.

When they had searched the whole house they met in the atrium by the household shrine.

'Before we begin the search outside,' said Flavia's father, gravely removing his garland, 'have we checked every room?'

'Yes,' said the children.

'Yes,' nodded Mordecai.

'No,' said Caudex slowly, scratching his armpit.

They all gazed at the big slave.

34

'Scuto is still shut up in the storeroom,' he mumbled. 'He was whining and scratching to be let out but – '

'Yes?' they cried.

'Then he went very quiet.'

They all hurried to the storeroom and cautiously Captain Geminus opened the door. By now it was dusk and the storeroom, which had no windows, was dim and shadowy. They could just make out the shapes of dozens of storage jars full of wine and grain, half-buried in the sandy earth to keep them from toppling over.

'I think I see him,' said Flavia's father. 'Bring a lamp.'

Alma rushed to hand him a clay oil-lamp and the captain stepped into the storeroom.

'Great Neptune's beard!' he exclaimed softly.

In the golden lamplight they saw Nubia and Scuto curled up asleep on the sandy floor. The girl's dark head rested on the dog's broad, woolly back. She had placed her flowered garland on his head. As they all crowded into the doorway, Scuto raised his big head, with the garland slightly askew. He looked at them drowsily, sighed deeply and went back to sleep.

One bright afternoon, a few days later, Flavia's new friends accompanied her to the river harbour to see her father off on a voyage.

Doctor Mordecai and Captain Geminus led the way.

They looked an unlikely pair, Flavia thought, as she watched them walking and talking together: her fair-haired Roman father in his tunic and blue cloak, the doctor with his exotic turban, robe and beard. But they had a common passion: travel. Mordecai had lived in

Babylon and Jerusalem, two cities her father had never visited, and Captain Geminus had seen many countries which Mordecai had only read about.

Flavia was glad they liked each other because in only a few days she and Jonathan had also become firm friends.

Jonathan had been coming to her house every morning to help teach Nubia Latin. He and Flavia had been reading the *Aeneid* to her, often stopping to explain or act out words. Jonathan was very funny and made them both laugh. Flavia thought it was good for Nubia to laugh.

Now, as they made their way towards the River Tiber, Nubia was walking between Flavia and Jonathan, holding Scuto's lead. Since the night of the dinner party, the slave-girl and the dog had been inseparable. She even refused to sleep in the new bed they had brought up to Flavia's room. Instead, Nubia curled up every night in the garden with Scuto, and slept under the stars.

Also walking with them to the docks was her father's patron, Titus Cordius Atticus, who had chartered her father's ship for a two-week voyage to Greece. He intended to visit the town of Corinth to buy pottery, perfume and bronzes.

Cordius was a very wealthy merchant who lived opposite them, in one of the largest and most beautiful houses in Ostia. He also had a town house in Rome and an estate in Sicily. But despite his wealth he always seemed very sad.

Flavia's father had once told her the reason: while Cordius had been serving as a officer in Germania, his whole family had been slaughtered by barbarians. A lovely wife, three fine young sons and a baby girl, now all gone to the underworld, and no one to leave his great riches to.

'Cordius doesn't need to work as a merchant,' her father had said, 'but since he lost his family there is a deep restlessness in him. I think he travels to get away from his empty houses. All the wealth in the world is no good if you don't have a family.' Her father had hugged her tightly.

Recently, however, Cordius had seemed more cheerful. Sometimes his stern face even relaxed into a smile. Flavia knew why, but she had been sworn to secrecy: Cordius was considering adopting his young freedman Libertus. She had overheard the rich merchant discussing it with her father.

'You mustn't tell a soul,' Flavia's father had warned her. 'He is still thinking about it and no one knows, not even Libertus.'

Previously a slave in Cordius's household, Libertus had shown such skill and promise that he had been set free. Now a freedman, he still lived and worked in his patron's house, but was paid for it.

Flavia considered that Libertus would make some girl a fine husband. He had straight black hair, clear skin and dark blue eyes. He was young, intelligent and charming. Furthermore, if Cordius adopted Libertus, one day he would be incredibly wealthy.

And so Flavia was delighted to see Libertus walking beside Jonathan's sister Miriam. She thought they made a dazzling couple and wondered if the young freedman was telling Miriam that her eyes were like amethysts and her skin like alabaster. Then she heard him say something about 'slavery in Judaea', and sighed. Libertus was definitely not wooing Miriam.

As they emerged from between two warehouses and stepped onto the quayside, Flavia took a deep breath of the salty air. Seagulls and swifts soared and swooped above the river. Sailors and dockers rolled barrels and wine jars, slaves loaded crates on carts, and soldiers marched past. And this was the quietest time of day.

The harbour always made Flavia feel both excited and sad. Excited because every ship promised a new adventure, sad because her father so often went away.

The sight of her father's small ship, the *Myrtilla*, also made Flavia sad. Myrtilla had been the name of her mother, who had died in childbirth when Flavia was only three years old. The twin baby boys had died, too. Flavia had been left alone with only her father and nurse Alma.

As they approached the *Myrtilla*'s berth, three burly Phoenician brothers shouted their greetings from various parts of the ship. They were called Quartus, Quintus and Sextus. The fourth crew member was an Ethiopian named Ebenus. His oiled, cheerful face rose up from the hold when he heard the others.

Her father and the merchant Cordius had already stowed their belongings on board the ship. They had visited the temple of Castor and Pollux, to make sacrifice for a good and profitable journey. Now, the wind was favourable and it was time for them to depart.

Captain Geminus bounded up the boarding plank to make some last-minute checks aboard the ship, while

Cordius gave Libertus some final instructions. Flavia was disappointed to see the handsome freedman hurry home shortly afterwards. She noticed Miriam watching Libertus until he was out of sight.

Suddenly, Flavia noticed that Nubia had begun to tremble uncontrollably. The docks obviously upset her. The slave-girl hugged Scuto for reassurance and his wet kisses seemed to calm her.

A few moments later, Captain Geminus came down the boarding plank and put one arm around Flavia's shoulder.

'Time for me to go,' he said with a smile, and then added gravely, 'you know, I'm a little worried about your safety since that incident with the dogs. Your tutor isn't here to look out for you this month, Caudex can be terribly slow and I don't know what Alma would do to protect you against a pack of wild dogs, or even kidnappers . . .'

'Don't worry, pater. I'm not alone. Doctor Mordecai lives next door and I have Jonathan and Nubia to keep me company now. And there's Scuto.'

'Ah yes. The fierce watchdog.'

They looked down at Scuto, who was lathering Nubia's face with his wet tongue. Smiling, Captain Geminus shook his head.

'Well, if I hear you've been in the least danger, I'm packing you off to my brother's the next time I go on a voyage!'

'Don't worry, pater. Jonathan and I will sit quietly in the garden all day and take turns reading the *Aeneid* to Nubia. We're teaching her Latin.' She pulled Nubia close and put a protective arm around her.

'Good, good . . .' Flavia's father quickly kissed her on the top of her head, said goodbye to the rest of them and then he and Cordius boarded the ship.

Using oars, the crew soon manoeuvred the small ship out of her berth and into the river channel. As the swift current carried the *Myrtilla* down towards the river mouth, Flavia's father stood at the helm, holding the steering paddle.

Although Flavia usually stayed to watch until the *Myrtilla* passed right out of sight, Nubia was trembling again, so Flavia decided to take her home quickly. Her father was busy at the helm, but just before they started back Flavia saw him turn and wave one last time.

It was still early afternoon when they returned to Green Fountain Street. Theirs was one of the few quiet residential streets in the bustling town, and now, at the hottest time of the day, it was almost deserted: only Libertus stood at the communal fountain in the middle of the crossroads. They waved as they walked past, and Flavia noticed Miriam give him a shy smile.

As soon as they had left the docks, Nubia had stopped trembling. Now, Jonathan was walking beside her and teaching her words in Latin by pointing at objects and saying their names.

'Door,' he said.

'Door,' she repeated.

'Lion.' He indicated a bronze door-knocker.

'Lion.'

'Kerb.'

'Kerb.'

'Fountain.'

'Fountain. Water?'

'Yes! Water! Good!' encouraged Jonathan. 'Street.'

'Street.'

'Don't step in that!'

'Don't step . . .?'

'Well, that looks like horse dung, but people empty their chamber pots here and it's pretty wet so I think we'd better go back on the pavement.'

Nubia looked at him solemnly.

'Pavement,' said Jonathan

'Pavement,' repeated Nubia.

'And what's this? Blood?'

'Blood,' said Nubia, and pointed at the trail of drops that led to Jonathan's front door.

SCROLL VI

The spots of blood, each about the size of a small coin, were a startling and vivid red. Flavia stooped to touch one, but Jonathan ran ahead, following the drops to his front door.

'Father, the door's open!' he called over his shoulder.

'Don't go in,' shouted Mordecai, 'there may be robbers still in the house!'

But he was too late. Jonathan had disappeared inside. Mordecai and Miriam hurried forward.

As they reached the door, Jonathan stepped back out, his face drained of all colour. He looked at them silently for a moment and then bent over and was sick in the road.

'Stay back, everyone,' began Mordecai in alarm, but Miriam had already pushed past him. Her scream broke the stillness of the afternoon.

'He's dead,' they heard her sob.

Mordecai rushed after her into the house. Flavia, Nubia and Scuto all moved forward to follow him, but Jonathan's arm – surprisingly strong – blocked their way.

'It's our watchdog Bobas,' he said quietly. 'You don't want to look. Someone has cut off his head and taken it away.'

'Who else was in your house?' asked Flavia an hour later.

She and Nubia were sitting with Jonathan in her garden, trying to comfort him. Miriam had been so upset by the bloodstain on the floor that Mordecai had taken her across town to stay with relatives for a few days.

Nubia had one arm around Scuto's neck. They had managed to make her understand what had happened to Bobas and she seemed determined to protect Scuto from a similar fate.

'No one else was in our house,' Jonathan answered grimly.

'What about the slaves?'

'We don't have any slaves. My father doesn't think it right to keep them.'

'But you told me your mother died when you were very young. Don't you even have a nursemaid or cook?'

'No. It's just the three of us.'

'Who does your cleaning?' gasped Flavia in amazement.

'I do,' replied Jonathan, almost proudly. 'And I garden. Miriam does the shopping and a little cooking. And Bobas was our doorkeeper and protector . . .' He bit his lip, and Flavia said quickly:

'Was anything stolen?'

'No. After we buried Bobas's body in the garden we looked everywhere. But nothing is missing. In fact, I found this in the atrium, not far from his body . . .' He held out a little quartz cube with circles scratched on its surface. Nubia took it from his hand and looked at it in puzzlement.

'What this?' asked Nubia.

'It's one of a pair of dice,' explained Flavia. She mimed throwing it and said in Greek: 'For gambling. For money.'

'It's not ours,' said Jonathan. 'My father would be very upset if he ever found me or my sister gambling,'

'Keep it safe,' said Flavia, handing it back to him, 'it may be a clue.' She looked up at the fig tree thoughtfully.

'If nothing was stolen, why did they kill Bobas?'

'Well . . .' Jonathan began, and then stopped. He pulled a twig off a bush and scratched idly at the ground.

'Why? Tell me,' insisted Flavia. She thought of pretty Bobas, with his lovely brown eyes and friendly nature.

'We . . . you've probably guessed that we are different from you. We have a different religion.'

'You're Jewish, aren't you?' said Flavia. Jonathan nodded.

'The people where we used to live didn't like us. That's why we moved here, to the edge of town, where no one would know who we were . . . where no one would bother us. Our old neighbours wrote things on the wall of our house and once they threw rotten eggs at father.'

'Do you think your old neighbours killed Bobas?'

'Maybe . . .' shrugged Jonathan. He seemed reluctant to talk about it.

'Why do they hate you so much?' Flavia asked. 'There are many Jews here in Ostia. I've seen their temple down by the docks.'

'Synagogue,' corrected Jonathan quietly and continued to scratch at the ground. It was obvious the subject made him uncomfortable.

'Well, I intend to solve this crime,' announced Flavia firmly. 'Whoever did this is wicked and should be caught.'

Nubia had been listening to their conversation attentively. Now she surprised them both by saying vehemently:

'Bad man. Kill dog. Find him.' Her amber eyes blazed with passion and she was squeezing Scuto's neck so tightly that he whimpered and rolled his eyes at her.

Flavia looked at Nubia and then turned to Jonathan.

'Do you want to find the person who killed your dog?' she asked him.

He looked up at her, and his eyes were blazing, too. 'Yes.'

'Then it's settled,' said Flavia calmly. 'We will solve this mystery and together we will find the killer.'

Flavia decided that they should begin their quest for justice by interviewing possible witnesses.

Wax tablet in hand and flanked by Jonathan and Nubia, she began in the kitchen. Alma assured them that she had heard nothing suspicious while they were out, though she did remark that Bobas barked so often she barely noticed it.

Next they looked for Caudex. They found him in the garden, snipping the dead heads off roses. When questioned, he confessed he had been dozing.

'Just a little nap in my room as I usually have after lunch,' he admitted, and after a pause, 'I could easily have heard if anyone had knocked on our door.'

The only other possible witness was Libertus, Cordius's freedman. Flavia remembered that he had been standing by the fountain on the corner when they had returned from the river harbour.

They caught Libertus just as he left the house, on his way to the baths.

'Around noon?' he said, as they fell into step beside him. 'Yes, as a matter of fact I did see someone. It was just before you came back from the harbour. I was drinking at the fountain and a man went running past. He looked very frightened and he was carrying a leather bag. I distinctly remember the leather bag. For some reason it reminded me of Perseus with the head of Medusa.'

'What Perseus?' whispered Nubia to Flavia.

'Perseus was a hero who had to kill a monster named Medusa. He cut off her head,' Flavia made a chopping motion with her hand, 'and he put it out of sight in a bag.' She mimed that, too, and then added in Greek: 'In myth. Monster's head in bag.'

Nubia understood: 'Perseus killed.'

'Yes, Perseus killed her.' Flavia turned back to the freedman. 'Libertus,' she said gravely, 'today someone killed Jonathan's watchdog and cut off its head. The head is still missing.'

'By Hercules!' gasped Libertus, and stopped dead in

his tracks. 'That is exactly the impression I got: of a head in a bag.'

'What did the man look like?' Jonathan asked.

Libertus shrugged and began walking again. 'Just average, really. Clean-shaven, medium height, light tunic, short dark cloak – I can't remember much more than that.'

They were approaching the centre of town and the streets were becoming more crowded. They all stood back to let a man pushing a handcart full of melons go past.

'I really must hurry,' said Libertus. 'I'm meeting someone at the baths . . .'

'Just one more question,' said Flavia. 'Do you remember which way he went at the crossroads: to the port, to the graves or towards the forum?'

'Yes, I do recall that,' said Libertus, frowning pensively. 'I remember I thought it curious at the time. He was running towards the tombs.'

It was the hottest time of the day. Hidden in the sun-bleached grasses of the necropolis, the cicadas made their sleepy creaking noise. Flavia, Jonathan and Nubia – with Scuto romping ahead – proceeded somewhat fearfully along a dirt road flanked by cypress trees and tombs.

Although their houses backed directly onto the graveyard, they had approached by means of the gate and road that the running man must have taken. The road was not much used and the tombs on either side of it were overgrown and untended.

Here and there were the usual piles of rubbish that

accumulated outside the gates of any Roman town: pottery shards, old sandals, broken furniture and clothes too tattered for the secondhand stall.

'What about the wild dogs who attacked us a few days ago?' Flavia looked around nervously. 'I don't want to meet them again.'

'I've been hunting lots of times in the graveyard and that was the only time I've seen them. We'll just have to take the risk. Besides,' Jonathan added, 'we want to find clues while they are fresh.'

As they walked, they looked right and left and especially down, for any telltale drops of blood. Scuto, who had begun by running back and forth to smell interesting smells, was now plodding down the middle of the road with his tail down, panting in the afternoon heat. Suddenly he stopped, looked to his left and wagged his tail.

'Over there,' said Jonathan, pointing. 'He sees something.' Scuto, tail still wagging, led them through the tombs to a small clearing among the pine and cypress trees. Beside a miniature tomb lit by dappled sunlight sat a man with short dark hair and a pale yellow tunic. He sat cross-legged with his back to them, and they could hear sobs and see his shoulders trembling.

As they came nearer, the man heard them and turned. His face was red with crying and his mouth turned down like an actor's tragic mask. Heavy eyebrows joined above his nose to form one dark line. Flavia had never seen such misery before.

But his misery turned to rage when he saw the little

group. He rose to his feet and pointing a finger at Scuto he screamed:

'Get that animal away from me. Get him away or I'll kill him. I hate dogs. I hate them all!'

SCROLL VII

The weeping man wiped his nose angrily on his arm and then bent down. He picked up a pine cone, drew back his arm, and threw it at Scuto. It fell short and the man sobbed again, 'Get away!'

He began looking around for other missiles but the three of them had already turned and were running back towards the road. Scuto loped behind them, still wagging his tail as if it were a game.

'Is the man following us?' gasped Flavia when they reached the road again.

'No, I don't think so,' said Jonathan. He was wheezing a bit. While she waited for him to catch his breath, Flavia joined Nubia in patting Scuto.

'Don't worry, Scuto,' she said in a soothing voice, 'we won't let the bad man get you.'

'Not bad man,' said Nubia.

Flavia and Jonathan both looked up at her in surprise.

'Sad man,' said Nubia quietly.

'But that's probably the man who killed Bobas!' Jonathan cried.

'You may be right,' agreed Flavia.

'But how can we be sure?' mused Jonathan.

'I know!' Flavia said, after a moment's thought.

'We'll all hide, and wait for him to go back into the town. When he does, you follow him, Jonathan. Try to find out who he is and where he lives. Nubia and I will go back to the little tomb and look for clues there. Then we'll meet back at my house. All right?'

'Yes, that sounds like a good idea. Let's wait beside that tomb in the shade . . .'

The three of them sat on a soft layer of dust and pine needles, and rested their backs against the shady wall of a large, decrepit tomb. Fragrant dill and thyme bushes screened them from the road, but they could see anyone who came along. For a long time no one passed. The only sound was the slow creaking of the cicadas and Scuto's steady, rhythmic panting.

Flavia gazed at the tombs around them. They were like small houses, with doors, so that new urns could be added. Some had inscriptions above the doors, others had pictures painted on their outer walls, like the two faded gladiators shown fighting on a tomb near the road.

Flavia's own family had a tomb further down the road, for the Gemini family had now been in Ostia for three generations. She often went there with her father to honour her mother and tiny twin brothers.

Half buried amphoras marked the graves of poorer people. Wine could be poured into their necks to refresh the ashes of the dead below.

Presently an old man leading a tiny donkey passed slowly down the road towards the town. He had loaded the little beast high with firewood. They could hear him singing snatches of a song and talking to himself. Then he was gone and the road was empty again.

'I don't think he's coming this way,' Flavia whispered to Jonathan at last. 'Unless we've missed him . . .'

'No, we haven't missed him. Wait here. I'll see if he is still at the tomb . . .'

He crept off but a few minutes later he stood before them.

'He's gone,' said Jonathan. 'But you must come and look at the tomb. Come quickly!'

'To the gods of the underworld,' Flavia read. 'Sacred to the memory of my poor Avita, eight years old . . .'

The three of them – and Scuto – stood before the little tomb while Flavia read out the Latin inscription painted over the tiny door.

'There's a picture on this side,' said Jonathan. They all moved round to the side of the tomb. Someone had painted a fresco of a little girl lying on a funeral couch surrounded by mourners. The colours looked strangely bright and cheerful.

'Little girl,' said Nubia sadly.

'Yes,' said Flavia softly. 'Probably his daughter. But where did he go? The only way back is along the road.'

'Unless . . .' said Jonathan. 'Unless *his* house backs onto the graveyard like ours.'

'But that would mean he lived on our street,' said Flavia.

'I wonder how we could find out,' mused Jonathan, nibbling a stalk of dried grass.

'I know just the person to ask!' cried Flavia.

*

They stood in Flavia's kitchen, munching grapes and sipping cool water from ceramic cups. Scuto was drinking long and deeply from his water bowl.

Alma bent over the kitchen hearth, stirring a pan of chicken barley soup and nodding her head.

'Yes, I remember something about a little girl. Her father was a sailor. They lived just up our street. The father adored the girl. Hated to be away from her. That's right, the girl's name was Avita. Avita Procula. And his name was Publius. Publius Avitus Proculus. Came back from a voyage a week or two ago to find she'd died.'

Alma reached up and took a pinch of rosemary from a dried bundle which hung from the ceiling.

'She lived just up the road?' asked Jonathan.

'Yes,' said Alma, crumbling the herb into the soup, 'the house right on the bend.'

'How did Avita die?' asked Flavia. 'Do you know?'

'Oh my, yes,' sighed Alma as she resumed stirring. 'But I never mentioned it to you, dear. I didn't want to give you nightmares . . .'

They all looked at Alma. She stopped stirring for a moment and faced them gravely. 'She died horribly, in great pain, of hydrophobia.' And when they continued to stare at her blankly, she explained in a whisper, 'A mad dog bit her!'

'Hydrophobia,' said Mordecai, 'is a terrible disease.' He was leaning over the marble-topped table in his study, examining medical scrolls.

'The word "hydrophobia" means "a fear of water". People suffering from hydrophobia are terrified of water, even of their own saliva.'

Jonathan, standing behind his father, allowed some spittle to bubble out of his mouth, looked down at it and opened his eyes wide in mock horror. Flavia and Nubia tried not to giggle. Mordecai went on:

'Victims also lose their appetite – '

Jonathan pretended to refuse an imaginary plate.

' – suffer hallucinations '

Jonathan opened his eyes wide again and screamed silently, brushing wildly at imaginary insects crawling on his arms. Flavia bit her lip to stop from laughing. Nubia covered her mouth with her hand.

' – and eventually become paralysed.'

Jonathan clapped his arms to his sides, went stiff as a plank and crossed his eyes. The girls, unable to contain themselves any longer, burst out laughing. Mordecai glanced up at them briefly.

'Jonathan, please,' he said without looking round, 'it's not a laughing matter.' He read on. 'The disease is also known as rabies, which means "a raging". Hmmmn. Let's see what Pliny has to say – I have his new volume here somewhere – '

'Who is Pliny?' asked Flavia.

'He's the admiral of the Roman fleet and a brilliant historian,' said Mordecai as he shuffled through the scrolls on the table. 'He's just written a superb natural history in thirty-seven volumes . . . Lives just down the coast from here . . . Ah!'

Jonathan's father held a scroll to the lamp, for it was nearly dusk and the light was fading quickly.

'Yes! Here's what Pliny says about rabies: "greatest danger of humans catching it when the dog-star is shining" – that's now – "it causes fatal hydrophobia . . .

to prevent a dog from catching this disease, mix chicken dung in its food." '

Jonathan screwed up his face and stuck his tongue out.

Mordecai smiled indulgently at their laughter, then suddenly hissed at them to be quiet.

They all heard a strangled cry and the sound of barking.

'They're in the graveyard again,' cried Mordecai between clenched teeth, 'but this time I'm ready.'

The doctor hurried out of the study and ran upstairs, almost tripping on his long robe. Jonathan, Flavia and Nubia followed him into a narrow bedroom with one small window. Under the window a small pile of stones lay on an octagonal table, and next to them a bow and arrow. Mordecai pushed his head out and they heard him grunt.

'There they are!' He reached for the bow and arrow and aimed it through the window.

Jonathan and Flavia jostled to see, but the window was too small. Mordecai was blocking their view.

'Quickly!' cried Jonathan. 'The other bedroom has a window. Follow me!'

SCROLL VIII

The girls followed Jonathan into a second narrow bedroom with bright, mustard-yellow walls. They ran to the window and Jonathan yanked out a wooden lattice-work screen that fitted into its frame. Peering through, they were just in time to see Mordecai's arrow fly into the midst of the pack of dogs which surrounded a tall umbrella pine.

The arrow missed.

The dogs swarmed around the tree, barking loudly and gazing up into it.

'Use your sling,' Flavia urged Jonathan.

'I can't. There's not enough room in here to swing it. I need to be outside.'

Their three faces crowded into the tiny window frame.

'What are they barking at?' asked Jonathan.

'There's something up that tree.'

'Yes,' agreed Jonathan. 'There's something on the other side, clinging on – ' It was difficult to see in the fading light.

'I can see hands. Or maybe paws,' said Flavia.

'Boy,' said Nubia.

'No, it can't be a boy. Look how fast it's climbing now,' cried Jonathan.

'It must be a monkey,' gasped Flavia.

The dogs had stopped barking and were watching the climber with interest, too.

Suddenly the creature moved round the trunk and they could all see its silhouette against the yellow sky of dusk. The creature was not a monkey, but a boy no more than eight years old.

As they watched in amazement, he shouted incoherently down at the dogs: not a scream of fear, but a mocking taunt. This enraged the dogs, who began to bark furiously again.

Another arrow whizzed down from the window. This one found its mark. One of the dogs yelped, leapt into the air, then fell back with a shaft in his gut. The others sniffed at him and, when a second arrow struck the leader, they ran off into the woods. Two dogs with arrows in them lay writhing on the ground. High up in the tree, the small boy clung to the trunk.

'Let's help the boy,' cried Jonathan, and ran downstairs with the girls close behind him.

Mordecai followed them down the stairs.

'Wait!' he cried. 'Don't go out! The dogs aren't dead yet. They may still be dangerous.'

'But we have to help the boy,' protested Jonathan.

'Yes, I know,' his father reassured him, as they reached the bottom of the stairs. 'That's why I brought this . . .'

They all looked at the object Mordecai held in his hand. It was a large, curved sword. The blade was polished to mirror brightness and its edge was sharp as a razor.

★

The back of the house had no windows at ground level, so the three of them ran back upstairs to the yellow bedroom in order to watch. In the twilight, they saw Jonathan's father emerge cautiously from the back door beneath them. The white oval of his turban gleamed in the dusk. Below it they could see his blue shoulders and the flash of the sword.

He moved slowly towards the pine tree, occasionally glancing up at the boy, but keeping a closer eye on the wounded dogs. The leader lay panting quietly, pinned to the ground by an arrow in his leg. The other – a bitch – writhed in agony with an arrow in her belly. The blade flashed as Mordecai cut the she-dog's throat with a single stroke, putting her out of her misery.

But his action caused the leader to twist with alarm, and in doing so the huge black mastiff freed himself from the ground. The wounded beast faced Mordecai and crouched. His lip curled back to reveal sharp, pale fangs dripping with saliva. The broken shaft protruded from his hind leg.

Mordecai murmured something soothing, though they could not make out the words, but the wounded hound was not pacified.

With an ugly snarl, he leapt directly at Mordecai's face.

Jonathan's father reacted by instinct. The bloody sword flashed again and the dog's head and body fell in two separate places.

For a moment, no one moved. Then Flavia and her friends raced downstairs and out of the back door.

When they reached Mordecai, he was standing in

the same spot, looking down at the two dead dogs and trembling.

'Let me have the sword, father,' said Jonathan quietly.

Mordecai shook his head emphatically. 'No! If these dogs are rabid, even the blood from the sword might be dangerous.' He moved over to a clump of horse-grass and began wiping the blade clean.

Flavia felt a tug at her arm. Nubia was pointing up at the tree. The boy, instead of coming down and thanking them for saving his life, was shimmying higher up the tree.

'Come down,' called Flavia, 'the dogs are dead. It's safe – '

'They can't hurt you now,' Jonathan added.

But the boy had reached the larger limbs and was inching his way along one. His bare feet gripped the branch almost as tightly as his hands. They watched in fascination as he slowly stood up on it, remained still for a moment and then leapt six feet towards another umbrella pine nearby. He caught hold of a branch with one arm, but it was a small one and began to bend alarmingly. They gasped but the boy had already moved on, using his momentum, and swung to the next branch.

There was an even larger gap between the tree he was in and the next one, which led to the woods beyond.

'He'll never make it,' gasped Flavia in horror, as the boy swung from the pine branch, preparing to jump.

'He just might,' breathed Jonathan.

The boy leapt.

He seemed suspended in air for a moment and the four faces watching him seemed frozen, too.

Then, impossibly, he had grasped one of the pine's outermost branches and was swinging for the next, sturdier limb. But as he swung forward they all heard an ominous crack. The branch – and the boy with it – plummeted to the earth below.

'It's a miracle, but it seems no bones are broken,' murmured Mordecai as he examined the boy. 'Jonathan, could you bring the lamp-stand a bit nearer?'

They were all standing round the boy, who lay on a couch in the mustard-yellow bedroom. The boy's eyes were closed and his face was very pale, but he was breathing. Jonathan pulled a standing lamp closer to the bed, carefully, so that the hot oil wouldn't spill.

The light now shone full on the boy's face, and they could see he was exceedingly grubby. Smears of dirt streaked his face and his tangled hair was full of dust and twigs. His tattered tunic smelled curiously of sour wine and pine resin.

Abruptly the boy opened his eyes. They glittered sea-green in the lamplight and for a moment they registered fear. But only for a moment. Then they grew alert and wary.

'Peace be with you,' said Mordecai with a little bow, and added, 'every stranger is an uninvited guest.'

The boy started to rise but Mordecai pushed him gently back against the striped cushions piled on his bed.

'Careful, my boy,' he said softly. 'You've taken a nasty fall. It's a miracle you've no broken bones.'

The boy settled back on the pillows and looked round at them, almost as if judging his chances of escape.

'Jonathan, the bread please . . .' said Mordecai.

Jonathan handed his father a plate with a flat, round loaf of bread on it. Mordecai tore a piece from the loaf and handed it to the boy.

The boy didn't hesitate. He reached a hand out from under the covers, took the piece of bread, sniffed it quickly and swallowed it almost whole. Flavia noticed that his fingernails were cracked and filthy.

Mordecai set the plate carefully on the couch. The boy took another hunk of bread and devoured it. He ate like a dog, chomping once or twice with his molars and then throwing his head back and swallowing the half-chewed bread in one gulp. Between bites he looked constantly round at them: warily, suspiciously, as if at any moment one of them might suddenly lunge forward to steal his food.

When he had finished the loaf, and drained a beaker of cold water, he wiped his mouth with his bare arm and pushed back the cover as if to go.

'No, no,' Mordecai said gently, pressing him back on the bed. 'You can't leave now. It's already dark outside. Let me get word to your family that you are all right. What is your name, and where do you live?'

The boy looked at him silently, his mouth firmly closed.

'We have shared bread together,' explained Mordecai solemnly. 'You are now under our protection. Please tell us your name.' He smiled encouragingly.

The boy said nothing.

'He doesn't understand us,' said Jonathan.

The boy shot him a furious look.

'Oh, but I think he does,' said Mordecai. 'Young man,' he said gently, 'please open your mouth for me.'

The boy glared at him.

'Please,' said Mordecai softly.

The boy opened his mouth slowly. Mordecai carefully held the boy's chin between thumb and forefinger and lowered it even more. Then he looked into the boy's mouth.

After a moment he closed it again and looked gravely at the three of them.

'He understands well enough,' said the doctor, 'but he is unable to reply. You see, someone has cut out his tongue.'

SCROLL IX

There was a stunned silence as they looked in horror at the boy. He glared defiantly back at them and Flavia saw angry tears fill his eyes. She realised his pride must be injured, and thought quickly.

'I've seen you near the forum, haven't I?' she asked in a conversational tone. 'You often sit by the junk man's stall . . .' She didn't add that she had seen him begging.

The boy looked at her suspiciously for a moment and then gave a small nod. Jonathan followed Flavia's lead.

'How did you learn to climb trees so well?' he asked. 'I've never seen anything like it. Could you teach me?'

The beggar-boy looked pleased, in spite of himself, and shrugged.

Then Nubia spoke:

'What name?' she asked and then corrected herself: 'What your name?'

The others looked at her in horror. Didn't she realise the boy couldn't speak to tell his name?

The boy looked at Nubia for a moment and then growled and snarled like a fierce dog.

'Sorry!' Flavia apologised to the boy.

'We didn't mean to upset you,' added Jonathan hastily.

'Dog?' said Nubia.

Ignoring Flavia and Jonathan, the boy beckoned Nubia on with one hand: she understood what he was trying to say.

'Lion?' she asked.

The boy shook his head, but his gleaming eyes urged her on.

Flavia and Jonathan finally caught on.

'Tiger?' asked Flavia. 'Is Tiger your name?'

The boy shook his head.

'Horse?' suggested Jonathan. The boy looked at him, rolled his eyes heavenward and snarled again, curling his lip back from his teeth.

'Oh, I know!' cried Flavia. 'Wolf!'

The boy gave an emphatic nod of assent.

'Lupus? Is that your name?' asked Flavia. The boy nodded again, folded his arms and sat back on the cushions.

Nubia turned to Flavia.

'What is Lupus?'

'Wolf,' said Flavia, 'like a fierce wild dog.' Then she remembered the word in Greek: 'Lykos!'

'Ah! Lupus!' said Nubia, and gave the boy a radiant smile. The boy raised his eyebrows questioningly, and pointed back at them.

'I'm Flavia.'

'Jonathan.'

'My name is Nubia,' said the slave-girl. And automatically added, 'How may I please you?'

Lupus dropped his jaw at her in mock astonishment, and the others burst out laughing, even Nubia.

After another hour of questioning, with much nodding and shaking of Lupus's head, they had discovered several facts about him.

Lupus was an orphan. He had no family. He had no home. He spent much of his day searching in the rubbish tips behind the tombs. The junk man occasionally gave him small coins for what he found. With those coins, together with any he received from begging, he bought food. During the summer, when the nights were warm, he slept outside, often among the tombs. In the winter, when it was cold or damp, he slept beside the furnace of the Baths of Thetis. He thought he was about eight years old, but did not know for certain.

None of them dared to ask how he had lost his tongue.

Throughout their exchange, Mordecai had been sitting quietly in a shadowy corner, watching and listening. They had almost forgotten his presence, and when he stood up and came into the circle of lamplight, Flavia jumped.

'Children, it is well past sundown,' he gently reminded them, 'and time for you all to go to bed. Flavia, you and Nubia should go home now, or your nurse will worry. Lupus, you are welcome to spend the night here. Would you like that?'

Lupus considered this proposal for a moment and then nodded.

'Good,' smiled Mordecai.

He pinched out all but one of the wicks on the lamp stand and left the room. Jonathan and Nubia said goodnight to Lupus and went out. Flavia trailed behind on purpose, and as she reached the door, she turned and whispered to the boy:

'Lupus, Jonathan's dog was beheaded this morning. We are trying to find out who killed it. Will you help us solve the mystery?'

Lupus's green eyes glinted in the dim lamplight and she saw him nod.

'See you in the morning then,' said Flavia.

'We're just finishing our breakfast,' said Jonathan the next morning as he led Flavia and Nubia through the atrium and corridor towards the garden.

'Miriam's still at my cousin's house and father went to the forum early to report the crime to the magistrates, and also to tell them about the pack of wild dogs. He says soldiers will probably deal with them. Father told us not to go anywhere until he comes back,' Jonathan added as they stepped into the garden.

It was only an hour after dawn and the garden was still in shadow, though the sky above was clear blue. Lupus was sitting cross-legged on a faded red and blue carpet spread on the garden path. Although the low table before him was loaded with food, he wasn't eating. He was sipping a thick, creamy liquid from a clay beaker.

'It's buttermilk,' explained Jonathan. 'He had some bread and honey, but this is easier for him to eat.'

'Good morning, Lupus,' said Flavia. 'Are you feeling better this morning?' The mute boy greeted Flavia and

Nubia with a half smile and nodded. Jonathan and the girls sat around the table on the carpet.

Flavia pulled a wax tablet and stylus from her belt. 'Let's make a plan for today. Jonathan, have you told Lupus everything?'

'Yes,' nodded Jonathan. 'Everything I could remember. How we all went to the harbour with you, leaving Bobas here alone and how we found him when we got back . . .' His voice caught and Flavia asked quickly,

'How do you think the killer got in?'

'Father rarely locks the door,' Jonathan admitted. 'We have no door-slave and in our old community, no one ever locked their doors.' He paused and added softly, 'We'll never make that mistake again.'

'Who lives on the other side of this house, Jonathan?'

'A banker and his family, I think, but they shut it up last week and went to Herculaneum for the summer.'

'Hmmm.' Flavia made a few notes on her wax tablet. 'No one *heard* anything, no-one *saw* anything – apart from Libertus – and nothing was stolen . . .'

'The dice!' cried Jonathan. 'I forgot about the dice!'

He fished in the pouch tied to his belt and showed Lupus the quartz dice. Lupus blew on it, rolled it on the carpet and scowled as it came up one.

'The dog throw,' observed Flavia absently, and then: 'Wait! When you throw a one it's called the dog throw! It's the worst score. Do you think it means something?'

Jonathan shrugged, and Lupus scratched his head.

'Probably not . . .' Flavia chewed the end of her stylus. 'I think the killer was the man crying beside the tomb,' she said finally. 'He hates dogs and he fits Libertus's description. Did you tell Lupus what the man looked like?'

Jonathan started to reply, but suddenly Lupus grabbed Flavia's wax tablet and stylus and rubbed out her notes with his thumb.

'Hey!' said Flavia in protest.

Lupus ignored her and began to make a few quick marks on the tablet. He grinned with delight as the tip of the ivory stylus pushed back the soft beeswax to reveal blackened wood beneath. Flavia was about to snatch it back when she saw that he was drawing something. After a moment, the boy held it up for them to see.

With confident black lines etched in the yellow wax, Lupus had drawn a man. The portrait was simple but clear: a square face, clean-shaven, short hair brushed forward and heavy eyebrows that met above his nose.

'That's him!' exclaimed Flavia with a squeal of excitement. 'That's the man we saw at the tomb!'

SCROLL X

'That's amazing!' breathed Jonathan, admiring Lupus's sketch of the man. 'Who taught you to draw?'

Lupus pushed out his lower lip and shrugged, as if to say it was not difficult.

'Do you know this man?' asked Flavia.

Lupus shook his head.

'Then how could you draw him?'

Lupus jerked his thumb back towards the graveyard. Then he mimicked someone weeping.

'You've seen him crying at his daughter's grave, too!'

Lupus nodded.

'When?' asked Jonathan.

Lupus thought for a moment, flicked up three fingers, then four.

'Four different times?'

He nodded.

'My old nurse Alma told us that his name was Publius Avitus Proculus,' Flavia said to Lupus. 'He's a sailor and he lives further up this street.'

'Why kill dog?' asked Nubia suddenly.

'He hates all dogs because his daughter was killed by one,' explained Jonathan. 'Hates dogs. Thinks dogs bad.'

'No, wait,' said Flavia. 'Nubia's right. Why *did* he kill

Bobas? Bobas was a tame dog, not a wild one. And he was shut up here in the house.'

'Perhaps Bobas looked like the dog who bit his daughter,' suggested Jonathan. 'Or maybe he was passing by, and heard Bobas bark and became mad with grief and killed him . . .'

'Maybe . . .' said Flavia. 'Still, we've got to be sure it was him, before we accuse him of such a crime . . .' They were all silent for a few moments.

'I know!' cried Flavia, suddenly. 'Let's show your drawing to Libertus across the street, and see if he thinks it's the same man he saw running away.'

'Good idea,' agreed Jonathan, and then his face fell. 'But my father told me to stay inside until he got back. Lupus, too. And I have to do my chores.'

'Then Nubia and I will go!' announced Flavia, and seeing Jonathan's disappointed face, she added, 'Don't worry. We'll come straight back.'

Flavia hesitated for a moment before Cordius's house and then rapped on the door. The knocker was a fat bronze dolphin whose nose banged loudly on a bronze scallop shell.

'Knocker,' said Flavia to Nubia automatically, as they waited for a reply. Then: 'Dolphin. Shell. Green. Green door. Dog barking. Peephole. Opening . . .

'Hello!' she said politely to the beady eyes that appeared in the tiny window. 'I know your master is away, but may we speak to Libertus please?' The eyes regarded her suspiciously.

'My father is your master's client,' added Flavia.

After a moment, the sliding door of the peephole

shut and they heard the grate of the bolt sliding back. An extremely thin slave with a sour face opened the door.

Straining against a leash wrapped round his hand was a large red hound who snarled and bared his teeth at them.

Flavia shrank back in alarm, but Nubia slowly extended the back of her hand to the dog and spoke softly in her own language. Immediately, the dog stopped snarling and sniffed her hand. Then he licked it.

The doorkeeper cursed the dog under his breath, and beckoned the girls in. Flavia hesitated on the threshold. On the floor was a mosaic. Tiny pieces of coloured clay and stone showed a fierce black dog against a red background. The mosaic dog was straining against his lead and baring sharp teeth, and below him were the words CAVE CANEM: 'Beware of the dog!'

'I certainly will!' muttered Flavia under her breath.

'Wait here,' grumbled the sour-faced porter, and went off with his dog to find Libertus.

While they waited in the atrium, Flavia and Nubia looked around in wonder. Flavia had never been in Cordius's house before. It was the home of a very wealthy man: at least three times as big as hers.

The atrium had a beautiful floor of black and white marble, and in its middle – under the open skylight – a fountain bubbled in a gold-tiled impluvium. On the walls around them were frescoes depicting scenes from the travels of Aeneas, the legendary hero who founded Rome.

'Look,' pointed Nubia. 'Dog with three heads.'

Flavia gazed in delight at the pictures on the wall. 'Yes, it's Cerberus. Cerberus. He is very fierce. He's the hound who guards the gates of the underworld. Land of dead people.'

'Cerberus,' said Nubia in wonder and walked over to the wall. Flavia followed her and they both examined the three-headed hound opening all his mouths at a startled Aeneas. Behind Aeneas, a woman held out her hand to the dog.

'I don't remember that part of the *Aeneid*,' murmured Flavia to herself.

'Book six,' said a man's voice behind them, and they both started guiltily. It was Libertus, but he did not seem angry. His dark blue eyes sparkled as he quoted: ' "Huge Cerberus makes the caves of the underworld echo with his three-throated barking . . ." '

Libertus pointed.

'That's the scene where Aeneas's guide gives the hellhound a drugged biscuit, so that he can pass by . . .'

Libertus nodded at the frescoes with approval. 'They're beautiful, aren't they?' he said.

'Very beautiful,' agreed Flavia.

'Come through to the garden,' he said with a smile. 'As you know, Cordius is away, and in his absence I am the master of his house.'

He led them out of the atrium and down some steps into a beautiful garden as big as Flavia's entire house. At its centre was a large ornamental pool with two bronze dolphins spouting water at each other. Six laurel trees, trimmed into perfect balls, had been planted on either side of the pool, and at one end stood an elegant palm tree, its top half lit gold-green by the early morning sun.

Flavia could see mosaic patterns on the garden paths and bronze statues half hidden in the fragrant shrubbery. She heard the snip of a gardener's shears and then noticed another slave sweeping the peristyle – the columned walkway that surrounded the garden. There was not a leaf out of place and even the dew on the mimosa seemed to sparkle like diamonds.

'Please sit.' Libertus gestured to a cedarwood couch with orange linen cushions. Taking a seat on a similar couch opposite the girls, he leaned forward, elbows on knees, and smiled.

'How may I help you, Flavia Gemina?'

'Remember we told you yesterday that Jonathan's dog was killed?'

'Yes,' he replied gravely and a frown creased his smooth forehead, 'a terrible matter.'

'And you saw a man running?'

'Yes. Carrying a leather bag . . .'

'Well – is this the man you saw?' Flavia pulled the wax tablet from her belt and showed it to him.

Libertus took the tablet from her and examined it carefully.

'Yes,' he said slowly, 'clean-shaven, hair combed forward, and those heavy eyebrows – yes!' He nodded. 'I remember the eyebrows, how they met over his eyes. And I think he was wearing a pale tunic.'

'Pale yellow?'

'It *was* pale yellow, now that you mention it. Yes! I'm certain this is the man I saw running down the street yesterday!'

⋆

The girls had just told Jonathan and Lupus their exciting news about the running man when they heard a knock on the door and Mordecai's voice calling his son.

'We really must get a new watchdog,' sighed Mordecai as they let him in. 'I do miss Bobas,' he added sadly.

Jonathan had cleared away the breakfast things and now he brought his father a cup of mint tea. They all sat on the carpet in a sunlit corner of the garden.

Mordecai was wearing a Roman-style tunic and mantle, presumably to impress the city officials, and for the first time Flavia saw him without his turban. His hair was black, streaked with grey, and quite long. He had tied it all back, including the distinctive locks which usually fell in front of his ears.

'The magistrates have received other complaints about the wild dogs and they assured me that they have men out looking for them even now. They promised they would bury the dogs I killed last night. As for the crime of Bobas's killing, it's not so simple. They're reluctant to get involved.'

Mordecai sipped his mint tea reflectively.

'I have an appointment to see an official later this morning and then I must visit some patients, so I may be out all day. Flavia, may Jonathan and Lupus stay at your house? I don't want to leave them here alone . . .'

'Of course,' said Flavia. 'They'll be perfectly safe at our house.'

⋆

'I've locked our door,' said Mordecai to the four of them a short time later. They were standing on the hot pavement outside Flavia's house.

'Here's the key, Jonathan. Keep it at Flavia's, and only use it if you need to get in urgently. With any luck I'll be back shortly after midday, but who knows? With city officials, anything is possible. Now promise me you won't get into trouble and that you won't go far.'

'I promise that we won't even leave this street, father,' said Jonathan earnestly.

'Very well,' smiled Mordecai. 'Peace be with you, my children.'

'Peace be with you,' they answered, and watched him hurry up the road.

As soon as he turned the corner by the green fountain, Flavia turned to Jonathan.

'We promised not leave our street,' she said, 'but Avitus's house is on this street and I've just thought of a brilliant plan for getting in!'

SCROLL XI

'Avitus might recognise the three of us from the graveyard yesterday,' Flavia began, 'but if I pinned my hair up and put on a nice stola, and went with Lupus, I don't think he'd recognise me.'

The four of them were sitting on the marble bench in Flavia's garden while she told them her plan to find out more about Avitus, the man they had seen weeping in the graveyard.

'A disguise!' cried Jonathan. 'What a good idea!'

Flavia explained the rest of her plan and the others agreed it was a clever one.

'There's only one problem,' he pointed out. 'For your plan to work, we'll have to clean up Lupus. I mean *really* clean him up . . .'

They all looked at Lupus.

'You're right,' agreed Flavia. 'It'll take a little extra time, but it has to be done. You'll have to take him, Jonathan, and Caudex can go with you.' She turned to Lupus.

'I know you've slept outside the Baths of Thetis,' she said with a grin, 'but have you ever been *inside* them?'

A few hours later, at mid-day, Flavia was reading book six of the *Aeneid* to Nubia. Suddenly Scuto, curled up at their feet, lifted his head and uttered a bark, and shortly afterwards they heard a knock at the front door.

'We'll get it, Alma!' Flavia called, and hastily put down the scroll. 'They're back!' she exulted. 'Oh, I can't wait to see this!'

The girls hurried to the door. Scuto sensed their excitement and ran barking after them, his claws skittering on the marble floor.

Flavia slid back the bolt and threw open the door to reveal Caudex and the two boys. All three wore large grins.

'Lupus!' cried Flavia. 'You're clean! Your skin is three shades lighter! And they've cut your hair!'

'Shaved it more like!' said Jonathan, patting Lupus's fuzzy stubble. 'His head was crawling with nits!'

'Even that old tunic looks cleaner,' marvelled Flavia.

'They cleaned and pressed our clothes while we were in the baths,' said Jonathan, stepping into the atrium. 'Show them your hands, Lupus!'

Lupus held out his hands reluctantly as he followed Jonathan in. They were almost spotless and the nails neatly manicured. Nubia commented shyly,

'Smell nice!'

Scuto sniffed at Lupus's foot and then sneezed.

Caudex, who smelled strongly of rose oil, closed the door behind them and took up his usual post.

'I don't think Lupus liked the steam room much,' said Jonathan over his shoulder, 'but I couldn't get him out of the pool. He's a brilliant swimmer and he was as happy as a newt in a puddle. Weren't you, Lupus?'

Lupus nodded as they went into the garden.

'You're not limping any more!' cried Flavia.

'We both had a long massage,' said Jonathan. 'I thought it might ease his aches and bruises.'

'And did it?' Flavia asked Lupus.

For a reply, the beggar-boy nodded again.

'Hmmmn,' said Flavia. 'The only thing he needs now are sandals. He can't go in bare feet!'

'I have some at home. I outgrew them last year, but they're still in good condition . . .' suggested Jonathan.

'You and Lupus take the key and get them,' said Flavia, 'while I change into a different person, too!'

A girl and a boy stood outside a house with a red door at the bend of Green Fountain Street. The girl had clear grey eyes and wore a white stola. Her light brown hair was neatly coiled on top of her head, though one or two strands had already escaped. The boy had green eyes and very short brown hair. His tunic was faded but clean. Both wore bullas around their necks, marking them out as freeborn.

The girl knocked again. Presently, an old man opened the red door and after a moment they all disappeared inside.

Meanwhile, behind the same house in the graveyard, another boy and girl were climbing a tall poplar tree. The girl moved up quietly and fluidly, as if she had climbed trees all her life. She was beautiful, with very short black hair, dark brown skin and golden eyes. Among the dark leaves of the poplar, she was almost invisible. The boy who followed her had dark, curly hair, a strong, straight nose and eyes so dark they were almost black. Unlike the girl, he was not a graceful climber: he kept getting poked in the eye with twigs and leaves. And under his breath he uttered words a polite Roman boy should not even have known.

Flavia looked around the atrium. It had originally been the same size as the one in her house, but flimsy rooms had been constructed on either side, making it a narrow, dark corridor. An entire family seemed to occupy the atrium. She could hear a child singing tunelessly behind one of the curtained doorways, and a woman was washing nappies in the impluvium. Beside her squatted two runny-nosed toddlers, intent on a game they were playing with seed-pods and pine cones.

'Avitus and his wife have the balcony rooms,' mumbled the toothless old man. 'Go through the garden and up the stairs . . .' He didn't wait for a reply, but shuffled back to his cubicle and disappeared behind the curtain.

The woman washing clothes nodded at them as they squeezed by and Flavia murmured a polite greeting. Damp laundry hung from a washing line beneath the skylight, blocking off what little sunshine managed to enter the dismal room. A faint odour of stale sweat and frying onions hung in the air.

Flavia tugged Lupus's hand and they moved hesitantly down the corridor into what should have been the garden. Here too, old rooms had been enlarged and new rooms built, so that the garden had shrunk to a few paving stones with weeds pushing between them. A wizened vine struggled up a rickety trellis towards what little light there was.

It was hotter in the garden than in the atrium. The

family who occupied this part of the house had left the curtains of their cubicles open to catch any breeze. It was still siesta time and Flavia glimpsed suspicious eyes watching her from low beds in the dim rooms.

As she and Lupus started up the stairs a young woman in a black stola appeared on the balcony above them. She had a long nose and small mouth, and large, moist brown eyes.

'Have you come to see me?' The woman called down.

'We've come to see if Avita can play,' said Flavia in her little-girl voice. 'My name is um . . . Helena, and this is my brother Lucius. We have just returned from a voyage.'

'Oh!' cried the woman, and then said, 'You'd better come up.'

She met them at the top of the stairs and led them into a small, stuffy room with a low couch against one wall and a table against the other. A few flies buzzed round the remains of a meal on the table. The woman in black perched on a stool and invited the two of them to sit on the couch. Flavia noticed that some of the plaster was missing from the ceiling and one or two cracks snaked along the walls.

'My name is Julia Firma,' said the woman. 'I have some very sad news. My daughter died several weeks ago.'

Lupus burst into tears, quite convincingly, Flavia thought. She pretended to pat him consolingly. Then she said to Julia, 'But Avita always seemed so healthy.'

'I'm afraid she was bitten by a rabid dog. '

'Oh how awful!' cried Flavia. 'How did it happen?'

'It's so crowded here, as you can see.' Avita's mother waved vaguely towards the garden. 'My daughter loved to play in the graveyard among the trees and I never thought . . .'

Her voice trailed off and she swatted absently at a fly. 'One day she came home complaining of a dog bite. She was very brave. She cried a little but it was not deep, so I merely put ointment on it and didn't think about it again.' The woman closed her eyes for a moment and then continued.

'After a few days, we suspected something was wrong. First, Avita lost her appetite and then she began to be terrified of the sight of water. She even refused to drink. Finally she began to see things that weren't there. The end, when it came, was peaceful.'

Julia looked down and brushed some plaster dust from her dark stola.

'The tragedy was that her father was away on a voyage when it happened. Avita was our only surviving child and when my husband returned and discovered that we had lost her, he was inconsolable. He doesn't share my faith,' she added quietly.

'Your faith?' asked Flavia.

'I believe that after we die, we will go to a place more wonderful than we can imagine. Not the cold, dark underworld, but a sunny garden – a paradise. I trust Avita is there now. She was also a believer.' Julia Firma gazed at the faded plaster wall with a smile, as if she could see through it to a world beyond. Lupus and Flavia exchanged glances.

'Would you children like to see her room?' Avita's mother asked suddenly.

'Yes, please.' Flavia nodded politely, remembering to use her little-girl voice.

Julia Firma rose and led them next door into a tiny bedroom. A small window looked out onto the graveyard and the walls were decorated with faded frescoes of trees, shrubs and birds.

'She loved this room,' sighed Julia, and looked around with a sad smile. 'She used to tell me paradise would be like this.'

A narrow bed occupied most of the cubicle, which was tiny but spotlessly clean. At the head of the sleeping couch was a low table with Avita's possessions still laid out: a clay lamp, a few tiny glass bottles, a bronze mirror, and a wooden comb. On the bed lay a small painting of the girl.

Flavia and Lupus gazed at the portrait of Avita. Coloured wax had been applied to a flat piece of limewood with such skill that the face painted there seemed about to speak. The girl wore small gold earrings and a bulla round her neck.

The face gazing back at them seemed so cheerful and alert that Flavia's throat tightened painfully: for the first time she really felt the tragedy of the girl's death.

Lupus picked up the portrait to examine it more closely and Flavia gazed out of the window into the graveyard. She couldn't see Jonathan or Nubia anywhere, but as she pushed her face further out, she caught a spicy whiff of grasses and pine needles. She breathed the scent of life gratefully and then turned back to look for clues on the table.

The clay oil-lamp caught her eye. Its design was one she had never seen before. On its top – where most lamps had a cupid or a leaf – was a beardless man with a lamb across his shoulders.

'The shepherd,' murmured Julia, stepping in from the doorway. 'He has carried my little Avita home, like that lamb.'

'The shepherd?' said Flavia.

'Our God,' Julia replied simply. 'See the Greek letters alpha and omega on the spout? They mean . . .'

But Flavia never heard what she was going to say.

At that moment an angry voice behind them cried, 'What are you doing in my daughter's room? I warned you!'

Lupus whirled round and Flavia dropped the little clay lamp onto the floor. There in the doorway stood Publius Avitus Proculus. And he was very angry.

SCROLL XII

'I told you never to come in here,' shouted Avitus. He was rigid with anger and his heavy eyebrows made him look very fierce. But his anger was directed at his wife, not at Flavia and Lupus.

'But Publius!' Julia protested. 'These children were her friends. I was just showing them – '

'Get out!' Avitus commanded his wife.

For a tense moment they stared at one another.

'No I will not!' Julia finally said. 'She was my daughter, too. You're not the only one who misses her!'

'Yes, but *you'll* see her again one day in paradise, won't you?' There was bitter sarcasm in Avitus's voice.

'That doesn't mean I don't miss her now, Publius . . .' A tear slipped down her cheek. '. . . just as much as you do.'

Suddenly her husband sagged. The anger drained from his face and he began to weep.

'It's my fault she died!' he cried. 'If I had been here . . . I wasn't even here when she . . .'

Julia Firma went to her husband and put her arms round him. 'Of course it wasn't your fault. It wasn't anyone's fault. You must forgive yourself, Publius.'

Avitus and his wife wept in each other's arms and Flavia felt her own eyes prickle with tears. Lupus cleared his throat to attract her attention and made a tiny movement with his head towards the stairs.

Flavia nodded, and the two of them squeezed past the weeping couple and hurried quietly downstairs. They passed through the narrow garden and dark atrium, stepping carefully over the toddlers, and let themselves out.

As the door closed behind them, Flavia shivered and stood silently for a moment in the hot street, soaking up the intense warmth of the afternoon sun.

The next moment they heard the sound of feet pounding the pavement and looked up to see Nubia and Jonathan running towards them.

'Head gone!' said Nubia who reached them first.

And when Jonathan stood before them – wheezing and unable to speak – she said again, 'Dog's head is gone!'

The four friends stood in the graveyard and looked at the bodies of the two dead dogs under the tree. The corpses had already been picked at by crows. Now ants were doing their work, too. Flavia instinctively averted her eyes and then forced herself to look back. There were two bodies, a brown one and a black one, but only one head: the mastiff's big head had disappeared.

'Perhaps a crow carried it off,' Jonathan suggested.

Flavia gave him a sceptical look. 'Too heavy. It's more likely that your father took it to the magistrate for some reason.'

'I don't think so. Remember, he said even the blood might be dangerous.'

'Perhaps one of the dogs from the pack carried it off.'

'Perhaps.' Jonathan sounded doubtful.

Lupus cautiously searched the dry weeds around the leader's headless body. Then he crouched down and sniffed.

'Any clues, Lupus?' Flavia asked him.

He shook his head.

'Better get away from those corpses,' said a deep voice.

The four of them jumped. Behind them two soldiers stood leaning on shovels and perspiring heavily in the heat.

'We're to dispose of them as soon as possible,' said the taller of the two. 'Orders of the magistrate.' He thrust his shovel into the dry ground.

'Did you take the black dog's head?' Flavia asked when she had recovered from her surprise.

'No, sweetheart! Why should we do that?' His shovel sliced into the ground again.

'Well, it's not here and I just wondered – '

'She's right, Rufus!' said the short one, who was leaning on his spade. 'There's a missing head.'

'You'll be missing a head, too, if you don't start helping me dig!'

'What did you find out at Avita's?' whispered Jonathan as they stood in the shade of a pine, watching the soldiers work.

'Nothing much. Her parents both miss her, but her mother believes she's gone to some wonderful garden with a shepherd.'

Jonathan gave Flavia an odd look. She added,

'Avitus came in when we were in her room and got very angry. He does have a bad temper . . .'

'We already know that,' murmured Jonathan, and then added thoughtfully, 'we must find out more about him. If only we could follow him.'

Lupus tugged hopefully at Jonathan's tunic and pointed eagerly at himself.

'Thanks for offering to follow him, Lupus, but I think he'd recognise you now that he's seen you.'

Lupus's response was to bend down, pick up a handful of twigs and dust, and smear them over his face.

'Oh, Lupus!' cried Flavia. 'Just after we got you cleaned up!'

'He's right!' cried Jonathan. 'Everybody knows the beggar-boy at the junk man's stall. And no one ever takes any notice of him. Dressed like a beggar, Lupus is as good as invisible.' He slapped Lupus on the back and said, 'Better take off those sandals and my bulla and put on your own tunic again.'

When Lupus had been restored to his former filthy state, they left him sitting in the shade of a mulberry tree within sight of Avitus's front door. Flavia gave him his last instructions.

'When Avitus comes out of his house – *if* he comes out – follow him at a distance and look for any suspicious behaviour. If he leaves, use this piece of chalk to make an arrow on the tree trunk to show which way you've gone. Here's some bread and cheese in case you get hungry. Better put them out of sight.'

Lupus slipped them into a little cloth pouch tied to the belt of his tunic.

'You're sure you don't mind just sitting here and waiting?' asked Jonathan.

Lupus shook his head.

'We'll try to find out more about Avitus, too,' Flavia told Lupus. 'We'll all meet back at my house an hour before sunset to discuss our findings. Agreed?'

Lupus nodded. Flavia, Nubia and Jonathan set off back down the road. As they passed their house Nubia said to Flavia, 'Take Scuto?'

Flavia hesitated. Someone was killing dogs and she didn't want anything to happen to him. Her father had always told her never to venture into the city without Scuto, but surely if there were three of them they wouldn't come to any danger.

'I think he's safer at home with Caudex and Alma,' she decided.

'Shouldn't you tell them where you're going?' suggested Jonathan.

'If I do, they'll never let us go!' said Flavia. 'Come on!'

Lupus sat under the shade of the mulberry tree and looked up and down the street. It was the hottest part of the day. Most people would be napping in their cool gardens or relaxing at the baths. The street shimmered with heat as Lupus watched the others disappear round the bend in the road.

A flash of movement caught his eye as a slave emptied a chamber pot from an upstairs window. A splash and the squeak of wooden shutters being shut again, and then silence, apart from the chirring of the cicadas.

Lupus thought about Flavia and her friends for a while. Then he thought of all the food he'd eaten in the past few hours.

He usually hated food. He couldn't taste it, it was difficult to chew, and every bite threatened to choke him if he didn't swallow carefully. But when he had been presented with grapes and bread and honey and buttermilk, his body had craved it so badly that he had eaten in spite of the danger.

Now his belly was full and content. He felt sleepy, too. The slow rhythmic creaking of the cicadas in the hot summer afternoon made him feel drowsy. His eyelids grew heavy and almost shut. He shook himself awake angrily.

That was one advantage to being hungry all the time: it gave you an edge, an alertness. His sense of smell was always sharper if he hadn't eaten for a day or two. His eyesight was keener, too.

Was this how ordinary people felt most of the time, full and content and muzzy? He had smeared his face with dust and dirt but under his dirty old tunic his skin felt soft and clean, his muscles loose and relaxed. He could still smell the sandalwood oil they had massaged him with. It made him feel soft and vulnerable. The itching of vermin always used to help him stay alert and awake. But now there were no lice in his clothing and no nits in his hair.

He reached up and stroked his head and felt the soft stubble. It felt nice. How good it would be to live in a beautiful house like Flavia's and always have a full belly and clean clothes and to be able to nap during the hottest part of the afternoon in a cool garden by a splashing fountain. Or go to the baths whenever you wanted and swim in pools of crystal clear water with mosaics of sea nymphs at the bottom, and have all your aches massaged away.

How wonderful never to have to worry about where your next meal would come from. Never to have to worry about people who wanted to hurt you. Never to have to worry about being lonely. Lupus's eyes closed and for a moment he began to slip into the delicious oblivion of sleep.

Suddenly he started awake. Something had moved in the hot, deserted street. The red door was opening. A man closed it behind him and turned to go north towards the Roman Gate. It was Avitus and he was alone.

SCROLL XIII

'Where are you taking us?' Jonathan hesitated as they reached the green fountain that marked the end of their street.

'To the marina forum. The harbourmaster is my father's friend. He might know more about Avitus.'

'But I promised my father we wouldn't leave the street.' Jonathan shifted uneasily on the hot pavement.

'Come on, Jonathan,' Flavia said in her most persuasive voice. 'Don't you want to find out who killed Bobas?'

'Of course I do. But father trusts me.'

'He trusts you to help him,' Flavia said softly. 'It won't take long. I promise.'

Nubia looked from one to the other. After a moment Jonathan said abruptly:

'All right. Let's get this over with.' He set off down Fullers Street at a quick pace, and the girls hurried after him.

Apart from one or two slaves running errands for their masters, the whole town had gone indoors to seek refuge from the heat. Flavia and her friends were damp with sweat by the time they reached the Marina Gate. Through the marble arch, brilliant white against the azure sky, they could see the darker cobalt blue of the sea.

'The harbourmaster's name is Lucius Cartilius Popli-cola,' said Flavia as they all paused for a moment in the cool shade beneath the arch. Flavia pointed to the left.

'I think he works there.'

The marina forum was an open square surrounded on three sides by a covered, column-lined walkway.

In the mornings and late afternoons, stalls set up in the shade of this colonnade did brisk business selling select goods fresh off the ships: fish, exotic fruit, jewel-lery, perfume, wine and fabrics.

Now most of the stalls were closed for the long afternoon lunch. Only one or two remained open. Somewhere a flute warbled and nearby a fishmonger was calling, 'Fresh squid! Last of the catch! Fresh squid!' in a sleepy voice. At the far end of the square stood an imposing brick and marble building.

'His office is in there?' asked Jonathan.

'I think so,' replied Flavia, her confidence faltering. The door was guarded by a soldier on either side.

'Well, come on, then,' said Jonathan, and headed for the building.

As the three friends hurried under the shady col-onnade past mostly empty stalls, the sound of the flute grew louder. Suddenly, Flavia felt Nubia grip her hand.

'Look!' Nubia whispered.

Behind one of the stalls stood a tall, handsome African. His skin was deep brown, like Nubia's, and he had the same neat ears and amber eyes. He was blowing into a little flute made of dark wood.

The three friends stopped before his stall. On a large piece of peacock-blue silk lay flutes of many different shapes, sizes and colours. When the flautist saw them he put down his instrument and smiled with perfect white teeth. He addressed Nubia in a soft, fluid language.

Nubia's face lit up and she replied in the same tongue. As she and the young man conversed, Flavia and Jonathan looked at her in amazement. Speaking her own language, she seemed completely different: confident and proud.

Nubia and the young man spoke together for a few minutes and then the slave-girl pointed to a small flute, like the one he had been playing. The man smiled apologetically and said something to her. Then he turned to Flavia and Jonathan:

'The one she is asking about is made of lotus wood from my country. Very expensive. One gold piece. One hundred sesterces.'

Flavia gasped. One hundred sesterces was a soldier's monthly wage.

'Come on, Nubia,' she said, 'you can come back and talk to him another day soon.'

Nubia followed the others towards the harbour master's office. She only looked back once.

'Avitus?' bawled out the captain of the *Triton* to Flavia and her friends an hour later. 'He wouldn't hurt a fly. Very moody, though. Always writing poetry. About dolphins and waves and sea nymphs. Laughing one minute, crying the next. Doted on that little girl of his, though. I've never seen anyone so affected by the death of a child.'

Flavia, Jonathan and Nubia were standing on one of the small piers of the marina watching a ship called the

Triton undergo repairs. They hadn't been able to see Poplicola, but an ancient porter in the harbour offices had told them the name of Avitus's ship and even where it was berthed. Captain Alga was halfway up the mast of his ship but his voice was so loud that they could hear him even over the jingle of tackle, the slap of waves against the pier and the shouts and hammering of the sailors.

'Have you seen him recently?' shouted Flavia.

'Avitus?' Captain Alga yelled back. 'No, he's on leave until tomorrow. Then we're off to Sicily again. We've been stuck here for two weeks trying to get our mast refitted. The old one was shattered in a storm. Most amazing storm I've ever experienced. Really thought we were going to Neptune's palace, if you know what I mean. All of us thanking whatever gods we believe in that we're alive and no sooner does he step off the ship than he's greeted with the news of his daughter's death. Told me he wished he had drowned in the storm and had never known what happened to her. Poor little thing – '

The captain would have bellowed on, but Flavia hastily shouted her thanks and led the others back up the pier.

'Well, *he* didn't seem to think Avitus was dangerous,' mused Flavia. 'But Libertus saw Avitus running with a bag, and . . .' Her voice trailed off as she considered the problem.

A fishing boat had just docked and the fishermen were unloading the day's catch. Two lean young men, naked apart from loincloths and as brown as chestnuts, were carrying baskets of gleaming fish down a wobbly boarding plank. One of them nearly slipped and fell, but he regained his balance and leapt lightly onto the pier while the other cursed him good-naturedly.

Nubia stared at the gangplank and shivered. It reminded her of the first time she had been forced to board a ship, at Alexandria. Venalicius had cracked his whip and forced them towards a narrow piece of wood which bridged the land and the boat. The gangplank rose and fell as if it were breathing and Shanakda – a girl from her clan – had screamed hysterically and refused to go up it, alarming all the others. Without warning, Venalicius had furiously unlocked her collar and pushed her into the water, though her hands had still been tied.

Nubia would never forget the sight of bitter sea-water filling Shanakda's screaming mouth and silencing her forever. They had all been quiet after that. Quiet and cowed for the whole voyage to Italia.

Nubia shivered again and felt Flavia's arm around her shoulders.

'I know you don't like boats, Nubia,' whispered Flavia. 'We'll go home right now . . .'

But as they turned left and started back towards the Marina Gate, Nubia saw a sight which made her heart pound. Three large men were sauntering straight towards them. Nubia knew them immediately. Their faces appeared often in her nightmares. They were Venalicius's henchmen, from the slave ship.

Nubia stopped short and looked frantically round, squinting against the glare of the sun on the water. The slave ship *Vespa* was berthed in the marina! She would know that hateful black and yellow striped sail any-where. And there was Venalicius himself, leering at her from the deck with his one good eye.

'Run for your lives!' cried Nubia. She gripped Flavia's arm tightly, 'Venalicius has seen us and sent his men to capture us!'

'What? What about Venalicius?' Flavia frowned at her.

Nubia suddenly realised she had been speaking in her native language. Now she tried to remember the Latin for 'run' but her mind had gone blank.

The men were getting closer. One of them was looking directly at her and smiling an evil smile.

In desperation, Nubia pointed towards the men, and then towards Venalicius.

Flavia saw the slave-dealer watching them from his ship and understood at once.

'Run, Jonathan! Run!' She grabbed his arm and pulled.

They turned and began to run back along the water-front away from the Marina Gate: Flavia first, then Nubia, then Jonathan.

'Why are we running?' shouted Jonathan, leaping over a rolled up fishnet.

'Venalicius's men are after us!' Flavia dodged a sailor.

'Who's Venalicius?'

'Slave-dealer!' shouted Flavia. 'If he catches us, he'll sell us on the far side of the world, where nobody will ever find us.'

She led them round a half-loaded cart, under an unmanned customs stall, and past the building site of the new marina baths.

'Are they still after us?' Flavia called over her shoulder.

'Yes!' gasped Jonathan.

Flavia's ankle started to ache and she realised Jonathan was wheezing. She had to find them some way of escape quickly. The marina piers were on the right. They'd be trapped if they went down one of those. There were some brick warehouses on the left, but again, if they went into one of those there might be no way out. The beach lay ahead of them, but there was no shelter there.

Suddenly Jonathan cried:

'I know where we can hide! Follow me!'

He turned and raced up the narrow alley between the last two warehouses on the waterfront. The alley was narrow and dark. It smelled of urine and vomit and worse. The ground was slippery with rotting fish scales and garbage.

Flavia hoped Jonathan knew what he was doing.

If he didn't, and if Venalicius's men caught them, she knew the three of them would be tied up in the hold of the slave-ship Vespa by that evening.

SCROLL XIV

Slipping from shadow to shadow, Lupus silently followed Avitus to Ropemakers Street. Red brick tenement houses three and four storeys high rose on either side of the street. Their ground floors were all taken up by one-roomed workshops which sold rope, nets, canvas and basketry. These shops were shuttered up, for the shopkeepers had retired to their apartments to rest until the day grew cooler.

Squeezed between two workshops at the end of the street nearest the theatre, was a narrow doorway. A wooden bead curtain hung in this doorway, and above it someone had painted an Egyptian eye. At least a dozen cats, half-starved and half-wild, napped in the bright sun beside the doorway. The timid creatures scattered as Avitus approached this doorway and pushed through the curtain.

Lupus knew almost everyone in this part of town, and he knew the woman who occupied the tiny room behind the bead curtain. She was an Egyptian soothsayer who called herself Hariola.

As quietly as a grass snake, Lupus slipped across the street, closer to the doorway. Then, making himself as small as possible, he sat in the narrow shadow cast by the overhang of one of the shops.

No one would notice him, and even if they did, they would just see a sleepy beggar-boy. He listened as hard as a rabbit, but although he could hear a man's muffled voice and then Hariola's husky croak, he could not make out their words. The voices went silent for a while. Lupus guessed the soothsayer was poking at chicken entrails or staring into a sacred bauble. Presently the woman's voice rang out, it sounded dramatic and false. Then he heard the man replying angrily and now he could hear the words clearly.

'You're lying! You don't know a thing about it!' Avitus shouted.

Abruptly, there was a clatter of beads as Avitus pushed through the curtain. A moment later the wooden beads rattled again and at the same time the sickly-sweet aroma of cheap musk filled Lupus's nostrils: the soothsayer had come out, too.

'Where's my money?' she hissed. 'That's three sesterces you owe me!'

Lupus did not dare put his head round the wall to look. Then he heard Avitus's retreating footsteps and Hariola's rasping voice: 'Unless you offer a sacrifice to the god Anubis, your daughter's spirit will never be at rest!' There was a pause and then he heard the woman shriek:

'May the gods curse you!' She muttered something in a language he could not understand.

As soon as he heard the bead curtain rattle again, Lupus quickly ran off to follow Avitus.

After Avitus left the soothsayer, he went straight to a tavern. Lupus rounded the corner just in time to see him disappear through the door. It was an inn Lupus was familiar with, and he hesitated a moment before entering.

The Medusa Tavern smelled of sour wine and fish soup. As his eyes grew accustomed to the gloom, Lupus saw several drinkers slouched over trestle tables. Avitus stood at the bar, already draining his first beaker.

Lupus took an empty wine cup from one of the tables, sat cross-legged in the sawdust on the floor, and placed the cup in front of him. Then he hung his head to make himself look more pathetic. He didn't expect to receive any coins, but there were three coppers in his cup by the time Avitus moved unsteadily out of the dim tavern into the blazing heat of the afternoon.

Lupus shadowed Avitus from one inn to the next, all the way to the docks. By the time Avita's father staggered into an inn beside the mouth of the river Tiber, Lupus had made nearly two sesterces from begging.

The Grain and Grape was a favourite of the soldiers stationed in Ostia: their barracks were nearby. An entire cohort from Rome – six hundred soldiers – patrolled the town in shifts. They worked hard keeping law and order, and guarding against fires. In their spare time, many of them liked to relax at the waterfront taverns with a cup of spiced wine and a game of dice.

A group of off-duty soldiers were there now, gaming with a few civilians at a table overlooking the river harbour. Unlike the other inns Avitus had visited, the Grain and Grape was light and airy. Large open windows offered views of the Mediterranean on one side and the mouth of the Tiber on the other. The late afternoon breeze, which sailors called Venus' Breath, had just started to rise off the sea. It brought a delicious coolness to the inn.

As the gamers called loudly for grilled sausages and honeyed wine, Lupus scanned the room for Avitus: predictably, he was hunched over a drink at the bar.

Hearing the clatter of dice and the laughter of the soldiers, Lupus judged they were in just the right mood to be generous. It would be a shame to miss this opportunity.

Keeping his head down, the beggar-boy approached the soldiers' table, and pitifully held out his empty cup. Most tossed in a few small coins, and one civilian put in half a spiced sausage. Satisfied, Lupus sat on the floor in the sawdust.

Avitus hadn't budged. He was still leaning on the bar pouring wine from a flagon. It was his ninth or tenth drink in under two hours.

Lupus emptied the coins into his cloth pouch and put the empty cup in front of him. He tossed in a coin – one always encouraged more – and munched the sausage carefully.

He found himself thinking about the portrait of Avita, the little girl who had died of a dog bite. He thought of the way the artist had added a tiny white dot to each of her eyes to make them sparkle. He wondered how the paint was made, and how painters were trained. And who were they? Greeks, like the potters? Alexandrians, like the glassmakers? Ephesians, like the silversmiths?

He was studying a fresco of Bacchus and Ceres on

the opposite wall when a scuffle broke out at the end of the table nearest to him. A soldier and his young civilian gaming partner were arguing.

The burly soldier grasped a handful of his companion's tunic, pulled him across the table and growled threats into his ear. The others laughed and ignored them, but Lupus saw what they did not: the soldier's dagger glinting beneath the table.

Drops of red liquid spattered onto the sawdust. Lupus stiffened. Then he relaxed as he realised it was only wine; the big soldier had knocked over the civilian's wine cup.

The young man pleaded with the soldier in an urgent whisper. Lupus pricked up his ears, and leaned a little closer.

'. . . at the house of the sea captain Flavius Geminus,' he heard the young man hiss. 'I swear it! A vast treasure! I promise I'll have the money I owe you by tomorrow!'

A vast treasure!

Lupus had never met Flavia's father, but he knew his name was Marcus Flavius Geminus, and that he was a sea captain. There couldn't possibly be two captains by that name in Ostia.

Out of the corner of his eye, Lupus saw the young man relax back onto his bench as the soldier released him. He was well-dressed and, judging from his voice, well-educated, too: probably a young patrician who'd gambled away his allowance. For the next ten years.

The soldier resembled the statue of Hercules near the forum, only bigger and uglier.

'Tomorrow then,' growled the soldier, and Lupus saw the knife go back into its sheath.

Suddenly Lupus remembered what he was supposed to be doing in the tavern. He glanced at the bar, just to make sure the man he was following was still there.

But Avitus had gone.

SCROLL XV

As Jonathan ran up the narrow alley, with Flavia and Nubia close behind him, his mind was racing. Just beyond this warehouse, where the piers ended and the beach began, was the synagogue. Although his family had not been welcome there for several months, he knew it as well as he knew his own house. If only they could get there before the slave-dealers' men caught them.

'Can you see them yet?' he gasped back to Flavia. He was finding it hard to breathe.

'No . . .' he heard her answer, then, 'yes! They're still chasing us!'

Jonathan nearly slipped on something slimy and wet, but he felt Flavia's arm steady him.

'Thanks!' he said, and heard the wheezing in his own voice.

A moment later the three friends shot out of the alley and were nearly trampled by a two-horse carruca. They had come out onto the main coastal road.

'Watch where you're going!' cried the angry driver of the wagon, trying to calm his horses.

'Sorry!' gasped Jonathan over his shoulder.

They ran down the road, overtaking a creaking mule-drawn cart and almost trampling three slaves napping in the shade behind a warehouse.

Jonathan knew exactly where he was going. When he had attended school at the synagogue, he and his friend David had discovered a way out via the courtyard. They would climb onto a branch of the fig tree, walk along the wall, and jump down onto a pile of stone blocks left behind by builders. If only the blocks were still there, he could lead Flavia and Nubia to safety. Once inside the synagogue, they should be safe. Even if the men followed them, Jonathan knew a dozen hiding places.

'Please God, may the blocks be there,' Jonathan prayed silently.

As they rounded the corner of the warehouse, Jonathan breathed a sigh of relief. Although half hidden by weeds, the blocks were visible, still piled against the side wall of the synagogue.

Jonathan sprinted across a short stretch of sandy waste ground and was up the blocks and onto the wall in moments. Straddling the top of the wall and gasping for air, he helped Nubia and Flavia up.

'It's a long drop,' said Flavia dubiously, looking down into the courtyard.

'Along wall . . . to fig tree,' wheezed Jonathan, fighting for breath. 'Then climb down.'

Nubia, holding her arms out like an elegant tightrope walker, began to move quickly along the top of the wall towards the tree. Flavia followed, scooting rapidly instead of walking. By the time Nubia had reached the tree and had gracefully lowered herself down, Flavia was only halfway there.

'Hurry, Flavia!' gasped Jonathan as he rose to stand on top of the wall.

'I am!' she muttered between gritted teeth.

Flavia stretched forward, grabbed a branch and swung down. For a moment she hung from the fig tree, then dropped down into the courtyard.

'Ow!' she cried. 'My sore ankle.'

Jonathan looked down. The girls' faces seemed very small as they watched him balance on the wall. He felt dizzy and out of breath, but he had done this many times before. Only a few steps and then he would be safe.

He took one faltering step, then another. The trick was not to look directly down, but to fix your eyes on a point some distance ahead.

Another step. He was almost there.

Suddenly he heard a cry to his left. Jonathan's head jerked round: Venalicius's three henchmen had just rounded the corner of the warehouse and had caught sight of him. They were running towards him.

He shouldn't have looked. It broke his concentration and he felt himself losing his balance. Flapping his arms wildly, Jonathan uttered an involuntary cry and tumbled off the wall.

Flavia screamed as Jonathan fell, but by some miracle one of his flailing hands caught a branch and he managed to hold on. For a moment he swung wildly among the leaves, startling a sleeping blackbird which flew up out of the tree with a staccato warning cry. Jonathan reached up with his other hand and grasped the branch. He hung for a moment, wheezing and gasping, trying to think what to do next.

Another shrill scream pierced the air. This time it was Nubia.

An ugly face had appeared over the wall. It was one of Venalicius's men!

The three of them gazed in horrified fascination at his ugly face: he had a broken nose and eyes that pointed in different directions. One eye seemed to be looking at Jonathan, as he dangled from the tree. The other gazed fiercely down at the two girls.

Then the ugly eyes opened wide and he looked past the girls at something behind them.

Flavia and Nubia turned and screamed again.

Looming above them was a huge figure in a black robe and turban.

For a split second, Flavia thought it was Mordecai. Then she realised this man had a longer beard. Also he was taller, heavier and much fiercer-looking. Venalicius's henchman must have thought so, too: his unpleasant face disappeared back down behind the synagogue wall.

The man in black gave the girls a cold look and then turned his gaze on Jonathan, still hanging limply from the fig tree.

'Shalom, Jonathan,' he said in a dry voice, and then moved underneath the boy and added something in Hebrew.

'Shalom, Rabbi,' wheezed Jonathan. He let go of the branch and fell into the man's strong arms. The rabbi lowered him gently to the ground. Jonathan stood gasping and trying to catch his breath.

The rabbi looked sternly at the girls and said in Latin, 'What are you doing here?'

'I'm sorry, sir,' said Flavia, 'but we were being chased.'

'Yes,' replied the rabbi, 'so it would appear.'

He glanced at Jonathan.

'This boy is not welcome here,' he said tersely. 'His father teaches dangerous lies and has disturbed many.' He looked at Jonathan, who was breathing marjoram oil, and Flavia saw his face soften a fraction.

'It is hard enough for us as it is,' said the rabbi, 'without being associated with these . . .' he hesitated and then said bitterly: '. . . these Christians.'

Flavia gasped and looked at Jonathan. 'You're a Christian?'

Jonathan nodded miserably.

Nubia tugged at Flavia's tunic.

'What Christian?' she asked.

'I'll tell you later,' said Flavia grimly.

Jonathan turned to the man in black.

'I'm sorry, Rabbi,' he pleaded, 'we didn't know where else to hide.'

The rabbi's face relaxed and he said to Jonathan,

'I suppose you can't be blamed for your father's misguided beliefs. Besides, the Master of the Universe, blessed be he, tells us to act justly and to love mercy . . .'

He tugged at his thick beard.

'However, I'm afraid there are others who would not be so understanding if they knew you were here. You must leave now.'

Jonathan nodded. 'Of course. We'll go immediately.'

'Just a minute.' The rabbi put his hand on Jonathan's shoulder. 'Let me check to see if it's safe.' He unbolted the double doors on the eastern side of the courtyard and peered out. Then he turned to them.

'No sign of any pursuers,' he said, and held open the doors.

As each of the three passed through the doorway he touched their heads and murmured a blessing.

'Go in peace,' he said gruffly, and then added, 'and go quickly.'

As the synagogue door closed behind them, Jonathan turned to Flavia. 'Which way shall we go?' he asked her.

'They might be waiting for us back at the docks.' Flavia frowned.

'The quickest way home is over the dunes through the graveyard,' said Jonathan.

'But what if we meet the wild dogs again?' asked Flavia nervously.

'Which would you rather meet again?' said Jonathan, starting across the coastal road, 'A few dogs, or those men?'

'A few dogs, I suppose . . .'

'Why didn't you tell us you and your family were Christians?' Flavia asked Jonathan as they set off across the dunes. 'I thought you were Jews.'

The sun threw their shadows ahead of them and a light breeze ruffled their tunics. After a moment Jonathan spoke.

'It's hard to explain. We *are* Jewish, but Christus is

the Latin name for our Messiah, so they call us Christians.'

Flavia said in a low voice:

'I've heard that Christians eat their God and my father says they burned Rome the year he put on the toga virilis, the year he was sixteen.'

'That's not true,' said Jonathan angrily. 'Everyone knows Nero only blamed the Christians for burning Rome so that people wouldn't be angry with *him*. Christians are peaceful. We are taught to love our enemies and pray for them.'

'You love your *enemies*?'

'We try to,' Jonathan sighed.

'But isn't it dangerous being a Christian?'

'Yes, it is. We can't worship openly because so many people hate us.' He trudged up a sand dune, wheezing a little, then added bitterly, 'They don't even take the trouble to find out what we believe.'

Flavia was about to ask Jonathan what Christians *did* believe when he stopped short.

'Uh-oh,' he said quietly. They were almost out of the dunes, and he had stopped to look up towards the graveyard. 'Here they come.'

Trotting out of the shimmering heat to meet them, almost like old friends, was a pack of six or seven panting dogs. The friends froze and looked around, but out there on the dunes there was nowhere to run and nowhere to hide.

SCROLL XVI

Lupus rushed out of the tavern and almost collided with Avitus, who was bending over the road. The boy jumped back just in time to avoid being spattered with vomit. Avitus didn't notice the beggar-boy who had been in his daughter's room earlier that day. He wouldn't have noticed a sea nymph riding by on a centaur. He was being violently ill.

Lupus backed off and hid behind a statue of the Emperor Claudius.

Avitus was sick until finally he was retching up nothing. At last he stood, looking pale and haggard, his heavy eyebrows a dark line across his brow. He wiped his sweaty forehead with his arm and turned north towards the new imperial harbour.

It was a beautiful blue afternoon, and as the day cooled, the port was coming to life. Venus' Breath had whipped up the sea beyond the river mouth and it was a deep sapphire colour. The sails of ships moving to and fro on the water made triangles of white and yellow against the blue.

The air was so clear that almost every brick of the distant lighthouse was visible against the afternoon sky. It was as if Lupus was seeing the structure for the first time. The tower looked like three huge red dice piled one on the other, each smaller than the one below, with a great plume of smoke furling away from the cylindrical platform at the very top.

Perhaps Avitus was also seeing the lighthouse as if for the first time, for presently he set off straight towards the ferry which would take him across the Tiber to the new harbour. Somehow, Lupus knew the little girl's father was heading for the lighthouse. And somehow, he thought he knew why.

'Sit down on the sand,' said Flavia firmly to her friends as the dogs approached.

'Sit *down*? Are you mad?' Jonathan's voice was a bit too shrill. 'A pack of wild dogs are heading straight for us, about to chew us to pieces and you say sit down?'

'That's what Pliny says to do,' said Flavia. 'Your father lent me his book about natural history. Pliny says, "An angry attack can be averted by sitting on the ground".'

'Dogs not angry,' said Nubia, gripping Flavia's arm.

'What do you mean, the dogs aren't angry?' yelled Jonathan. 'They're wild, rabid, mad, hydrophobic killers!'

He pulled his sling from his belt. The slave-girl knew immediately what it was and put a restraining hand on his arm.

'No throw rock. Make dogs angry,' she pleaded.

Jonathan hesitated and then looked to Flavia for guidance. The dogs were almost upon them.

'She's been right about everything else so far,' said Flavia. 'Let's trust her!' She paused. 'And let's trust Pliny, too. Sit down.'

Flavia sat cross-legged on the sand, pulling the other two down beside her. Jonathan closed his eyes and began muttering something in his native language. Flavia suspected he was praying.

The dogs were now so close that she could see their eyes and pink tongues. The lead dog had something in its mouth. Flavia was afraid to look. She closed her eyes but then opened them a crack to peep through. The thing in the dog's mouth looked like a child's arm, or maybe a dirty leg-bone.

She closed her eyes again and waited for the inevitable chomp of jaws on flesh. Now the creatures were so close that she could hear their tongues panting and smell their doggy breath. She stifled a scream as several cold noses prodded and sniffed her, but she felt no pain.

Presently she heard a low growl. The new leader, a brown dog with pointed ears and face, stood before them, his tail wagging. He had dropped the mysterious object on the sand.

Flavia peeked with one eye, then opened the other.

'A stick!' she gasped. 'It's only a stick!' And then, as the realisation dawned, 'They want us to *play* with them, to throw the stick!'

'That's all they've ever wanted!' laughed Jonathan, and Nubia began to laugh, too.

'And we thought they wanted to kill us!'

With tears of laughter and relief flowing down her face, Flavia knelt and reached for the stick. The leader watched, alert and panting eagerly. Flavia stood, drew back her arm as far as she could and then threw the stick towards the blue line of the sea beyond the dunes.

Like arrows released from a bow, the dogs were after it, barking and yelping with delight.

'Run!' laughed Jonathan, scrambling to his feet and helping Nubia up.

The three of them ran as fast as they could away from the dogs, towards the tombs.

But before they had reached the harder ground which bordered the necropolis, the dogs were back again, surrounding them.

Again, the leader dropped the stick. This time, however, Flavia reached for it too quickly. The leader lunged forward snarling, and almost seized her hand.

'Oh!' cried Flavia, 'I startled him!'

'Let Nubia do it,' said Nubia softly. She reached for the stick carefully, and threw it hard towards the sea. Again the dogs went one way and the children the other.

Again, they were soon surrounded by the dogs.

'Now it's not so funny,' gasped Flavia, as she threw the stick again. 'At this rate, it will take us hours to get home.'

'And the sun will be setting soon,' added Jonathan, whose asthma was making him wheeze again. 'Father will murder me when I get back.'

'Cheer up, maybe the dogs will kill you first,' joked Flavia, and was relieved to see Jonathan grin back.

Once again they were surrounded by a solid, panting mass of dogs and presented with a wet stick.

It was Jonathan's turn to throw the stick. He gingerly picked up the sopping piece of driftwood and allowed some of the saliva to drip off it. 'What does Pliny say about mad dog's slobber?' he asked, wrinkling his nose.

The leader growled. The dogs were becoming more and more impatient, more and more demanding. Something had to be done.

'Nubia has idea,' ventured the slave-girl, 'of escape from dogs.' The others turned and looked at her hopefully.

Just as Lupus was about to slip through the gate of the low wall surrounding the lighthouse, one of the guards playing dice looked up.

'Hey, you!' he bellowed, jumping to his feet. 'Get away from here!' The other two glanced over. They looked bored.

Lupus grunted in protest and pointed urgently at the lighthouse. Avitus had passed through the gate unchallenged only a moment before. The soldiers had been so intent on their game that they hadn't noticed him.

'I said get out!' The guard lumbered over and thrust his face into Lupus's. His breath reeked of garlic and his tunic stank of sweat.

Lupus lowered his arm, and then opening his eyes wide as if in surprise, he pointed again. At last the guard turned to look, but Avitus had just disappeared into the lower entrance of the tower.

Lupus let his shoulders slump and turned as if to go. Then he whirled around and darted through the gate while the soldier's guard was down.

Lupus was quick, but the soldier was quicker, and Lupus felt the air knocked out of him as the soldier grabbed his belt from behind. The other two guards rose to their feet and sauntered over.

'Look, you!' said Garlic-breath, holding Lupus aloft

by his belt. 'I'm going to count to ten and when I finish I don't want to see your snotty little face anywhere around here. Or else I'll throw you in the harbour. *Do you understand?*' He dropped Lupus onto the hard concrete of the breakwater.

On his hands and knees, Lupus nodded, and glanced quickly up at the lighthouse. There must be slaves at the top to feed the fire, but he couldn't see anyone. A great plume of black smoke was being fanned towards the town by the stiffening offshore breeze. From this close, the top seemed an immense height above him.

At that moment, Lupus saw Avitus appear on the second level. He seemed very high up.

Lupus scrambled to his feet and tried pointing again, but the soldier had already begun counting in a loud voice: 'six, seven, eight – .'

'Wait, Grumex!' said one of the other soldiers. 'I think I just saw someone up there.'

Garlic-breath whirled round, but Avitus had disappeared again. They all squinted up at the red brick tower, looking for movement. Apart from the smoke billowing far above them and a few gliding seagulls, there was nothing. In the silence, Lupus could hear the waves slapping against the breakwater and he felt a fine spray on the side of his face.

'You're crazy!' said Grumex after a few moments, but he sounded doubtful. 'Better go and check anyway . . .' he added after a moment. Then, noticing Lupus, he snarled,

'Go on! Get out of here!'

Lupus was backing off when suddenly, behind him, a woman carrying a fishing net screamed. At the edge of the highest tier of the lighthouse, a figure stood silhouetted against the sky.

'A man!' the woman shrieked, dropping her net and pointing. 'There's a man on the lighthouse and I think he's going to jump!'

SCROLL XVII

The dogs' leader growled low in his throat. Jonathan dropped the slimy stick and looked at Nubia.

'OK,' he said. 'What's your idea?'

The slave-girl closed her eyes.

She began to hum: softly at first, then louder. Then she took a deep breath and started to sing a strange, tuneless song. It made the fine hairs at the back of Flavia's neck stand up. The dogs began to whimper. Presently one or two of them sat.

Nubia was singing a song her father had taught her: the Dog-Song. She sang the story of how dogs had once been like jackals, wolves and desert foxes, hunting in the cold night. She reminded the dogs of how their ancestors used to howl at the moon from loneliness and hunger and a yearning for something they had never known.

The dogs began to howl with Nubia. Jonathan and Flavia exchanged wide-eyed looks, then turned back to watch her in fascination.

Gradually Nubia's song changed. She began to croon the story-song, relating how dogs discovered man and fire and warmth and safety. How they no longer had to roam cold and hungry at night, but could curl up beside the fire with a full belly and someone to scratch them behind their ears.

The dogs had stopped howling now, and were settling down. One or two were actually lying on the ground panting, their eyes half closed. The others were sitting. The leader whined and half stood, as if he felt his power fading.

But now Nubia was singing of warmth and love and loyalty and devotion, and finally he too settled down, rested his sharp, brown muzzle on his paws, and listened.

Bathed in the red light of the setting sun, the sea was the colour of purple wine. Lupus knew his friends would have been expecting him for some time now, but he could not leave the great curving breakwater on which the lighthouse stood.

Quite a crowd had gathered by now. The lighthouse was a dark shape against the blood-red sun, and the great plume of smoke from the bonfire at its top was as black as ink.

A hundred feet above them stood two tiny figures, silhouetted against the fading sky. One was poised at the very edge of the platform. The other figure, a soldier, stood on the same level, but further away. Every time he started to move, the man on the edge swayed forward as if to jump, and the crowd gasped.

A centurion was moving through the crowd asking if anyone knew who the man on the lighthouse was. Lupus considered trying to catch his eye, but even if he managed to communicate with him, what would he say? That the man's name was Avitus? That he was consumed with grief for his dead daughter and had been drinking wine all afternoon? What good would that do?

Lupus hung his head as the officer pushed past. But he needn't have bothered: the centurion didn't even glance at him.

The crowd suddenly gasped again and Lupus looked up. High above them, the soldier was finally approaching Avitus with his hand extended.

It was at that moment that the tiny black figure swaying on the edge silently pitched forward and fell through space. There was a cry from the onlookers as the figure struck the edge of the first tier, bounced and tumbled like a rag doll down to the concrete below.

Humming softly, Nubia stepped carefully around the dogs. Flavia and Jonathan followed her. Resisting the urge to run, the three friends made their way through the necropolis, now full of long, purple shadows. Behind them, the dogs sat or lay, almost as if they had been drugged. One, a heavily pregnant bitch, followed them for a while and then turned back with a wistful whine.

Flavia suddenly realised she was so thirsty she could hardly swallow. She tried not to think how wonderful a cup of cool water would taste. She would even drink the water at the green fountain, though it always tasted slightly mouldy.

Up the dusty road the three of them went, past trees whose leaves glowed like emeralds in the light of the setting sun, past the cooling glade where Avita was buried, past the tomb of fighting gladiators, and on through Fountain Gate.

As soon as they had passed beneath its arch, they knew they were safe. Without a word, they ran to the green-tiled fountain in the centre of the crossroads and plunged their dusty faces into the cold water. Then, each chose a spout and drank deeply. Flavia had never tasted anything as delicious as that water, even with its slight taint.

At last they turned their tired feet for home, dreading the reception they would get.

Rounding the corner, they were surprised to find a group of soldiers standing outside Cordius's house. An official-looking person, a magistrate, was deep in discussion with Libertus himself. Several passers-by had stopped to watch. Among them Flavia noticed the fat merchant in the grubby toga whom she'd seen laughing with Venalicius at the slave market.

Suddenly Libertus glanced up and saw Flavia.

'Those are the children I was telling you about!' she heard him say to the official. The young freedman smiled and beckoned them over.

'Their dog was killed, too,' Libertus was telling the magistrate, 'and beheaded! Just like Ruber!' He turned his dark blue eyes on Flavia. 'Avitus has just killed Ruber!'

'Ruber? Who's Ruber?' asked Flavia. But at that moment Cordius's front door opened and two soldiers emerged. Between them walked the sour doorkeeper who had let the girls in earlier that morning. Tears streamed down his hollow cheeks and in his arms he carried the headless body of a red hound.

'These children know who killed the dogs!' Libertus repeated to the magistrate. 'They know the man who knocked my porter unconscious and killed my watchdog. They know his name and even have a portrait of him on a wax tablet.'

'But – ' said Flavia.

'Your dog was killed as well?' asked the magistrate. 'And you think you know who did it?' He was a short man with thinning hair and pale, intelligent eyes.

'Well . . .' began Flavia, thinking of Avitus sobbing in his wife's arms and writing poetry about dolphins. 'We're not *positive* – '

'I still think he did it,' said Jonathan.

'And so do I!' agreed Libertus. 'I saw him running away from this boy's house yesterday, and it must be the same man who killed my dog. There can't be two dog-killers on the same street!' He turned to Flavia. 'Do you still have the drawing?'

Flavia pulled the wax tablet from her belt and showed the magistrate Lupus's sketch.

'He lives just up the road and his name is Publius Avitus Proculus,' said Jonathan firmly. 'His daughter was killed by a mad dog several weeks ago.'

'Well,' said the magistrate to the captain of the soldiers, 'I think we'd better interview this Avitus. Can you take us to his house, young man?'

'Yes, I can,' said Jonathan importantly, and led the way up the road to the house with the red door. Then he stood back while the magistrate pounded the knocker. Gradually the small crowd grew silent, and fixed their eyes on the door, waiting for someone – perhaps even the dog-killer himself – to answer.

As they waited, Flavia felt a touch on her arm. Nubia was pointing to the mulberry tree. On its trunk was scrawled a faint chalk arrow: it pointed north, towards the Roman Gate.

'That means Lupus *did* follow Avitus,' whispered Flavia. 'I wonder if he's back yet?'

'You wonder if who's back yet?' said a man's voice behind her.

Flavia jumped, then relaxed to see it was only Mordecai.

'Peace be with you.' He gave his little bow. 'Where is Jonathan?' he asked, 'and what is going on?'

'He's right there, by those soldiers.' Flavia pointed. 'He's helping the magistrate. Cordius's watchdog has just been killed and beheaded.'

At that moment the red door opened and the crowd held their collective breath. In the darkening twilight, Flavia could just make out Julia, Avitus's wife, at the door. They all saw her shake her head.

It was becoming too dark for any further investigation. Slaves were lighting lamps in the houses nearby. The magistrate and the soldiers marched past them back to their barracks.

Mordecai glowered at them as they passed.

'I spent nearly one whole day in a clerk's office only to be told nothing could be done,' he grumbled. 'But when a rich man's watchdog is killed the crime is under investigation within minutes!'

'Father!' cried Jonathan, running up. Mordecai was

surprised to find his son's arms around him. 'Father, don't be angry!'

Flavia secretly gave Jonathan's arm a pinch. 'Your father has only just now returned,' she said with a significant look. She didn't want him to tell Mordecai they had broken their promise.

'Why should I be angry?' asked the doctor.

'Er, no reason,' Jonathan said. 'It's just that our house key is still at Flavia's!' Mordecai looked sharply at Jonathan, so Flavia said quickly,

'What did you find out from the magistrate?'

'Well,' said the doctor, as they began to walk back down the street, 'he told me the dogs here in Ostia aren't truly wild. Most of them used to be tame, but their masters either died or abandoned them. They became feral, that is half-wild, and they began to run together in a pack. One clerk I spoke with said they weren't really dangerous, but just a nuisance.

'He also told me that dogs with hydrophobia, or mad dogs, always run alone. Because, you see, even the other dogs are afraid of them.'

The street had emptied and total darkness had descended by the time they reached Flavia's house. The double doors of Cordius's house opposite had been shut and bolted. Two blazing torches had been set on either side. They lit up the porch as if it were day.

'Should we light our torches, too?' said Flavia, almost to herself.

'No need,' said Mordecai, 'Cordius no longer has a watchdog, but you still do.'

An awful thought suddenly struck Flavia and Nubia

at the same time and they looked at each other fearfully.

'I *hope* we still have a watchdog!' cried Flavia, and pounded hard on her door.

SCROLL XVIII

Flavia banged the bronze figure of Castor hard against the bronze Pollux again and again, frantically calling Caudex.

'Listen!' said Nubia suddenly, putting her hand on Flavia's arm.

From deep inside the house they heard the wonderful sound of Scuto's bark.

A moment later Caudex slid open the peephole and blinked sleepily at them. Now they could hear Scuto's claws scrabbling on the inside of the door.

'Open up, Caudex!' cried Flavia. 'We're hungry and tired and, oh hurry!'

At last the door swung open and Scuto joyfully greeted everyone, licking and pawing and wagging his tail. Even Mordecai got a sloppy wet kiss. As they all moved into the atrium Alma bustled up, scolding them for being so late.

'What do you mean, staying out after dark?' she cried, hugging Flavia hard. 'I nearly died of worry.' She gave Nubia a squeeze and complained, 'Caudex was beside himself, too. Weren't you, Caudex?'

The slave yawned and nodded.

'I've made enough dinner for you all,' Alma announced. 'Come and eat it before it gets cold.'

Jonathan was hanging back, hoping to avoid Alma's enthusiastic welcome, but she caught sight of him and enveloped him in a squishy embrace.

'And where's Wolfie?' she asked, looking hopefully past Mordecai and out through the open door.

'Isn't Lupus back yet?' cried Flavia.

'No, not a trace of him,' frowned Alma.

They were all sitting around the table, just finishing their soup, when Scuto uttered a loud bark, leapt up from under Nubia's feet and scampered out of the dining room. A few minutes later he trotted back with a tired and hungry Lupus in tow. Flavia quickly drew up another chair and Alma brought the boy a bowl of warm broth, the last of the chicken soup.

The others waited for Lupus to finish before they began their fish and leek pie.

'We have news for you!' Flavia said, as Lupus pushed away his empty soup bowl.

Lupus pointed at himself and then back at her, as if to say, And I have news for you, too!

'Do you remember we told you about the red watchdog we saw at Cordius's house this morning?'

Lupus nodded and took a bite of fish pie.

'Well, someone killed him a few hours ago!' breathed Flavia. 'And they cut off his head!'

'Like Bobas. Dog of Jonathan,' added Nubia.

Lupus choked on his mouthful and had to be pounded on the back by the doctor, who was sitting beside him.

When Lupus had recovered, Mordecai turned to Flavia.

'You went to Cordius's house?'

'Yes, Nubia and I went this morning. We wanted to speak to his freedman Libertus, because he is our only witness. Remember he was standing at the fountain just before we found Bobas's body?'

'Yes,' said Mordecai slowly.

'Well, while he was at the fountain, Libertus saw a man running away from your house. The man was carrying a bag, and it could have had a head inside.'

'Like Perseus,' said Nubia.

Flavia continued,

'Nubia and I went round to Libertus's house this morning, and he said that the man in the drawing was the man he saw that day. The running man was Avitus!'

'Wait.' Mordecai looked confused. 'What drawing?'

'This drawing.' Flavia showed him the wax tablet, now very smudged but still quite recognisable. 'Lupus drew it.'

'You drew this?' Mordecai asked in amazement, taking the tablet. 'It's excellent!'

'That was the man we saw crying in the graveyard. Lupus knew who he was and drew him,' explained Flavia.

'It must have been Avitus who killed the dogs!' exclaimed Jonathan.

Lupus made a strangled noise and when they looked at him he was violently shaking his head.

'Let's see what Lupus has to report,' said Flavia. 'You followed Avitus today, didn't you? We saw your chalk arrow on the tree.'

Lupus nodded. All eyes were on him.

'How soon after we left you did Avitus come out of his house?'

Lupus held his thumb and forefinger close together.

'A short time?'

Lupus nodded.

'And what did he do?' asked Mordecai, with great interest.

Lupus imitated someone drinking and then becoming drunk. He held up five fingers.

'He had five beakers of wine?' asked Flavia.

Lupus shook his head and held up ten fingers.

'Ten beakers of wine!' shouted Jonathan.

Lupus nodded emphatically.

'He had ten beakers of wine?' said Flavia, amazed. 'And what's the five?'

Lupus made his fingers walk around the table: first they walked onto Nubia's empty plate, then onto Jonathan's plate, then Flavia's.

'Five taverns!' shouted Jonathan.

Lupus nodded.

'But ten beakers!' exclaimed Mordecai. 'A man wouldn't be able to walk after drinking that amount.'

Lupus imitated someone throwing up. They all wrinkled their noses and nodded.

'He could still have killed Ruber the watchdog,' insisted Jonathan, 'maybe in a drunken haze.'

Lupus shook his head and drew the side of his hand across his throat. They all stared at him in silence. Then Flavia whispered:

'He's dead?'

Lupus nodded.

'Avitus?' asked Jonathan.

Lupus nodded again.

'How?'

Lupus walked his fingers up the wine jug and then made them jump off and splat onto the table.

'Where?' asked Mordecai. His voice was grave.

Lupus looked around and then caught sight of the wax tablet. He rubbed out his drawing of Avitus and with the tip of his knife he scratched something into the wax.

Mordecai took it, nodded and showed it to the others.

'The lighthouse!' breathed Flavia. She looked at up Lupus, 'And you saw him jump?'

Lupus nodded gravely.

'Then that means Avitus couldn't have killed Ruber,' said Flavia slowly. 'He hasn't been near our street all afternoon. But if he didn't do it, who did?'

Everyone was too tired to think clearly. Flavia and Jonathan were yawning over their dessert of apples stewed in honey and pepper. Nubia had actually fallen asleep in her chair.

'Come, Jonathan,' said Mordecai. 'We must go home to bed now. Lupus, will you be our guest again tonight?'

In reply, Lupus looked at Flavia, raised his eyebrows and pointed down.

'You'd like to spend the night here?' asked Flavia. 'Of course! Alma, may Lupus spend the night here?'

Alma was clearing away the dinner plates.

'Of course, dear. He can sleep in Aristo's bedroom.'

'Very well,' said Mordecai. 'We will say goodnight. Peace be with you.'

'I'll just fetch your house key,' said Alma and disappeared into the study.

After Jonathan and his father had left, Caudex bolted the door after them. A yawning Nubia had already disappeared into the garden with Scuto, so Flavia showed Lupus to the spare room.

'Here's a clay lamp for you,' she said, 'I always keep one lit in my room. There's a copper beaker of cold water on that shelf and a chamber-pot under the bed, in case you can't be bothered to go downstairs to the latrine in the middle of the night.'

Although Flavia was utterly exhausted, she couldn't sleep. The house was quiet and dark. Everyone had gone to bed. Lupus had begun snoring even before she was out of the bedroom. Nubia was snuggled up with Scuto under the fig tree in the garden. Alma and Caudex were sleeping in their rooms off the atrium. Outside, in the graveyard, the tree-frogs had taken over from the cicadas and were croaking slowly and rhythmically, as if urging her to sleep.

The rising moon shone through the lattice screen of her window and made silver diamonds on her bedroom wall. There was even a sea breeze drifting in from the south to soothe her. It smelled of pine and salt water, and made her think of the ocean.

She thought of her father, somewhere far out on the inky waves, perhaps pacing the deck and gazing at the same moon that shone through her window. She offered up a prayer to Neptune, god of the sea.

Then she turned her thoughts to the events of the past days. Had it only been two?

Poor Avitus was dead now, unable to live with his grief, and it was suddenly clear to her that he had never killed the dogs. He hadn't even been able to hit Scuto with a pine cone. How could he have coolly killed and beheaded Bobas?

But that brought her back to the puzzle that was keeping her awake. If Avitus hadn't killed Bobas and Ruber, who had? And who had taken the mastiff's head away from the graveyard?

Outside in the necropolis she heard an owl hooting. People said owls were bad luck, but her father always called her his 'little owl' and so she liked them. Besides, the owl was the bird of Minerva, the goddess of wisdom.

Wisdom made her think of Aristo, the young Greek who had been her tutor for the past two years. She tried to think in the way he had taught her: using both logic and imagination.

'If Avitus didn't kill the dogs, then who did?' she thought. 'We first thought Avitus killed them because he hated all dogs. But if someone else killed the dogs, they probably had another reason. Why would someone want to kill dogs?'

At that moment Scuto began barking downstairs, and as his barks set off all the other dogs in the neighbourhood, Flavia suddenly had the answer. She sat up in her bed.

'Of course!' she breathed. 'That's why!'

But just then she heard Nubia scream.

SCROLL XIX

'Thief!' said Nubia, as Flavia hurried down the stairs, carefully holding her lamp. 'Thief!' she repeated, and pointed to the storeroom. Flavia saw what had alarmed her: there was a sliver of light all around the edge of the storeroom door.

Scuto was wagging his tail and sniffing at the door. He barked again cheerfully.

Caudex ambled into the garden, carrying a torch and looking no more sleepy than he did the rest of the time.

'Caudex!' cried Flavia. 'There's a thief in the store-room!'

'Nothing in there worth taking,' mumbled the slave. 'Just grain and wine and some bits of old furniture . . .'

'Person go in there!' said Nubia.

'And I can see a light!' insisted Flavia.

Caudex squinted at the door, and scratched his head.

'All right,' he said with a shrug, and moved towards the door. The flames of his torch threw flickering bars of shadow from the columns onto the wall. Flavia and Nubia clung to each other as Caudex cautiously opened the door, and Scuto wagged his tail.

'What's all this noise?' Alma padded in, carrying a clay lamp. She was barefoot and had tied her hair up with a scarf. The lamp, lighting her face eerily from below, made her look like a stranger.

'There's a thief in the storeroom!' said Flavia, 'and I'm sure it's the person who killed the dogs.'

Suddenly, from the storeroom came two yells, one high and one low. Scuto, standing just outside the doorway, began to bark again.

'Got him!' they heard Caudex grunt, and then in a slightly muffled voice. 'Got your thief.'

He emerged from the storeroom. In one hand he held the flaming torch, and in the other he carried a squirming boy.

'Lupus!' exclaimed Flavia and Nubia together.

Lupus was struggling in Caudex's grip and incoherent sounds were coming out of his mouth. The words were garbled, but the sense of them was clear: Put me down, you big oaf!

'Caudex! Put him down!' cried Flavia. 'Lupus isn't a thief!'

Lupus's eyes blazed green in the torchlight, but Caudex did not put him down. Instead, he set the torch into one of the brackets on the wall. Then he took Lupus in both hands, held him upside down by the ankles, and gave him a good shake. Flavia and Nubia squealed and covered their eyes: Lupus's tunic had flopped down and he was wearing nothing underneath.

Then they heard the jingle of coins on marble and they opened their eyes in astonishment.

When Caudex had finished shaking Lupus down, he set the boy on his feet. Lupus stood hanging his head in shame: there on the walkway bordering the garden lay a dozen gold coins, glowing and winking in the flickering torchlight.

They all stared at Lupus in dismay. The coins on the marble pathway and his miserable expression confirmed his guilt.

'Lupus!' whispered Flavia after a moment. 'Where did you find that gold? Was it in the storeroom?'

Lupus nodded.

'Then you *were* stealing from us. We trusted you and opened our home to you and . . . THAT'S IT!'

They all stared at her, even Lupus raised his head.

'I think I've solved the crime!' cried Flavia.

She turned to Lupus.

'Lupus, you've *got* to help us. Where did you find that gold and how did you know it was here? We never keep that much gold in the house.'

Lupus glared at her. He was deeply ashamed and embarrassed.

'Please, Lupus! Everything makes sense now. We'll forget that you tried to steal the money, if only you'll help us!'

Lupus gestured sullenly for them to follow him. Caudex took the torch from the wall. The girls and Alma took their lamps, and they all followed Lupus back into the storeroom.

The boy led them to three large amphoras near the darkest corner. The jars were half-buried to keep them standing upright and looked just like all the others, except that they were set a little apart. One of them was closed but not sealed. Flavia went to this amphora and removed the lid.

Everyone gasped. This big jar did not contain grain or wine or olive oil like the rest. It was filled nearly to the brim with gold coins.

'Why, it's enough to buy our house a dozen times over,' breathed Flavia, dipping her hand in and letting the heavy coins sift through her fingers. 'And look! This seal isn't ours.' She picked up a blue wax seal about the size of a coin which had fallen to the store-room floor. She held it up to her lamp and examined it. 'It's not the twins. It's a dolphin!'

'That'll be the seal of Cordius, your father's patron,' said Alma. 'Perhaps he didn't have enough room for all his treasure and asked Captain Geminus to store some of it.'

'Alma, I think you're right!' said Flavia. 'This treasure certainly isn't ours, and the seal is probably Cordius's. But if none of *us* knew it was here, how on earth did Lupus know?'

She turned to the boy, who was still hanging his head.

'Lupus,' she said softly, 'did someone tell you about the treasure?'

Lupus hesitated and then waggled his head, neither nodding or shaking it, but something in between.

'Someone sort of told you about it?' she offered.

He nodded.

'Who?'

Lupus hesitated, then imitated someone drinking.

'Avitus?'

Lupus shook his head and sighed.

'I know! Someone you saw at one of the taverns!'

Lupus nodded.

'Who? Who was it?'

Lupus shrugged.

'Lupus, I think I know who it was but I want to be sure . . .'

Abruptly, Nubia slipped out of the storeroom and reappeared a few moments later with a wax tablet.

'Nubia, you're brilliant!' cried Flavia. 'Lupus, can you draw what he looked like?'

Lupus shrugged again.

'Just do the best you can,' she pleaded. 'Please . . .'

Lupus slowly took the tablet and stylus from Nubia. He squatted on the sandy floor of the storeroom and started to draw. Everyone moved their torches closer, so that he could see as clearly as possible. Lupus stopped, scratched his head thoughtfully, rubbed out the lower half and started again.

Finally he finished and held the tablet out to Flavia. She took it with a trembling hand and looked at the face he had drawn.

'I knew it!' she breathed. 'It had to be him. I should have guessed before.'

She had solved the mystery, but nothing could be done about it until morning. Flavia crawled back into bed and was sure she would lie awake all night going over the clues in her mind.

But she was wrong. She fell asleep the moment her head touched the pillow, and soon she began to dream.

She dreamt about Avita Procula.

In the dream, the little girl was being chased by wild dogs. Suddenly a huge magpie flew down and carried Avita up into the air. Avita was laughing and waving at

Flavia who stood on the ground. As Flavia watched the girl disappear into the heavens, she realised the dogs were now coming towards her. She turned and ran, but although her heart was pounding she ran slowly, as if she were moving through sticky honey.

In her dream she heard the dogs' barking grow closer and imagined she felt their hot breath on her legs. She had dreamt this dream before and she knew she always woke just as the animals leapt for her with open jaws. But this time something was different. Without turning around, she realised that there was now only one dog pursuing her: one dog with three horrible heads. Cerberus, the hound from hell. In her dream she heard someone screaming again and again, and the screaming didn't stop.

Flavia woke up sweating. Her heart was pounding and her whole body trembling. She was groggy and confused and wondered how she could be awake when she still heard screaming.

It was an awful scream, a woman's hysterical expression of pure horror. Strangely, it sounded like Alma.

Flavia swung her feet out of bed, but she was clumsy and half-asleep, and she banged her toe on the bedside table. Automatically, she took up her clay lamp before she stumbled out onto the balcony.

The moon was almost directly overhead. It poured a wash of eerie light onto the garden below, making the shadows inky black. By the stars in the sky and the damp in the air, Flavia knew it was the middle of the night.

She stood hesitating, and while she stood, she heard

a man's cry, short and involuntary. Caudex? Although she was trembling, she made her way carefully downstairs and crossed the garden by the moonlit path. The pebbles hurt her bare feet but she didn't want the dangerous black shadows behind the columns to touch her.

'Nubia?' she whispered. 'Alma?'

Up ahead a flickering light moved and the scent of a pitch pine torch reached her nose. Another moan echoed from the atrium. The corridor looked like a gaping throat ready to swallow her with shadows, so she ran down it as fast as she could. A wave of relief swept over her as she saw four familiar figures and one dog silhouetted by the orange light of a torch.

They were standing at the open front door and when they heard her feet pattering on the marble floor of the atrium they all turned to look at her.

In each of their faces was reflected a different kind of horror. Even Scuto was whimpering. They were so stunned that none of them made a move to stop Flavia from looking at the thing in the street. She passed between Nubia, who was trembling, and Lupus, who crouched like an animal about to flee. Flavia stopped in the doorway.

There in the moon-washed street stood a trident, the kind fishermen use to catch fish. Its base was wedged tight between paving stones and its three prongs pointed up towards the cold stars. On each of the three points was planted a severed dog's head. One was white, one black, and one red. Each pair of milky, blind eyes was staring directly at Flavia.

She heard a scream and realised it was coming from

her own throat. A wave of black nausea washed over her as the unseeing eyes of the hounds impaled on the trident stared into hers. The dogs' heads filled her vision and became the three heads of the undead creature who guarded the underworld. The blood pounded in her ears like rhythmic thunder as the heads of Cerberus receded until they were three points at the end of a long tunnel. Finally, even the three pin-sized heads were snuffed out and she was sucked down after them into the darkness.

SCROLL XX

'Flavia? Flavia, are you all right?'

A familiar accented voice sounded in Flavia's ear. She kept her eyes closed for a minute, considering the red-brown light beyond her eyelids. Was it morning? It still felt like night. Then she smelled oil-lamps and cinnamon and mint tea, and Flavia knew she was safe in Jonathan's house.

She opened her eyes to see Mordecai standing over her with a gentle smile. His hair hung loose and long about his shoulders.

'What happened?' Flavia asked him.

'You fainted,' the doctor explained.

'Then it wasn't a dream?'

'I'm afraid not. The thing you saw was real.' Mordecai held out a cup of steaming mint tea and urged, 'Drink this.'

Flavia sipped the hot, sweet drink and looked around. She was in Mordecai's study on the striped divan, propped up by cushions. The room was blazing with light. She guessed he had lit every candle and lamp in the house.

Nubia was sitting on the floor with Scuto, hugging an orange blanket around them both. Jonathan stood nearby, looking pale and concerned. Alma perched on the edge of the divan. She, too, was wrapped in a thick blanket and sipping mint tea.

'That's right, drink the tea,' said Mordecai gently to Flavia. It occurred to her that mint tea was Mordecai's cure-all. It would be easy to be a doctor: you just had to know how to brew mint tea. She smiled at the thought.

'That's better.' Mordecai helped Flavia sit up a bit more.

'Where's Lupus?' she asked suddenly.

Jonathan and his father exchanged quick looks. Mordecai answered softly:

'Alma told us what happened: how you found him stealing the gold . . .'

'He's gone!' Jonathan blurted out. 'He just ran out into the night after we came to see what had happened.'

'Did you see Cerberus? I mean the *thing*?' Flavia couldn't bring herself to say the words.

'Yes,' said Jonathan, swallowing and looking sick. 'Alma told us how she heard a moan outside her window, and when she looked out . . . Some fiend had stuck Bobas's head, and Ruber's and the missing head from the graveyard, on a trident.' He shivered in the flickering candlelight.

'Caudex is taking the . . . three heads through the house to put outside in the graveyard,' said Mordecai. 'He'll bury them tomorrow.'

'I thought I had gone to the land of the dead. Or that it was some horrible nightmare,' Flavia whispered.

'It wasn't a nightmare!' said Alma suddenly, putting her cup down decisively and rising to her feet. 'It was real and it was an omen of death!' There was a note of hysteria in her voice. 'Tomorrow we are leaving this town until your father returns!'

'No!' cried Flavia, sitting forward. 'That's exactly what the killer wants. He wants to frighten us away so that he can get at the gold.' She chewed her lower lip thoughtfully. 'But we must *pretend* to go away. Yes! That's it! We'll set a trap for the thief.' She took a gulp of the sweet tea.

'Tomorrow we'll all pack and make a big show of leaving. But we'll leave the back door unbolted. We'll go out of the city gate, then double back through the graveyard and keep watch. Then, when he comes, we pounce!'

Caudex came in, looking slightly queasy and wiping his hands on his tunic.

'Who will we pounce on?' he asked thickly.

'The thief, of course,' said Flavia. 'But we need some way of proving his guilt. Something which will prove beyond a doubt he was after the money . . .' Suddenly she remembered the magpie's inky footprint on her father's parchment.

'Doctor Mordecai,' she said excitedly, 'do you have a medicine or potion which would stain someone's hands?'

Mordecai thought for a moment and then his face lit up.

'Yes,' he said. 'I have just the thing to catch your thief . . .'

'But who *is* the thief?' asked Jonathan, bursting with curiosity.

'Yes, who?' they all echoed.

'Do you mean you haven't guessed yet?' asked Flavia, and the sparkle returned to her eyes.

The next day around noon, a two-horse carruca clattered up Green Fountain Street and stopped in front of the house of Marcus Flavius Geminus. The blue door of the house swung open, and the door of the neighbouring house, too, and for the next half hour people moved noisily in and out of the two houses, packing the carriage with chests and travel bags.

Up and down the street shutters squeaked open as curious neighbours satisfied themselves that nothing was amiss. A family was just going on a trip. Those who peeped out saw an oriental-looking man in a black turban directing a large slave in the loading of a cart. They heard the voices of children and the snorting and stamping of horses. Presently the neighbours closed their shutters again and returned to their midday siestas.

When the luggage was stowed in the carruca, a rather plump female climbed up beside the driver and sat sobbing noisily into a handkerchief. Three children and a sheep-like dog scrambled up onto the carriage behind the chests. Presently the carruca moved off slowly towards the marina. The big slave and the man with the turban followed on foot.

The clop of the horses' hooves and the grating of the iron-rimmed wheels grew fainter and soon the afternoon throbbed again with heat and the cries of cicadas. Once more Green Fountain Street was quiet and peaceful.

★

The carruca rattled away from Flavia's house towards the marina. As it passed the Laurentum Gate, Flavia and Jonathan slipped off the back of the carriage and landed lightly on the street.

'Look after Scuto, Nubia,' whispered Flavia.

'Look after Nubia, Scuto,' grinned Jonathan.

The cart clattered and creaked on its way. Caudex continued to walk behind it, but Mordecai joined Flavia and Jonathan as they hurried towards the brick arch of the gate.

'Where is he?' muttered Flavia, looking around nervously.

'Here I am.' A figure stepped out from behind one of the columns which flanked the arch. It was the magistrate they had seen the previous afternoon. His pale eyes looked them over.

'Marcus Artorius Bato,' he said, introducing himself. 'I received your message. Your charge is a serious one.'

'Yes, we know,' replied Mordecai, 'and we pray that we are not wasting your time.'

'So do I,' said the young man drily. 'Lead on.'

'This way!' said Flavia, and led them out of the gate and back along the outside of the city wall. They moved quickly, pushing through the dry grasses and thistles, startling dozens of tiny brown grasshoppers. They soon crossed the dusty road which led back into the city through Fountain Gate and stood at Flavia's back door.

Bato shook his head disapprovingly.

'There's a regulation against building into the city walls, you know. This door should be blocked up.'

'We're not the only ones.' Flavia gestured towards Jonathan's door.

'Thanks, Flavia.' Jonathan glared at her.

'We'll block up our doors if necessary,' said Mordecai politely, 'but just now we have a thief to catch!'

Bato gave a curt nod.

Flavia had left the back door wedged open with a twist of old papyrus. Now she put her eye to a gap about the width of her little finger. Between the columns surrounding her garden she could just see the storeroom door.

Jonathan crouched down below her to look, too. He wobbled a little and put out his hand to steady himself.

'Careful!' hissed Flavia. 'If you push the door shut we'll be locked out and we'll never catch him!'

'Sorry!' Jonathan grinned sheepishly.

'It may be a long wait,' said Flavia, glancing up at the young magistrate.

'As if I have nothing better to do,' Bato remarked sarcastically, mopping his forehead with a cloth. It was like an oven in the midday sun.

'I suggest that Marcus Artorius Bato and I wait in the shade of that pine,' whispered Mordecai. 'You two can take turns keeping watch . . .'

'No, wait!' breathed Flavia, putting up her hand. 'He's there!' She gazed up at them in wonder: her trap had worked!

'What's he doing?' mouthed Jonathan.

Flavia put her eye to the crack again.

'He's in the study . . . looking behind scrolls, under the desk . . . He's being very careful: trying not to disturb anything . . .' She was silent for several moments, moving her head slightly to get the best view.

'What?' cried Jonathan. 'What's he doing now?'

Flavia stood and faced them. Her heart was thumping and her knees trembling. 'He's just gone into the storeroom,' she breathed. 'This is it!'

Quietly, inch by inch, Flavia began to pull open the back door. Suddenly one of the hinges gave a squeak. Flavia froze. Then she continued opening the door as carefully as she could. Tiny drops of sweat beaded her upper lip and a trickle of it ran down the back of her neck.

At last the door was open enough for each of them to squeeze through. Flavia went last, carefully easing the door shut behind her.

The others waited in the shade of the peristyle, each one standing behind a pillar. It was blessedly cool there and Flavia breathed a sigh of relief. For a moment she pressed her cheek to one of the cool, plaster-covered columns. Then, heart pounding, she began to tiptoe towards the atrium.

'Quick!' she mouthed to the others. 'Through the study to the atrium. We don't want him to get away! Jonathan, you stay here and guard the back door.'

Jonathan nodded and pressed himself behind the column closest to the back door.

Quickly and quietly, the two men followed Flavia past the dining room and into the study. As they moved past the desk, Bato accidentally jogged the pink marble column which held the marble bust of the Emperor. They all froze as the bust slowly wobbled one way and the column the other. Then Bato reached out and caught the heavy sculpture just as it was about to crash to the marble floor. He set it carefully back on its pedestal and let out a sigh of relief. The stone Vespasian seemed to scowl as the magistrate mopped his forehead again.

They tiptoed forward through the folding doors and into the atrium. At that moment, they heard the storeroom door open and then close. The three of them pressed themselves against the atrium wall. Footsteps moved along the corridor towards them and then, just as they expected the culprit to round the corner, the footsteps stopped.

'By Hercules!' said a man's voice, in a tone of mild surprise.

Bato stepped forward, followed by Mordecai and Flavia.

In the shadow of the corridor stood a man in a yellow tunic, with a heavy leather bag slung round one shoulder. The thief was staring at his hands, which were stained a vivid reddish purple colour. As the three appeared, he raised his head and looked at them with dark blue eyes. It was Libertus.

'Titus Cordius Libertus,' said the magistrate in a loud official voice, 'I arrest you in the name of the Emperor Vespasian, for attempted theft and for destruction of private property.'

Libertus smiled ruefully and gazed at his hands.

'It seems you've caught me red-handed!' he confessed. He slipped off the bag and eased it to the floor. It settled heavily, the clink of many gold coins muffled by the leather. Flavia and Mordecai glanced at each other.

'Hold out your hands,' commanded Bato.

'What is this?' Libertus asked calmly, referring to the stain on his hands.

'Just a vegetable dye,' replied Mordecai as Bato put stiff leather manacles round the freedman's wrists. 'It will wear off in a few days.'

Jonathan came up behind Libertus. The freedman glanced round at him and gave a puzzled half-smile.

Bato pulled the heavy leather bag from the shadow of the peristyle into the sunny garden and squatted beside it. He opened the leather flap and cautiously poked at the gold with his finger. In the brilliant light they could see that some of the coins were thinly coated with red dye.

'Why did you do it?' Flavia blurted out. The sight of Libertus standing meekly, so handsome and vulnerable, made tears sting her eyes.

'I needed money badly,' he replied quietly. 'And my life depended on getting it quickly.'

'Gambling debts?' Flavia asked, suddenly remembering the dice.

He nodded.

'Why didn't you throw yourself on the mercy of your patron Cordius?' asked Mordecai.

'That stingy old miser wouldn't have given me anything,' snarled Libertus, and for a moment the bitterness made his face looked ugly. 'That's why he moved all his money over here. So no one could touch it.'

A tear rolled down Flavia's cheek. She swiped at it angrily. Libertus saw her concern and his face relaxed.

'I didn't want to *hurt* anyone,' he said earnestly. 'I just needed some cash.'

Bato looked up sharply. 'The gold in this bag is worth nearly a million sesterces,' he commented dryly.

'And you *did* hurt somebody!' said Jonathan angrily. 'You killed two dogs and nearly frightened us to death.'

'It seemed the best way at the time.' Libertus shrugged. 'I needed to make sure this house was empty long enough for me to search it and to silence that noisy dog next door.'

'Why didn't you just give him a drugged dog biscuit, like the woman in the fresco?' asked Flavia.

'That's a very good question,' remarked Bato, closing the bag and rising to his feet. 'Why did you kill the poor creature? And in such a barbaric manner?'

'I needed him silenced for more than just a few hours,' Libertus replied evenly. 'I removed the head to add an element of fear. Later, when I was investigating the back of this house, I found another dog's head and that gave me my brilliant idea.' For a moment he looked pleased with himself, then he frowned.

'And I almost got away with it.' Libertus glanced resentfully at Mordecai. 'If you hadn't found me out I'd be on my way to Hispania right now, debts paid and with enough money left over to buy a nice little farm . . .'

'You think I found you out?' said Mordecai in

surprise, and then laughed. 'No, my dear fellow.' He gestured.

'The person who guessed your plan and set the trap was this young lady here: Flavia Gemina!'

SCROLL XXI

It was late morning. A hot June had become an even hotter July.

The week before, the Emperor Vespasian had passed away with the words 'Oh dear, I think I'm becoming a god.' His son Titus had succeeded him quietly and without bloodshed, much to the relief of all. Flavia's father had already commissioned a sculpture of the young Emperor to join the bust of Vespasian in the study.

Flavia and Nubia were sitting in the garden preparing garlands for the evening celebration. The girls bent their heads, one fair and one dark, over their work. A cool breeze touched Flavia's hair and she brushed a strand from her eyes.

'Look, Nubia,' she said softly, 'you can weave the jasmine into the ivy, and then you put the grape hyacinth in like this. There!' She put her finished garland beside her on the marble bench and counted on her fingers. 'Let's see, how many will we need? One each for me, you, and Jonathan. And Miriam's back now, so that's four. One for my father and one for Doctor Mordecai: that's six. And one for Cordius. Oh, and Aristo! That's eight. A good number, though nine is the perfect number for a banquet . . .'

'Lupus?' asked Nubia quietly.

'Why do you keep bringing him up?' Flavia scowled. 'He ran away the night he stole – all right, *tried* to steal the gold, and he hasn't come back since. I'm not going to go chasing after a thief. Oh, Pollux! Now look what I've done!' She put down the ruined garland and stared at it absently.

Scuto, lying at their feet, pricked up his ears, lifted his head from his paws and gazed towards the front of the house. Then he uttered a loud bark.

'That will be Jonathan,' said Flavia. She pushed the glossy piles of ivy and jasmine off her lap and followed Scuto out of the garden and into the atrium.

Caudex was just opening the door. Flavia ran forward to greet her friend.

'Hello, Jonathan! Oh, hello Doctor Mordecai!' Jonathan's father entered behind his son.

'Father has something he wants to say to us.' Jonathan rolled his eyes. 'He won't tell me what it is yet . . .'

'Is Nubia here?' asked Mordecai pleasantly. He was wearing a pale blue turban and a white robe, and Flavia thought the colours made him look milder than usual.

'Yes. She's in the garden. We're making garlands. Please come through.' She led the way into the garden and then ran to get two chairs. As she passed the open door of the kitchen she whispered, 'Alma, could you bring us some peach juice?'

'Of course, dear,' her old nurse replied. 'I'll be there in a moment.'

Flavia set the chairs by the bench and they all sat down. The three friends looked at Mordecai and he looked back with his heavy-lidded eyes. The fountain splashed and a bird repeated the same clear note high in the fig tree. Nervously, Flavia picked at a strand of ivy.

Mordecai cleared his throat.

'Miriam and Jonathan and I are very honoured to have been invited to your father's homecoming dinner this evening,' he began.

'Even though he's been home for three days now,' broke in Flavia, and then bit her lower lip.

'Yes,' smiled Mordecai. He cleared his throat again. 'However, I was sad to hear from Jonathan that you haven't invited Lupus.'

Flavia stared at Mordecai with open mouth for a moment before she remembered herself and closed it. Then she shot a glare at Jonathan. But he was gazing bleakly at Scuto, who lay panting at their feet.

'Lupus tried to steal from us!' was all she could say in her defence. 'That's why he wanted to spend the night here. He . . . he betrayed us!'

'Flavia.' Mordecai twisted a gold ring on his finger. 'And Jonathan,' he added, looking up at his son, 'do you have any idea what kind of life Lupus has led?'

'No,' admitted Flavia, hanging her head.

Jonathan just shook his miserably.

'He's been on his own in this city for as long as he can remember. He has no mother or father, as far as we know. No home, no place to be safe, no family of any kind. As if that weren't bad enough, he hasn't even got a tongue with which to communicate. You were probably the first real friends he's had in his life.'

Flavia swallowed. Her throat hurt.

'His entire life has been a fight to survive, and he must have fought very hard to have stayed alive this long. He has had to beg or steal every bite of food that's come into his poor mouth.' Mordecai sighed, and softened his tone.

'Can you not find it in your hearts to forgive him? I admit he did something that was wrong. He was tempted to steal and he gave in to that temptation. But haven't you ever given in to temptation? Haven't you ever done anything wrong?'

None of them spoke.

'Jonathan, you broke your promise to me the day you were almost kidnapped. You promised you would stay on this street. Flavia, your father told you never to go into the graveyard but you have gone there repeatedly. You know what you did was wrong, don't you?'

Flavia nodded and then blurted out, 'What about Nubia? You haven't said anything to *her*.' She immediately regretted saying such a spiteful thing and bit her lip. But Mordecai surprised her by saying,

'You're right, Flavia, I'm sure Nubia *has* done things in her life that she is ashamed of.'

Nubia raised her head and nodded. Her eyes were full of tears.

'Well,' said Mordecai gently, 'our faith teaches that if you say sorry to God for the wrong things you have done, *and* if you forgive the people who have done wrong things to you, you will be forgiven. Would you like that?'

Nubia and Jonathan nodded immediately. After a moment Flavia did, too. It sounded suspiciously easy.

'Are you sorry for all the wrong things you've done?' asked Mordecai. They all nodded this time. 'Then say sorry to God.'

'How?' asked Flavia.

'Jonathan?' said his father.

Jonathan closed his eyes and said, 'I'm sorry for all the wrong things I've done, Lord.' and then added, 'Amen.'

Straight away, Nubia closed her eyes and imitated Jonathan. 'I'm sorry for wrong things also. Amen.'

'What does "amen" mean?' Flavia asked cautiously.

'It's like saying: I really mean it,' said Mordecai with a smile.

Flavia closed her eyes and tried to imagine which god she was speaking to. Finally she settled on the beardless shepherd with a lamb over his shoulders.

'I'm sorry for all the wrong things I've done,' she whispered to him, and then added, 'amen.' When she opened her eyes a moment later she felt lighter some-how.

'And now,' said Mordecai, 'will you forgive Lupus?'

They all nodded.

'Then what are you doing sitting here? Get down to the forum and find him and invite him to your party!'

The three of them jumped up and began to run for the door.

'Wait!' said Mordecai.

They all ran back. Mordecai slipped Jonathan some coins. 'You'd better take him to the baths again.'

'Yes, father!' Jonathan grinned, and they all charged off toward the door.

'Wait!' cried Mordecai. They all ran back.

'You'd better take Caudex *and* Scuto with you this time.'

'Yes, Doctor Mordecai!' Flavia nodded vigorously, while Nubia ran to get Scuto's lead.

'Wait!' shouted Mordecai. They all ran back.

'Who's going to drink all this peach juice?' he asked, gesturing at Alma coming towards them with a tray.

'You are!' they laughed, and ran out of the garden.

It was a perfect summer evening. The warmth of the late afternoon sun had released all the scents of the garden and a sea breeze touched the leaves just enough to make them tremble. The sky was lavender and the garden was deep green, filled with cool shadows.

The nine of them were sitting or reclining in the dining room.

Miriam had been counted an adult, because at thirteen she was legally old enough to marry. Wearing a dark blue stola which set off her glossy black curls and pale skin, she reclined next to Aristo. Flavia felt a pang of jealousy. Aristo, her tutor, had sailed back from Corinth with her father. He was young and handsome with olive skin and curly hair the colour of bronze. Flavia had always imagined she would marry him when she was older.

But Miriam had been silent, as usual, and Aristo was not even looking at her. He was chatting to the merchant Cordius, who as the guest of honour reclined on the middle couch. On the third couch Mordecai reclined next to Flavia's father.

Flavia, Jonathan, Nubia and Lupus all sat round a table in the middle, so that they could be part of the conversation. All nine diners were bathed and perfumed, wearing their garlands of ivy, jasmine and grape hyacinth.

Cordius had brought along a young slave named Felix, who was helping Alma serve dinner. They had just finished the first course: bite-sized parcels of peppered goat's cheese wrapped in pickled vine leaves. Felix removed their empty plates as Alma brought in the main course, rabbit with onion and date gravy.

'This is delicious, Alma!' said Flavia's father. 'I always miss your cooking when I'm at sea.'

'I caught the rabbits this morning with my sling,' said Jonathan proudly.

'It *is* delicious,' agreed Cordius. 'Congratulations to both hunter and cook!' He lifted his wine cup.

Flavia tried not to look at Cordius. The sight of a flowered garland above his mournful face made her want to giggle. But she couldn't avoid looking at him when he said,

'I owe a great debt of gratitude to you four children.'

He made a gesture to his young slave Felix, who quietly moved to stand near the table.

'I knew there was a thief in my household. That's why I removed the gold from my strongbox. But it was your quick action that exposed him and the crime. I know you expected no reward, but I would like to give you one.' He nodded to Felix, who handed a heavy gold coin to each of the four friends.

They all gasped. Flavia and Jonathan thanked Cordius warmly. Lupus automatically put his coin between his teeth and bit it in order to test it was really gold. His face went red as everyone laughed, but when he saw they weren't offended he smiled furtively. Nubia was staring at her reward with eyes almost as round and gold as the coin.

'You might also like to know that Avitus's widow will be looked after,' said Cordius. 'Doctor Mordecai told me about the tragic loss of her daughter and husband. She is an excellent seamstress and I have offered her a place in my household and a small allowance.'

'Very gracious of you.' Mordecai bowed his head to the merchant.

'What will you buy with your newfound riches?' Cordius asked Flavia with a rare smile.

'A complete set of Pliny's *Natural History*,' she announced without a moment's hesitation. Everyone laughed.

'Nubia?' said Captain Geminus.

'Lotus wood flute,' the girl said softly.

'Ah! We have a budding musician in the household,' Aristo leaned forward on one elbow with interest. 'I'll look forward to accompanying you on my lyre.'

'Lupus?' asked Mordecai.

Lupus shrugged. He had an odd smile on his face.

'What will you buy with *your* coin, Jonathan?' asked Flavia's father in a jolly voice, a bit too loudly.

'I'd like to buy a new watchdog,' said Jonathan. 'I've been reading Pliny's *Natural History*, too, and he writes about a kind of watchdog from India. Its mother is a dog, but its father is a tiger. It is the fiercest watchdog in the world, but they cost a fortune. I couldn't buy one before, but now perhaps I can. A watchdog that fierce would never let anyone hurt the people it protected. And nothing could hurt it either. Don't you agree, Nubia? Nubia?'

But once again, like a shadow, Nubia had disappeared.

SCROLL XXII

'How does she *do* that?' marvelled Jonathan, scratching his curly head.

'Shall we search for her?' asked Aristo from the couch.

'No,' said Flavia. 'She'll come back. She's probably just taken Scuto a bit of rabbit.'

Scuto had been shut in the storeroom as he always was when a party was given. Otherwise he would disgrace himself by begging for morsels or tripping up Alma as she came in with the soup.

'I must ask you,' said Cordius to Flavia as he took a sip of wine, 'when did you first guess the true motive for the killings?'

'Well, it was thanks to Aristo,' said Flavia shyly. Everyone looked at the young Greek tutor in surprise.

'He always tells me to use imagination as well as reason.' Flavia looked down at her plate and then back up at Cordius.

'I was lying in bed, trying to think like Aristo: if Avitus hadn't killed the dogs, then someone else must have. And if someone else killed the dogs, then what was their motive? It probably wasn't because they hated dogs!'

Everyone was listening intently, and Flavia noticed that Aristo's eyes sparkled with delight.

'Just as I was trying to imagine what motive there could be for killing dogs, Scuto barked. And I suddenly knew. It had to be the obvious motive.'

'To silence the watchdog!' cried Aristo.

'Exactly,' exclaimed Flavia. 'But why silence Jonathan's watchdog, or the watchdog across the street, or even our watchdog?'

' "If the owner of the house had known at what time of night the thief was coming, he would have kept watch and not let his house be broken into",' quoted Mordecai.

Aristo looked at him curiously. The young Greek was very well-read but did not recognise the quote.

'Yes,' Flavia was saying. 'The main reason for silencing a watchdog is to break in and steal something. But Jonathan's family doesn't have much worth stealing, and I thought we didn't either, so I concluded the target must be Cordius.'

'Logical,' murmured Aristo.

'Then, when Lupus discovered all the gold in our storeroom, I realised that *we* were the intended victims and that either Scuto would be killed, or the thief would try to frighten us away.'

'But you knew who the thief was before Lupus told us,' said Jonathan. 'How did you work that out?'

The evening sky had darkened from violet to purple and the dog-star winked brightly above the tiled roof. Caudex came in to light the lamps and Felix cleared away the remains of the rabbit stew.

'It was simple,' Flavia ventured. 'If Libertus was telling the truth, Avitus *had* to be the killer.'

Jonathan nodded.

'If Avitus wasn't the killer, then Libertus was probably lying. And if Libertus was lying, it must have been to protect himself. Libertus said he had been drinking at the fountain. But who would drink that smelly old water when there's sweet water in your house just a few yards up the road?'

'Unless you're very thirsty!' interjected Jonathan.

'Or unless you had to wash blood off your hands or dagger! You wouldn't do *that* in front of the slaves, would you?'

'He had the head with him as we passed by,' added Jonathan. 'Probably wrapped up in his cloak. But he was standing on the other side of the fountain and we couldn't see it.'

Flavia took a sip of her watered-down wine.

'When we first went to Libertus, he gave a description which could have been almost anyone's, to throw us off the track. To make it convincing, he made up the bit about the bag, because he knew a head was missing. Later he added details which pointed to Avitus, but only after I showed him the drawing and described what Avitus had been wearing.'

'Why didn't you suspect Libertus earlier?' asked Aristo with interest.

'Well, he was so polite and handsome,' she said, reddening slightly. 'It just never occurred to me he might be bad.'

'An understandable error,' Cordius murmured, and Flavia remembered that he had been prepared to make the young freedman his son.

' "Man looks at the outward appearance, but the Lord looks at the heart",' Mordecai quoted again, and everyone nodded their agreement, though Aristo gave him another keen look.

Flavia concluded. 'As soon as I knew the culprit was Libertus, and that he probably wanted to get rid of the dogs in order to steal the treasure, I knew the real crime would soon be committed.'

'I don't understand something!' said Flavia's father in the rather loud voice he used when he'd had too much wine. 'Lupus overheard Libertus in the tavern, correct?'

'Yes,' Flavia answered.

'Then why didn't he tell you that the man he overheard was Libertus from across the street?'

'Because Lupus had never actually seen Libertus,' explained Flavia. 'Overhearing Libertus was just a piece of good luck. But if Lupus hadn't told us, or shown us what he looked like, we might never have solved the crime.'

Cordius toasted Lupus and the rest followed suit.

At that moment Alma came in with their dessert course. She held a tray of hot pastry cases filled with honey and walnuts, each of them in the shape of a little dog.

Everyone made noises of great approval and appreciation. They each took one, and sucked the honey off their scalded fingers.

Bright stars pricked a sky which was not yet quite black, but deepest blue. The sweet fragrance of the jasmine and hyacinth garlands filled the air.

Suddenly Nubia stepped into the soft golden lamplight of the dining room.

'Nubia!' they all greeted her.

'Have a honey and walnut dog!'

'Have a drop more wine.'

'Where have you been?'

'Graveyard,' said Nubia and crouched in the centre of the dining room. Carefully, she placed her woollen cloak on the marble floor. In its folds squirmed two small creatures.

'Oh!' breathed Miriam, jumping down from her couch. 'They're adorable!'

Everyone leaned forward to see the two little puppies, only a few weeks old, which lay squeaking on Nubia's cloak.

'They're wonderful!' said Jonathan in an odd, choked voice. 'Was the father . . .?'

Nubia looked at him and nodded. The puppies looked like miniature versions of the fierce black hound who had first led the feral pack.

'What will you do with them, Nubia?' laughed Captain Geminus.

Nubia held one up and hugged it.

'I keep it?' she asked.

'Of course!' Flavia and her father answered together.

Nubia, her head bent, hugged the puppy as tightly as she dared. After a moment she looked up, with tears sparkling on her eyelashes and said, 'I name him Nipur. Name of my dog at home.'

'Nipur it is then,' said Captain Geminus, in a hearty, booming voice, and wiped something out of his own eye.

'And the other one,' said Jonathan quietly. 'What will you name him?'

'I don't name him. You name him,' said Nubia,

handing the other puppy to Jonathan. 'Don't get tiger dog.'

Jonathan took the small, squeaking bundle carefully, almost reverently, and kissed its wet black nose.

'I will name him Tigris,' said Jonathan solemnly, 'and he will be my tiger dog. Oh, Pollux! He's just peed on me!'

They all burst out laughing and Felix came round with the wine again.

'I'm afraid we must go soon,' said Mordecai apologetically, and winced as he waited for his children to protest.

But they were too busy cooing over Tigris, who was licking rabbit gravy off Jonathan's finger.

'Before you go,' said Captain Geminus to Mordecai, 'I have a proposal for you. I must be off again soon, making the most of the sailing season. After all that's happened this past month I would like to send Flavia and Nubia somewhere safer.

'My brother has a large villa south of here on the bay of Neapolis, and he says he would be delighted to receive a houseful of people for the month of August. Your children are both invited, and you are very welcome, too.'

'Would we be able to take the puppies with us?' asked Miriam, looking up from Tigris.

'Of course!' said Flavia's father. 'Scuto will be going, though Alma and Caudex will remain here to keep an eye on things. I think they deserve a rest, too.'

'Oh please, can we go father?' begged Miriam and Jonathan.

'I'll think about it,' said Mordecai, with a smile.

Captain Geminus turned to Lupus, who was stroking Nipur and keeping his head down.

'Lupus, we would be honoured if you would come, too.'

Flavia, Nubia and Jonathan cheered and urged Lupus to come.

Lupus looked up at them and nodded once, gruffly. Then he lowered his head again and examined Nipur's tail with intense concentration.

'Of course,' added Captain Geminus, 'Aristo will be accompanying you, so there will be lessons in Greek, philosophy, art and music every morning . . .'

They all moaned.

'Then we shall definitely come!' announced Mordecai.

They all cheered.

'To a peaceful August in Pompeii, then,' said Flavia's father, and raised his cup in a toast.

'Pompeii,' they all echoed, and raised their wine cups.

FINIS

THE LAST SCROLL

Ostia, the port of ancient Rome, was and is a real place.

Today, it is one of the nicest ancient sites in the Mediterranean. Located about sixteen miles outside Rome, Ostia Antica (ancient Ostia) is not to be confused with the modern town of Ostia Lido (Ostia beach).

If you visit the site of Ostia Antica, you can see the remains of many warehouses, inns, temples, public baths and houses.

Some places in this story are real: the theatre and synagogue, for example. Other places are made up, like Flavia's house and Aurarius's workshop. But they *could* be there, we just haven't found them.

THE SECRETS
OF VESUVIUS

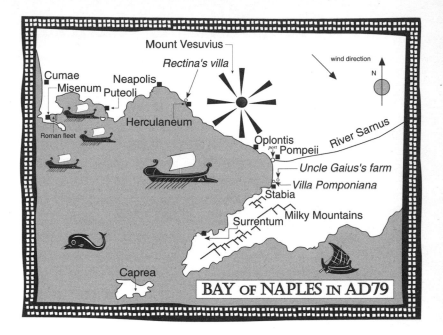

Mount Vesuvius
Rectina's villa
wind direction
N
Cumae
Misenum
Neapolis
Puteoli
Roman fleet
Herculaneum
Oplontis
port
Pompeii
River Sarnus
Uncle Gaius's farm
Villa Pomponiana
Stabia
Milky Mountains
Surrentum
Caprea
BAY OF NAPLES IN AD79

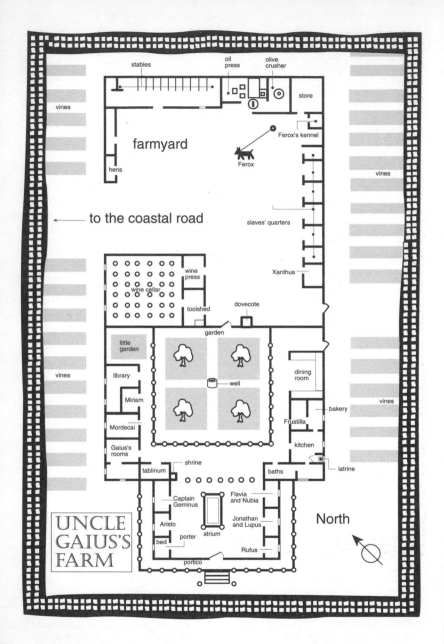

stables

oil press

olive crusher

store

vines

farmyard

Ferox's kennel

hens

Ferox

vines

to the coastal road

slaves' quarters

Xanthus

wine press

wine cellar

toolshed

dovecote

garden

little garden

well

dining room

library

Miriam

bakery

Mordecai

Frustilla

vines

Gaius's rooms

kitchen

shrine

baths

tablinum

latrine

Captain Geminus

Flavia and Nubia

Aristo

Jonathan and Lupus

North

bed

porter

atrium

Rufus

UNCLE GAIUS'S FARM

portico

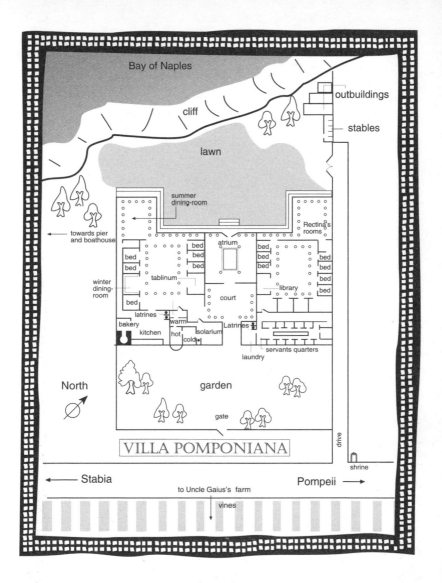

Bay of Naples

cliff

outbuildings

stables

lawn

summer dining-room

Rectina's rooms

towards pier and boathouse

bed
bed
atrium
bed
bed

bed
bed

bed
bed

bed

tablinum

winter dining-room

library

bed
bed
bed

court

bed

latrines

Latrines

bakery

kitchen

warm

hot

cold

solarium

servants quarters

laundry

North

garden

gate

VILLA POMPONIANA

drive

shrine

← Stabia

Pompeii →

to Uncle Gaius's farm

↓ vines

*To all my students
past, present and future*

SCROLL I

'Jonathan, look out!' screamed Flavia Gemina.

Jonathan ben Mordecai – hip deep in the blue Tyrrhenian sea – didn't see the horrible creature rising out of the water behind him.

'Arrrgh!' The sea monster seized Jonathan round the waist.

'Aiieeee!' cried Jonathan. But his scream was cut off as he was pulled under, and salt water filled his mouth and nostrils. A moment later the surface of the water sparkled peacefully under the hot summer sun. Flavia and her slave-girl Nubia stared in horror.

Suddenly Jonathan shot up again in an explosion of spray and foam, gasping for air. He spat out a mouthful of seawater.

'Lupus, you fool, I could have drowned!'

Another figure popped up out of the water beside him, laughing hard. It was Lupus the sea monster, naked as an eel. Although Lupus was only eight years old, Flavia squealed at the sight of his nakedness and shut her eyes. She heard Lupus splash through the waves onto the beach.

When she thought it was safe to look, Flavia opened one eye.

Lupus was tying the cord belt of his tunic.

Flavia opened the other eye.

Jonathan was creeping up behind Lupus with a large scoop of wet sand in one hand. Before he could drop the sand down the back of Lupus's tunic, the younger boy spun round and tackled Jonathan. They fell onto the sand, where they rolled around like a pair of wrestlers in the palaestra.

Finally Jonathan, who was older and bigger, ended up on top. He straddled Lupus's waist and held the younger boy's wrists hard against the hot sand. Lupus struggled and strained, but although he was strong and wiry, he couldn't budge Jonathan.

'Ha!' crowed Jonathan. 'The warrior Achilles has overpowered the fierce sea monster. Beg for mercy. Go on. Say *pax*!'

Flavia sighed and rolled her eyes.

'Jonathan, you *know* Lupus can't speak. He doesn't have a tongue. How can he beg for mercy? Let him go.'

'No,' insisted Jonathan. 'No mercy until he begs for it. Do you want mercy?'

Lupus's green eyes blazed. He shook his head defiantly as he tried to struggle free.

'Then you will receive the punishment!' Jonathan let a glob of foamy saliva emerge from his mouth. It hung over Lupus's face.

Lupus looked up in alarm at the dangling spit. Flavia and Nubia squealed. Suddenly a furry wet creature hurled itself at Jonathan, barking enthusiastically.

'Scuto!' laughed Jonathan. He fell off Lupus as the dog covered his face with hot kisses. Two wet puppies scrambled after the bigger dog.

Scuto waited until the four friends had gathered

around him. Then he shook himself vigorously. The puppies followed suit, shaking their small bodies from head to tail.

'*En!*' said Nubia. 'Behold! My new tunic is be-spattered.'

Jonathan laughed. 'I think we've been reading you too much Latin poetry.'

Flavia looked down at her own tunic, which was also spotted with salt water. 'Oh well, only one thing to do . . .'

She ran squealing into the water, tunic and all. The other three yelled and followed her.

For several minutes they splashed and dunked each other. Then Lupus gave the older children their daily swimming lesson. He showed them how to move through the water by pulling with their arms and making their legs move like a frog's. Nubia, who had grown up in the African desert, where water was rare and precious, had been shy of the sea at first. Now she loved swimming. Jonathan was making good progress, too. But Flavia couldn't get her arms and legs to work together.

At last they all emerged from the sea and fell in a row onto the soft, warm dunes. Breathing hard, the four of them closed their eyes and let the hot August sun dry them. The sea breeze was deliciously cool against their wet bodies. Scuto and the puppies, Nipur and Tigris, lay panting on the sand.

When she'd caught her breath, Flavia lifted herself on one elbow and squinted up the beach. Sextus, one of her father's sailors, lay dozing under a papyrus parasol meant for the two girls.

Having their own private bodyguard was more than a luxury. Only a few weeks earlier, Flavia and her friends had narrowly escaped capture by Venalicius the slave-dealer. If he had caught them, he could have taken them anywhere in the Mediterranean and sold them as slaves, never to be found again. But Sextus was nearby, and for the moment they were safe.

Flavia lay back on the warm sand and gazed up at a seagull drifting in the pure blue expanse of the sky. She could taste the salt on her lips and hear the whisper of waves on the wet sand. Her friends lay beside her and the dogs dozed at her feet.

Flavia Gemina closed her eyes and sighed. She wished every day could be like this. But her father had decided that Ostia was not a safe place for them to spend the rest of the summer. In two days they would sail south to her uncle's farm near Pompeii.

That was a pity. The farm was safe. But dull.

Flavia sighed again.

She had enjoyed her first taste of detective work, when she and her friends had discovered and trapped Ostia's dog-killer. She wanted more mysteries to solve. And there were plenty here in Ostia. A nine-year-old girl named Sapphira had gone missing a few months earlier. Alma's favourite baker had been robbed three times. And there were always mysterious strangers lurking near the harbour, hoping to catch a fast boat away from Italy. Living in a busy seaport like Ostia, you needed to use all your senses and be constantly on the alert.

'What is it, Jonathan?' said Flavia. 'Why do you keep poking me?'

'You were snoring,' he said. 'And I think someone's in trouble.'

Flavia sat up and shaded her eyes with her hand.

Far out on the vast expanse of glittering blue water, she could just make out the curve of an upturned rowing boat. And clinging to it was a tiny figure frantically waving for help!

SCROLL II

The four friends scrambled to their feet and gazed out to sea.

'Behold. A sturdy vessel has capsized!' said Nubia.

'Sextus!' cried Flavia. 'Quick!'

The big bodyguard scrambled to his feet and looked around in alarm.

'A boat's capsized!' she yelled.

The three dogs barked and bounced round the sailor as he ran up to them. He was tanned and muscular, and would have been good-looking if most of his teeth hadn't been missing.

'What?' he said, and then, 'Where?'

They all pointed.

It took Sextus only a moment to assess the situation. Cursing under his breath, he stripped off his tunic, ran splashing through the shallow water and then swam towards the upturned boat with strong, powerful strokes.

Lupus ran to the water's edge, hesitated, then took off his own tunic.

'Lupus, no! It's too far,' they cried.

Lupus ignored their shouts. He plunged into the water and began to swim after Sextus.

To Flavia, it seemed ages before Sextus reached the upturned boat. She breathed a sigh of relief as Lupus's smaller head finally joined the other two. But instead of swimming back at once, the three figures stayed with the boat, bobbing up and down.

'What are they doing?' said Jonathan.

Finally the two larger heads began moving back towards the beach. After a moment the smaller head followed, but more slowly than before.

Nubia gripped Flavia's arm anxiously. 'Lupus getting tired.'

'You're right,' said Flavia. 'He'll be exhausted.'

'I have an idea,' said Jonathan. 'I'll run to the marina and hire a litter to carry them home. Father can treat them.'

'Good idea,' said Flavia. 'But what about your asthma? I'd better go. I can run faster.' When she saw the expression on his face she gave his shoulder a quick squeeze. 'You stay and protect Nubia. Scuto will protect me.'

Flavia's bare feet slapped against the wet sand – she had left her sandals on the dunes. Never mind, no time to go back now. Scuto ran beside her, his tongue lolling. Soon she could see the marina where fishing boats and smaller merchant ships were docked.

Her heart was beating fast as she and Scuto ran over the softer dunes, past the synagogue and up towards the quay. A boardwalk separated the marina on the left from warehouses and temples on the right. As Flavia ran past the piers she looked to see if the slave-ship *Vespa* was moored there. Thankfully, its hateful yellow and black sail was nowhere in sight. Venalicius and his crew must be on their way to Delos, or one of the other slave-trading centres.

The area around the Marina Gate was crowded. Flavia hooked her finger through Scuto's collar as she dodged sailors, shoppers, soldiers and slaves. She needed a litter, and she needed one quickly. There were usually one or two under the arch of the gate. They offered lifts around Ostia for a few sestercii.

She kept her left hand tightly over her money pouch. In this crush, thieves would be everywhere.

At last she spotted a litter in a patch of shade near the Marina Gate. Beside it lounged two muscular young men eating their lunch: greasy pieces of meat on wooden skewers.

'How much . . . to hire your litter . . . for half an hour?' She stood breathlessly in front of them.

'What, darling? Want a ride, do you?' grinned one of the litter-bearers. His ears were shaped like broccoli.

'Capsized boat,' Flavia gasped. 'My friends are rescuing him. How much to carry him . . . to a house near the Laurentum Gate?' She jingled her coin purse urgently.

'Four sestercii, sweetheart,' said the other one, whose nose was not unlike a turnip. 'I'm giving you a special rate because it's a good deed we're doing.'

'And because it's been slow all morning,' grumbled Broccoli-ears under his breath, and tossed the last greasy gob of meat to Scuto.

Flavia and her hired litter-bearers were about a hundred yards up the beach when she saw Sextus stagger out of the water and onto the shore, half pulling and half carrying a portly man.

Barking loudly, Scuto raced ahead towards the

group on the shore. As the dog approached, the stout man abruptly sat down on the sand. Scuto, his tail wagging vigorously, licked the man's face and then hurried on to greet the others.

'You're just in time,' cried Jonathan, running to meet Flavia and the litter. 'His lips are turning blue. We need to wrap him in a blanket and get him to my father as quickly as possible.'

Broccoli-ears and Turnip-nose knew their job. They lifted the man and helped him into the litter. He was stout and tanned, with a fringe of white hair round his bald head. And he was wheezing, the way Jonathan sometimes did. As Flavia helped the litter-bearers tuck a faded green blanket around him, she noticed a heavy gold ring on his finger.

'Do you want the curtains open or shut, darling?' asked Turnip-nose.

'Open,' said Flavia. 'So we can see how he's doing.'

'Wait,' gasped the man. It was the first time he had spoken. 'Where is my bag?' His voice was high and breathy.

'He insisted we take it,' explained Sextus, coming up to the litter. 'Lupus has it.'

Flavia turned to see Nubia helping Lupus out of the sea. The boy staggered across the sand to the litter and held out a dripping oilcloth bag. The man, now comfortably propped up on his cushions, grasped it eagerly.

'Thank you, thank you,' he cried in his light voice. 'This is all that matters.' He reached into the bag and they all waited to see what priceless treasure he would pull out of it.

It was a wax tablet and stylus. The man grunted

with satisfaction, opened the tablet and shook drops of water from it. Then he began to write. They all stared at him. After a moment he looked back at them.

'Well, why are we waiting?' he wheezed cheerfully. 'Off you go, bearers, to wherever you are taking me.'

'Wait!' cried Flavia. 'I know who you are!'

SCROLL III

'You're Pliny, aren't you?' said Flavia. 'The man who wrote the *Natural History*.'

'Why, yes. Yes, I am,' said the man in the litter. 'How did you know that?'

'Well –' began Flavia, and then caught sight of Lupus, dripping and shivering. 'Please may Lupus share your litter?'

'Of course, of course!' Pliny gestured to the litter-bearers.

Broccoli-ears and Turnip-nose helped the exhausted boy climb up onto the other end of the couch. They settled him against a cushion facing Pliny. Then Broccoli-ears took the two poles at the front of the litter and Turnip-nose took those at the rear. When the strong young men had adjusted the balance, they set off back up the beach.

'Tell me how you guessed my identity.' Pliny closed his wax tablet and looked at Flavia.

'Well,' she began, jogging a little to keep up. 'You sat on the sand when Scuto ran up to you. In volume eight you say that the best way to calm an attacking dog is to sit on the ground.'

'You've read volume eight of my book?'

'Yes, I have the whole set,' admitted Flavia with a

shy laugh. 'It's a pleasure to meet you, sir. My name is Flavia Gemina, daughter of Marcus Flavius Geminus, sea captain.'

'It's a pleasure to meet you, too, Flavia Gemina,' said Pliny. 'But I am not the only person who sits down when a fierce dog approaches. You must have had other clues . . .'

'I did. I know the author of the *Natural History* is an admiral who lives just down the coast. Your face is tanned as if you've spent time in the sun, but your hands are soft and ink-stained, like the hands of a scholar. I can tell from your ring that you're rich and high-born.' Flavia took a breath and carried on.

'I also heard that a killer whale was spotted in the harbour yesterday. You wrote a book about natural history. So that would explain why you were out in a small boat with your tablet and stylus.' Most of this was occurring to Flavia as she spoke, but the old man's shining eyes encouraged her.

'Furthermore,' she proclaimed dramatically, 'I think the killer whale surfaced near your boat and . . . and capsized it with his tail.'

'Extraordinary!' cried Pliny, clapping his hands. 'What a superb mind you have for deductions. However, I am afraid you are incorrect about the cause of my accident. We never saw the killer whale. Rather, my stupid slave panicked when a wasp flew too near. He stood up and flapped his arms about, with the inevitable results. I'm afraid he has paid dearly for his fear of being stung. I shouldn't have taken a mere household slave.'

'You mean your slave is dead?' gulped Jonathan, jogging on the other side of the litter.

'Yes, indeed. I'm afraid he now lies at the bottom of the Tyrrhenian Sea. But who are you, young man, and where are you taking me?'

'I'm Jonathan ben Mordecai. My father is a doctor. He'll help you recover.'

'Ah!' said the admiral. 'A Jew! Jews make extraordinarily good doctors. I look forward to meeting him. However, I don't think there is anything wrong with me that a cup of wine and a piece of cheese won't cure. I've been floating in that water since two hours past dawn. I'm as wrinkled as a raisin and ravenously hungry.'

'I'm sure my father has some wine,' said Jonathan, and then added, 'I've read some of your book, too.'

'How gratifying! I am surrounded by fans. Do you also enjoy my writings, young lady?' This last was addressed to Nubia, who smiled shyly and then looked rather frightened.

'Nubia has only been here in Italy for two months,' Flavia explained, 'She's learning to speak Latin but can't read it yet.'

'And you, young man, the brave and aquatic hero who rescued my precious tablets and notes. What is your name?'

'His name is Lupus,' answered Jonathan. 'He is an orphan and can't speak. His tongue was cut out.'

'Poor boy!' said Pliny, 'How did it happen?'

Lupus's grin instantly faded and his green eyes stared coldly into the admiral's. Pliny's cheerful gaze faltered and he looked uncertainly at Flavia.

'We don't know how Lupus lost his tongue,' she whispered. 'He lives with Jonathan now, and has lessons with us. We hope one day he'll be able to tell us in writing. But he doesn't like people talking about it.'

They had just passed through the cool shade of the Marina Gate. Now the litter emerged into the bright, hot sunshine and turned right onto Marina Street, just inside the city walls. Although many people were making their way home or to taverns in order to eat the midday meal, it was still crowded.

Lupus's face brightened again and he beamed around at the lesser mortals who had to walk on foot. Suddenly he startled them all by crowing like a rooster at two scruffy boys loitering in front of a snack bar. The boys saw him and whooped back.

'Lupus in a litter!' cried one of them.

'Are you rich, now?' yelled the other.

Lupus nodded smugly and stuck his nose in the air in a parody of a rich man. One of the boys picked up a rotten lettuce from the gutter and threw it at the litter. The soggy green missile struck Jonathan on the back.

'Hey!' Jonathan turned around, but the boys had darted out of sight.

'Perhaps we should close the curtains now,' Pliny said to Flavia.

Lupus clutched Pliny's ankle and shook his head imploringly.

'Very well,' said Pliny. 'But if you ride in a litter you must behave with decorum and not bellow out at your comrades.'

Lupus nodded meekly and behaved himself for the rest of the journey home.

'Well, that was delicious,' said Pliny, patting his ample

stomach. 'I owe you all a great debt – you saved my life. But even more importantly, you fed me. I hate missing my midday meal.'

They were all in the cool triclinium of Flavia's house: the adults reclining on couches against the wall, Flavia and her friends sitting round a table in the centre. The dining-room opened out onto a bright inner garden with a fig tree, fountain and scented shrubs.

Reclining on Pliny's right was Flavia's father. Marcus Flavius Geminus was tall and tanned, with light brown hair and the same clear grey eyes as his daughter. His hand trembled nervously as he refilled the admiral's wine cup. He could scarcely believe he was entertaining the Commander-in-Chief of the Roman imperial fleet.

Admiral Pliny nodded his thanks and then turned to Jonathan's father Mordecai, who reclined on his left.

'Thank you for looking after me, doctor.'

'It was nothing.' Mordecai bowed his turbaned head. 'I merely prescribed mint tea and a light lunch to revive you.'

'And it has. Particularly this delightful wine.' Pliny lifted his cup towards Captain Geminus. 'Is it from the Vesuvius region?'

'Why, yes.' Flavia's father looked impressed. 'My brother Gaius has an estate near Pompeii. This wine is from his vineyards.'

'I know the region well. In fact, I am going down to Misenum in less than a week, as soon as the festivals have finished.' Pliny folded his napkin and smiled at them all. 'And now, much as I'd like to stay and chat, I must be getting back. My household will begin to worry and I am a busy man. However, I would like to invite you four children to dine with me at my Laurentum villa tomorrow evening. Will you come?'

'We'd love to come,' Flavia said, flushing with pleasure.

'Excellent,' said the admiral. 'I'll send my carriage for you at the ninth hour. You see, I've already thanked your bodyguard for rescuing me, but I'd like to give each of you a small reward, too.'

SCROLL IV

The following afternoon, soon after the four friends returned from the baths, a two-horse carruca pulled up outside Flavia's house.

It was only a few miles from Ostia to Laurentum, a pleasant drive along the coastal road. The carriage crunched up the gravel drive of Pliny's seaside villa less than half an hour after they had left Ostia. A door-slave in a red tunic met them on the steps of the butter-coloured villa and led them through cool rooms and sunny courtyards to a breezy dining-room.

Flavia and her friends gazed around in amazement.

The room they stood in was surrounded on three sides by water. Only a low wall and spiral columns separated them from the blue Mediterranean. Jonathan and Lupus immediately went to the marble parapet and leaned over.

'Careful!' wheezed Admiral Pliny, shuffling into the room. 'We're right above the sea.'

'*Salve!*' they all said, and he returned their greeting.

'These halls are fair,' said Nubia.

'It is a rather fine triclinium, isn't it?' Pliny was wearing a faded purple tunic and leather slippers. He held a wax tablet in one hand. 'When the wind's from the south-west you can actually feel the spray from the breakers.'

'And look at that view!' Flavia pointed back the way they had just come. A slave had opened the double front doors and they could see all the way back through the house to the gravel drive and green woods beyond.

'It's the most beautiful villa I've ever seen,' said Jonathan.

Lupus nodded vigorously.

Pliny smiled.

'My only complaint,' he said, 'is that there is no aqueduct to supply us with running water. It makes a bit more work for the bath-slaves. But there are several wells and springs on the property.'

'You have your own private baths?' Jonathan's jaw dropped.

'Oh yes. Steam room, cold plunge, heated swimming pool . . . I simply can't do without my bath.'

A handsome slave in a red tunic hurried into the room. Around his neck hung a scribe's inkpot on a chain.

'Ah, Phrixus! Just in time.'

Admiral Pliny turned to Flavia and her friends.

'Please be seated.' He gestured towards a table set with five places. 'I prefer to sit for my meals rather than recline. I usually have a slave read to me while I eat and it's easier to take notes sitting down.'

Two female slaves in blue entered the sunny dining-room on bare feet, holding silver basins and linen napkins to wash the diners' hands. Nearby, in the shadow of a column, a fair-haired boy in a red tunic played soft music on pan pipes.

The food was simple but delicious: hardboiled eggs

to start, chicken and salad for the main course and sweet red apples for dessert. The two serving-girls kept the cups filled with well-watered wine and passed out rolls made from the finest white flour.

As they ate, Pliny told them amusing stories about the Emperor Vespasian, who had been his friend. Occasionally the admiral turned to his scribe and dictated a few lines. The young slave had smooth, tanned skin and dark curly hair. He reminded Flavia of her tutor, though Aristo's hair was lighter.

Finally, as they munched slices of apple, Pliny leaned back in his chair.

'Now, Flavia Gemina, I believe you recently solved the mystery of Ostia's dog-killer!'

'You know about that?' Flavia felt her face grow pink.

'Of course. Research is what I do best.' The admiral's eyes twinkled, and he added, 'I know Ostia's junior magistrate fairly well. He was very impressed with your detective work. Tell me how you did it.'

A sea breeze ruffled their hair and garments.

'Well, I couldn't have done it without my friends.'

For the first time that evening, Pliny ignored his Greek scribe and gave them his undivided attention. His eyes shone as Flavia and Jonathan took it in turns to tell the story. He laughed at Lupus's sound-effects and when, after much coaxing, Nubia shyly sang her haunting Dog-Song, the admiral wiped a tear from his eye.

'Extraordinary,' said Pliny. 'You are quite remarkable children.'

He glanced at his scribe and Flavia thought he was

going to resume his dictation. Instead, the young man slipped out of the dining-room and returned a moment later with three small pouches and a papyrus scroll.

'Thank you, Phrixus.' Pliny looked around the table at each of them. 'I promised you all a reward for rescuing me yesterday and I hope my modest gifts will not disappoint you.

'First, to Lupus, the brave young swimmer who rescued my precious research . . .' Pliny nodded at Phrixus, who presented Lupus with a small, blue silk pouch.

Lupus opened it with eager hands and tipped out the contents. A gold ring set with an engraved aquamarine fell into his palm.

'What is it?' Flavia asked.

'It is a signet ring with a wolf carved upon it,' said the admiral. 'Most suitable for someone whose name means "wolf".'

Lupus passed it around. They all admired the miniature wolf's face cut into the gem. Lupus looked at Pliny with bright eyes and nodded his head respectfully.

'You're most welcome,' said Pliny in his breathy voice. 'Next, the dusky Nubia. Unwillingly taken from your desert home, you bravely face the future as a stranger in a strange land.'

Phrixus presented Nubia with a tiny pouch of orange silk. Inside were two earrings: golden brown gems in gold settings.

'The stone is called "tiger's-eye",' explained the admiral, 'because the yellow streak looks like a cat's eye.'

'Thank you, sir,' said Nubia, putting in the earrings. They gleamed in her neat ears, perfectly matching the colour of her eyes.

'Jonathan,' continued Pliny, 'I understand you suffer from asthma, as I do.'

Phrixus handed Jonathan a small leather pouch on a black silken cord.

'In this pouch are exotic and rare herbs for your shortness of breath. Such a bag of herbs has brought me relief on many occasions. Always wear it round your neck. When you feel the tightening in your chest, breathe into it.'

'Thank you, admiral,' said Jonathan. He gave the sack a tentative sniff.

'And finally, a gift for you, my dear.' Pliny smiled at Flavia. 'Something which I hope will appeal to your enquiring mind.'

Phrixus handed Flavia a papyrus scroll, tied with a blue ribbon. As she untied the ribbon, Pliny explained,

'It's an unpublished work of mine, written in my own hand when I was younger. It's a short account of some of the great mysteries of the past. I meant to include it as an appendix to my book *The Scholar*, but in the end I left it out.'

Wide-eyed, Flavia unrolled the scroll carefully. Minuscule writing covered the sheet from margin to margin.

'Thank you,' breathed Flavia. 'I love mysteries.'

The admiral nodded. Then he narrowed his eyes and stroked his chin thoughtfully.

'I think I might have a real mystery for you to solve. You say you are travelling to the Pompeii region soon?'

'Yes,' replied Flavia. 'My uncle Gaius lives between Stabia and Pompeii.'

'Perfect!' exclaimed the admiral. 'Phrixus, do you have –' but the Greek scribe was already holding out a scrap of papyrus.

'What a marvellous servant you are, Phrixus,' said Pliny with a smile. 'You anticipate my every wish. Please give it to our young detective.'

Flavia eagerly took the piece of papyrus and read it. Then she looked up at Pliny, a frown creasing her forehead.

'It's only a riddle,' she said. 'A child's riddle.'

'Yes,' said Pliny, 'but it may lead you to a great treasure!'

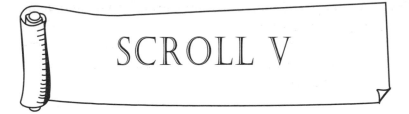

SCROLL V

'Read us the riddle,' said Jonathan, leaning forward in his chair.

'*Littera prima dolet, secunda iubet, tertia mittit, quarta docet, et littera quinta gaudet,*' read Flavia. 'My first letter grieves, my second commands, my third sends, my fourth teaches, and my fifth letter rejoices.' Flavia frowned at the piece of papyrus.

'I know this kind of puzzle!' cried Jonathan. 'When you guess all the letters, they spell out a word. And I think I know what the first letter is. "My first letter grieves" means the letter *A*, pronounced "ah!", because that's the sound you make when you're sad. May I see it?'

'Do *you* know the answer, Admiral Pliny?' asked Flavia, handing Jonathan the papyrus.

The admiral shook his head. 'I'm afraid I don't. The riddle is a bit of graffiti I saw about a month ago, on the wall of a blacksmith's workshop in Pompeii. The young smith who repaired my cart-wheel saw me studying the riddle. He assured me that the answer would lead me to a most valuable treasure. "A treasure beyond imagining" were his precise words.'

Pliny took the papyrus scrap from Jonathan and studied it thoughtfully.

'I should very much like to know the answer to the riddle,' he said, 'because I believe it is genuine. There was something special about the blacksmith . . . I went back the following week to speak to him, but he wasn't there. If you should find him, or solve the riddle, send a messenger to me at this address in Misenum. I'm going down after the festival of Jove.' The admiral handed the riddle to Phrixus, who dipped his pen in the hanging inkpot and wrote the address on the back.

'So you see,' said the admiral, blowing on the ink and flapping the papyrus, 'this is a two-part mystery. Solve the riddle. And find the blacksmith.'

'Do you happen to know –' began Jonathan.

'The blacksmith's name?' Pliny rose smiling from his chair. 'I do indeed – it is Vulcan, a most suitable name for a blacksmith.'

'Vulcan?' said Nubia.

'The god of blacksmiths and metalworkers,' said Flavia. 'Vulcan!'

Two days later, Flavia and Jonathan lay on their backs on a sun-warmed ship's deck, gazing up at the blue sky and the taut canvas sail. Beneath them, the merchant ship *Myrtilla* rose and fell, almost like a living creature.

A strong breeze had filled the ship's sail and for two days the *Myrtilla* had ploughed a creamy path through the sapphire sea. On the previous evening, the *Myrtilla* had anchored in a cove and they had spent the night sleeping on a crescent beach under a million stars.

There were seven passengers on board: Flavia and her three friends, plus Jonathan's father Mordecai and sister Miriam, and Flavia's young Greek tutor Aristo.

Flavia's father, the owner and captain of the ship, sat at the helm with the steering paddle in his right hand. Occasionally he barked a command to his four crew members, the Phoenician brothers Quartus, Quintus and Sextus, and an Ethiopian named Ebenus.

'Nubia seems to have got over her fear of ships,' Jonathan observed.

Flavia's slave-girl was high in the rigging with Lupus. Earlier in the day, the two of them had seen one of the Phoenician brothers go up and had followed him like monkeys. Now Nubia was playing her lotus-wood flute while Lupus drummed a beat on the oak mast. Their music seemed to fill the sail and carry the ship forward.

Mordecai and Aristo sat chatting in the shade of the cabin, near Scuto and the puppies. For their own safety the dogs had been housed in a wooden cage with a straw-covered floor. They were not enjoying themselves and stared out resentfully at their owners. Miriam stood alone at the front of the ship. The wind whipped her curly dark hair and violet mantle as she leaned over the prow.

'Let's get back to Pliny's riddle,' said Flavia. 'You say the first letter is *A*, the sound for sadness. But then what?' They had been trying to solve the puzzle since the evening of Pliny's dinner party.

'I was thinking about it last night on the beach,' said Jonathan. 'The sound for rejoicing might be the letter *E*, pronounced "eh!".' He punched the air, as if his favourite chariot team had just won.

'So it starts with the letter *A* and ends with *E*.' Flavia thoughtfully picked at one of the gummy ridges of pine pitch which sealed the planks of the deck.

'And I think "my third letter sends" means the letter *I*, because *"i!"* means "go!". If you tell someone to go, you send them away.'

'So it could be a word spelled *A*-something-*I*-something-*E*.' Flavia frowned. 'What's a Latin word that ends in *E*?'

'There are hundreds. Lots of words end in *E* when you are speaking to someone –'

'Or praying to one of the gods! Of course! Why didn't I think of that?' Flavia sat up so that she could think more clearly. 'So we only need letter two and letter four: "my second commands" and "my fourth teaches" –'

'*En!*' cried Nubia, high in the rigging. 'Behold!'

'She's right!' cried Flavia. '*En* means "behold" or "look". The riddle says "my fourth teaches": so *N* could fit, because in a way, it teaches. So we have *A-something-I-N-E . . .*'

'*En!*' cried Nubia again, more urgently: 'Behold!' She was pointing back and to the left. Then Lupus pointed, too, and suddenly Quartus cried,

'To port, to port!'

'She's not giving us the next clue,' said Flavia, scrambling to her feet. 'She really wants to show us something!'

Flavia ran to the side of the ship and Jonathan followed, staggering a little as the deck rose and fell beneath him.

They leaned over the polished oak rail and gazed back.

A long, low warship was moving up quickly behind them. With its bristling oars and the eye painted on the prow, it reminded Flavia of some kind of dangerous insect.

'Like bug.' Nubia's voice from above echoed Flavia's thought.

The warship was already beside them, so close that they could see the water dripping from the flashing oars and hear the song of the oarsmen. The officer leading the chant was walking forward, so that he seemed to be overtaking the *Myrtilla* on foot. At the ship's stern a figure sat in the shade of the open cabin.

Flavia squinted. 'Maybe it's Pliny.'

'I don't think so.' Flavia's father joined them at the rail. 'The admiral said he was coming down tomorrow. But that ship is certainly one under his command, probably on manoeuvres from the naval harbour at Misenum.'

They waved as the warship slid past and the singing young officer grinned and waved back. The oarsmen were too intent on their rowing even to look at the ship they were overtaking. Soon the warship had pulled far ahead and disappeared behind a honey-coloured shoulder of rock.

'By Hercules, they're fast,' said Aristo.

'Superb!' agreed Mordecai.

'They have the benefit of eighty oarsmen as well as the wind full in their sail,' said Captain Geminus with a grin.

As they approached the promontory, the *Myrtilla*'s crew had one of its periodic bursts of activity when Captain Geminus bellowed and three of the crewmen swarmed over the rigging.

When the activity finally subsided, the *Myrtilla* had changed direction and was sailing into a vast blue bay.

'There it is,' said Flavia. 'The great bay of Neapolis.'

SCROLL VI

Jonathan had never seen so many boats in his entire life. Not even in the port of Ostia. They had passed the naval harbour of Misenum and the port of Puteoli on their left, and were now sailing towards a large mountain.

'That, of course, is Vesuvius,' said Flavia's father. 'It's covered with vineyards; which is why it's so green. You can see a few red roofs among the vines. Those are villas of the very rich.'

'How great and marvellous are your works,' murmured Mordecai. A breeze touched the two locks of grey hair which hung from his black turban. 'Truly this place is like paradise.'

'Pliny says this is the most fertile region in the whole world,' said Flavia.

'Does your uncle own one of those villas on the mountain?' Jonathan asked her.

'No,' said Flavia, 'he lives further south, between Pompeii and Stabia.'

'Where?'

Captain Geminus pointed again: 'See the town at the foot of Vesuvius?'

'Yes.'

'That's Herculaneum. Then . . . look right – no

further – yes, there. That's Pompeii and then . . . do you see that small cluster of red roofs a bit further to the right? That's Stabia. My brother lives nearer to Stabia than Pompeii. But we'll disembark in Pompeii. The harbour at Stabia is murder to get in and out of.'

It was late afternoon by the time the *Myrtilla* sailed into the port of Pompeii. The vast blue bowl of the sky was filled with the piercing cries of swifts, which had begun to fly lower as the day cooled.

Pompeii was built on a hill, and they could see the imposing town walls across the water, orange in the rays of the sinking sun. The red roofs of the tallest buildings peeped above.

Using the large paddle at the back of the ship, Flavia's father guided the *Myrtilla* into the harbour. When the ship was moored, they all made their way carefully down the boarding plank.

'I must organise my berth with the harbourmaster,' said Captain Geminus, looking around. 'Ah, here he comes. Can you wait at that tavern over there across the square, the one with the yellow awning and plane trees? We'll bring the baggage and dogs over in a few minutes.'

The seven passengers made their way slowly past a forest of elegant masts. Coloured pennants fluttered and the tackle jingled musically in the late afternoon breeze. After two days on the springy wood of the *Myrtilla*'s deck, the pier felt hard and unyielding under Flavia's feet, and jarred her heels as she walked.

The harbour shrine of Castor and Pollux was wreathed with garlands, for it was the Ides of August, a day sacred to Jupiter, Diana and the Twins. The shops and taverns around the square were all clean and swept. Many had hanging baskets of violets and daisies.

Fresh from an afternoon at the baths and still dressed in their festive clothes, the young Pompeians strolled along the waterfront as the day cooled, perfumed girls in wisps of silk and young men in sea-green tunics with their hair slicked back. Some wore flowered garlands on their heads. Flavia wondered whether Vulcan the blacksmith was among them.

At the tavern with the yellow awning, Mordecai ordered two jugs of well-watered wine. The serving-girl brought the wine immediately and returned a few moments later with bowls of nuts.

'Mmmm, pistachio nuts!' said Jonathan, taking a handful. 'You don't get free nuts with your wine in Ostia.'

'That's because Pompeii is a much more elegant place than Ostia.' Aristo lifted his wine cup towards the city walls.

'And more expensive, too,' grumbled Mordecai, as he counted out coins for the girl.

'Here comes your father already,' Jonathan said to Flavia, spitting out a shell. Then he frowned: 'He's changed his clothes!'

Nubia frowned, too: 'He's had his hairs cut.'

'And it appears he's bought himself a new pair of boots, as well.' Mordecai tugged his beard in puzzlement.

Lupus grinned and shook his head, as if to say they were all mistaken.

'Uncle Gaius!' squealed Flavia. She jumped up from

her chair, vaulted over a planter full of daisies and threw herself into her uncle's arms.

Gaius Flavius Geminus Senior was ten minutes older than his twin brother Marcus, who hurried up a few minutes later, followed by Quartus with the luggage and Sextus with the dogs.

'Gaius!' Flavia's father dropped the sea bag he was carrying and embraced his brother. 'You got my letter! I wasn't sure I'd sent it in time. I was going to take rooms in a tavern and organise a carriage tomorrow!'

'Your letter came yesterday. Xanthus has the cart ready and waiting, with a couple of horses tethered behind. If we go now we'll be home before dark.'

'But Uncle Gaius!' said Flavia. 'I wanted to spend the night in Pompeii. I wanted to look around the town. There's someone here I want to find.'

'Don't be silly.' Her uncle ruffled her already tousled hair. 'We're expecting you at the farm. You can see Pompeii any time. Now, aren't you going to introduce me to your friends?'

The sun had just set and all the colour had drained from the hot summer sky when Xanthus the farm manager drove them into the dusty farmyard. Xanthus was a short, leathery freedman with thin fair hair and a permanently worried expression. As the cart rocked to a halt, he jumped down to wedge the wheels. Flavia and the others climbed out of the carriage, stretching and groaning.

The jolting of the cart had produced the usual effect on Flavia: she was bursting to use the latrine. Scuto's intention was the same as hers. He scampered round the farmyard, wagging his tail and sniffing out a suitable spot to relieve himself. He finally decided to take revenge on the big wooden box which had jostled and jolted him for nearly an hour.

Flavia's dog had just lifted his leg against one of the cart's rear wheels when there was a terrifying snarl. Out of the evening shadows streaked an enormous creature.

A huge black wolf was heading straight for Scuto!

SCROLL VII

As the snarling wolf tore through the farmyard, every-one froze. Even Scuto – one leg still lifted – seemed paralysed by fear as the savage creature bore down upon him.

'Ferox! No!' bellowed Flavia's uncle Gaius.

The enormous beast jerked to a halt, as if it had been pulled up short.

Flavia looked closer: it *had* been pulled up short. The monster strained against a leather collar attached to a long iron chain. His eyes bulged with fury and his claws scrabbled at the earth.

Scuto gulped, lowered his leg and backed off. Jon-athan and Nubia clutched their own puppies tightly. Nipur was whimpering and Tigris expressed his un-tigerlike terror by wetting his master's tunic.

'Oh Pollux!' swore Jonathan. 'He's widdled down my front.'

As if a spell had been broken, everyone laughed and began to move again. Ferox was the only one not amused. He uttered a series of deep barks which echoed off the farm buildings and stables.

'Come bathe and have some dinner,' shouted Fla-via's uncle over the din. 'The slaves will unpack. And don't worry about Ferox. Once he gets to know you, he's no trouble at all.'

Gaius's farm was an ancient but cheerful building with white walls and a red-tiled roof. The living quarters were built round an atrium and a large inner garden. A high wall separated the house from the farmyard and outbuildings.

Next to the kitchen was a simple two-roomed bath-house. Gaius's house-slaves had heated the water so that the travellers could wash off the dust of the journey and soak their aching limbs. The girls went first, followed by the boys and men.

Clean and refreshed, hair still damp, they found their way to the garden triclinium just as the first few stars pricked the violet sky.

'It is our Sabbath,' Mordecai said to Flavia's uncle. 'Do you mind if Miriam lights the candles?'

'Of course not,' said Gaius, and Mordecai gave him a small bow of thanks.

As the adults reclined and the children took their seats, Miriam remained standing. Pulling a lavender scarf over her curly hair, she recited a Hebrew prayer and lit the candles with a taper.

For a moment everyone was silent. The scent of rose and jasmine drifted in from the inner garden and somewhere a bird sang one sleepy note. The moon hung like a pearl crescent above the cool green leaves of a laurel tree.

Then Gaius's ancient cook Frustilla shuffled in with hot black-bean soup, cold roast chicken and brown bread, while a half-witted house-slave named Rufus began to light the oil-lamps.

As they ate, Gaius asked Flavia if there was anything special she and her friends would like to do while they were in Pompeii.

'We'd like to visit a blacksmith's shop by the Stabian Gate.'

'That's an unusual request for a ten-year-old girl.' Her uncle raised an eyebrow. 'May I ask why?'

'Well, a few days ago we rescued Admiral Pliny –'

'What!' Gaius nearly choked on his soup. 'You rescued Admiral Pliny? The Emperor Vespasian's friend and advisor?'

Flavia nodded. 'He asked us to solve a riddle and find the man who gave it to him.'

'A *riddle*? Before you tell me how you rescued Pliny, can you tell me why on earth the Commander-in-Chief of the imperial fleets wants to solve a riddle?'

Flavia and Jonathan looked at each other and grinned.

'The treasure!'

Jonathan's eyes opened with a start. His heart was pounding and his body was drenched in sweat. At first he thought he was still dreaming. The ceiling of his bedroom was too high and the walls were too close together. The faint scent of fermenting wine drifted through the high window. Somewhere a cock crowed.

Then he remembered. He was at Flavia's uncle's farm. The previous day, the Sabbath, had been a quiet one. They had unpacked and explored the farm. Today they were going into Pompeii to look for the black-smith called Vulcan.

'Lupus?' he whispered. There was no reply.

Jonathan lifted his head. He was surprised to see Lupus's bed was empty. Tigris was gone, too.

After a moment Jonathan got up and slipped on his tunic and sandals. Groggily he pulled back the curtain in the doorway and walked from the dim atrium into the bright garden. It was a few minutes past dawn and the sky above was lemon yellow. Birdsong filled the air and the cock crowed again.

'Good morning, Jonathan!' said Flavia. 'We were just going to get you.'

'Breakfast is ready.' Miriam smiled at him.

They all sat around a white-painted wrought-iron table under a laurel tree near the well, eating flat brown bread, dates and white cheese. The dogs sat attentively nearby, hoping for scraps. Miriam was pouring out barley water from a jug and Aristo was making notes on a wax tablet.

Jonathan pulled back a chair and sat down heavily.

'Are you all right, Jonathan?' asked Flavia, passing him the plate. 'You look a bit pale.'

'Just a bad dream.' He tore off a piece of bread and tossed it to Tigris. Then he took a handful of dates. 'Are we having lessons today? I thought we were going into Pompeii to find Vulcan.'

'Uncle Gaius says he'll take us later,' said Flavia, 'when he takes my father back to the harbour.'

'Don't worry.' Aristo had seen the look on Jonathan's face. 'It's only a short lesson today.'

The young Greek put down his wax tablet and lifted

a large orange and black ceramic pot from the ground. He set it carefully in the centre of the table. On its side was painted a scene from Greek mythology.

Scuto had wandered off with the puppies to explore the garden. Jonathan watched them wistfully.

'This Greek vase is an antique – almost five hundred years old,' Aristo was saying. 'It was used for mixing wine at dinner parties. Flavia's uncle very kindly said I could show it to you this morning. You may look, but – no, Lupus! Don't touch it! It's worth over four hundred thousand sestercii.'

Jonathan sat up straight. 'That's nearly half a million!'

'Precisely,' said Aristo. 'Not only is it old, but it is the work of a master. The artist has decorated this vase in a very clever way, painting the space *behind* the figures black, so that they show up red-orange, the colour of the clay. Then, with a fine brush, he has added the eyes, mouths and other details. This, of course, is the way all the Greek potters decorated their vases five hundred years ago.'

Jonathan and the others brought their faces closer to look at the figures on the big mixing bowl. Suddenly Lupus giggled and pointed.

'Yes,' admitted Aristo ruefully, 'those satyrs are a bit rude. But when you are half-man, half-goat, I suppose you don't need to wear any clothes.'

Flavia giggled, too, and Miriam blushed. Jonathan grinned; he felt better already.

'However,' said Aristo, clearing his throat. 'I haven't brought out this vase to show you naked satyrs. I know you're looking for a blacksmith named Vulcan and I thought you might like to hear the story of his name-sake. This figure here – the man riding the donkey – is Vulcan, blacksmith of the gods.'

SCROLL VIII

'Vulcan,' began Aristo, 'was the son of Jupiter and Juno. As the son of the king and queen of the gods, he should have been very fine to look at, but baby Vulcan was small and ugly with a red, bawling face. Juno was so horrified that she hurled the tiny baby from the top of Mount Olympus.'

'What is Muntulumpus?' asked Nubia.

'Mount Olympus,' enunciated Aristo, 'is a mountain in the north of Greece. It's the home of the gods.'

'What happened to the baby?' asked Miriam, her violet eyes wide with concern.

'The baby fell down for a day and a night. Luckily, he landed in the sea. Even so, his legs were damaged as they struck the water and they never developed properly. Baby Vulcan sank like a pebble into the cool, blue depths, where the sea-nymph Thetis found him and took him to her home – an underwater grotto. There she raised him as if he were her own child.'

Aristo paused to take a sip of barley water. 'Vulcan had a happy childhood. Dolphins were his playmates and pearls his toys. Then one day, when he was about your age, he found the remains of a fisherman's fire on the beach. The young god stared in amazement at a single coal, still red-hot and glowing. After a world of cool, watery blues and greens, it was more lovely to him than any pearl.

'Vulcan carefully shut this precious coal in a clam shell, took it back to his underwater grotto and made a fire with it. On the first day, he stared at this fire for hours on end, never leaving it. He fed the flames with seaweed, driftwood, coral and stones. On the second day, he discovered that when he made the fire hotter with bellows, certain stones sweated iron or silver or gold. The third day he beat the cooled metal into shapes: bracelets, chains, swords and shields.

'Vulcan made pearl-handled knives and spoons for his foster-mother. He made a silver chariot for himself and bridles so that seahorses could transport him quickly. He even made slave-girls of gold to wait on him and do his bidding. From that day onwards, he and Thetis lived like royalty.'

Aristo pointed to the vase.

'See, he holds hammer and tongs. That's how you can recognise him. And if you look carefully, you can see that the artist has painted his legs to look too small for his body.'

'He looks sad,' said Miriam.

'But he looks nice, too,' decided Flavia.

'Where's he going?' asked Jonathan.

'He's being escorted back to Mount Olympus. Here's how it happened.

'One day Thetis left her underwater grotto to attend a dinner party on Mount Olympus. She wore a beautiful necklace of silver and sapphires, which Vulcan had made for her. Juno admired this necklace and asked where she could get one.

'Thetis became flustered and Juno grew suspicious. At last the queen of the gods discovered the truth: the baby she had once rejected had now grown up to become the most gifted worker in precious metals the world had ever seen.

'Juno was furious and demanded that Vulcan come home. The smith god flatly refused. However, he did send Juno a most beautiful chair. Made of silver and gold, inlaid with mother-of-pearl, it had a seat like a shell and arms like dolphins.

'Juno was delighted when she received it, but the moment she sat down, her weight triggered hidden springs: metal bands sprung forth to hold her fast. The more she shrieked and struggled, the more firmly the mechanical throne gripped her. The chair was a cleverly designed trap!'

Lupus gave a triumphant bark of laughter and slapped his thigh.

'Serves her right,' agreed Jonathan.

Aristo smiled.

'For three days Juno sat fuming, still trapped in Vulcan's chair. She couldn't sleep, she couldn't stretch, and she couldn't eat.'

'Ewww!' said Jonathan. 'She couldn't use the lavatory either.'

The girls tittered and Lupus guffawed. Aristo gave them a stern look and waited until they were quiet.

'It was Jupiter who finally saved the day. He promised that if Vulcan would return to Mount Olympus and release Juno from the chair, he would give him a wife. And not just any wife, but Venus, the goddess of love and beauty. What man, or god, could resist?'

Aristo pointed to the big vase. 'Here he is riding his donkey back to Olympus, where his mother sits trapped on her throne.'

'Where is Venus?' asked Nubia.

'Probably getting ready for the wedding.'

'Did she love Vulcan?' asked Miriam.

Aristo shrugged. 'Perhaps. But she loved many others too, after all, she is the goddess of love. Later, Vulcan built a smithy under a huge mountain on the island of Sicily. They say that whenever Venus is unfaithful, Vulcan grows angry and beats the red-hot metal with such force that sparks and smoke rise up from the top of the mountain. We call mountains which send forth smoke and fire "volcanoes", after Vulcan.'

'Not really,' snorted Jonathan. 'That's just a story.'

'Is it? If it's not the god Vulcan at his forge which causes mountains to send up smoke and flames, then what does?'

Flavia raised her hand. 'Pliny says that earthquakes make volcanoes. And earthquakes are caused when the wind is trapped and there is no escape for it.'

'A reasonable explanation,' said Aristo. 'Though I think the myth is more romantic.'

'What about Thetis?' asked Miriam. 'Didn't she miss Vulcan after he went back to Olympus?'

'Vulcan never forgot his foster mother,' answered Aristo. 'He often visited her underwater grotto and that is why he is a god of sea as well as fire. And later – much later – he made her warrior son Achilles the most beautiful armour in the world. But Juno was Vulcan's real mother, and it was right and proper that they be reunited.'

The young Greek leaned back in his chair and smiled at them. 'Lesson finished! I hope it helps in your search for Vulcan.'

It was late morning by the time they set out on their quest for Vulcan.

Flavia and her three friends had settled themselves in the cart along with forty amphoras of wine and a soft layer of sawdust. They had convinced Scuto and the puppies to stay in the cool garden with Miriam. Xanthus drove the cart and the Gemini brothers rode behind.

As they turned off the farm track onto the main road to Pompeii, they passed a farmer driving his empty cart back from market. He sat beside his young son, and Flavia heard him whisper that Castor and Pollux were in town. The little boy gazed back at the twin riders with his thumb in his mouth and eyes as round as coins.

'Uncle Gaius, why aren't you married?' Flavia leaned back against an amphora and gazed up at her uncle as he rode behind.

Gaius looked down at her in surprise. Then he glanced at his brother.

'Well,' he began, 'When we were younger, we both loved Myrtilla –'

'You loved my mother?' Flavia sat up straight in the cart.

'Yes,' said her uncle Gaius. 'Yes, I did. But she preferred your father.'

SCROLL IX

'It's not quite that simple,' said Flavia's father. 'When pater died, Gaius inherited the farm because he was the eldest. That didn't bother me. I wanted to sail the world.'

'But I prefer plants and animals. I could never dream of making my life on board ship,' said Flavia's uncle. 'I get seasick just watching ships in the harbour.'

'And I'd be a terrible farmer. Your uncle was very generous. He sold some antique vases, and he gave me enough money to buy my ship.'

'I thought if I got Marcus out of the way, I'd have a better chance with Myrtilla,' admitted Gaius with a grin.

'What he didn't realise,' said Flavia's father, 'was that your mother was an adventurer like me. I named my ship after her, and promised to show her the world if she'd marry me.'

Gaius sighed. 'I offered her life on a farm in the most beautiful bay in the world. But . . .' he shrugged.

'And that's why you never married?'

Her uncle nodded and Flavia felt the odd sensation she sometimes got when she really focused on him. He looked so much like her father.

Flavia settled back against her amphora again, and considered that had fate been different, Gaius might have been her father. Her name might have been Julia or Helena. Perhaps she'd be older or younger, with darker hair or different-coloured eyes. But then would she still be Flavia? It made her head hurt just to think about it.

Abruptly, another thought occurred to her: if her mother had married Gaius instead of her father, maybe she wouldn't have died in childbirth. Maybe her mother would still be alive.

There were no festive strollers in the port of Pompeii that morning; it was a busy market day. The *Myrtilla*'s crew and Xanthus loaded the wine aboard the ship, while Flavia's father sacrificed a dove at the harbour shrine of Castor and Pollux. By the time Flavia and her friends had waved the *Myrtilla* out of the harbour, it was almost noon. The sky above was a hard blue, and the heat like a furnace.

Carts were not allowed into Pompeii via the Sea Gate, so Gaius instructed Xanthus to meet them outside the Stabian Gate in an hour.

As they walked from the harbour up the steep incline to the Sea Gate, they had to make way for groups of men in white togas going to the marine baths, just outside the town walls.

'The law courts have probably just finished for the day,' said Gaius, mopping his brow. 'Everything will be closing for lunch soon, so we'll have to hurry. I just want to show you the forum.'

The shade under the arch of the Sea Gate was blessedly cool, and Flavia noticed that the paving stones were wet.

'This town's built on a hill and the fountains constantly overflow,' her uncle explained. 'That's why
Pompeii has the cleanest streets in the Roman empire.'

As they emerged from the shadows into the brilliant
light of midday, the heat struck Flavia like a blow.
Crowds of sweaty men and perfumed women pushed
past her on their way home or to the baths.

She tried to keep up with her uncle, but he was used
to walking quickly, and already he was disappearing
from sight. Flavia grabbed Nubia's hand and looked
round for the boys. Lupus was lingering behind, pointing out rude graffiti to Jonathan. At the entrance to the
forum, they had to step over a beggar who showed
them his diseased leg. Flavia caught a glimpse of red,
open sores and her stomach clenched.

Suddenly they were in the forum, a bright open
space surrounded by temples and porticoes.

'There's the Temple of Jupiter.' Her uncle gestured
towards the north. 'A beautiful sight, isn't it, still
decorated for the festival and with Vesuvius rising up
behind it . . . Flavia, are you all right? You're as white
as a candidate's toga!'

'Yes, Uncle Gaius. I'm just thirsty.'

'Well, come on, then. There are public fountains on
the other side of the forum. Follow me.'

Animals were not allowed into the forum and there
were barriers to prevent carts from entering. This
meant that many people left their horses and donkeys
just outside the entrances, causing an almost perma-
nent bottleneck. As the four friends hurried after
Gaius, Flavia found herself squashed between a group

of bankers in togas and two half-naked slaves carrying the bankers' tables.

'The Stabian baths are to the left there,' Flavia heard her uncle say, but all she could see was a big plank of wood and the folds of togas.

'Absolutely magnificent, but since the big earthquake they still haven't completed all the repairs. Can you imagine? After seventeen years?'

Flavia jumped up and down a few times. When she was up, she could just see Gaius's light brown hair above the other heads in the crowd.

Someone took her right hand. Jonathan. He shouldered one of the bankers aside and moved in front of Flavia, to protect her from jostling.

She could still hear Uncle Gaius up ahead;

'I remember that earthquake well. I was about thirteen, a little older than you. I'll never forget the smell of the sulphur. Like rotten eggs. Up near Misenum a whole flock of sheep was killed by sulphur fumes. Imagine. Five or six hundred sheep, all killed by a smell.'

'I think *I'm* about to be killed by a smell,' muttered Jonathan.

Flavia swallowed and tried to smile. The stench of sweat was overpowering and the blazing sun made it worse. Her heart pounded and her stomach clenched.

Suddenly there was a scuffle somewhere up ahead.

A woman screamed.

The crowd parted to reveal a man wearing a dark turban and robe. He stood in the street looking around with mad eyes. The woman screamed again as the man grasped one of the bankers and shook him by the shoulders.

'God's judgement!' he cried in a hoarse voice. 'It's coming upon us all! The abomination that causes desolation!'

He released the startled banker and clutched at a slave's wrist.

'Doom! Death! Desolation!' he rasped. The slave shook him off with an oath, but the madman persisted. He looked round as the crowd shrank back, then stared straight at Flavia and her friends.

'You!' He pointed towards them. 'You know it, too!'

Please not me, Flavia prayed.

He flung his arms wide in a sweep of black robes ands swooped down on them. His face came nearer and nearer. And stopped inches from Jonathan's.

Flavia saw his red-rimmed eyes stare into Jonathan's and when he opened his mouth to prophesy doom, she smelled garlic and fish on his breath. 'You know it, too!' he said to Jonathan.

Flavia knew she was going to faint.

Suddenly a fist shot out. The madman's chin flew up and back, carrying him with it.

Lupus had knocked him flat.

SCROLL X

Lupus winced and blew on his smarting knuckles.

'Thanks, Lupus,' said Jonathan.

Lupus shrugged and grinned. One of the things he had learned on the streets of Ostia was the effect of a swift blow where chin met neck.

The turbaned man lay in the wet street, staring up at the blue sky and moaning: 'Doom. Death. Desolation.'

'Jupiter's eyebrows!' Flavia's uncle rushed up to them. 'Are you all right? Did that madman hurt you?'

'It's all right, Uncle Gaius. We're fine.' Flavia clutched her uncle's arm and leaned on it gratefully.

'He must be some kind of soothsayer,' said Gaius. He made the sign against evil and guided them around the turbaned man to a nearby fountain.

Lupus plunged his hand into the overflowing fountain basin while the others took turns at the spout. He drank last and as he raised his dripping mouth he heard a woman's voice.

'That man's a Christian. I'm sure of it!'

Lupus wiped his mouth and glanced at Jonathan, who was watching two soldiers push their way through the crowd.

'The soothsayer's a Christian!' someone else cried out.

'Always prophesying doom!' said the first woman.

The soldiers bent down and the metal strips of their armour flashed as they lifted the turbaned man and dragged him back towards the forum.

'You know the punishment for practising an illegal faith!' called the banker angrily. 'The amphitheatre!'

'Lunch for a hungry lion!' someone else quipped. There was laughter as the crowd began to disperse.

'I think *we* need some lunch,' said Gaius, looking around. 'Ah! That corner snack bar does wonderful chick-pea pancakes. How about it?'

Lupus was hungry, but he wanted to find the blacksmith too, and he knew the shops would be closing soon. He caught Flavia's eye. She nodded to show she understood.

'Uncle Gaius, we're all hungry, but if we don't hurry we might miss Vulcan.'

'All right. Let's find your blacksmith and then we'll eat.'

Even as he finished speaking the gongs began clanging noon; it was time for shops to close and the baths to open.

They followed Gaius as he hurried past several more fountains to the Stabian Way. As soon as they turned onto it, Lupus saw the gate at the bottom. Keeping to the cool shadows beneath overhanging roofs, he ran ahead, past townhouses on the left and the theatre on his right.

Just before the gate, on the left, were three shops in a row. In the window of the middle shop, above the counter, hung a dazzling selection of pots, pans, lamps and bath scrapers, all bronze, all flashing in the sunlight.

Hearing Lupus's footsteps, a dwarf in a sea-green tunic emerged from the doorway and clanked a string of bronze cowbells.

'Best pans here!' he called out cheerfully. 'Please come in!'

'We're looking for a blacksmith named Vulcan,' cried Flavia, running up.

Lupus grunted at her urgently and pointed to the shop next to it. It did not have a window or a counter, just an open door. But above this doorway someone had painted a scene from Greek mythology: a young man, riding a donkey and carrying his tools. It was the god of blacksmiths: Vulcan.

'Hello?' Flavia peered into the dark smithy. 'Is anyone there?'

'We're closing for the day!' came a gruff voice from inside.

Flavia stepped in, so that she could see better. Nubia and Jonathan stayed behind her, but Lupus squeezed through and slipped into the shop. It was as hot and dark as Hades. The only light came from the doorway behind them and from coals glowing redly on an open hearth.

'We're looking for Vulcan,' she called, feeling foolish even as she said it.

A figure moved out of the darkness – a huge muscular man in a leather apron. He was totally bald and the red coal-light gleamed off his shiny scalp and shoulders.

'Vulcan, is it?' said the gigantic blacksmith in a low growl.

'Yes, please,' replied Flavia politely and took an involuntary step backwards onto Nubia's foot.

'Are you one of them?'

'What?' said Flavia.

'Do you know the way?' The smith bent forward to peer at the three of them. They backed hastily towards the door and into Gaius who stood solidly behind them.

The big smith lifted his head to see Gaius filling the doorway. He straightened himself and for a moment he studied their faces. Then he folded his arms.

'Vulcan doesn't work here any more and don't ask me where he's gone, because I don't know.'

'But we have to find him,' protested Flavia.

'Closing up shop now. You'll have to go. All of you!' The big blacksmith glared at Lupus, who was pointing at some graffiti on the smithy wall. Flavia squinted at it. In the dim red coal-light she could just make out the first two lines: 'My first letter grieves, my second commands . . .'

Suddenly, Flavia knew the answer to the riddle.

Heart pounding, she turned back to the giant, took a deep breath and said:

'*Asine!* You jackass!'

SCROLL XI

'*Asine*,' Flavia repeated loudly. 'Jackass!'

'Flavia!' she heard her uncle's horrified voice behind her. 'Apologise at once!'

But the giant's scowling face had already relaxed into a gap-toothed grin.

'Shhh!' he placed a meaty finger against his lips. 'We can't be too careful, you know.' He glanced around and bent nearer. 'I wasn't lying when I told you Vulcan doesn't work here any more. But he *does* stop in from time to time. You see, he's a travelling smith these days. I could give him a message next time he passes by.'

'A message . . .' said Flavia. 'Yes! We have an important message for him. If you see him, tell him to come to the Geminus Farm on the road to Stabia. We have work for him, don't we, Uncle Gaius? Important work.'

'So the answer to the riddle was *asine*, "jackass",' said Jonathan as they rode home in the cart. 'How did you solve it?'

'Well,' said Flavia, popping the last of a chick-pea pancake into her mouth. 'When we had all the letters but one, I went through the alphabet: *Abine, acine,* and so forth.'

'I did that, too, but I didn't get the answer . . .'

'I thought of *asine*, but it didn't make any sense,' said Flavia, 'until we were in the smithy. Then I remembered the donkey Vulcan rides on, and I knew that must be the word.'

'Of course!' Jonathan hit his forehead with the heel of his hand. 'The missing letter is S which sounds like *es* – "be!", "My second commands . . ." But what does it mean?'

'It's obviously a password or codeword of some sort,' said Flavia. 'It worked with the big blacksmith!'

'I know that!' said Jonathan. 'I mean: how does it help us find a treasure beyond imagining?'

'I don't know,' said Flavia. 'But I'll bet Vulcan the blacksmith does.'

'This was an excellent idea,' said Jonathan later that afternoon. He was testing the weight of a leafy branch.

The four friends were back on the farm, in a fig tree so ancient that it had long ceased to bear fruit. From its upper branches came the liquid notes of Nubia's flute.

Jonathan pushed some large green leaves aside. 'Look!' he said. 'From here we can see anyone coming to the farm, and anyone travelling on the road from Stabia to Pompeii. But they can't see us!'

The old fig tree grew near the edge of an olive grove surrounded by Gaius's vineyards.

'My uncle says we can use those old planks in the tool-shed by the wine press,' added Flavia.

'I've always wanted to build a tree fort,' Jonathan said. 'I'll draw up plans and we can take turns building it and keeping watch.'

Abruptly the flute music stopped and Lupus grunted urgently above them. All Jonathan could see of him were his grubby feet in their too-large sandals.

'What is it, Lupus?' he asked. 'Is Vulcan coming?'

Lupus grunted no. The leaves parted and he pointed to the vines below them.

'You see something in the vineyard?' asked Flavia.

Lupus grunted yes.

'Behold!' said Nubia. 'An orange tunic. But it is now gone.'

'Scuto!' scolded Flavia. 'You're a pathetic watch-dog!'

Scuto, tussling with the puppies in the shade beneath the fig tree, looked up at his mistress and wagged his tail.

'They're all useless,' said Jonathan with a grin.

'It couldn't have been one of my uncle's slaves,' mused Flavia, 'they all wear brown.'

'Then it must have been someone spying on us!' said Jonathan. 'We'll have to keep a sharp lookout from now on.'

Over the next few days they spent every free minute working on the tree fort.

At the hottest time of the day, when the adults bathed or napped, the four friends hurried to the leafy coolness of the fig tree to hammer planks, make rope ladders and watch for Vulcan's approach. Once they invited Miriam to help them, but she preferred to stay in the shady house and garden, picking flowers and weaving with Frustilla.

Then, late one morning after their lessons, as they

were hurrying off to the tree fort, Gaius's guard dog Ferox finally had his revenge.

After the first evening, Scuto had been careful to give Ferox a wide berth. At first he had behaved in a sensible manner, hugging the farmyard wall fearfully, with his tail firmly between his legs. But as the days passed, his confidence increased.

On the morning in question, Flavia's dog pranced into the farmyard with his tail held high, barked amiably at the hens and began to sniff out an interesting smell. As usual, Ferox shot to the end of his chain and erupted with a torrent of furious barks which Scuto totally ignored. Nose down, Flavia's dog continued to sniff closer and closer to the watchdog, now almost hysterical with rage.

Ferox strained so hard at his collar that his eyes bulged from their sockets and his deep barks were reduced to wheezing gasps. Scuto wandered off nonchalantly, as if the slavering beast at the end of the iron chain were no more threatening than one of the brown hens.

Then Scuto made his mistake. He squatted thoughtfully by the chicken coop, intending to relieve himself of some deep burden. This Ferox could not tolerate. With a last mighty effort, using every fibre of strength in his huge body, he pulled at his iron chain. After a moment there was metallic *ping* as a link of the chain broke.

Like an arrow released from a bow, Ferox sped towards the hapless Scuto.

Flavia had just turned back to call her dog when she saw a golden-brown blur pursued by a huge black streak. They were heading through the vines, towards the coast, and in the time it took Flavia to blink, they had vanished from sight.

SCROLL XII

It was easy enough to follow Ferox's trail: the hound was dragging two yards of iron chain behind him. The four friends and their puppies tracked its snaking path in the dust between the vine rows. Flavia tried not to think of what Ferox might do to Scuto if he caught him.

After half a mile, the trail emerged from the vineyard and ended at the coastal road which marked the border of her uncle's land. There was a distant rider approaching from the direction of Pompeii, but otherwise the road was empty. Across the road and set back from it were the imposing backs of opulent villas overlooking the bay.

The road from Pompeii to Stabia was not wide, but it was well-paved, with tightly fitted hexagonal stones. The daily sea breeze had blown all the surface dust away, and the track left by Ferox's chain ended there.

'Now where?' said Flavia, close to tears. 'Where could he be?'

'Behold!' Nubia pointed. 'Nipur something smells.'

Nipur had been sniffing round the base of a roadside shrine to the god Mercury on the other side of the road. Now he nosed his way through dried grasses and thistles towards the back of one of the seaside villas.

The puppy led them to a high white wall with ancient cypress and cedar trees rising up behind it. In the centre of the garden wall was a solid-looking, wooden door with the words 'DO NOT ENTER' in faded red letters on the wall next to it. Despite the warning, a gap had been scraped in the earth beneath the door.

Flavia uttered a cry. Half of Ferox protruded from this gap. The rear half.

'Your dog is stuck,' came a piping voice from above them. Flavia and her friends looked up in astonishment to see a small girl sitting on the high wall, half hidden in the shade of an umbrella pine.

'I've been waiting for you,' remarked the girl, and added, 'I thought this was the safest place.'

'Have you seen another dog pass this way?' called Flavia desperately. 'One with curly light brown fur?'

The little girl regarded Flavia with eyes as dark and bright as a sparrow's. She was barefoot and dressed in a bright orange tunic.

'Don't worry about Scuto. He's safe inside with my little sisters.'

Flavia whispered a prayer of thanks.

'Wait!' cried Jonathan. 'How did you know Scuto's name?'

'The same way I know you're Jonathan, and you're Flavia and Nubia and Lupus –'

'You're the one who's been spying on us!' cried Flavia.

The little girl smiled brightly. 'Not spying exactly – just watching. My name is Clio.'

At the sound of their voices, Ferox had begun to

squirm. He was wedged as tightly beneath the door as a cork in a wine skin. Clio grasped a pine branch and pulled herself up. 'I'll get help,' she offered.

'Wait!' said Jonathan. 'See if you can find some strong rope and – no! get a fishing net!'

Clio grinned, nodded, and scampered off along the top of the high wall as confidently as if it were a broad pavement. Lupus watched her in admiration.

As soon as she was out of sight, the four friends turned their gaze on Ferox, wedged beneath the door. Flavia almost felt sorry for him, but when he began to whimper and scrabble feebly with his hind legs the sight of his quivering black bottom reduced her to helpless laughter.

Impulsively, Lupus picked up a piece of gravel and flicked it at the animal's vulnerable rear.

'Lupus, don't!' giggled Flavia nervously. 'You'll just make him angrier!' Lupus gave her an impish grin. He took another stone and fitted it into the sling Jonathan was teaching him to use.

He had obviously been practising.

The stone hit the watchdog squarely on the bottom. Ferox yelped like a puppy and they all collapsed with mirth.

Suddenly, Ferox began to growl and squirm. This time he tried retreating, inching back towards his tormentors. And this time he succeeded.

Nubia had seen this coming.

As Ferox shook himself off and began to turn, she scooped up Nipur and thrust him at Flavia.

'Hold puppies. Nobody is moving!'

Jonathan nodded and clutched Tigris tightly.

Ferox crouched. A low growl rumbled in his chest.

But before he could leap, Nubia caught his gaze, held it and murmured soothing words in her own language.

After a few moments, she slowly extended her hand – palm down – and took a small but confident step forward. Ferox growled again, but with less conviction. Nubia continued to reassure him. Presently, she took another step forward. The huge dog's hackles gradually flattened and he rose from his crouching position. Nubia took another step.

Ferox sniffed her fingertips, gave a half wag of his tail and allowed his gaze to flicker sideways for a moment. Without taking her eyes from Ferox's face, Nubia crouched and groped in the dust. When her hand closed around the metal links of his chain, she stood again and breathed a small sigh of relief.

It was at that precise moment that Tigris, squirming in Jonathan's arms, uttered several sharp, defiant barks.

Ferox crouched again, opened his dripping jaws and launched himself at Jonathan.

Flavia screamed and Jonathan instinctively threw himself to one side.

Nubia tried to hold the huge animal back, but was jerked off her feet as the iron chain whipped out of her grasp. Ferox's sharp teeth missed Tigris by a whisker. Snarling with rage, the big dog skidded in the dust and turned to attack again.

As Ferox gathered himself to leap, something like a spear struck him hard on the side. It knocked him to the ground. A heavy oak staff lay in the dust beside the stunned dog.

'Quickly!' called a man's voice. 'The net! Throw the net!'

Flavia looked up in time to see Clio standing on the wall above them. A motion of the girl's arm unfurled a yellow fishing net.

It floated to the ground.

Clio's aim was perfect: as Ferox struggled to his feet, the net enveloped him.

Then Flavia saw a young man lunge forward, grasp the net and give it a deft tug. Ferox's legs flew out from under him. Confused and stunned, the big dog tried to right himself, but the more he thrashed, the more hopelessly entangled he became.

'Get right back, Lupus!' Jonathan scrambled to his feet. 'He might still get loose! Tigris! Come here! You bad dog!' Jonathan gave his puppy a fierce hug.

Flavia helped Nubia up from the ground. 'Are you all right?'

Nubia nodded, but she was trembling.

The garden gate squeaked open and Clio rushed out. She stood with her hands on her hips, looking down at Ferox. 'He's wrapped himself up as tightly as a sausage in a vine leaf,' she observed.

Lupus guffawed and Clio grinned at him.

As Gaius's watchdog thrashed furiously on the ground, Flavia looked up at the strong youth. He wore the one-sleeved tunic of a tradesman and had a chest and arms like Hercules.

'Thank you,' she said solemnly. 'You saved our lives.'

The young man limped cautiously towards Ferox to retrieve his staff. Flavia saw that one of his leather boots was an odd shape. Glancing back towards the road, she saw a donkey tethered to the shrine of Mercury. In its basket-pack were a workman's tools: tongs, a hammer and an axe.

'Vulcan!' she squealed, jumping up and down and pointing at him. 'You're Vulcan the blacksmith!'

SCROLL XIII

Scuto had escaped Ferox only to be captured by Clio's younger sisters. They had pounced on him with cries of delight. After they had bathed, combed and brushed him, they had anointed him with scented oil. Clio rescued him just in time; her sisters had been about to tie pink ribbons to his fur.

Now he hurried furtively through the vineyard, trailing a cloud of jasmine perfume and a small procession.

First came the two puppies, stopping to roll in the dust whenever Scuto did.

Then came Vulcan, riding his grey donkey and pulling Ferox – still cocooned in the yellow fishing net – on a makeshift stretcher of pine branches. Nubia walked beside Ferox, softly playing her flute. Whenever she stopped playing, the big dog began to thrash and moan.

Clio had fallen into step beside Lupus, and was chattering away to him non-stop, waving her arms expansively.

'I wonder how long it will take Clio to realise that Lupus can't speak,' Flavia said to Jonathan with a grin. They took up the rear of the procession.

One of her uncle's field-slaves must have run ahead

to alert the farm, for when they emerged from the vines, most of the household was waiting in the farmyard.

Nubia's flute music trailed off and Ferox began to moan again.

'What happened?' said Aristo.

'Are you all right?' asked Mordecai.

'Where's Ferox?' said Gaius.

'Uncle Gaius!' Flavia squealed. 'Ferox broke his chain and we followed him to a villa and he got stuck but then he wiggled out and attacked us but Vulcan saved us!'

'Ferox broke his . . . Who?' said Gaius.

'Vulcan the blacksmith,' said Flavia. 'The one we've been looking for!'

'You're Vulcan the blacksmith?' Gaius asked the youth on the donkey.

But the young man did not reply. He was gazing over their heads, towards the garden. There was a look of awe on his face, as if he had seen something miraculous. Flavia and the others turned to see what he was staring at.

Miriam had just emerged from the garden, her arms full of ivy and fragrant honeysuckle. Dressed in a lavender stola, with her glossy, dark curls pinned up at the neck, Venus herself could not have looked more beautiful.

Although the farmyard was like a furnace in the noonday heat, Flavia and her friends gathered round Vulcan to watch him mend Ferox's chain. He was crouched over the chain with a pair of pliers. His one-sleeved tunic revealed tanned, oiled shoulders gleaming with sweat. The powerful muscles of his arms and chest bulged as he squeezed the link.

'There. That should hold him.' Vulcan glanced up at Jonathan and Lupus, who were gazing at him with open-mouthed admiration. 'Could one of you bring me a cup of water? I'm very thirsty.'

The boys nodded and both ran off towards the house.

Flavia couldn't take her eyes off the blacksmith. Somehow his neat head seemed all wrong on the powerful body. With his sensitive mouth and long eyelashes, it was as if a sculptor had wrongly put the head of a poet on the body of Hercules. His dark eyebrows met above his nose, giving his face a mournful, brooding look.

And Flavia's gaze kept straying to the strangely shaped boot he wore on his right foot.

Jonathan and Lupus ran empty-handed back out of the garden. 'My sister's drawing cold water from the well,' said Jonathan.

Vulcan nodded and turned to Flavia's uncle, who stood leaning against the shady doorway of the olive press. 'You can put his collar on again, now.'

It had taken Gaius a good half hour to calm his dog and cut off the fishing net.

'I think I'll leave him in his kennel to calm down.' Gaius stepped forward. 'Thank you for saving the children, and for repairing his chain.'

The young blacksmith acknowledged Gaius's thanks with a nod. He wiped the sweat from his forehead with the back of his forearm.

Flavia was desperate to ask Vulcan about the riddle, but there were too many people within earshot, including Clio and some of her uncle's farm slaves.

So she decided to try the codeword.

'*Asine!* You jackass!'

Vulcan turned slowly and looked at her, his eyes smouldering under his single eyebrow. Then he looked back at Miriam, coming towards him with a shy smile and a cup of cold water.

Flavia shivered. It felt as if he had looked right through her.

'Thank you,' Vulcan said quietly to Miriam, and without taking his eyes from her face, he lifted the cup to his lips and drank. Jonathan's sister lowered her gaze.

The shrill cry of the cicadas had ceased some time earlier, and the hot afternoon seemed to be holding its breath. The only sound Flavia could hear was Vulcan swallowing great gulps of cold water.

Suddenly, she felt dizzy and unbalanced, as if she were about to faint. She gasped and reached out for Nubia, who reached for her in the same moment. Clutching at each other, the two girls looked up just in time to see Miriam fall forward into Vulcan's arms!

'What in Hades?' Jonathan lay flat on his back in the dust, and wondered why Vulcan was holding his sister.

It felt as if the farmyard court had been given a brisk shake by a giant's hand. They had all staggered, Jonathan and Clio had fallen down. Doves exploded out of the dovecote and the hens ran clucking out of their coop. In their stables the horses whinnied and in the garden the dogs began to bark.

Vulcan gently set Miriam back on her feet. Her face was as pale as alabaster.

Fine dust from the farmyard had risen in a golden cloud. Now it began to settle again.

'Earth tremor,' explained Flavia's uncle, helping Clio up. He extended his hand to Jonathan and pulled him to his feet. 'Nothing to worry about. We've had quite a few minor quakes this summer. That one wasn't too bad. All the same, Xanthus and I had better have a quick look round the farm to make sure nothing's been damaged. Xanthus!' he called.

Gaius turned away and then turned back.

'I imagine you're all feeling a bit shaken. Miriam, perhaps you could ask Frustilla to prepare lunch now? I'll join you presently. Vulcan and Clio, I hope you'll both join us.'

Lupus followed Vulcan through the garden, admiring the smith's muscular back and wondering why he limped. Jonathan's father must have wondered the same thing, for as Vulcan came into the dining-room, Mordecai stepped forward with a look of concern on his face:

'You've hurt yourself. You're limping.'

Vulcan looked flustered. 'It's nothing. I've had it from birth.'

'Please,' insisted the doctor. He gestured for Vulcan to recline and then nodded at Miriam, who had just come in with a copper pitcher and basin. She poured a stream of water onto her father's hands, catching the overflow in the basin. Mordecai dried his hands on the linen napkin over her arm. Then he turned back to Vulcan, who was reclining on one of the low couches.

Lupus and the others tried to see what Mordecai was doing, but he kept his back to them and allowed his loose blue robes to screen Vulcan's foot from their view. Lupus saw the doctor put the blacksmith's boot on the floor and bend his turbaned head over the foot.

'Ah,' murmured Mordecai, almost to himself, 'Clubfoot. Not a terribly bad case . . .' He examined it for a few minutes and then helped Vulcan put the boot back on.

'This could have been corrected shortly after birth, when your bones were still soft.' He dipped his hands in the basin and then turned back, drying them on a napkin. 'It could have been corrected! Did your parents not know that?'

Tears filled Vulcan's eyes, but they did not spill over. His voice was steady as he looked up at Mordecai.

'I don't know who my parents are, sir. I was abandoned at birth.'

SCROLL XIV

Flavia felt miserable. She had called a poor, orphaned, clubfoot a jackass! How could she ever ask him about the treasure now?

Listlessly, she pushed some black olives around the rim of her dish. It was terribly hot and suddenly she had no appetite.

Her uncle Gaius strode in from his inspection of the farm and quickly rinsed his hands in the copper basin. He threw himself on the couch next to Aristo and helped himself to a slice of cheese.

'Not too much damage to the farm,' he remarked through his first mouthful. 'A few shattered roof tiles and a crack in the olive press. I'm glad you got our message, Vulcan. I really could do with the services of a blacksmith for a few days. I hope you don't mind staying in the slave quarters?'

'Not at all,' said the smith, with a quick glance at Miriam.

There was another pause.

Nubia broke the silence. 'Are you the god Vulcan from Muntulumpus?'

Vulcan almost smiled.

'No. Vulcan is just my nickname. It's not hard to

guess how I got it. I don't like it, but it's something I have to live with.'

Flavia swallowed. If he didn't like being called Vulcan, he probably didn't like being called a jackass.

The smith took a small piece of cheese and then put it down again. 'I don't know my real name,' he said. 'They say a slave-girl found me wrapped in swaddling clothes beside the banks of the river Sarnus. She gave me to her master and he gave me to one of his freedmen, a blacksmith. My adoptive parents didn't mind my foot. They loved me as if I had been their own son and they gave me the name Lucius. But no one has called me that since my parents died.'

'I'm adopted, too,' said Clio. She was sitting at the table between Lupus and Flavia. 'We're all adopted. All nine of us.'

'Extraordinary,' murmured Mordecai, and then to Vulcan. 'Please continue.'

'There's not much more to tell. We moved to Rome when I was still a baby. I grew up there. My father taught me to be a blacksmith and my mother taught me how to read and write. They died a year ago, when I was sixteen. After I settled their affairs, I moved back here to search for my real parents.'

'*My* real parents are dead,' said Clio, taking a handful of olives. 'Father says they died in a plague. I never even knew them.'

'Do you want revenge on your parents for abandoning you?' Jonathan asked Vulcan.

'Jonathan!' chided Mordecai.

Vulcan lowered his head and then looked at Jonathan from under his long eyelashes.

'No. I don't want revenge. I have forgiven my true parents. But I want to find them. That's why I came back to Pompeii. For the past year I have looked everywhere in the town, but haven't found them yet. So when Brutus the travelling blacksmith died last month, I bought his donkey. Now I can visit all the farms and villages in the area. If my parents are still here, I know I will find them!' The muscles of his arm bulged as he clenched his fist.

'But how will you recognise them?' asked Jonathan.

'I believe . . .' said Vulcan, and stopped. 'I don't know,' he said finally, 'but I must find them. I must!'

'Why haven't you asked Vulcan about the treasure yet?' Jonathan asked Flavia after lunch.

They had taken Clio to the tree fort, while the adults were having their midday siesta. Jonathan sat crosslegged on the newly-built wooden platform. He was sharpening the point of an arrow with a small knife.

'Treasure?' came Clio's voice from the leaves above. 'What treasure?'

Flavia rolled her eyes at Jonathan. 'That's one reason I haven't mentioned it! Also, I think he's angry with me for calling him a jackass.'

'That was pretty . . . bold of you,' admitted Jonathan.

'Treasure?' said Clio again, and jumped onto platform beside Flavia.

So Flavia told Clio all about the riddle and the treasure.

'That's why you called him a jackass,' said Clio, and tipped her head to one side. 'Who did you say gave you the riddle?'

'Our friend Pliny. He's a famous admiral who's written dozens of books.'

'He told us about the riddle because we saved his life,' added Jonathan.

Clio's eyes sparkled. 'Is he a fat old man with white hair and a funny voice?'

Lupus barked with laughter from his treetop perch, and Nubia giggled behind her hand.

'He's not fat!' cried Flavia, sitting up a little straighter. 'He's just a bit . . . stout.'

'Do you know him?' Jonathan asked Clio.

'Of course' she chirped. 'He knows my parents and often stays at our villa. In fact, he's coming to dinner in a few days.'

'He is?' cried Flavia. 'I wish we could come, too. Then we could tell him we've found his blacksmith and almost solved the riddle!'

Clio looked at Flavia with her bright black eyes and tipped her chin up decisively. 'Then I'll send you all an invitation.'

'In that case,' said Flavia, 'we'd better find out about the treasure!'

'You'll find the blacksmith in the toolshed by the wine cellar,' said Xanthus the farm manager.

Flavia knew the toolshed. It was a dark, cool room full of pruning hooks, plough shares, hoes, picks and various pieces of tackle for cart and horse. When they opened the battered wooden door and peeped in, Vulcan was nowhere in sight. But someone had been there recently. The puppies pushed through Flavia's legs and sniffed round a newly cleared space and a half-built brick furnace against one wall.

'Shhh!' said Jonathan suddenly. 'Do you hear that?'

They all listened. From the cellars on the other side of the toolshed came a bubbling groan, interspersed with curses and mutters.

'It's horrible,' said Clio. 'What is it?'

A shudder shook Nubia and she gripped Flavia's arm.

Even Scuto whimpered.

Jonathan swallowed and looked at them. 'It sounds like someone is being murdered!'

SCROLL XV

Flavia laughed. 'Don't worry,' she said. 'It's just the grape juice in the barrels. It makes that noise as it turns into wine. Sometimes the barrels practically shout. Come on!'

She led them across the beaten earth floor of the toolshed and pushed open the door to the cellars. It was a vast room with thick walls: cool, dark and musty. As they stepped inside, the damp scent of fermenting wine filled Flavia's nostrils and made her slightly dizzy.

Vulcan was there in the gloom, leaning on his staff and speaking quietly to three farm-slaves. When he saw Flavia he stopped talking to them.

'We were just getting more bricks,' he said to Flavia, and nodded towards a pile of bricks. The three slaves hurriedly began taking bricks for the furnace back into the toolshed. Vulcan limped to the doorway to supervise them.

'Did you want me?' he said to Flavia. Although his voice was soft, his dark eyebrows made him look quite stern.

The farm-slaves were passing bricks through the doorway. Behind them the wine in the barrels snarled and groaned. Despite herself, Flavia shivered, too.

'No, it doesn't matter,' she said, backing out of the room. 'It can wait.'

'What's the matter?' said Jonathan, a minute later. 'Why didn't you ask him about the treasure?'

'Um . . . the slaves,' said Flavia. 'I couldn't ask him in front of them. We'll have to get him alone.'

But as the day progressed the young blacksmith always had at least one slave nearby and Flavia had to resign herself to waiting.

That night Flavia dreamt of her dead mother Myrtilla.

In her dream, they were back in her garden in Ostia, on a summer's evening. Her mother and father sat beneath the fig tree by the fountain, laughing, talking and watching Flavia play with the twins, now Lupus's age.

Flavia had woken at the darkest hour, full of despair, knowing that her mother and dead brothers were only shadows, wandering the cold grey Underworld and chirping like bats. She had tried to replace that terrible image with her dream of them all in a secret, safe and sunny garden. But it was no good. Hot tears squeezed out from the corners of Flavia's eyes, wetting her cheeks and running down into her ears. As she stared into the darkness she knew that she would give all the treasure in the world, everything she had, even her life, if only she could make that dream come true.

The morning of the Vinalia – the late summer wine festival – dawned a glorious pink and blue, but Flavia awoke feeling drained after her restless night. Nubia and the dogs were already up, presumably gone to breakfast. Listlessly, Flavia splashed lukewarm water on her face from the jug in the corner and padded out to the garden for lessons.

The others were crowding round the wrought-iron table examining something. Even the dogs seemed interested. As Flavia approached, Nubia lifted her neat, dark head and called out:

'Flavia! Come see what appears outside Miriam!'

Flavia sighed and quickened her step. The others moved aside to let her see.

On the table was a small wooden cage with a tiny door on one side and a handle on top. Inside perched a bright-eyed little sparrow.

'Oh!' cried Flavia. 'He's lovely! Where did he come from?'

'He just appeared outside Miriam's bedroom door this morning!' said Jonathan, and added, 'Aristo says it means Miriam has an admirer!'

'Who is it, Miriam?' asked Flavia; already her dream was fading. 'Who is your admirer?'

Miriam flushed. 'I don't know.'

Aristo smiled at Miriam. 'A sparrow is the traditional gift of a man to his sweetheart,' he said. 'The poet Catullus even wrote a poem about a sparrow that he gave to his beloved. He talks about the little bird on his girlfriend's lap, hopping about now here and now there.'

'Oh, do you think it's tame?' breathed Flavia.

'Probably,' said Aristo. 'Shall we see?'

He eased open the delicate cage door and held his forefinger just outside. The sparrow cocked his head and regarded the large finger with a bright eye. He hopped to the door and cheeped. Then he hopped onto Aristo's finger. Flavia started to squeal with excitement, but Nubia put a restraining hand on her arm.

Very slowly, Miriam put her elegant white finger next to Aristo's, so that they barely touched. After a moment, the sparrow hopped on to Miriam's finger. Scuto, his eyes fixed on this feathered morsel, gave a wistful whine.

'Oh!' giggled Miriam. 'He tickles.'

'Sit down,' whispered Jonathan. 'See if he hops on your lap now here and now there!'

'Not with the dogs licking their chops like that.' Flavia laughed.

'I take dogs away,' said Nubia solemnly.

'I'll come with you.' Flavia felt much more cheerful. Now she had two mysteries to uncover: Vulcan's treasure, and the identity of Miriam's secret admirer.

There were many things Nubia did not understand about the new land she lived in.

When Flavia's uncle took them all into Pompeii later that morning to celebrate the Vinalia, Nubia did not understand why the priest on the temple steps crushed a handful of grapes over the bleeding carcass of a lamb. When they went to the theatre, she did not understand why the men on the stage wore masks while the women in the audience left their faces uncovered.

Afterwards, when they returned to the farm, she did not understand why on this particular day they ate roast lamb outside, sitting on old carpets near the vines beneath the shadows of the olive grove. She did not understand how Flavia could hand her uncle a piece of bread with the left hand. In her country this was a grave insult, for the left hand was used to wipe the bottom. And she did not think she would ever understand how the Romans could allow a wise old woman like Frustilla to wait on strong young men like Aristo and Vulcan.

But one thing Nubia did understand was the look between a girl and her lover. She had seen the same look many times at the spice market, when all the clans met together to trade.

By the end of the day, as they all walked back through the cool vine rows beneath the pale green sky of dusk, Nubia knew not only that Miriam was in love, but with whom.

SCROLL XVI

Clio had promised them an invitation to the dinner party and sure enough, just as they finished their music lesson the next morning, they heard a banging on the rarely-used front door. Presently a spotty teenaged slave in a white tunic wandered into the garden. For a few moments he stared at Miriam open-mouthed. Then he remembered himself.

Gaius and Mordecai appeared in the library doorway as the young slave recited his message in a loud voice:

'Titus Tascius Pomponianus invites his neighbour Gaius Flavius Geminus Senior to dinner at the Villa Pomponiana.

'Please bring your family and house guests to my home at the tenth hour tomorrow for a light dinner. The starter will be mussels in sweet wine sauce and the main course a fine turbot caught only yesterday. There'll be quails' eggs, camel's cheese and imported Greek olives.

'My children will play music for your entertainment and our guest of honour will be the Admiral Pliny, on active command of the fleet at Misenum.'

The slave glanced at Miriam, licked his lips nervously and continued,

'My young mistress Clio Pomponiana adds that the

young ladies of Gaius's household are invited to bathe . . .' here the young slave's voice broke and he continued an octave higher, '. . . to bathe with her at the ninth hour in the private baths of the villa.'

'I think he means us,' Flavia giggled to Nubia and Miriam.

'Can we go, father?' Miriam said. 'Tomorrow's the Sabbath.'

'Is the villa near enough to walk to?' asked Mordecai.

'Easily,' said Gaius.

Mordecai smiled. 'Very well. I should like to meet Admiral Pliny again.'

'Tell your master we accept his kind invitation with pleasure,' said Gaius with a solemn bow.

After the blushing slave left, Flavia's uncle clapped his hands and rubbed them together energetically. 'Tascius has been in that villa for over a year and this is the first invitation I've had. I owe it all to you and your friends, Flavia!'

Flavia still hadn't been able to get Vulcan on his own, but the next morning there was another clue about Miriam's secret admirer.

Jonathan's sister had just set the breakfast platter on the table. She was wearing a grey-blue stola with a lilac shawl tied round her slender waist, humming to herself. Flavia sighed: she would never be that elegant and graceful.

Suddenly Jonathan caught his sister's wrist and held it for a moment. Miriam was wearing a silver bracelet set with amethysts.

'It's beautiful,' said Flavia. 'Is it new?'

Miriam blushed and then nodded.

'Who gave it to you?' asked Jonathan sharply.

Miriam shrugged.

'It appears outside your bedroom?' Nubia asked.

Miriam nodded.

'Why are you getting all these presents?' scowled Jonathan. Flavia knew his nightmares had put him in a bad mood.

In the fig tree above them a bird trilled sweetly as Aristo rushed into the garden. He looked sleepy and rumpled, but handsome in a fawn coloured tunic with matching lace-up boots.

If Miriam was silver, thought Flavia, Aristo was bronze.

'Sorry,' he said, pulling back his chair. 'I had a broken night, and I'm afraid I overslept.' He glanced at Miriam.

'Lovely bracelet,' he said. 'Is it new?'

Later that day, a few hours after noon, Nubia ran into the garden from the farmyard. As the gate banged shut, Flavia looked up from Pliny's scroll of famous mysteries. The boys had taken the dogs hunting and all the adults were still resting after lunch.

'Vulcan is in the stables,' said Nubia breathlessly. 'Being all alone.'

'At last!' said Flavia. She left the scroll on the table and ran after Nubia.

Vulcan nodded at the girls as they pushed open the stable door. He had taken his donkey from one of the stalls and was grooming it.

Nubia went straight to the creature to watch Vulcan

brush it, but Flavia hoisted herself up on one of the stalls, and drummed her feet on the wooden half-door. She hoped he'd forgiven her for calling him a jackass in front of Miriam.

'Vulcan . . .' She casually nibbled a piece of straw, 'have you ever met Admiral Pliny?'

'I don't think so.' Vulcan was brushing the donkey's back with long firm strokes.

'He knows you.'

Thin shafts of golden sunlight pierced the dusty air and made coins of light on the stable floor. There was a pungent smell of sweet hay and sour mash, of horse dung and saddle oil.

'I might have met him,' said the smith carefully. 'Many of the rich and famous have summer houses in Pompeii.'

Flavia took a deep breath. 'Do you remember giving any of them a riddle?'

Vulcan stopped brushing and looked up at her. 'So that's why you called me a jackass . . .'

'Pliny said you told him that solving the "jackass riddle" would lead to "a treasure beyond imagining" . . .'

Vulcan handed Nubia the curry comb and indicated that she should take over. Nubia happily brushed the donkey's velvet-grey coat.

'I call him Modestus,' Vulcan said, stroking the donkey's long nose, 'because he is a humble creature. He will carry any burden you care to put on him. At the baker's, he will patiently circle a millstone for his whole life, never complaining, just walking. And in the spring, when the donkey gets a new coat, there is a cross on his back. See? Just there where Nubia is brushing. The cross, too, is a symbol of sacrifice and submission.'

Nubia stopped brushing for a moment. 'What is submission?' she asked.

'It's when you allow people to do things to you even though you are strong enough to resist. Like some slaves.'

Vulcan turned to Flavia.

'The donkey is also a symbol of peace. If a king rides on a horse, that means he comes to make war. But if he rides on a donkey, he comes in peace.'

Flavia frowned and jumped down off her perch.

'But how does the donkey lead to treasure?'

Vulcan turned his dark eyes on her. 'You seem to be a rich girl, Flavia Gemina. You are of good birth. You have your own slave. Why do you need riches?'

The question stumped Flavia.

'Tell me, Flavia Gemina,' continued Vulcan, folding his muscular arms. 'What would be your greatest treasure?'

'A roomful of giant rubies and emeralds and pearls. And gold coins . . .'

'That's what most people say. But think again. What, for you, would be the best treasure, a real treasure, a treasure beyond imagining?'

Behind Flavia the stable door squeaked open and Vulcan looked over her shoulder. His expression changed.

Flavia turned to see Miriam standing in the stable doorway. She was wearing her prettiest violet stola with an apricot shawl. 'Hello, Vulcan,' she said softly, and then to the girls, 'I've been looking for you every-where. It's almost the ninth hour and time for us to go to Clio's. If we don't hurry, we'll be late!'

Flavia, Nubia and Miriam hurried through the hot vineyards and across the coastal road to find Clio waiting by the back gate of the Villa Pomponiana. An older girl stood beside her.

'Oh good! You're here,' cried Clio. 'I was beginning to worry . . . This is Thalia, my eldest sister. She's fourteen. That's about your age isn't it, Miriam?'

Miriam nodded.

'Thalia's engaged to be married!' said Clio. 'Show them your ring.'

With her protruding eyes and wide mouth, Thalia reminded Flavia of a cheerful frog. She proudly held out her left hand and they all admired her engagement ring: two clasped hands engraved in a garnet. Then Thalia took Miriam's arm and led the way through the shady garden to the bath complex.

Entering the baths of the Villa Pomponiana was like stepping underwater. Painted fish swam across blue walls. On the floor, black and white mosaic tritons pursued laughing sea nymphs. The girls stripped off, and two female bath-slaves took their clothes to be hung, brushed and scented.

Shyly at first, the naked girls made a circuit of the four rooms.

In the first room, they soaked in a green marble pool full of warm, vanilla-scented water. Then they moved into the steam room, where they sat for as long as they could bear on hot cedarwood benches. After the cold plunge they hurried into the last room, where the two slave-girls were waiting with soft linen bath-sheets.

The solarium, with its thick glass skylight, marble slabs and resting couches, was where bathers were scraped, massaged, manicured and coiffed. It led back into the warm room, and the circuit could be done all over again.

Once relatively dry, the girls rubbed scented oil over their bodies.

'Your heels are a bit rough,' commented Thalia, eyeing Flavia's feet. 'Would you like Gerta to pumice them?'

'What's pumice?'

'It's a special stone imported from Sicily,' said Thalia, beckoning one of the slaves with her finger.

'Oh!' cried Flavia, taking the small grey brick. 'It's so light! But it's hard. It looks like an old sponge!' She let Nubia hold it and then gave it back to Gerta.

'It tickles!' Flavia laughed as the slave-girl briskly rubbed the pumice-stone against her heel, but afterwards her heels felt silky smooth. She lay back on one of the couches, wrapped in a soft linen bath-sheet, and as she waited her turn for a massage she pondered Vulcan's question.

Presently the bath-slaves proved their skill as hairdressers. Quickly and confidently, one pinned up Miriam's cloud of black curls in a simple but beautiful style and the other arranged Thalia's rather frizzy brown hair to look almost as elegant as Miriam's. Nubia watched them with interest.

When their hair was done, Thalia looked at Miriam and sighed. 'You're disgustingly beautiful,' she said cheerfully. 'I'll bet you could win any man you wanted to.'

'Miriam already has dozens of admirers!' said Flavia. She tried to look at Thalia without moving her head because Gerta had begun to arrange her hair. 'Someone gave Miriam a sparrow and a bracelet and all my uncle's farm-slaves stare whenever she goes by.'

'Are you in love, Miriam?'

Miriam blushed.

'Don't try to hide it,' said Thalia. 'I can always tell.'

Miriam gave a tiny nod.

Flavia jerked her head round and she got an ivory hairpin in her scalp.

'Ow! You're in love? Who is he, Miriam?'

But at that moment the table began to shake and tremble. Flavia stared as a bronze hand-mirror shimmied across its surface, slid over the edge and clattered onto the mosaic floor. Her chair was shaking, too. She was just about to ask the slave-girl to stop when Thalia screamed,

'Earthquake! Run! Run for your lives!'

SCROLL XVII

Clean and perfumed, but naked apart from the bath-sheets clutched round them, the girls stood in the hot courtyard while the villa shuddered around them.

'Father! Help!' screamed Thalia. 'FATHER!'

Within moments, a man with fierce eyebrows and short grizzled hair rushed into the courtyard. The quake had obviously interrupted his preparations, too. He was wearing a tunic, but he was barefoot and his toga was slung over his shoulder like a blanket.

'Don't panic, girls!' he commanded. 'Remain in the open. Nothing to be frightened of. Just a tremor. Look! It's over already.'

Thalia had thrown herself sobbing into her father's arms.

'There, there. Told you not to worry about these tremors. Look! Clio's not afraid . . .' He held Thalia at arm's length and examined her red and swollen face. 'Better now, my beauty?'

Thalia sniffed and nodded, and her father turned to Flavia and Miriam.

'Hello, girls!' His broad smile revealed a finely crafted set of wooden false teeth. 'Titus Tascius Pomponianus, master of this household. Sorry your bath was interrupted by tremors. They're common in this part of the world. Now. I suggest you put some clothes on. The other guests have arrived. Nearly time for dinner!'

The vast, airy dining room of the Villa Pomponiana was open on three sides. Its roof was supported by tall white columns with painted black bases. Gauzy linen curtains could be drawn to dim the room if the light was too bright, but now the setting sun was screened by seaside pines, so the curtains were open.

Flavia's jaw dropped as she gazed out between the columns.

The view was stunning. A sloping lawn glowed yellow-green in the late afternoon sunlight and drew her gaze down to the indigo blue bay with Mount Vesuvius beyond.

As she turned away from the view, Flavia saw that everyone else was already there. Lupus and Jonathan, dressed in their best white tunics, were seated at a large marble table with seven dark-haired girls. Mordecai, Aristo and her uncle were reclining. And there was another familiar face.

'Admiral Pliny!'

The admiral was just as Flavia remembered him: plump and cheerful, with a white fringe of hair and intelligent black eyes. His faded purple tunic was the same one he'd worn at his Laurentum villa, and the same Greek scribe stood behind him with a portable ink pot.

'Flavia Gemina!' wheezed Pliny. 'How delightful to see you again.'

Flavia flushed with pleasure, delighted that the admiral had remembered her name.

'Admiral Pliny, we've solved your riddle and found –
hey!' A steward was guiding her firmly towards the
table and Pliny had turned away to speak with Tascius.

'Flavia, Miriam and Nubia, I'd like you to meet my
sisters,' said Clio, 'Melpomene, Calliope, Euterpe,
Terpsichore, Erato, Polyhymnia, and – Urania leave
Lupus alone! Besides, that's my seat, so move over!'

'Your sisters are named after the nine muses?' asked
Flavia as she took her seat.

Clio nodded and turned to Lupus. '*I'm* named after
the muse of history.'

Three female kitchen-slaves padded back and forth
across the room, bringing in appetisers and wine. The
prettiest one handed out fragrant garlands of dark ivy
and miniature white roses. There were garlands on
nineteen heads, and a twentieth garland lay between
Pliny and Tascius on the central couch. It should have
adorned the head of Tascius's wife, but she was late
returning from an outing.

Frog-faced Thalia was the only daughter old enough
to recline. She had found a place on the couch beside
Aristo. Flavia noticed that although she was engaged,
she kept fluttering her eyelashes at him.

Behind each of the three couches stood a slave,
ready to cut meat from the bone, retrieve a fallen
napkin, refill the empty wine-cups or, in the admiral's
case, take notes.

'You must forgive me,' Pliny announced to the
company in his light voice, 'if I dictate the occasional
line to my scribe. I am completing a study of Roman
religion and have vowed to finish it before the Saturnalia four months hence.'

Tascius showed his wooden teeth in a rather stiff smile. 'We know you hate being separated from your stylus and tablets, admiral.' He turned to the others. 'The admiral's written seven complete works. At least a hundred scrolls altogether. His first book was a biography of my father. That's how we met.'

Pliny waggled his forefinger. 'Not quite accurate, my dear Titus. My first book was a manual on how to throw javelin from horseback.'

'I know the one,' said Flavia's uncle from his couch. 'It was required reading when I did my military service.'

Pliny looked pleased. 'I dare say the book I'm writing now will be my greatest yet. My *Natural History* was only thirty-seven volumes. This is now approaching fifty.'

He paused as the slave-girls served the starters: honey-glazed quails' eggs in fish sauce, squares of camels'-milk cheese and purple olives from Kalamata.

As the others ate, Clio stood up to sing. She was accompanied by Erato on the lyre, and her younger sister Melpomene on the double flute. Clean and with her hair pinned up, Clio looked like a different person. Her voice was high and sweet, and as she confidently sang a popular song called 'The Raven and the Dove', the diners nodded their approval at one another.

Tascius gazed at his adopted daughters affectionately and when Clio finished singing he clapped almost as enthusiastically as Lupus.

'Tell us how you come to have such a large family,' Flavia's uncle Gaius said to Tascius, when the applause had died down. 'And such a talented one!'

The former soldier rubbed the palm of his hand over his short cropped hair.

'My wife,' he said. 'All due to her soft heart. We had a baby, but he was stolen in infancy. Slave-traders, we presume. Never received a ransom note.'

'Your baby was stolen?' cried Flavia, sitting up straight. 'How did it happen?' She noticed her uncle Gaius shaking his head at her and frowning. But Tascius didn't seem offended.

'We were at our Herculaneum villa,' he said. 'Rectina – my wife – was sleeping in her bedroom with the baby. We think there were two of them. One must have passed the baby through the window to his accomplice. When Rectina woke from her nap, the baby was gone. We punished the household slaves, posted a reward, but he was never found.'

'It was a boy?' Flavia asked, ignoring her uncle's warning scowl.

'Yes' said Tascius. 'Just a few weeks old. Rectina was devastated.'

'I apologise for my niece's curiosity,' said Gaius. 'As your guests it's not –'

'No, no. Not offended. Reason my wife and I adopted all these beautiful children. At first we thought we could have others. But they never came. A few years after we lost our son, Rectina brought home a baby girl. An orphan. I called her Thalia.' He smiled at his eldest daughter.

'After that, people kept bringing us abandoned children. I'm a keen musician. Named my girls after the Muses and taught them how to play.'

'Don't you have any sons?' asked Jonathan.

'Baby boys aren't often abandoned,' said Tascius. 'Besides, we always hoped to find our own son.'

He was interrupted by murmurs of approval as the three serving-girls struggled into the dining-room with the main course: an enormous turbot on a silver platter.

'Excuse me,' Pliny said, licking creamy dill sauce from his thumb. 'This delicious turbot has just reminded me of something.'

He snapped his fingers and said over his shoulder. 'Phrixus. New heading: the Vulcanalia. Vulcan, the god of fire and the forge, is important in the months of late summer, when the ground is driest and a careless spark can set a granary on fire and destroy its contents in minutes. During his festival – the Vulcanalia – living fish are thrown on a fire as a substitute for the life of each person. The festival is particularly prominent in the town of Ostia, whose many granaries are the basis of its wealth.'

'We celebrate the Vulcanalia, too,' said Tascius. 'It's the day after tomorrow. Why don't you join us, admiral? Why don't you all come along?'

He looked around at them. 'We hold the fish sacrifice down on the beach. I'm the priest of Vulcan for this region. Because the god requires only the lives of the fish and not their flesh, we provide plenty of wine and make quite a feast of it. Everyone comes, rich and poor.'

'Why, yes!' The admiral clapped his hands in delight. 'I'd love to come.'

'And we will bring Vulcan,' announced Flavia.

They all stared at her.

'Do you mean a statue of the god?' Tascius frowned.

'I do believe she means the blacksmith they call Vulcan,' said Admiral Pliny in his breathy voice, dabbing his mouth with a napkin. 'Have you located him?'

Flavia nodded. 'We solved the riddle you gave us and we found the blacksmith named Vulcan.'

'Remarkable!' said the admiral. 'And the treasure?'

'Well,' said Flavia. 'We're not exactly sure what the treasure is yet . . . But Vulcan's at our farm right now.'

'I look forward to seeing him again,' said the admiral. 'Now, Flavia Gemina, tell us how you and your friends solved the riddle.'

SCROLL XVIII

The sun had long set and the white columns surrounding the dining-room glowed gold in the light
of a dozen oil-lamps. Through the columns and
beyond the pine torches which illuminated the
lawn, the bay gleamed like wet black marble, reflecting a thousand spangles of light. It was difficult to
see where the lights of luxury villas stopped and the
stars began.

Tascius had just ordered torch-bearing slaves to
escort Gaius's party home and everyone was rising
from couch and chair, when a tall woman in a peacock
blue stola and black shawl swept into the room.

'So sorry I'm late, everyone,' she said in a gracious,
well-modulated voice. 'I've been settling affairs at my
villa.' She was a dark, attractive woman in her early
forties, with a straight nose, long eyelashes and dark
hair piled high in a complicated arrangement of curls.

'My dear Pliny.' She kissed the admiral's cheek, then
turned to smile at Gaius and Mordecai.

'Rectina,' said Tascius. 'Don't believe you've met our
neighbours. Gaius Flavius Geminus. Owns the estate
which backs onto our villa. His niece Flavia. His guest
Doctor Mordecai ben Ezra . . .'

Flavia stared at Rectina. There was something terribly

familiar about her. She was certain she had seen her before. But where?

In the middle of the night, Jonathan woke Flavia. He nudged her shoulder, careful not to spill any of the hot oil from his clay lamp.

'What? What is it, Jonathan?' she mumbled. 'Have you had another nightmare?'

Jonathan shook his head and put his finger to his lips. 'Lupus has something to show you.'

At the foot of Flavia's low bed, Scuto blinked and yawned. Then he rested his head on his paws and sighed. Nubia yawned, too. She pushed back her covers, rose stretching and sat beside Flavia.

'Go on Lupus, show them,' whispered Jonathan. Lupus emerged from the shadows by the door and squatted beside Flavia's bed. He flipped open his wax tablet and began to draw.

'You've drawn Vulcan!' Flavia yawned. 'It's good!'

'He's not finished,' said Jonathan. 'Watch.'

Lupus glanced round at them, eyes glittering sea-green in the flickering lamplight. With a few strokes of the stylus he made Vulcan's mouth fuller and more feminine and thinned out the eyebrows. Finally he added elaborately curled hair and a head scarf.

'Great Neptune's beard!' said Flavia. 'With that mouth and hair, Vulcan looks just like Clio's mother . . . her adoptive mother, I mean.'

'Rectina,' said Jonathan.

'But that can only mean –'

Jonathan nodded. 'Rectina must be Vulcan's mother and –'

'Tascius must be his father!' cried Flavia. 'We've found Vulcan's long-lost parents!'

Long after Nubia's breathing had become slow and regular again, Flavia lay awake thinking about the plan she had devised.

She was far too excited to sleep.

Besides, she needed to use the latrine.

She got up and padded soundlessly through the atrium and into the kitchen. Ashes still glowed deep red on the hearth but they didn't provide much light. Flavia felt her way through to the latrine, with its polished wooden seat and hole.

She was just coming back out of the kitchen when she heard a noise – the sound of footsteps and the garden gate.

It must be Miriam's secret admirer leaving another token of his love!

The sky above the garden was charcoal grey, with one or two stars still burning faintly in the west. The chill breeze that often heralded sunrise touched her face and bare arms. Flavia crept silently along the columned walkway, the luminous white chips in the mosaic floor guiding her way.

When she reached the gate, she carefully undid the latch and opened it. Peering through the predawn gloom across the farmyard, she was just in time to see a figure disappear into the stables. Quietly Flavia eased open the gate and stepped out.

Suddenly she remembered Ferox and froze. But he was nowhere in sight. Someone must have locked him in his kennel.

Flavia crept across the farmyard, the powdery dust cool between her toes. As she drew closer, she heard voices. A light flared and then burned dimly from the small stable window.

Peering through the window, she could just make out a figure standing beside the donkey's stall.

It was Mordecai.

An oil-lamp hung from a hook on the rafters above him and lit an open scroll in his hands. His eyes were closed and he was rocking forwards and backwards with little movements, chanting. A few other oil-lamps created globes of light in the dim space and Flavia caught a whiff of frankincense.

The others, facing Mordecai with their backs to Flavia, were harder to make out. Flavia could distinguish Miriam by the pale scarf draped over her head. And Jonathan stood next to her. The bent figure was probably the old cook Frustilla, and Flavia thought she saw Xanthus, too.

Mordecai stopped rocking and chanting. He briefly bowed his head and kissed the scroll. Then he stood to one side as another figure limped towards him.

It was Vulcan.

The smith stood at the front and began to sing in a light, clear voice. The others joined him, lifting their hands in the air. They were worshipping something.

Flavia knew that Jonathan and his family were Christians. She remembered Jonathan telling her about a shepherd god, but she saw no image. She squinted to find the altar or statue they were praying to. But the only thing they were facing – apart from

Vulcan and Mordecai – was the donkey Modestus, dozing peacefully in his stall.

Suddenly she understood.

One of their gods must be a donkey.

They were worshipping a jackass!

SCROLL XIX

Flavia intended to ask Jonathan about the donkey-god later that morning, but before she could, an argument broke out between them.

Their lessons were over and Flavia had explained her plan for reuniting Vulcan and his parents.

'No, absolutely not.' Jonathan shook his head. 'It's a bad idea. And what if we're wrong?'

'But if we're right, he'll be so grateful that he'll forgive me for calling him a jackass and he'll tell us about the treasure.'

'Then you should tell him about his parents today,' said Jonathan. 'Why wait until tomorrow?'

'Because tomorrow is the Vulcanalia,' said Flavia. 'It will be perfect – just like the picture on the vase. What do *you* think, Lupus?'

Lupus scowled at Flavia.

'He doesn't like your plan because we can't tell Clio.'

'That's because she's always chattering. She wouldn't be able to keep it a secret. Besides, Rectina's her own mother and she didn't even notice the resemblance. Clio should have seen it for herself like I did.'

'You didn't figure it out,' said Jonathan. 'Lupus did!'

'I knew Rectina looked familiar,' said Flavia hotly. 'I was about to figure it out.'

'No you weren't!' said Jonathan.

'Yes I was!'

'Weren't!'

'Was!'

'You don't care about people's feelings,' said Jonathan. 'All you care about is that stupid treasure.' He stood abruptly. 'I'm going hunting. Come on Lupus!'

'I'm doing my plan whether you like it or not!' Flavia shouted after them.

'Fine! But don't expect us to help you!' The garden gate slammed behind the boys.

'Fine!' yelled Flavia, and brushed hot tears from her eyes.

The omens for the Vulcanalia were not good. Jonathan overslept and woke with a headache. Flavia and Nubia had apparently gone on ahead and the others were already leaving, so Jonathan grabbed Tigris and hurried after them through the vineyards.

It was a cool, grey morning with a sullen wind. As they crossed the coastal road and came over a rise, Jonathan saw that Titus Tascius Pomponianus and most of the inhabitants of Stabia had already gathered on the beach for the ceremony.

The most important people sat on a low wooden stage. In addition to Rectina and Tascius, who had paid for the ceremony, there were two local magistrates, a senator from Rome and Admiral Pliny. A painted wooden statue of the god Vulcan smiled down on a long brick altar covered with hot coals. Near the altar were several oak barrels. Jonathan wondered what they were for.

He looked for Flavia but couldn't see her anywhere. Then he saw Clio waving at them. She was standing with her sisters beside the platform, dressed in her favourite orange tunic. As they hurried to join her, a hush fell over the crowd. Tascius had risen and covered his head with a fold of his toga. The ceremony was about to begin. Everyone pushed closer to watch.

'Great Vulcan, god of fish and fire, anvil and anchor,' pronounced Tascius in his loudest military voice, 'be merciful this year. Protect us against the twin dangers of flame and water. And keep the grain in our warehouses from fire and damp.' The wind moaned and he raised his voice even more to be heard above it.

'Merciful Vulcan, we offer you these creatures as a living sacrifice, as substitutes for our own lives. Please accept their lives for ours. Grant that we may live another year in peace and prosperity.' Tascius paused and looked around at the crowd. Rectina smiled up at her husband and Pliny scribbled notes on his wax tablet. The crowd on the beach murmured with excitement as everyone craned for a view.

His head still covered with his toga, Tascius approached one of the oak barrels beside the platform.

'If father drops the fish, it's bad luck!' Clio whispered to Lupus and Jonathan. 'He was practising all yesterday afternoon.'

Tascius pushed the folds of his toga up over his shoulder, leaving his entire right arm bare. With a dramatic flourish he lifted his arm in the air for all to see, then plunged it into the oak cask. The crowd grew silent again. For a long moment, the only sound was the wind snapping togas and cloaks. Finally, Tascius held a live, dripping fish in the air.

'This life for my life, Great Vulcan!' he cried, and threw the fish onto the coals. The crowd cheered.

The fish, a medium-sized mackerel, thrashed for several moments and then sizzled on the red-hot coals, one eye staring glassily up at the grey sky. Jonathan stared in horrified fascination and beside him Miriam screamed and covered her eyes. Jonathan saw the fish give a few more convulsive shudders before it died.

Tascius shot Miriam a glare. Then he pulled the toga back from his head, stepped away from the barrel and turned to the crowd.

'Let us each offer a fish as substitute for our lives!' he cried. 'And let us celebrate with grain, grape and fish!'

Immediately the people on the beach surged forward and crowded round the barrels. Jonathan had to scoop up Tigris to keep him from being trampled.

Soon fish were flying through the air and dropping onto the coals. Above, seagulls circled and swooped. One bird caught a small mackerel mid-air and flew away with its prize, to the great delight of the crowd.

Some of the fish flipped out of slippery hands and fell thrashing onto the beach, only to be scooped up and thrown onto the coals, sand and all. For the sacrifice to be effective, the fish had to be alive.

Clio had just thrown her fish and now Lupus was up to his armpit in one barrel. He finally extracted a mackerel as long as his forearm. Although he could not say the words, he uttered an enthusiastic grunt as he threw the dripping creature.

'Aren't you going to sacrifice a fish, Jonathan?' laughed Clio, wiping her hands on her tunic. 'It's fun! And we get to eat them in a few minutes!'

Jonathan cradled Tigris protectively. He shook his head. 'I'm not really hungry.'

Suddenly Clio pointed up the beach.

'Here come the entertainers!' she squealed.

A fire-eater dressed in a scarlet tunic was first. He was followed by five midgets who formed a pyramid. The most popular performer was a young man dressed as the sea-nymph Thetis. He juggled four live fish while singing in a falsetto voice.

Then Jonathan heard the crowd chanting.

'Vulcan! Vul-can! Vul-*can*!'

Jonathan turned towards the coastal road. Over the dunes came a figure on a donkey. It was Vulcan the blacksmith, and on either side of him walked Flavia and Nubia.

SCROLL XX

Flavia and Nubia had hidden in the tree fort until the others left, then found Vulcan at his furnace in the tool-shed. He had mentioned earlier that he would not attend the Vulcanalia, but when Flavia told him that his long-lost parents might be on the beach, he saddled his donkey at once.

But Flavia felt uneasy.

She had envisaged a bright, sunny morning like all the other mornings so far. Vulcan and his parents would fall joyfully into each others' arms. It would be just like Vulcan's return to Mount Olympus. Then, in gratitude, he would tell her about the treasure.

Instead, the day was grey and heavy, with a peevish offshore breeze that blew fine grit and sand into their faces.

It was not a good omen.

The smell of charcoal-grilled fish and the sound of laughter reached them before they topped the sandy rise that led down to the beach.

Things seemed to improve as Vulcan came into sight. The crowd was already extremely merry due to the free wine. One or two people knew the smith's name and cried it out. Soon everyone took up the chant:

'Vulcan! Vul-can! Vul-*can*!'

As the people crowded round him, cheering and chanting his name, Vulcan smiled and looked up hopefully. Flavia's heart was pounding and she knew his must be, too. She pointed to the stage and shouted over the noise of the crowd.

'On the stage. The woman in dark blue and the man with short grey hair. No, not the stout one; that's Pliny. The tall one in the toga. Titus Tascius –'

'Pomponianus.' Vulcan's dark eyes were shining as he urged the donkey on towards the stage.

Flavia saw the crowd part before him. The faces around them were laughing and chanting Vulcan's name. Some people rose to their feet, others seemed more interested in their grilled fish.

Vulcan halted his donkey a few feet from the stage and dismounted awkwardly with the help of his staff.

Rectina had been watching his approach. When she saw the young man limping towards her, she rose unsteadily to her feet.

'Do I know you?' she asked, looking from his face to his foot and back.

But before Vulcan could answer, she fainted into her husband's arms.

'Oops,' said Flavia under her breath. 'That wasn't supposed to happen.'

Tascius, kneeling on the stage with his wife in his arms, looked up in confusion at Vulcan. 'What have you done to her? Who are you?'

'By Jove!' cried Admiral Pliny, stepping forward and peering at the blacksmith. 'It *is* him. It must be. Don't you realise who this is, Titus? It's your long-lost son!'

Tascius looked at Pliny and then back at Vulcan. A strange look passed across his face.

'My long-lost son? No, it's some sort of monstrous joke,' he said through clenched wooden teeth. 'Get him away! Get him away before she sees him again!'

The festival of Vulcan did not end well.

Everyone saw Tascius take his wife away in a curtained litter. Their daughters hurried after them on foot. Someone said Rectina had been taken ill and soon the rumour spread that she had eaten bad fish. The senator and magistrates made hasty exits, leaving Pliny to conclude the ceremony on his own.

As the admiral attempted to read out the final invocation from his notes, the crowd grew angry.

'Where's our money?'

Flavia saw Pliny consult his notes nervously and heard him ask Phrixus, 'What money? What do they want?'

'He always gives us coppers!' shrieked a woman.

'Throw coins to the crowd!' yelled another helpfully.

'By Jove,' Pliny muttered, 'I don't have any . . . I mean . . . Phrixus, do you see a bag of coppers around here?'

One of the revellers had drunk too much free wine and he vomited noisily beside the platform.

'He's been poisoned, too!'

'It's bad luck!' someone shouted.

'Bad luck and bad fish,' said a fisherman, and spat on the sand.

'Where's our money?'

'Come on, Phrixus,' Pliny wheezed to his scribe.

'Let's get back to the ship, back to Misenum. Quickly . . .'

Flavia looked at the angry crowd and turned to Nubia. 'We'd better go, too. It might get nasty. Where's Vulcan?'

'He left just now, riding fastly his jackass.'

'You were right, Jonathan. I should have listened to you. Now I've ruined everything!'

Jonathan could see that Flavia felt miserable. They had left the angry crowd on the beach and hurried back to the farm. Now they sat at the wrought-iron table in the garden. The day was still grey and overcast, with a vicious wind that whined petulantly and rattled the leaves of the trees and shrubs.

'When a mother sees the son she thought was dead . . .' Jonathan said quietly.

'And now Vulcan's run away.'

'And you'll never find the treasure?'

'Oh Jonathan! I don't really care about the treasure. I just wanted to be able to solve the mystery for Admiral Pliny. But now he's sailed back across the bay and Vulcan has gone, too.' The moaning wind rose in volume for a moment, sounding almost angry. It whipped stinging strands of hair across Flavia's face.

'I'm sure we'll see Pliny again,' said Jonathan, patting her on the back. 'Now let's go and try to find Vulcan.'

In the middle of the night the sound of dogs barking woke Flavia from a deep sleep. She sat up, puzzled and disoriented. Then she remembered. Her plan had gone wrong. Vulcan had disappeared and they hadn't been able to find him.

Scuto's reassuring bulk was missing from the foot of her bed and Nubia's bed was empty. Flavia rose and stumbled groggily towards the sound.

She found her dog in the moon-washed farmyard. Scuto, the puppies and Ferox stood barking, their noses to the sky. The other members of the household were coming into the farmyard, holding lamps and rubbing sleep from their eyes.

The strange wind was still moaning. It blew low, fast-moving clouds across the sky towards the mountain, and the moon kept appearing and disappearing.

'You understand animals, Nubia,' whispered Flavia. 'Why are they barking?'

'The moon is not being full. I don't know.'

As her eyes adjusted to the darkness, Flavia saw a small figure shuffle out of the garden and into the farmyard. It was Frustilla. Muttering to herself, the ancient cook hobbled forward and hurled an entire bucket of cold water over the dogs.

It did the trick.

Ferox stopped barking and retreated hastily to his kennel. The other three dogs whimpered and shook themselves. Scuto trotted over to Flavia.

'What on earth has got into you, Scuto?' Flavia squatted down and ruffled the damp fur of his neck. He rolled his eyes and looked embarrassed.

'Shhh!' hissed Jonathan. Everyone was quiet.

Above moaning wind they all heard it. Faintly but unmistakably, from all the neighbouring farms and villas, the sound of dogs barking.

'Great Jupiter's eyebrows,' whispered Gaius.

And there was another sound.

'I hear squeakings,' whispered Nubia, picking up Nipur and clutching him tightly.

Lupus uttered a strangled yelp and pointed to the open garden gate. Flavia squinted. And gasped.

Emerging from beneath the myrtle and quince bushes, pattering across the mosaic walkways, skittering down the dusty paths came dozens of tiny dark shapes. There were mice, rats and even a snake.

Everyone stared as the creatures emerged from their hiding places in house and garden, and made their way out of the garden gate and through the vineyards towards the sea.

SCROLL XXI

'I had the dream again last night.' Jonathan's face was pale and there were dark shadows under his eyes. It was a heavy, colourless dawn, the second day of the Vulcanalia. The previous day's wind had died and there was a faint, unpleasant smell in the air.

'I think the dogs must have had bad dreams, too,' said Flavia.

The puppies and Scuto lay dejectedly under a quince bush, chins on paws.

'At least they're not barking any more,' said Jonathan.

Mordecai emerged from the kitchen with a tall brass pot and seven cups on a tray. 'The well was dry this morning so I've made mint tea with yesterday's water.'

Jonathan slumped at the table.

'Have dates.' Nubia held out a plate.

'She's right,' said Aristo. 'You'll feel better when you've eaten.'

Jonathan shook his head and closed his eyes. Then he opened them again, horrified.

'Now I see it even when I close my eyes.'

'What do you see, my son?' Mordecai poured hot water onto the mint leaves.

Jonathan closed his eyes and shivered. 'I see a city on

a hill, with a huge golden wall and towers. And there are legions and legions of soldiers, Roman soldiers, coming to camp around it.' He opened his eyes again. 'Something terrible is going to happen. I know it.'

'How many times have you had this dream?' asked Mordecai, gripping the back of an empty chair. In the white light of dawn his eyes seemed as black as the turban above them.

'This is the third or fourth time,' said Jonathan.

Mordecai sat heavily on the chair and stared at the steam coiling up from the cups.

'When you see Jerusalem being surrounded by armies,' he whispered, 'you will know that its desolation is near.'

'What?' Flavia frowned.

'I never said it was Jerusalem,' said Jonathan. 'I don't even know what Jerusalem looks like.'

'Yet the city you described was Jerusalem. I'm sure of it: Jerusalem the golden.' Mordecai looked at his son. 'And you *have* seen Jerusalem, you know, although you were just a baby. We were among the last people to escape before the siege began. And the fate of those left behind was truly terrible . . .'

He closed his eyes for a moment and then continued.

'I believe your dreams are from God, Jonathan. Through you he is sending a warning to us all. The prophet in Pompeii – the one you told me about – I fear he was correct. God's judgement is about to fall upon this country.'

They all stared at him.

The sound of brass curtain rings sliding along a

wooden rod cut through the heavy silence and they turned to see Miriam. She stood framed in her bedroom doorway, her cheeks wet with tears and her face as pale as marble.

'He's dead,' she whispered. 'Dead.'

'Who?' Jonathan cried. 'Who's dead?'

Miriam held up the bird cage. 'Catullus. I found him when I woke up.'

The feathered corpse of the once bright sparrow lay on the floor of the cage.

'Another portent,' said Mordecai. 'We must leave immediately. The Lord has warned us today as he once warned me, nearly ten years ago.'

In the trees above, a bird uttered a single, hesitant note, and then was silent.

Jonathan stood up and nodded. 'When I think about leaving I feel better.'

'Then pack your things. We must depart immediately.'

'No, father. I'm not going. There is no danger of besieging armies now.' Miriam had put the birdcage down. Her voice was firm.

Jonathan stared at her in amazement. Never before had he heard his sister defy their father. Her eyes were bright and a flush had crept into her pale skin.

Mordecai was staring at his daughter in disbelief.

'Miriam,' he said. 'You must come with us.'

'Father, please don't ask me to go.' The flush in her cheeks deepened. Miriam dropped her eyes and stammered, 'I want to stay here for a little longer.'

'Miriam, is there something you want to tell me?'

Again the absolute silence. Then she spoke quietly, without looking at him.

'Yes, there is. I am in love, father, and I wish to marry him. Please don't make me leave.'

'Marry? You have only just turned fourteen!'

'I'm a woman now.' Miriam lifted her eyes and looked directly at her father. 'And I'm ready to marry.'

'Yes. I suppose you are.' Mordecai's voice was barely more than a whisper. 'Well, who is it? Whom do you love?'

'She is in love with me,' came a voice from beneath the peristyle. 'And I would give my life for her.'

SCROLL XXII

The man who emerged from the house and stepped into the garden was the last person Flavia expected. She gasped:

'Uncle Gaius!'

Lupus choked in amazement and Jonathan's jaw dropped. Only Nubia seemed to accept this revelation calmly.

To Flavia, it seemed unbelievable. How could Jonathan's sister want to marry a man her father's age? But when he and Miriam looked at one another, Flavia saw the love in their eyes.

Mordecai's face softened. 'Then you must come with us, too, Gaius. We must all leave Italia. And quickly, I beg of you. We can discuss this matter later.'

Gaius took a few steps towards Mordecai and held his hands out, palms to the sky. 'But how? How can I leave my villa, my vines, the farm? If there's another strong earthquake I have to stay here to protect the house against looters and thieves. If I must face God's judgement, then I would rather face it here in the house where I was born.'

'No. Father's right.' Jonathan looked around at them all. 'We have to leave! Don't you understand?'

Mordecai nodded. 'Nearly ten years ago, when I saw Jerusalem beginning to be surrounded by armies, I remembered the words of the Shepherd: "Let those who are in Judaea flee to the mountains. Let no one on the roof of his house go down to take anything out of the house. Let no one in the field go back to get his cloak. For then there will be great distress, not seen from the beginning of the world until now."

'I felt a sense of dread then, just as Jonathan does now. And it was that sense of dread which saved our lives. My children and I left Jerusalem immediately. But their mother . . . their mother . . .'

To Flavia's dismay, Mordecai began to weep.

'She was so beautiful,' he said, and turned to Miriam. 'So much like you, my dear. She refused to go, just as you are refusing to go. We argued, and she decided to stay with her parents. I relented and I never saw her again.'

Mordecai held out his hands to his daughter.

'Miriam. What good is a warning from the Lord if we refuse to listen? You must come with us.'

Before Miriam could reply, something soft struck Flavia's bare arm.

'Oh!' she cried. A wren lay at her feet in the dust.

Flavia bent down and gently picked it up. 'I think it's dead,' she said. 'But it's still warm.' She looked up into the leaves of the laurel tree, just in time to see three more birds drop from its branches.

Suddenly all around them the trees were raining birds: a shower of wrens, thrushes and sparrows. Nubia knelt to pick up a tiny sparrow.

'Birds dead,' she whispered. 'All dead.'

'What on earth . . .' said Aristo, staring at the feathered corpses around them.

'Rotten eggs!' cried Gaius. 'I should have remembered!'

'You should have remembered what?' asked Flavia.

'Sulphur smells like rotten eggs,' said her uncle, 'and sulphur fumes are what killed the sheep up near Misenum in the big earthquake seventeen years ago.'

Flavia sniffed the air. There was a distinct scent of rotten eggs.

'But if the smell of sulphur can kill animals as large as sheep . . .' said Aristo. He didn't need to finish the sentence.

As they stood staring at each other, a voice broke the silence.

'My mother always told me that the smell of rotten eggs meant that Vulcan was angry.'

They all turned to see Frustilla standing in the kitchen doorway.

'My grandmother was from the island of Sicily,' quavered the old woman, shuffling into the garden, 'where the smith god has his forge . . .'

'And when the smith god is angry –' said Jonathan.

'There's a volcano!' cried Flavia.

As if to confirm Flavia's words, the ground rumbled beneath their feet, and they heard a sound like distant thunder.

'Of course,' said Mordecai. 'I should have guessed! You're right, Miriam. There are no besieging armies. This time God's judgement will come by natural disaster. He has been warning those of us with eyes to see.

The sulphur, the tremors, dry wells, the odd behaviour of the animals, Jonathan's dreams . . . Frustilla is right. They all point to one thing: a volcanic eruption.'

'But which mountain will erupt?' asked Jonathan.

'It has to be Vesuvius!' cried Aristo.

'But it's not a volcano. It's never erupted,' said Gaius. 'Has it, Frustilla?'

'Not in my lifetime,' said the old cook. 'And I've never heard of it being a fire-spitter. But there's a small volcano north of it, near Misenum. They say it smells of rotten eggs.'

'Vesuvius could be dormant . . . that is, a sleeping volcano . . .' Mordecai tugged his beard. 'I believe I know how we can find out! Gaius, do you have Pliny's *Natural History*? I'm certain there is a section on volcanoes . . .'

'There's a copy in the library,' answered Gaius.

They all hurried into the library and Flavia's uncle lifted down a fat cylindrical scroll-case marked 'Pliny'.

'Quickly!' said Flavia, hopping with impatience. 'I think there's something about Vesuvius in scroll three!'

Miriam gently pushed Gaius's fumbling hand away and swiftly unpicked the cord with her deft fingers. Together they eased off the leather lid.

Meanwhile, Aristo had moved to a dim corner of the library. He was passing a clay lamp along the wall and peering at the dangling leather labels.

For several moments the only sound was the crackle and rustle of papyrus scrolls being unrolled on the library table.

'Here's something about Vesuvius!' cried Flavia at

last. She scanned the passage. 'But Pliny doesn't say anything about it being a volcano.'

In his shadowy corner, Aristo pulled a scroll from its niche.

'Listen to this!' said Jonathan. 'In scroll two, Pliny lists some volcanoes around the world. He doesn't mention Vesuvius, but he says that there is a small fire in Modena that erupts every year on the feast day of Vulcan. That's now!'

Gaius shook his head. 'Modena is as far north of Rome as we are south of it.'

'Eureka!' cried Aristo from his corner. 'I've found it!'

He moved over to the doorway, set down his lamp and unrolled a scroll.

'Diodorus of Sicily tells about strange animal behaviour several centuries ago near my home town in Greece. I'd forgotten the exact details, but here it is!'

He read aloud. ' "In a town called Helice on the gulf of Corinth, there was a devastating earthquake. Before the earthquake struck, to the puzzlement of the citizens, all sorts of animals, such as rats, snakes and weasels, left the city in droves." '

'Exactly like last night,' said Jonathan.

Aristo was silent for a moment as he scanned the text. Then the colour drained from his face.

'What?' They all gazed at him anxiously.

' "Five days later",' he read, ' "the entire town was swallowed up by the sea." '

SCROLL XXIII

There was a long silence as they all looked at one another, broken only by Ferox barking in the farmyard.

'We must warn people,' said Mordecai, after a moment. 'I'm a fool. The Lord has been trying to tell us for days, but I didn't see the signs.'

'Neither did Pliny,' said Flavia, 'and he is the greatest natural historian in the world.'

'Do we escape by land or by sea?' said Aristo.

'The quickest route is always by sea,' Mordecai said. 'But we must escape any way we can . . .'

Suddenly the garden gate swung open.

'Vulcan!' cried Flavia.

'Clio!' said Jonathan.

'Modestus!' said Nubia.

The muscular blacksmith and the little girl in the orange tunic stood side by side, with the donkey's big head nosing between them.

Lupus ran to Clio and stopped shyly in front of her. Her face was blotched and tear-stained, but she smiled back at him.

'Vulcan, where were you?' Flavia asked. 'We looked everywhere for you.'

'I rode south,' he said. 'Modestus and I slept on the beach. Just now I presented myself at the Villa

Pomponiana, but Tascius refused to see me and Rectina wasn't there. On my way back here I found Clio.'

Mordecai stepped forward. 'Listen to me. We believe Vesuvius is going to erupt and that we must get as far away from it as we can.'

'The best route of escape is probably by sea,' added Gaius. 'Clio, you're lucky your family has a boat. You must all sail away as soon as you can.'

'But –'

'You must get out as soon as possible!' urged Mordecai. 'All of you!'

'We can't.' Clio's eyes filled with tears. 'Mother and Father had a horrible argument last night. Mother took my sisters and three slaves and she left for her villa at dawn. I jumped off the back of the carruca and came back to find out why, because Mother wouldn't tell us anything.' Tears ran down Clio's face. Lupus offered her a grubby handkerchief.

'Please, Clio,' said Mordecai. 'Try to be calm. Tell us again: where is your mother's villa?'

'Just the other side of Herculaneum,' said Clio, blowing her nose on Lupus's scrap of linen. 'Two miles north of the Neapolis gate.'

'Great Jupiter's eyebrows!' said Gaius. 'It's at the very foot of the mountain!'

Even as he spoke, the earth trembled and shook beneath them once more.

'We must warn those beneath the mountain,' said Flavia's uncle grimly.

He ran his hand through his hair just as Flavia's

father did when he was upset. 'I'll go to Pompeii immediately and tell the authorities what we've discovered. Then I'll ride inland to Nuceria and warn them, too. But someone will have to go to Oplontis and Herculaneum, and then on to Neapolis . . .'

'I will,' said Vulcan without hesitation. 'It may be the last chance I get to see . . . my mother.'

'Are you sure?' asked Mordecai. 'You may be riding to your death.'

'Deaths holds no fear for me,' said Vulcan bravely, and then swallowed. 'Well, only a little.'

'I know you can ride a donkey,' said Gaius. 'But can you ride a fast horse?'

Vulcan nodded.

'Good,' said Gaius. 'Then we must leave immediately.'

'I'll go too, if you need me.' Aristo stepped forward.

Gaius smiled. 'Thank you Aristo, but I need you and Mordecai to get my household to safety. Tell Xanthus to harness the mules to the carriage. Vulcan and I will take Celer and Audax.' He turned to the doctor.

'Mordecai, can you drive a carriage?'

'Yes, of course.'

'Will you drive Miriam and the children to Stabia? Take Frustilla, too, and Rufus. Drop Clio home on your way. Aristo, will you and Xanthus follow on foot with my other slaves? When you all get to Stabia, board a ship and sail away from here as soon as you can. I'll give you all the gold in my strongbox.'

'You don't have to go to Stabia,' sniffed Clio. 'Our boat is big enough for you all. Father will take you.'

'Are you sure?'

Clio nodded.

'Excellent,' Gaius said. 'Mordecai. Aristo. Get everyone to the Villa Pomponiana and sail as soon as you can. Don't wait for us.'

Suddenly Miriam threw her arms around Gaius. 'Don't go! Stay with us!'

'I must go, my darling,' said Gaius, softly, and brushed dark curls away from her face. 'How could you still love me if I didn't try to help all the people whose lives are in danger?'

'But what if you're wrong? What if it's all a mistake? What if they are just tremors?'

'Then no harm will come to us. Except perhaps from angry citizens.'

'But, Gaius –'

'Shhh!' he whispered. 'I've waited all my life for you and I'm not about to lose you now. I promise I'll return.'

As they embraced, Aristo and Vulcan glanced at each other.

'I gave her the bracelet,' confessed Vulcan. 'I made it myself.'

'I gave her the sparrow,' Aristo said.

Vulcan frowned. 'Then that means he –'

'*He* didn't give her anything,' said Aristo with a sigh.

At two hours past dawn, Vulcan and Gaius rode out of the farmyard to warn the towns near Vesuvius of the coming disaster.

Vulcan planned to tell the town magistrates of Oplontis, Herculaneum and Neapolis.

Gaius was heading for Pompeii and then Nuceria.

Ferox, freed from his hated kennel, ran joyfully beside his master. He easily kept up with the galloping horses. As soon as they were out of sight, Mordecai turned to the children.

'I'll give you half an hour to pack your things. Take only what you can carry. And hurry. I feel in my spirit that disaster is almost upon us.'

Flavia and Nubia had just finished packing when they heard Mordecai shouting. For a moment they stared at one another. They had never before heard his voice raised in anger.

'I couldn't stop him, father!' Jonathan cried.

The girls hurried out of their bedroom and into the garden. Jonathan and his father stood face to face.

'But why didn't you tell me immediately?' The anger in Mordecai's voice made his accent more pronounced.

'He made me promise.' Jonathan looked miserable.

'And Clio's with him?'

'No. *He's* with *her*. She's the one who insisted on going. He told me – I mean he let me know – that he was only going along to protect her.'

'Those two are the most stubborn, rebellious souls I've ever met,' said Mordecai. 'They're just the same!'

He noticed Aristo and the girls watching him open-mouthed.

'Lupus and Clio have taken – no, *stolen* one of the horses. Clio's gone after Vulcan to try to save her family. Of all the foolish . . . Lupus the eight-year-old has gone to protect Clio the seven-year-old. Dear Lord!' He looked up into the sky. 'What else could possibly go wrong?'

The garden gate opened and Xanthus staggered in. He was bloody and beaten, his clothing ripped and torn.

'The slaves,' he gasped. 'I tried to stop them but they've all run away. And they've taken the mules and carriage.'

SCROLL XXIV

Lupus and Clio had hoped to catch up with Vulcan on the road to Pompeii, but they were not the only ones to have a premonition of disaster. A steady stream of people moving against them made it difficult to travel quickly.

'Go back!' one or two travellers shouted at them. 'The god Vulcan has just told us that there's a furnace beneath Vesuvius. It's about to explode.'

'At least we're on the right track,' said Clio over her shoulder to Lupus.

Lupus grunted in response. He wasn't used to riding. Already his bottom ached from half an hour of bouncing.

At the harbour of Pompeii, half the ships were gone and scores of people were trying to board those that remained. Women and children were screaming and men were fighting. There was a sinister red stain on the pavement in front of the tavern with the yellow awning.

Passing between the harbour and the town walls, Lupus and Clio saw an official standing beneath the arch of the Sea Gate.

'By order of the magistrate,' he shouted, 'do not leave the city. The tremors are not dangerous! Stay in your homes, or they may be looted! Return to your homes immediately, I say!'

A few people hesitated when they heard his words, but most kept their heads down as they hurried past him through the gate.

'I thought Flavia's uncle was going to tell them about the mountain,' said Clio.

Lupus grunted yes.

'Then I don't understand why that man in the toga is telling people not to leave.'

At first sight, the Villa Pomponiana seemed deserted. It was now late morning, baking hot, with only a breath of wind from the bay.

Jonathan was sweating as he and Flavia helped Mordecai lift Xanthus off Modestus. Nubia led the donkey across to the stables while they carried Xanthus up the steps to the dining-room and eased him onto a dining couch. The farm manager's broken ankle and ribs would mend, but his punctured lung was grave.

Aristo had been carrying old Frustilla on his back. As soon as he set her down she and Miriam went off to find a basin and water so that Mordecai could treat Xanthus.

'Find Tascius, if you can,' said Mordecai, glancing up at Jonathan and Flavia.

They nodded and ran through the silent rooms and inner courtyards.

At last they found Tascius in the atrium, hunched in front of the household shrine. He heard them enter, and lifted his head from his hands.

'They've all left me. My wife, my daughters, most of

my slaves. Not even a live chicken to sacrifice to the gods.'

'We've got to get away from here,' said Jonathan. 'Something terrible is going to happen. We think Vesuvius is going to erupt. Flavia's Uncle Gaius and Vulcan have gone to warn people in the towns.'

Tascius looked at them stupidly.

'Vesuvius is a volcano,' said Flavia. 'It's going to erupt!'

'When? How?'

'Soon! I mean, we don't know exactly,' said Jonathan, 'but we must leave!'

'If you're right . . . Jupiter! My wife and daughters are in Herculaneum.'

'Can't we rescue them in your boat?' asked Flavia.

Tascius shook his head. 'Could have yesterday, when the wind was from the south. But not today. Can't even sail out of Stabia today.'

It was almost noon when Clio and Lupus rode their horse through the bright, sunny streets of Herculaneum. It was a smaller, prettier town than Pompeii, with red roofs and palm trees, but it seemed all the more vulnerable because of the huge mountain which loomed above it, filling half the sky.

'Until last year, we used to live here,' Clio said, looking around. 'I've never seen it so quiet.'

As they passed a tavern, two drunks called out from the shady doorway.

'Hey! Haven't you heard? The god Vulcan passed by earlier and told everyone to flee the city. And they all believed him. All except for us! We get free wine!'

His companion snorted. 'Ha! "Vulcan" is probably going through their money boxes right now.' He drained his wine-cup and stepped outside the tavern. 'Nice-looking horse . . . Want us to take her off your hands?' He nodded at his companion and the two of them lurched towards the children.

Clio stuck out her tongue at the men and kicked her heels. The tired mare trotted down the hill and out through the Neapolis Gate.

In the dining-room of the Villa Pomponiana, Nubia shivered and hugged Nipur tightly.

It was just past midday and she stood beside Flavia watching Mordecai try to save the farm manager's life. Xanthus had suddenly begun to cough blood and seemed unable to breathe. His face was a horrible blue colour. Nubia saw tiny beads of sweat on Mordecai's forehead as he and Miriam tried to staunch the flow of blood.

A moment earlier, the noonday heat had been stifling. Now the air around her was freezing cold.

Nubia shivered again.

She had felt this presence once before.

The day the slave-traders had burnt her family's tents and murdered her father. Was the presence death? Or something worse?

The floor vibrated under Nubia's feet, like one of Scuto's silent growls. The earth itself was angry, but no one else seemed to notice.

Nubia glanced back over her shoulder towards Vesuvius. And froze.

An enormous white column was rising from the mountain's peak.

The fact that it was rising in complete silence made it all the more terrifying.

Lupus hit the ground with a force that knocked the breath out of him. He was dimly aware of Clio beside him and the mare's bulk above them, blocking out the sunlight as she reared. For an awful moment he thought the falling horse would crush them both.

Then, with a scream of terror, the mare found her balance and galloped off towards the south.

Lupus had still not managed to get air back into his lungs. Finally it came in a great sobbing breath. Clio's body beside him remained terribly still.

He heard thunder and felt the ground shudder beneath him. Then Lupus saw what had terrified the horse.

Rising straight into the air from the mountain above him was a huge pillar of white smoke and ash.

Vesuvius was erupting, and he was at its very base!

SCROLL XXV

The thunder continued, rumbling up from the earth itself. Bits of gravel and tiny fragments of hot pumice began to rain down on Lupus.

Ignoring this stinging hail, he shook Clio and patted her cheeks. He tried to call her name, but the only sound that came from his mouth was an animal-like groan.

Lupus had never wanted his tongue back so badly. He wanted it back so that he could curse every god who existed.

But he didn't have a tongue and he couldn't curse the gods, even though Clio was dead.

The sound of the volcano reached Stabia a moment after Jonathan watched his father stab Xanthus.

The farm manager had been raving, calling out to the gods. Grimly, Mordecai had told Miriam to get the long needle from his capsa. She had reached into the cylindrical leather case and pulled out a long, wickedly sharp knife.

They stared in horrified fascination at Xanthus's blue, gasping face. Mordecai ripped open the injured man's tunic, fixed the point of the needle at his side between two ribs and pushed. There was a sound like air escaping as the needle pierced the dying man's lung.

Then Xanthus gasped and his chest seemed to swell. The colour began to return to his face.

'Thank God,' whispered Mordecai. 'Miriam, make a poultice to seal –'

At that moment the sound of deep thunder reached them. They all turned to look behind them.

'Oh no,' said Jonathan.

'Dear Apollo' Aristo said.

'Not now!' cried Mordecai. 'Not now!'

The thick column above the cone of Vesuvius, white against the brilliant blue sky, was already beginning to blossom.

Even as they watched, the top of the cloud spread and flattened, until it had taken the shape of an enormous umbrella pine.

The mountain had been thundering for an eternity.

He had been carrying her body forever. Chips of hot pumice and grit spattered him like hail, so that there were a hundred tiny cuts and burns on his arms and legs and face.

Sometimes he fell and sobbed, then he picked her up again and continued up the dirt path between black, flame-shaped cypress trees. If there was a place reserved in the afterlife to punish the wicked, this was it. He knew he had failed and deserved no less.

And so he carried her on up the path to the smoking villa and the waiting god, who stood staring at him in disbelief and amazement. Truly the smith god, whose dwelling place was beneath the earth in darkness and fire, must be king of this realm, and so he handed the little girl's body to Vulcan.

Then Lupus fainted.

Tascius stumbled down the steps and stood in the middle of the green lawn, staring at the volcano with his arms outstretched.

'The gods!' he cried. 'They can't bear our evil any more. They can't bear *my* evil. It's Vulcan. It's Vulcan's anger. The gods tested me and I failed.' He fell to his knees on the grass and began to scratch his cheeks.

The others looked at him aghast.

After a moment, Mordecai left Xanthus and went down the steps and into the hot sunlight. He tried to help Tascius to his feet.

'Tascius,' he said firmly, 'you are a Roman soldier and commander. You must take charge. You must get the household on board your boat and prepare to sail as soon as the wind shifts.'

'It's no use!' Tascius pointed at the volcano. 'Vulcan's anger has come upon me and I must die.' He grasped his own tunic and ripped it at the neck.

'Titus Tascius Pomponianus!' cried Mordecai, gripping the Roman's wrists, 'If it is indeed time for you to die, let your death be honourable. Set an example to these young people.'

They stared into each other's eyes for a long moment.

'Yes,' said Tascius at last, taking a deep breath and nodding his head. 'The gods may have taken everything else, but they cannot take my dignity. Not unless I allow it.' Slowly the old soldier rose to his feet. 'You are right, doctor. I'll prepare the boat at once.'

★

Someone was pouring cool water down Lupus's scorched throat. It went down the wrong way and he had to sit up to cough.

When he had caught his breath, he opened his eyes. Vulcan stood over him, with Rectina close beside him. Their brown eyes, so similar, were filled with tenderness and concern.

One of Clio's younger sisters, Urania, was clinging to Rectina's skirts. Thalia hovered nearby, her face swollen and blotched with weeping. Lupus was aware of a thunder in his ears and a sound like hail on the roof.

Rectina held the beaker out again and Lupus drained it.

'How did you find us?' asked Vulcan when Lupus had finished. 'God must have guided you.'

Lupus snarled and gave the rudest gesture he knew. He meant it for the gods, but Vulcan recoiled as if he had been struck. Then he swallowed.

'You have been through terrible things, Lupus. We all have. Don't be afraid.'

Lupus wanted to explain that he wasn't afraid – he was furious. But he couldn't, so he lay back on the couch and closed his eyes. The house rattled around them as if it were a moving carriage.

Lupus felt a cool, moist sea sponge on his forehead and he heard Rectina's gentle voice.

'Thank you for bringing my little Clio back to me, Lupus,' she said. 'At first we feared she was dead, but when Vulcan laid his hands on her and prayed –'

Lupus was off the couch in an instant. He pushed past Rectina and Vulcan and looked frantically around.

He stood in the middle of an elegant red and black atrium, with chairs and couches and easy access to the garden, but he saw none of it.

All he saw was Clio in her grubby orange tunic, sitting on the couch opposite him, smiling weakly. She was pale and dishevelled, but she was very much alive.

SCROLL XXVI

'My boat's ready to sail,' said Tascius, coming up the steps from the direction of the beach. 'Packed and provisioned with food and water.' He wiped his forehead with the back of his forearm.

'Most of my slaves have gone. I've posted the remaining few to guard the boat. Promised them a passage to safety and their freedom as a reward.' He slumped into a chair and turned his face towards Vesuvius.

Jonathan looked round at the others. 'If the boat's ready, shouldn't we go?'

'Wind's still against us,' said Tascius. 'Stronger now, too.'

'Maybe we could go to the harbour of Stabia and hire a boat there,' Jonathan persisted.

'They're at the mercy of the wind, just as we are. The only boats which might escape are small rowing boats or the big oared warships.'

'Couldn't we go in a carriage?' suggested Flavia. She had her arm around a whimpering Scuto and was trying to soothe him.

'Rectina has taken it,' said Tascius. 'I have a small cart and a chariot. But they're of no use.'

'Then we should walk.' Jonathan was finding it hard

to breathe, but it was not the asthma that pressed hard on his chest. It was fear.

'We can sail as far in one hour as we could walk in twelve,' said Tascius, and then added, 'if the wind shifts.'

'But what if the wind doesn't shift?' asked Jonathan.

'A gamble we'll have to take.'

'Father!' cried Jonathan in desperation.

Mordecai looked up from the couch. 'I'm sorry, Jonathan. This man can't be moved and if I leave him he'll die.'

'Then so will we,' said Jonathan bleakly.

'Lupus,' said Vulcan, raising his voice to be heard above the volcano's thunder. 'We need your help.'

Lupus looked up at him and nodded. He sat beside Clio, with his arm protectively round her shoulders, still amazed by what had happened to her. Had she just been unconscious? He was certain she had died.

'Lupus? Are you listening? Good. The road north has just been blocked by a landslide and my mother's only sailing boat has been stolen. We're trapped at the foot of a volcano.'

A sharp cracking sound cut through the steady background rumble and they all paused as the house shuddered. A marble statue in the garden toppled forward and crashed to the ground.

'My mother has an idea,' continued Vulcan. 'It's our one chance of escape. If we can get a message to Admiral Pliny across the bay, he might send war ships to rescue not just us, but all the others trapped here at the foot of the volcano. My mother is writing the message now.'

Lupus made a gesture with his palms up and grunted. The sense was clear: 'How?'

'Rectina has a small rowing boat in the boathouse down by the shore,' said Vulcan. 'I can row, but because of my foot I cannot run. When we reach Misenum, someone will have to take the message quickly to the admiral. Clio says you are fast and brave. Also, you know what Pliny looks like.'

A shower of gravel and pumice fragments rattled on the roof above them.

'I wanted to go,' said Clio. 'But they say I'm too weak. You'll go, won't you?'

Without hesitation, Lupus nodded.

'Good,' said Rectina, coming into the room. She staggered a little, for the earth was still vibrating beneath them. 'I've just finished writing this message. Pliny will not refuse me. He is a brave man.'

She handed Lupus an oilskin packet about the size of his thumb. It had been tied with leather cords, dipped in liquid wax and sealed with her signet ring, the coiling hearth-snake of good fortune.

'When you get to Misenum,' Rectina said, 'you must run as fast as you can to the admiral's house. It's at the very top of the hill. Three enormous poplar trees stand beside the entrance. Do you understand, Lupus? Vulcan will row. And you will run.' She kissed his forehead. 'May the gods protect you.'

At the Villa Pomponiana, they stared across the bay towards the mountain, praying for the wind to change. But the cloud of ash above Vesuvius was unfurling to the south and they could see their prayers had not yet been answered.

Presently, while Mordecai and Miriam quietly worked to keep Xanthus breathing, Tascius told them the true story of Vulcan's birth.

'I first met Pliny when he was a guest in this very house,' Tascius began, pouring himself a cup of wine.

'He served with my father in Germania. They grew close on campaign. Pliny was very like my father. A brilliant scholar as well as a man of action. I was a good soldier, but not clever. Pliny was the man my father always hoped I would be.'

He paused and looked around at them. Beneath the solid line of his eyebrows his eyes looked bruised.

'I've never spoken of this to anyone. Look who I'm telling now. Jews, slaves and children.' He made a dismissive gesture. 'Doesn't matter. I'll be dead soon.'

He took a sip of wine.

'When Rectina and I were first married, she lived here. With my parents. I was away on campaign most of the time. That was when Pliny came here as a guest, to finish his biography of my father. Pliny is old and stout now like me. But eighteen years ago he was in his prime.'

Tascius paused and stared into his wine-cup, as if he could see the past reflected in the dark liquid.

'I was often away. Pliny was always here. With my father. And with Rectina. Once I caught them speaking together, laughing. That was when I first suspected.'

'Nine months later, after Pliny went back to his dusty scrolls, Rectina gave birth to a son. A son born with a mark of the gods' disapproval. A clubfoot.'

'Do you mean . . . ?' Flavia gasped as she realised what Tascius was saying.

'Yes,' said Tascius. 'Vulcan is not my son. He is Pliny's!'

SCROLL XXVII

In a small rowing boat on the vast bay of Neapolis, Lupus watched the blacksmith in awe. Vulcan had been rowing for nearly an hour. He had only paused twice: first to shrug off the cloak meant to protect him from the rain of gravel and ash, and later to strip off even his tunic. Now he sat in a loincloth, his powerful chest and arms dripping with sweat. The veins stood out on his arms and hands, pumping blood to muscles that must be screaming with pain.

The blacksmith's gentle face was frozen in a grimace. It was bloody and blackened with a hundred tiny cuts and scorches. His lips were cracked and dry. Lupus knew that ashes had burnt the inside of Vulcan's mouth, as they had his, and that it must be agony for him to swallow.

Lupus took a swig from the water gourd Rectina had given them and then offered it to the smith.

His teeth bared, Vulcan shook his head and continued to pull with every fibre of his being towards Misenum, still four miles distant.

'Does Vulcan know that Pliny is his father?' asked Flavia.

Tascius shook his head. 'I don't believe he does

know. Unless of course he's reached Rectina at Herculaneum and she's told him.'

He gazed towards the blue bay and the volcano beyond. The tree-shaped pillar of ash which rose from Vesuvius was no longer white but a dirty grey. The ground still trembled beneath them.

'I suspected Rectina was pregnant with Pliny's baby. When he was born, I saw the clubfoot. That was when I knew he wasn't mine.' He drained his cup again. 'I named him Publius.' Tascius gave a hollow laugh. 'After my father.'

'Did you ever tell your wife what you suspected?' asked Aristo.

Tascius shook his head. 'I didn't want to lose her. I loved her, you see. Later I couldn't accuse her because . . .' Tascius refilled his cup with undiluted wine. 'The world will soon end. May as well tell you everything.

'Soon after the baby was born, I'd finished my military service. We decided to move to Rectina's Herculaneum villa. Only took two slaves with us. The rest were due to arrive in a day or two, with our belongings. It was a tiring journey. Rectina went to have a nap with the baby.

'Somehow I found myself in Rectina's room. The baby lay next to her on the couch. I remember he was wrapped up tightly in swaddling clothes. I picked him up. He opened his eyes. Great dark eyes like Rectina's.

'I carried him to the window. A low window with iron bars. Overlooking vineyards. I rested the baby on the sill against the bars. Then I went outside.'

Tascius got up from his couch and stood near the

colonnade, where the shade ended and the sunshine began. His back was to them now but they could still hear his voice.

'If the baby had cried, or made the slightest noise. But he didn't. From outside the window it was easy enough to pull him through the bars.

'I saddled a horse. Rode to Pompeii and left him in some bushes by the river. Slave-girls were washing their clothes nearby. He began to cry as I rode off. I knew he would be found.'

Tascius paused for a moment, resting his head against one of the cool white columns.

'On my way back to the villa, I stopped at Herculaneum to see an old friend. In case anyone should ask where I'd been. Had a cup of wine with him. When I returned at dusk, the house was in uproar. Rectina was . . . I thought she might be relieved to be rid of the baby. But her anguish was terrible. I never wanted to hurt her.'

There was a distant rumble from the volcano and another tremor shook the villa. Tascius's wine-cup, which he had left near the edge of the table, fell and shattered on the marble floor. Tascius did not turn around and no one else moved.

'The next morning I rode back to Pompeii. Searched the river bank. Made enquiries. Posted rewards. Punished our house-slaves. But the baby had vanished.

'Later, I thought that if Rectina had another child perhaps she would forget the first one. But there were no more babies. Rectina's womb had closed up with grief. Or perhaps the gods were punishing me.' He turned and looked at them.

'When Rectina took in that first little orphan girl, she seemed happy again. I allowed her to keep the baby. And eventually eight more. You've seen how I love them. How much they love me. I'm a good father.' His face relaxed for a moment. Then he frowned and walked over to the shattered wine-cup. He knelt beside it and began picking up the shards of clay.

'Then when *he* appeared at the Vulcanalia yesterday, she fainted. I brought her back here. When she revived she desperately wanted to know where he was. I told her I didn't know. She looked at me and said "It was our son, wasn't it, Titus?" and I said "Not our son, *your* son." She asked what I meant. At last I said what I had never said before: "That cripple was never mine. He was Pliny's child." She looked at me. And I think . . . For the first time she realised what I had done all those years ago.'

Tascius stood and squeezed his thumb where he had pricked it on one of the shards.

His voice faltered. 'Then Rectina asked me where he was. And may the gods forgive me. I said . . . I said, "Who? Pliny, or your son?"'

Tascius looked at the drop of red blood on his thumb.

'Early this morning she took my daughters and left me forever. Now I am truly alone.'

Lupus and Vulcan were less than two miles from Misenum, with the harbour in clear sight, when something struck the blacksmith's forehead and knocked him backwards.

At first Lupus thought Vulcan was dead. He crawled

forward and pressed his fingertips against Vulcan's neck, as he had once seen Mordecai do. After a moment he felt a pulse, weak but steady.

As he took his hand away, Lupus noticed his fingertips were covered in blood. The blow had left an ugly gash at Vulcan's hairline. He found the still smoking pumice and weighed it in his hand. It was an ugly chunk of rock, denser and heavier than the pumice which had fallen so far. It must have struck Vulcan a glancing blow. A direct hit would surely have killed him.

Lupus stood up, planted his feet apart to stop the boat from rocking and calculated the distance to the harbour. A mile. A mile and a half at most. He could try to row but first he would have to shift Vulcan's powerful body and that would take too long.

It would be quicker to swim. He had covered that distance a month before, but he had been strong then and it had been a fine, fair day.

Now the sky was raining ash and gravel. And ugly lumps of clay mixed with pumice, like the one that had struck Vulcan. Lupus fingered the oilcloth pouch around his neck, Rectina's message to Pliny. He knew it was the only hope for Clio and her sisters.

He stripped off his tunic, took a deep breath and jumped.

SCROLL XXVIII

As Lupus plunged into the bay he almost cried out. The salt water made every tiny cut and burn on his face and body sting. It felt as if a hundred needles were pricking his skin.

He knew salt water was good for surface wounds. He had heard Doctor Mordecai telling one of his patients, a man with sores on his skin, to bathe in the sea.

But this water had a scum of ash floating on its surface and his back was exposed to a steady rain of debris from the volcano.

Soon, Lupus began to tire. He had been up since before dawn, had ridden for two hours, had carried Clio at least half a mile. Now his arms ached and his lungs could not take in enough air.

He stopped to tread water for a moment. He could see a man-made breakwater no more than half a mile distant and beyond it the masts which marked the naval port. He could even make out the silhouette of three poplars on one of the hills overlooking the harbour. Those three trees marked his goal, the admiral's home.

Hundreds, maybe thousands of lives, depended on him. He took a breath and struck out again.

★

'Here! Give me your hand, boy. Up you come. By Hercules! What have you done to yourself? And what were you doing paddling about among the Roman fleet? This is a restricted area, you know. Soldiers and marines only. Caius! Have you got a blanket? An old cloak? Anything? Yes, that'll do. Wrap this round yourself, boy. Better? Now under ordinary circumstances I'd have to report you to – Hey! Where are you going? Come back, you mongrel! That's not your cloak!'

At the Villa Pomponiana in Stabia, Nubia ran to one of the dining-room columns.

'Bug-boats!' She cried and pointed towards the bay. From beneath a couch, Nipur sensed her excitement and began to bark.

'Bug-boats?' said Tascius, frowning at the slave-girl.

'There!' cried Jonathan. 'Coming out from behind the promontory. Warships! One, two, three, four . . .'

'By the gods, you have good eyesight.' Tascius squinted. 'Yes . . . yes! I see them. Looks like the imperial fleet!'

'Those ships are powered by oar, are they not?' asked Aristo.

'Yes,' replied Tascius, 'by both oar and sail.'

'Then they can go anywhere, even against the wind.'

'But where *are* they going?' asked Jonathan.

'I'd guess Herculaneum,' said Tascius.

'It's the admiral!' cried Flavia, jumping to her feet and clapping her hands. 'It's Admiral Pliny! He's launched the imperial Roman fleet to rescue the people at the foot of the volcano!'

Jonathan added, 'And please, God, to rescue us, too!'

Lupus sat on a couch in the warship's open cabin, wearing an oversized tunic and sipping warm honeyed wine. The sleek warship sped over the water, its banks of oars rising and falling in time to the rowers' chant. Behind them followed a dozen similar warships.

Admiral Pliny reclined beside Lupus. In his hand was Rectina's note. The admiral had read it several times but now he unfolded the papyrus again. Pliny's scribe Phrixus stood nearby, his stylus poised over a wax tablet.

'She writes that she is terrified by the danger threatening her and she begs me to rescue her and her daughters from an awful fate . . .' Pliny read it aloud and then looked down at Lupus. 'It's a good thing you came when you did. Phrixus and I were just about to take a much smaller boat to investigate the phenomenon. I had no idea the volcano posed such a threat to the inhabitants.'

As they passed the promontory of Puteoli, Lupus thought of Vulcan, lying unconscious in a rowing boat. He stood and gazed over the water, then grunted and pointed to his right.

'What is it? What do you see?'

Lupus walked back and forth in front of the admiral, imitating Vulcan's limp.

'Have you injured your foot? Are you hurt?'

Lupus shook his head vigorously, then snatched the wax tablet from the scribe's startled hands. Phrixus uttered an exclamation, but Pliny held up his hand. They both watched as the boy wrote something in the wax.

Lupus had been studying with Aristo for over a month and he had learned his alphabet and a few basic words. He had never written the name Vulcan before, but now he tried, sounding out each letter in his head as Aristo had taught him. Then he handed the tablet to Pliny. On it he had written in neat capitals:

VOLCAN

'Yes, my boy, very astute! The phenomenon we are witnessing is indeed a "volcano". I never suspected that Vesuvius –'

Lupus snatched the tablet back from the startled admiral and added two words. He showed Pliny the tablet again.

VOLCAN IN A BOAT

Then he pointed out to sea.

'Over there!' cried Phrixus. 'I see something. A small rowing boat! The blacksmith Vulcan must be in that boat.'

SCROLL XXIX

Flavia helped Jonathan tie a linen napkin over the lower half of his face. He had soaked it in water to stop the fine ash from filling his lungs.

She finished off the knot at the back and they rejoined Nubia between two pillars of the dining room. They watched the Roman fleet move across the bay like insects crawling across a polished jade table.

Occasionally, they felt the ground vibrate and saw the tree-shaped plume of ash thicken and change colour. The air had been growing denser, and it was harder to make out details.

'Have they reached the coast?' asked Aristo anxiously.

'Bug-boats stop,' said Nubia quietly.

'Are they disembarking?' Tascius asked.

'What are they doing?' Jonathan held Pliny's sachet of herbs under his napkin and Flavia noticed he wasn't wheezing.

'I don't know . . .' said Tascius, wiping the sweat from his face with his forearm. 'Perhaps the shore is blocked. It's hard to tell. It seems to be getting dark early today.'

'It *is* dark, isn't it?' murmured Aristo.

'Look at the sun,' said Flavia. 'It's as red as blood.'

'The sun will be turned to darkness and the moon to blood at the end of this world,' said a voice behind them and they all turned to look.

Mordecai slowly pulled the linen cloth over Xanthus's face. Then he bowed his head and recited the prayer for the dead.

Lupus watched as Pliny's sailors lifted Vulcan out of the rowing boat into the warship and laid him in the cabin, on the admiral's couch.

'By the gods, he looks dreadful!' wheezed Pliny.

The smith's burns and cuts had not been washed by salt water, as Lupus's had. His face and body were terrible to see. For a long moment the admiral stood looking down at Vulcan. Then he turned to Lupus.

'He rowed all this way from Rectina's villa? Impossible!'

Lupus shrugged.

'And then when he was hit by debris from the volcano you swam the rest of the way?'

Lupus nodded and Pliny frowned. 'If I believed in the gods . . .' The admiral shook his head and opened his canvas parasol. 'Come Lupus, if you're not too tired you can help us continue our observations.'

Lupus was exhausted, but he followed the admiral and his scribe to the front of the boat. The three of them leaned over the bronze beak of the ship and gazed across the water towards the volcano. Behind them the oarsmen sang their fast chant and the oars rose and fell in time.

The breeze was with them, too, and presently Lupus thought he could make out the red roof of Rectina's villa by a row of cypress trees. Was that a figure standing on the jetty? Or just a post? The ash made it hard to see.

The wind must have shifted slightly, for suddenly a shower of gravel and pieces of flaming rock rattled down onto the parasol.

'Fascinating,' murmured Pliny, and turned to his scribe. 'Phrixus, make a note of this: ashes falling hotter and thicker as we approach the shore, mixed with bits of pumice and blackened . . . um, stones, charred and cracked by the flames.' Pliny abruptly broke off in a coughing fit.

Suddenly the lookout cried, 'Shallow water and rocks ahead, admiral!'

Pliny leaned over the rail and then whirled to face the men.

'Stop!' he wheezed, holding up his hand and then, 'Back row, back row!' He collapsed into another fit of coughing.

The oarsmen deftly flipped their blades, then manoeuvred to stop the forward movement of the ship.

Lupus saw one of the officers quickly run a pennant up a rope. It fluttered at the top of the mainmast, warning the other warships of danger.

'By the gods,' muttered Pliny as his coughing subsided. 'The shore is blocked with debris. We'll never reach them now!'

As he spoke a flaming boulder the size of a millstone hit the water less than three yards ahead of them. Its impact rocked the boat and spattered them with hot water.

'The water's hot, almost boiling!' gasped Pliny. 'Phrixus, make a note of that!'

The scribe ignored his request.

'Master!' he cried. 'Your parasol is on fire! Quickly!'

Pliny hurled the flaming parasol overboard and the three of them hurried back to the shelter of the cabin as another shower of hot gravel rained down on their heads. Once under cover, the admiral turned and peered towards the shore again.

'We can't go forward,' said Pliny. 'I see no way to get to Rectina.'

Behind them, on the admiral's couch, Vulcan groaned.

'Admiral!' cried the helmsman. 'We must turn back now. The mountain is hurling down great stones at us and the shore is completely blocked by them. if we remain here the fleet will be destroyed. We must go back!'

'No,' wheezed Pliny after a moment. 'No retreat. I shall not go back!' He thought for a moment and then snapped his fingers.

'I know what we'll do! Send the other warships back to Misenum. They must take shelter there. I cannot afford to lose the entire imperial fleet. As for us, we will make for Tascius at Stabia, in case Rectina has been able to make her way back to him.'

Lupus grasped the admiral's arm and shook his head violently. He knew Rectina would wait for them at her villa.

'No! I've made up my mind,' announced the admiral, impatiently shaking Lupus's hand from his arm. He turned to the helmsman and said: 'The wind is behind us, we'll make excellent time. Those are your new orders: head for Stabia. "Fortune favours the brave",' he quoted. And added to Phrixus, 'You can write that down.'

'Behold!' cried Nubia. 'Bug-boats going home.'

'Are they?' cried Tascius, wiping his eyes with his hand, 'Jupiter! My eyes sting. Can't see properly. It does look as if – but the fleet hasn't had time to take on passengers.'

'Nubia's right,' said Jonathan miserably. 'They're turning back.'

'Jupiter blast it!' cursed Tascius, turning away.

'Be happy!' cried Nubia, still watching the bay. 'One bug-boat comes here!'

Lupus stood at the stern of Pliny's flagship and looked back across the water at Herculaneum, disappearing into the fog of ash behind them. The cloak drawn over his head and shoulders hardly protected him from the angry rain of hot gravel, but he did not care.

His eyes were fixed on a tiny figure in orange, where the silver-green olive trees met the water.

The ash in the air stung his eyes and made them stream, but he did not blink. He watched the figure grow smaller and smaller, until finally he could no longer see her.

SCROLL XXX

From a distance, the approaching warship had looked clean and sleek, but as it drew near, Flavia saw that it was smudged with soot and scorch marks.

She was standing between Jonathan and Nubia beneath the umbrella pines near Tascius's private jetty. The three friends and their dogs watched the oars rise and fall like the wings of a bird, then dip to slow the warship. Carried forward by its own speed, the warship slid up beside Tascius's private jetty, just nudging his private yacht.

The two slaves guarding Tascius's boat had also been sheltering under the pines. Now they ran onto the short pier, caught ropes thrown by the sailors, and tied them firmly to the docking posts.

There was a strong swell in the scummy water. The ship rose and fell as the water slapped against the jetty, making it difficult to disembark, but finally the sailors manoeuvred the boarding plank over the side. The first person off the ship was an exhausted boy in an oversized tunic.

'Lupus!' Flavia and her friends cried, and rushed forward to greet him.

Two sailors carried Vulcan's stretcher up the marble

steps and into Tascius's dining-room. The smith was still unconscious, so they lifted him onto a dining couch. Miriam propped him up on the black and white silk cushions and Mordecai began to bathe his head wound with vinegar and oil.

Lupus, red-eyed with grief and exhaustion, took a long drink of water, climbed onto another couch and instantly fell asleep.

A moment later Admiral Pliny puffed up the steps behind them. He went straight to Tascius, who was staring down at the unconscious blacksmith.

'Is Rectina here?' asked Pliny. 'Has she arrived back from Herculaneum?'

Tascius looked up at him, speechless.

'She sent word for me to rescue her,' said the admiral, 'but I'm afraid there was no way we could reach her. I'm sorry, old friend. I'd hoped . . .' He stopped to catch his breath and look around.

'Flavia Gemina! You're here! And Mordecai ben Ezra, too. Excellent. You can have a look at my sailors, doctor. Many are suffering burns and cuts.' He turned back to Tascius.

'My dear Titus. May we make use of your excellent baths before dinner?'

'A bath? You want a bath?'

'If you don't mind.'

'I've very few slaves left,' stammered Tascius, 'No one to light the furnace for hot water. There's always the cold plunge . . .'

'Excellent.' The admiral mopped his forehead. 'Just what's needed on such a hot and stifling day. Bring your tablet and stylus, Phrixus, we'll continue to take notes. Would anyone else like to accompany me?'

'Wait!' cried Jonathan, his voice slightly muffled behind his napkin. 'You can't just go and bathe as if nothing were wrong. There's a volcano erupting less than five miles away!'

'Aren't you going to rescue us?' Flavia asked.

'Sailing us away in your bug-boat?' said Nubia.

'Out of the question, I'm afraid,' wheezed the admiral. 'It's already growing dark. My men and I need to eat and by the time we've dined it will be night. I suggest we all get a good night's sleep and set off at first light tomorrow morning. It's really not too bad down here at Stabia, you know. Not compared to Herculaneum and Pompeii.'

The tree-shaped cloud which stood over the volcano was deep red in the light of the sinking sun. Jonathan, Flavia and Nubia stood watching it.

'If we had walked south along the coastal road,' Jonathan said, 'we would be miles away by now.' His voice was muffled behind his napkin.

'I think it's easing off,' said Flavia.

'What?'

Flavia lifted her own napkin away from her mouth. 'I said I think the volcano is stopping. The noise isn't as loud as it was before.'

'The floor is not shivering so much now,' said Nubia. She wore a napkin, too.

'I guess so.' Jonathan slumped against one of the columns. 'I just wish we were far away from here. I wish we were back home in Ostia.'

Flavia tried to cheer Jonathan.

'This was a good idea of yours, wearing napkins.'

After a hasty dinner of ash-coated bread and cheese, everyone had followed Jonathan's example and tied moistened napkins over nose and mouth to keep the fine ash out. Admiral Pliny, still damp from his bath, agreed that it helped his breathlessness. His sailors, playing dice on the floor, all wore napkins. Even Vulcan, eyes closed and face pale against the black silk cushions, had a cloth draped over the lower half of his face.

'That can't be a good omen,' said Jonathan, looking back into the dining-room.

A combination of the sun's horizontal rays and the fine ash created a thick red light which filled the dining-room.

'It looks as if the room is full of blood,' said Jonathan. 'And everyone looks like robbers. Robbers in a room full of blood. Or am I seeing things again?'

'You're not seeing things,' said Flavia. With napkins tied over the lower halves of their faces, they did look like masked bandits.

Flavia looked at the others. For the first time she really saw people's eyes and eyebrows. She had never noticed how pale and rumpled Pliny's eyebrows were, or how beautifully Miriam's dark ones set off her eyes. Mordecai and Jonathan had handsome brows, whereas Vulcan and Tascius each seemed to have one heavy, straight eyebrow that met above the nose.

Suddenly Flavia gasped as she had a flash of pure revelation. Taking a deep breath she turned to Pliny.

'Admiral Pliny,' she began, her heart pounding, 'what was the real reason you asked us to find Vulcan?'

SCROLL XXXI

Though the sun had not set, the red light in the dining-room had become a thick purple gloom. One of Tascius's three remaining slaves, the spotty messenger boy named Gutta, began to light the oil-lamps in the villa and the torches in the garden.

'Why did I ask you to find Vulcan?' said Pliny. 'Why do you think?'

'I think you knew he was the long-lost son of Rectina, my uncle's neighbour, and I think you hoped that we would lead Vulcan to her.'

'Very astute, my dear. You're almost right. I wasn't sure he was Rectina's long-lost son, but I suspected it.' Pliny's black eyes were bright above his napkin. 'The first time I saw him I knew he looked familiar. A few days later I realised who he reminded me of: Rectina! I felt sure he must be the kidnapped child of Rectina and Tascius. I went back to see him again but –'

'Liar!' Tascius's voice was muffled behind his cloth, but the anger in it was audible.

'What?' the admiral's eyes grew wider.

'Vulcan isn't *my* son, is he?' Tascius had risen to his feet.

'What do you mean?'

Tascius was trembling. 'He's yours!'

'I don't know what you're talking about.' Pliny sounded genuinely surprised.

'I know that you and Rectina were lovers! This *cripple* is the result of your betrayal!'

Pliny stood and pulled the napkin away from his nose and mouth.

'How dare you say such a thing? Who gave you such an idea?'

'You weren't content to steal my father's affections. You had to take those of my wife as well.'

A look of genuine dismay replaced the anger on Pliny's face. 'My dear Titus,' he said gravely. 'You are very much mistaken. Rectina and I have great affection and respect for one another, but we were never lovers.'

'Liar!' said Tascius, tearing his own cloth away from his face and throwing it onto the ground. 'This cripple is your son, not mine.' Tascius marched over to Vulcan's couch and wrenched the boot from his right foot. 'Look! Here is proof of the gods' displeasure!'

Everyone stared in horror at Vulcan's twisted foot. It was red and rounded like a clenched fist. Miriam stifled a sob and hid her face in her father's robes. On his couch, Vulcan stirred and groaned. His long eyelashes fluttered.

Mordecai stepped forward, his dark eyes angry between turban and napkin. 'You can't possibly take this as proof that he isn't your son.' He picked up the blacksmith's boot and struggled to replace it.

'But he isn't. He's not my son.'

Flavia turned towards Tascius.

'Yes he is!' she cried. 'Can't you see the resemblance between you? Look at his eyebrows! If he has Rectina's

335

mouth and nose and eyes, well, Vulcan has your eyebrows!'

'Eyebrows!' snorted Tascius. 'Eyebrows, indeed!'

'She's right, father.' Vulcan opened his eyes. 'Mother told me the truth. I am your son, your only son, whom you abandoned.'

Admiral Pliny stared at Tascius. 'You? *You* are the one who abandoned him?'

Tascius hung his head.

'You abandoned him because you thought he was mine?'

Tascius nodded.

'Do you realise what you've done?' said Pliny. 'You abandoned your own child, lived a lie for seventeen years, and ultimately drove your wife and daughters away, probably to their deaths.'

Tascius lifted his head and stared at Pliny stupidly, like a boxer who has received too many blows.

'Rectina never loved anyone but you,' said Pliny steadily. 'She was always faithful to you, just as a Roman matron should be.' He gestured towards Vulcan. 'And this young man . . . Titus. Listen to me. This is one of the most courageous young men I have ever known. He is your son, Titus, your own flesh and blood. And you should be proud of him. As proud of him as your own father was of you.'

Everyone stared at Tascius as he slowly turned to look at Vulcan. In the flickering lamplight his eyes were shadowed.

'Is it true?' he said. 'Are you . . . ?'

Vulcan turned his head away and closed his eyes. He

was weeping. To the north the volcano rumbled ominously.

Tascius took a faltering step towards the couch.

'Vulcan?'

The grey-haired soldier stood over the dining couch and took the young man's battered hands in his own. He studied them, then kissed them gently and pressed them to his face. His shoulders shook and soon Vulcan's hands were wet with his father's tears.

Presently, Tascius pulled the signet ring from the third finger of his hand and held it up for all to see.

'Great Jove!' he began, but his voice broke and he had to start again. 'Great Jove! I declare in front of all these witnesses that this young man is my true son and heir.' He gently pushed the ring onto the little finger of Vulcan's left hand. 'From this moment on, all that I have is his, and he shall no longer be known as Vulcan, but by his given name: Publius Tascius Pomponianus.'

'I can't think of him as "Publius",' whispered Flavia to Jonathan and Nubia. 'He'll always be Vulcan.'

'I know,' agreed Jonathan, and Nubia nodded, too.

It was long past sundown and outside it was pitch black, except for where the torches burned.

Admiral Pliny had gone to bed, but none of the rest of them could sleep. No one wanted to be far from the lamplight, and no one wanted to be alone.

Gutta was sweeping ash from the floor and some of Pliny's sailors were still playing dice at a low table.

Tascius had pulled a chair up beside his son's couch and for a long time the two of them had been deep in quiet conversation. Every so often Tascius raised a cup of well-watered wine to the young man's lips and helped him to drink. Sometimes they wept together. Presently they called Mordecai over and Flavia heard the three men discussing the meaning of the donkey riddle.

She approached them almost shyly.

Vulcan looked up at her and smiled.

'Hello, Flavia Gemina,' he said. 'I must thank you.'

'For what?' said Flavia. 'I didn't think about your feelings. All I cared about was the treasure.'

'I don't believe you,' smiled the blacksmith. 'I think you are a girl who seeks the truth. And your desire for knowledge helped me find my parents: my mother . . .' he swallowed, 'and my father.'

Tascius gripped his son's hand so hard that the knuckles grew white.

'How can I thank you?' whispered the young man.

'Will you tell me what the riddle really means, and what the treasure is?'

SCROLL XXXII

Lupus had finally woken from his deep sleep. Although the night was stifling and hot, he pulled a linen cover round his shoulders and came to sit with Flavia, Jonathan, and Nubia on the floor beside Vulcan's couch.

'So. You want to know the meaning of the riddle and what the treasure is?' The young blacksmith tried to sit forward and then sank back weakly against his cushions.

'Careful, Publius,' said Tascius, and patted his son's shoulder.

'I think I know what some of it means,' said Flavia. 'I think "jackass" is a password for Christians, because you worship the donkey.'

There was a pause. Then Jonathan yelped, 'What?'

'I saw you worshipping the donkey in the stables,' explained Flavia.

'We don't worship a donkey!' Jonathan cried. 'Our God is invisible.'

'Oh,' said Flavia.

'But you were right to think it's a password,' said Vulcan. 'Our faith is illegal so we must be careful. The donkey is just one of many codewords, which show us aspects of our God.'

'So your invisible God is a bit like a shepherd and a bit like a donkey?' said Flavia.

'And he's a bit like a dolphin and an anchor and an eagle and a warrior,' said Jonathan. 'That's my favourite: the warrior.'

'But how is he like a jackass?'

'You tell me,' said Vulcan.

'Gentle and patient and humble?'

'Exactly.'

'And with big ears and soft fur?' said Nubia gravely. Then she giggled.

'Hey! Nubia's first joke!' cried Jonathan, and slapped the African girl on the back.

Vulcan smiled, too. 'Also, each letter of the word jackass – *ASINE* – has another deeper meaning. If you study them, the letters show you how to journey along the Way.'

'What way?'

'The Way to joy and fulfilment in this life, and Paradise in the next.'

'That's the treasure beyond imagining?' said Flavia.

Vulcan nodded.

'So it's not *real* treasure?' She couldn't help feeling disappointed.

'Of course it is, Flavia!' said Vulcan. 'You of all people should know that sometimes the greatest treasure is knowledge. Knowing how to meet with God.' He looked at his father. 'Knowing how to forgive. Knowing how to find joy in a world of pain, and afterwards the greatest treasure of all. Eternal life. Not in a dark and shadowy underworld, but in a green and sunny Paradise, reunited with those we love. What treasure could be better than that?'

Behind them, Miriam had begun to weep.

Vulcan looked at her with concern.

'She's worried about Uncle Gaius,' explained Flavia.

'Where is he?'

'He went to Pompeii and Oplontis to warn the inhabitants about the volcano, remember?' said Flavia.

'And he isn't back yet?'

Flavia shook her head.

'It's dark now,' said Nubia. 'Miriam worried that dark.'

Vulcan nodded, and looked at Miriam for a long time.

'And you're worried about Clio, aren't you?' said Jonathan to Lupus.

Lupus nodded.

They were all silent for a few minutes. Then Nubia reached out and touched the finger on which Lupus usually wore his ring: 'Give wolf-ring to Clio?' she asked.

Lupus nodded again.

Suddenly, Tigris whimpered and emerged from beneath a couch where he'd been sheltering with Scuto and Nipur. He padded to the steps and sniffed the murky air.

'What is it, boy?' asked Jonathan, getting to his feet and following him. 'What do you see out there?'

The others peered out into the darkness towards the volcano.

Then they saw it too.

Moving straight towards them out of the ash-black night, illuminated by the torches on the lawn, were two gleaming yellow eyes: the eyes of a wounded beast.

Tigris barked and wagged his small tail, but the rest of them stood frozen as the creature moved into the torchlight.

'Ferox!' cried Jonathan. 'It's Ferox!'

From the other side of the room, Miriam gave a cry and ran to the step that led down into darkness. Then she screamed.

Ferox was bloody and wounded. One ear was torn from his head and his left rear leg hung useless. The foam round his muzzle was flecked with blood and his breath came in wheezing gasps. He looked up at them and whined.

'Master of the Universe!' whispered Mordecai and cautiously stepped forward to examine the wounded dog. Ferox whined again and wagged his tail feebly. As Mordecai reached out a hand to touch the matted fur on the dog's chest, Ferox growled softly and flinched. Mordecai looked down at his fingertips. They were smeared with blood.

'These wounds were inflicted by man and not by volcanic rock,' said Mordecai grimly.

'He must have been protecting Gaius!' cried Miriam. She clutched her father's arm.

Ferox turned as if to go back into the night, then looked over his shoulder at them and whined imploringly.

'Ferox want to follow,' said Nubia, turning her amber eyes on Flavia and Jonathan.

'No way I'm going out there,' muttered Jonathan.

'Uncle Gaius out there maybe,' suggested Nubia.

'Gaius?' cried Miriam. 'Out there? Then I'm going to follow Ferox!' She hurried down the steps onto the ash-covered lawn and wrenched one of the garden torches from its holder. Then she turned to look back up at them. With the yellow flames flickering on her black curls, and all but her eyes hidden by a cloth, she looked like a beautiful bandit.

'I'll come with you,' said Tascius. 'It's time I showed half the courage you all have.'

'We'll come, too!' offered two of the sailors. They were gazing at Miriam in awe, and as she moved off into the swirling ash they hurried after her.

Flavia and her friends looked at each other. Without a word they hurried down the steps, grasped torches and followed the others into the night.

As they followed the wounded animal into the darkness, the globes of light from their pine torches lit the falling ash. It floated down around them like warm black snow, muffling every sound except for the constant thunder of the volcano.

Chest deep in ash, Ferox limped ahead, his left hind leg dangling uselessly. Occasionally he would stop and utter a soft whine, looking back to make sure they were still following. Nubia whispered words of encouragement in her own language. They followed him across the ash-covered lawn, through the open gate and up the drive.

Presently, they could hear the noise of pack animals and carriage wheels and see the dim globes of torchlight through the ash. They were approaching the coastal road. A steady stream of refugees were making their way along it towards the south.

They found his body at the roadside shrine of Mercury. It was already covered with two inches of ash. Ferox nosed the still form of his master and whined up at them pitifully. Miriam cried out and ran forward. One of the sailors took her torch as she knelt and brushed away the ash.

'Gaius!' she cried, 'Gaius, my love. Speak to me. Tell me you're still alive!'

She pulled back the cloak from his head. Gaius's face was cut and bleeding. His nose had been broken and there was an ugly knife wound across his left cheek-bone. One eye was swollen shut but the other flickered and then opened. As he looked up at Miriam, one corner of his mouth pulled up in what looked to Flavia like a grimace.

But she knew it was a smile.

SCROLL XXXIII

'I don't know if he'll live,' said Mordecai gravely. 'The stab wound in his chest pierced a lung. His leg is broken and he has been badly beaten. He is also suffering from a number of dog bites.'

'But you have to save him, father,' cried Miriam. 'He saved Gaius's life. Without him Gaius would be dead now, buried by ash!'

They were back in Tascius's dining-room. Mordecai knelt on a blanket spread on the floor and examined Ferox. Jonathan assisted his father.

Flavia's uncle Gaius lay on a couch nearby. He had eaten some bread and cheese and had drained a jug of diluted wine. Now Miriam was gently sponging his cuts and wounds with a vinegar-soaked sea-sponge.

'He saved my life . . .' Gaius's lip was swollen where he had been hit. 'Four of them and a huge mastiff. Wanted the horse. Ferox killed the mastiff and wounded two of the men. Couldn't fight other two off. They beat me. Took horse.' He closed his eyes from the effort and Miriam put her cool finger gently on his battered lips.

'Shhh! Don't speak, my love,' she said. 'Father will do everything he can to save him.'

When Mordecai finished dressing Ferox's wounds he got to his feet. 'The only thing we can do now is pray.'

Ferox lay on the blanket, panting. He rolled his eyes up at the doctor and then over towards Gaius. He whined softly.

'Yes,' said Mordecai quietly. 'He's alive. You saved him. Good dog.' As he spoke, Jonathan bent and placed something in the folds of the blanket, then stepped back. Tail wagging, Tigris sniffed Ferox. Then the puppy licked the big dog's face and curled up beside him. Ferox lowered his big head, uttered a deep sigh, and slept.

It was after midnight when the mountain exploded. None of them were really sleeping, apart from Pliny, whose snores could be heard by those making their way to or from the latrine. The rest dozed in the dining-room or talked quietly together, waiting for the dawn.

Suddenly a brilliant orange flash lit the room and a moment later the whole house trembled under a deafening wave of sound. Everyone looked at the growing column of fire which rose slowly up from the mountain. In its light they could see that the top of Vesuvius was completely gone.

'Jupiter,' muttered Tascius. 'It's getting worse.'

Another quake shook the house and Flavia actually saw the columns sway back and forth. Some of the lamps fell to the floor and shattered, spilling hot oil. A snake of fire slipped from one shattered clay lamp, writhed across the floor and down the steps, then died.

Jonathan staggered into the room from the direction of the latrines.

'Come quickly,' he cried, his voice muffled behind his cloth. 'Pliny's door is blocked. He'll be trapped!'

Mordecai, Tascius and a dozen of Pliny's sailors hurried after Jonathan. Flavia and Nubia followed.

No one had swept the courtyard and it had quickly filled up with ash and bits of pumice stone. The level of the debris was almost up to Flavia's knees. The sailors tried to wade through the grey ash, cursing as they went.

'It's hardening,' said one of them.

'Like cement,' confirmed the other.

They tried to open the wooden door of the bedroom, but it wouldn't budge.

'He must be terrified!' cried Flavia. 'He's probably been crying out for hours.'

One of the sailors put his ear to the door and the other one pressed his forefinger to his lips. But there was no need. From right across the courtyard and even above the rumble of the volcano, they could all hear the admiral snoring.

After nearly half an hour, the sailors had chipped away enough of the hardened ash to open Pliny's door. The tapping had woken Phrixus, who helped by pushing the door from inside. At last he was able to help his master through the narrow opening and into the ash-filled courtyard.

'What do you want?' grumbled Pliny irritably. 'Why have you woken me?'

'Well, apart from the fact that the mountain is melting like wax, the house is falling down around us and you were about to be buried alive, no reason,' muttered Jonathan.

'Haven't you felt any of the quakes?' cried Tascius.

He helped his friend into the dining-room. 'And don't you see those sheets of fire flaring up on Vesuvius?'

The admiral peered through the columns towards the mountain.

'Bonfires,' he announced after a moment.

'Bonfires?' echoed Mordecai.

'Yes,' the admiral wheezed. 'No doubt they flared up when cowardly peasants left their homes in a hurry and their hearths caught fire.'

A huge flash lit the sky, silhouetting the decapitated cone of Vesuvius for an instant.

'And that?' asked Aristo.

'An empty house catching fire, from the sparks showering down upon it. Nothing to worry about. Let me go back to sleep and wake me at dawn.'

There was another explosion and again the sky was lurid red for a long moment. Far away they could hear people screaming.

'See,' gestured Pliny. 'Cowardly peasants. Nothing to worry about, I say. Back to bed . . .'

Abruptly, the whole house seemed to rock on its foundations. From somewhere nearby there was an enormous crash and a scream.

Gutta the slave-boy hurried in. 'The roof of the baths has just caved in!'

'Anyone hurt?' asked Tascius in alarm.

'No,' said the slave, and fainted.

'We must get out of here before the whole house comes down around our heads,' said Mordecai, passing a tiny bottle beneath Gutta's nose.

'But you're tending the ill and wounded,' wheezed

Pliny, gesturing at Gaius and Vulcan on their couches. 'How can they travel?'

'We could take Vulcan's donkey,' suggested Flavia. 'And your sailors could help, too.'

'Yes, very well,' said Pliny, staggering to remain upright as another quake shook the house. 'I suppose we could go down to the beach and see if it's possible to make our escape by ship.' He glared at the volcano. 'It does appear to be getting a little worse.'

SCROLL XXXIV

'Miriam, your hair is on fire!' screamed Flavia Gemina.

They had just set out for the beach when a shower of flaming pumice stones rained down upon them and Miriam's dark hair burst into flame.

Before Miriam could panic or run, her father had enveloped her head with his robes, smothering the flames.

'Father, it hurts,' Miriam sobbed, and Mordecai pulled her back up the steps into the dining-room. Everyone followed.

'See?' gasped the admiral. 'It's death out there. We'd do much better to remain here.'

'No,' said Mordecai. 'We must go, or I'll lose both my children.' He nodded at Jonathan, who was pale and wheezing. 'Can't you smell it?' said Mordecai. 'It's sulphur.'

'I know what we can do,' gasped Jonathan. 'Cushions! We'll tie cushions . . . to our heads. To keep off . . . the burning pumice.'

Pliny gazed at him for a moment. 'You really are the most resourceful children. Unless anyone has a better idea, I suggest we take young Jonathan's advice!'

★

With a striped silk cushion tied to his head and two across his back, Scuto led the way down to the shore.

Earlier, the fall of ash had been like silent black snow, now it was fiery rain. The volcano's rumble was deeper, angrier now, and flashes of lightning flickered ominously above its cone. Despite the muffling ash, they could hear women and children screaming and men crying out.

With cushions tied to their heads and the damp napkins still knotted to cover their noses and mouths, they made their way through the blackness down towards Tascius's jetty.

Flavia could see a line of torches extending ahead of her. There were at least fifty of them. Forty of Pliny's sailors headed the procession, followed by the admiral and Phrixus. Gaius rode the donkey, with Miriam and Mordecai walking either side of him. The sailors had chopped up the dining-room couches to make two stretchers. They carried Vulcan on one, Ferox on the other.

Nubia had showed Jonathan how to make slings for the puppies, like the ones the women in her clan made for their babies. Behind them stumbled Flavia and Lupus, flanking Aristo, who carried old Frustilla on his back. Taking up the rear was the slave-boy Gutta.

Most of them held a torch or lamp. Even so, it was darker than any night Flavia had ever known. Presently, the torches at the front slowed and stopped. Something was happening up ahead.

'What is it?' Flavia called out, then adjusted her cushion as a shower of sparks fell on her.

'Too rough,' came the reply from Mordecai, relaying

what he'd heard Pliny say. 'The sea is still too rough for sailing. There is no escape that way. We must go along the beach towards Stabia.'

Flavia had never been so tired. She tried to concentrate on just placing one foot in front of the other. She prayed to Castor and Pollux, and she prayed to Vulcan – the god of volcanoes – and not for the first time she prayed to the Shepherd. She prayed that she and her friends might live.

Earlier in the evening she had felt hopeful. It seemed as if the volcano was not going to be the disaster they had all feared.

Now she felt only despair. The sun should have risen by now, but it was darker than ever, and all her hope had been quenched by oppressive heat, darkness and exhaustion. She wished she had slept earlier, for now she could barely keep her eyes open.

The refugees had turned on their heels, so that now Gutta and Flavia led the way down along the beach while Pliny and his sailors took up the rear. It seemed as if they had been walking for hours.

There was another awful roar from the mountain behind them and everyone turned wearily to see what new terror the gods had dreamed up.

Although they were miles from Vesuvius, they all clearly saw what happened next.

Of all the horrors the volcano had produced so far, this was the worst.

As when soda is added to wine vinegar and it bubbles and froths over the edge of the cup, so a tide of fire poured down the volcano's cone. This was not a drift of warm ash falling gently from the heavens or a slow lava flow. This was a wave of yellow fire rushing towards them faster than galloping horses. The speeding flames lit up distant houses and olive groves and vineyards, and left them blazing as it passed.

Flavia saw a row of tall poplar trees explode and then burn like torches. The poplars were two or three miles distant but already the ring of fire was bearing down upon them.

'Down!' bellowed Tascius, in his commander's voice. 'Get down on the sand.'

Aristo had already eased Frustilla off his back. Now he pushed Flavia and Nubia face down onto the sand. Flavia's cushion slipped halfway off her head. She had just pushed it back in place when the wave was upon them. A roaring heat, almost unbearable, made her ears pop and sucked the air from her lungs. Then it had passed.

Hesitantly, Flavia opened her eyes. And cried out.

She was blind.

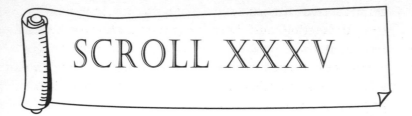

SCROLL XXXV

Men were screaming, crying to the gods for mercy or help. In her blindness, Flavia heard one of Pliny's big sailors cry out for his mother. Another shrieked, 'Let me die!' over and over.

Then a light flickered and flared and illuminated Aristo's wonderful face.

Flavia sobbed with relief. She wasn't blind. The blast of hot air had extinguished all the torches. Aristo had used a sulphur stick to rekindle his.

Soon they had all lit their torches and lamps from his one flame, and they could see each other again.

Some of the sailors hadn't been prompt in following Tascius's order. The wave of fire had knocked them to the ground, scorching their eyebrows and reddening their faces as if they'd been burnt by the sun.

'We're five miles from the mountain,' breathed Aristo, picking up Frustilla and dusting her off. 'What must that have been like for those at its foot?'

'Or those on the water,' said Mordecai grimly. His beard was singed and the locks of hair that hung from his turban burnt right away. 'It was a mercy we were not able to board the ship after all.'

'No one near Vesuvius could have survived that,' said Flavia, then bit her lip as she saw the look on

Lupus's face. Tascius stared bleakly at the mountain, too. If Rectina and her daughters had remained at Herculaneum . . .

As they turned to move south again, Flavia was aware of something holding her back. Nubia had gripped her cloak.

'Wait,' Nubia said.

Flavia looked wearily at her slave-girl, then beyond her.

Something was happening. A group of people had stopped further back along the beach.

'What?' groaned Flavia. 'What is it?'

'I think it is the old man,' said Nubia, pointing. 'The Pliny.'

The glow of several torches marked a group of figures huddled on the sand.

'Please, master.' They heard Phrixus's voice, exhausted but urgent.

Flavia turned and stumbled back towards the group on the beach. She hadn't even the strength to ask the others to wait.

The wave of fire seemed to have purified the air and for a moment she imagined it was easier to breathe. She could see the group clearly in the flickering torch-light. Someone had spread a sailcloth on the beach and the admiral was sitting on it. Phrixus knelt beside him, and as she came closer Flavia saw the slave's handsome face, smudged with soot and twisted in concern for his master. Three big sailors stood over their admiral, holding their torches and looking down helplessly.

Further back on the shore, a spark had ignited the sail of a beached ship. As the timbers caught fire it began to burn fiercely. The flames gave off a bright yellow light and illuminated the group on the sand.

Flavia sank onto the sailcloth beside Pliny and touched his shoulder. The old man lifted his head and gave her a feeble smile. The dark cushion on his head gave him an almost jaunty look. He had pulled the napkin away from his face and was breathing into the small sachet which hung from his neck. It was similar to the one he had given Jonathan, filled with herbs to bring relief for breathlessness.

Flavia suddenly felt her heart would break. What good would a little herb pouch do in this nightmare of ash, sparks and noxious gases?

The admiral tried to snap his fingers and both Phrixus and Flavia leaned nearer.

'What do you want, master?' asked Phrixus. Tears streaked the soot on his cheeks.

'Your wax tablets and stylus?' Flavia suggested.

Pliny gave another feeble smile and shook his head. His lips moved. Flavia and Phrixus both brought their ears closer. Flavia couldn't make out his words, but Phrixus understood.

'Water. He wants a little cold water . . .'

The scribe stood up and looked around desperately.

'Water!' he cried. 'Does anyone have water?'

Everyone shook their heads. Few had thought to bring water, though they would have given anything for a mouthful to wash away the ashes from their mouths. For ashes were the taste of death. Flavia suddenly saw from Pliny's face that he tasted his own death. Phrixus saw it, too.

'Water. Please bring him water!'

A short figure moved out of the gloom and knelt

beside the admiral. It was Gutta, the spotty slave from Tascius's villa. He uncorked a gourd and poured a stream of water into the admiral's thirsty mouth.

Pliny gripped the boy's wrist and drank the water greedily. At last he nodded his thanks to the slave and curled up on the canvas sheet. Flavia heard his voice, stronger now, but still barely audible. 'A little nap. That's all I need. Just a little nap.'

Suddenly the smell of rotten eggs hit the back of Flavia's throat and almost made her gag. She knew they must get away from the deadly fumes, or die.

'Sulphur!' cried Tascius, looming out of the darkness. 'We must go quickly, before we are overcome! Come on, old friend.'

Phrixus and Gutta helped the admiral to his feet. Pliny stood leaning on the two young slaves. The pillow tied to his head had slipped to one side.

'We must go, master,' cried Phrixus. 'The sulphur.'

The curtain of ash parted for a moment and they could all see the admiral, lit by the red and yellow flames of the burning boat.

Pliny gazed back at them and tried to say something. Then he collapsed, like a child's rag doll, into the arms of Phrixus and Gutta. They eased him back onto the sailcloth.

Mordecai was at his side in an instant. He loosened the admiral's clothing and pressed two fingers against the side of Pliny's neck. After a moment he put his ear to the admiral's mouth. Finally he looked up at them and slowly shook his head.

Pliny was dead.

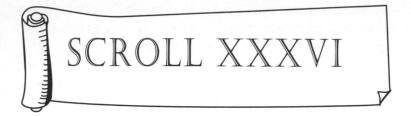
SCROLL XXXVI

They left the admiral's body there on the shore.

The sulphur fumes were still choking. Jonathan and Frustilla were both struggling for breath. One of the big Roman oarsmen took the old cook onto his back and jogged ahead, another carried Jonathan. Their fellow-sailors lit the way. Someone said the promontory was not far off. If they could get round it, the air might be clearer.

It was their only hope of survival.

To Flavia, dazed with exhaustion, everything was vague after that. They left the beach and made their way up to the coast road where the going was a little easier. Once round the promontory they found that the sulphur fumes were not as powerful, and the fall of ash was much lighter.

Beside a small cove was a seaside tavern with a boathouse attached. Many people were sheltering there, under the large brick vaults. They found a spot on the far wall and huddled against a rolled-up fishing net. Flavia was dimly aware of the faithful donkey Modestus standing patiently nearby. Then someone doused all the torches but one and she fell into a fitful sleep.

After a long time, Nubia shook Flavia awake. The tavern-keeper was bringing water round to the refugees. The small flame of his clay lamp illuminated the blackness around them.

Flavia waited for Nubia, then she took the clay beaker and drank. The water was cold and fizzy and smelled of eggs, but it washed the taste of death from her mouth. Vaguely, as if in a dream, she heard Mordecai's accented voice.

'How much is the water? I have gold.'

'Nothing. No charge,' said the innkeeper.

'But why?'

'The Master says: If you give even a cup of cold water, you will not lose your reward . . .'

Flavia drifted off into sleep again.

She dreamt of magpies carrying Rectina and her daughters up into the heavens.

She dreamt of Pliny, sailing away on a wax tablet with a sheet of papyrus for his sail. In her dream he turned back and waved at her cheerfully as he sailed towards a blue horizon.

She dreamt of Ferox playing with Scuto and the puppies in her sunny garden back home in Ostia.

She dreamt of a baby, with Miriam's dark curls and Gaius's grey eyes.

Finally she dreamt of Vulcan. He stood at his forge, his torso gleaming and polished as bronze. He looked happy. His burns and cuts had healed and both his feet were whole. He was forging armour for Achilles, the warrior son of Thetis. Then Achilles – golden Achilles – stepped into the darkness of the smithy. Vulcan handed him the armour of light and the warrior put it on.

Achilles turned to look at Flavia, who was now also in the dream. He smiled at her. Suddenly he was too bright to look at. Flavia squinted and tried to see his face. Dressed in his armour, he shone like the sun. Then she saw that he was the sun.

The endless night had ended and day had come again.

'Behold!' said a soft voice beside her. 'The sun.'

Flavia nodded and squeezed Nubia's hand.

They had survived the volcano.

FINIS

THE LAST SCROLL

Vesuvius is one of the most famous volcanoes in the world. But until it erupted in August AD 79, nobody suspected it was a volcano. We know about it from two sources.

First, we have archaeological evidence: the famous 'buried cities' at the foot of the volcano. Their remains give us a glimpse of a single day in the Roman empire.

Second, we have written evidence: two letters by Pliny's young nephew, who was staying with his uncle at Misenum when the volcano erupted.

Theories about the timing of the volcano are constantly being revised, but recent studies indicate that most people survived the first twelve hours of the eruption. It was only after midnight that a series of pyroclastic flows killed those closest to the volcano.

Admiral Pliny was a real person, as were Tascius and Rectina. Vulcan, Clio, and Phrixus were not real people. But they *could* have been.

Vulcan's riddle is also real. No one knows exactly what it means.

THE PIRATES
OF POMPEII

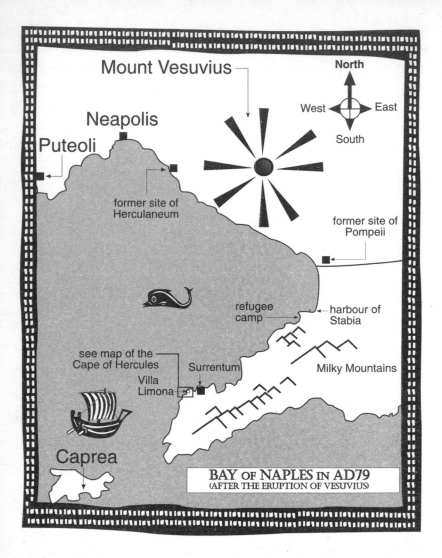

Mount Vesuvius

North

West — East

South

Neapolis

Puteoli

former site of
Herculaneum

former site of
Pompeii

refugee
camp

harbour of
Stabia

see map of the
Cape of Hercules

Surrentum

Villa
Limona

Milky Mountains

Caprea

BAY of NAPLES in AD79
(AFTER THE ERUPTION OF VESUVIUS)

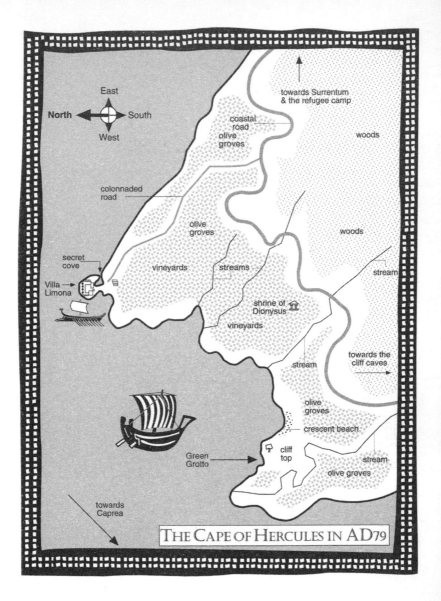

East

North ← ⊕ → South

West

towards Surrentum
& the refugee camp

coastal
road
olive
groves

woods

colonnaded
road

olive
groves

woods

secret
cove

vineyards

streams

stream

Villa
Limona

shrine of
Dionysus

stream

vineyards

towards the
cliff caves

stream

olive
groves

crescent beach

Green
Grotto

cliff
top

stream

olive groves

towards
Caprea

THE CAPE OF HERCULES IN AD79

To my husband Richard,
who feeds me

SCROLL I

The mountain had exploded and for three days darkness covered the land. When the sun returned at last, it was not the same golden sun which had shone down on the Roman Empire a week before. It was a counterfeit, gleaming dully in a colourless sky above a blasted world.

On a grey hillside ten miles south of the volcano, a dark-skinned slave-girl climbed a path in search of the flower which might save her dying friend.

Nubia turned her head left and right, scanning the ash-coated slope for a gleam of pink blossom. She did not know what Neapolitan cyclamen looked like, only that it was pink and had a remarkable ability to cure. The doctor had called it 'amulet'.

But there was no pink here. Only grey. Nubia climbed slowly past olive trees, figs, cherry, quince and mulberry, all covered with the same soft crust of chalky ash. Here and there, black stumps showed where falling drops of fire had set an olive or palm tree alight. Some of the charred tree trunks were still smoking. It looked like the land of the dead, thought Nubia: the Land of Grey.

The blanket of ash muffled sound, but Nubia heard a cry drifting up from the beach below. She stopped, turned, and looked back down. From this distance, the buildings around the cove seemed tiny.

Through the thin film of ash which still drizzled from the sky, she could make out the Inn of Pegasus on the right of the cove, by the headland. A few fishing boats, as tiny as toys, were drawn up on the beach near the boathouses where Nubia and the others had taken shelter from the eruption.

On the other side of the cove were the Baths of Minerva, the red roof-tiles pale pink under a coating of ash. Between the baths and the boathouses were hundreds of tents and makeshift shelters. The refugee camp.

Another wail rose from the beach below and Nubia heard an anxious voice behind her.

'Who's dead? It's not him, is it?'

Nubia turned to look at the girl with light brown hair who was hurrying back down the slope. Behind her, three dogs sent up clouds of ash as they pushed through the oleanders and myrtles on either side of the path.

'I don't think it is him,' said Nubia, turning back to gaze down on the beach.

'Doctor Mordecai said he wouldn't live much longer . . .'

The girls watched a coil of black smoke rise from the funeral pyre on the shore. Around it, tiny figures lifted their hands to the hot white sky and cried out to the gods. Nubia shuddered and reached for her mistress's hand.

Flavia Gemina was more a friend than a mistress. A freeborn Roman girl, she had bought Nubia in the slave-market of Ostia to save her from an unimaginable fate. Since then, Flavia's kindness had been like a drink of cool water in a desert of pain. Even now, Nubia took courage from Flavia's steady gaze and the reassuring squeeze of her hand.

After a moment they turned wordlessly and continued up the grey mountain, a dark-skinned girl and a fair-skinned one, wearing torn and dirty tunics, searching among the ashes for the plant which might save their dying friend Jonathan.

From the beach below, eight-year-old Lupus saw the girls start back up the path. They were easy to see: the only spots of colour on the grey mountain. Flavia wore a blue tunic and Nubia a mustard-yellow one. The golden-brown dot pursued by two tiny black dots must be Scuto and the puppies.

He was just turning back to the pyre, to watch the body burn, when he thought he saw something move much higher up the mountain. A person wearing brown. No. Two people.

Then a gust of wind blew acrid smoke from the funeral pyre into his face. His eyes watered and blurred. When he'd wiped them, he could still see the girls and their dogs, but the other figures had disappeared.

Lupus shrugged and turned back to the burning body.

The dead man's relatives were crying and moaning. Two professional mourners dressed in black helped the family express their grief with shrill wails. Lupus let their cries of pain wash over him. He didn't know who the dead man was. He didn't care. He only knew that the man's bloated corpse had washed up on the shore around noon. One of many in the past two days.

Lupus stood close enough for the heat of the flames to scorch him and he kept his eyes open, though the smoke stung. When the professional mourners scratched their cheeks, he scratched his. It hurt, but it brought release. He needed to feel the pain.

The heat of the flames seemed to make the blackened corpse shiver and for a moment Lupus imagined it was the body of Pliny, the great admiral who had treated him with courtesy and respect, but who had died gasping like a fish.

Then the body became that of Clio, seven years old, bright, brave and cheerful. Clio whom he had tried twice to save. And failed.

Finally he saw the body of his own dead father. The father whose murder he had witnessed, powerless to stop. The father whom he had never properly mourned. Lupus tore at his cheeks again, and let the pain rise up in him. Around him the mourners wailed. At last he, too, opened his tongueless mouth and howled with anger and grief and despair.

Flavia's keen grey eyes were usually excellent at spotting wild flowers.

In Ostia, whenever Flavia went to visit her mother's grave outside the city walls, she and her nurse Alma would gather herbs and wild flowers along the way. Flavia always left the prettiest ones at the tomb, to comfort the spirits of her mother and baby brothers. Later Alma would divide the remaining herbs into two groups. She used some for cooking and put the rest into her medicine box.

When Doctor Mordecai had asked the girls to find amulet, Flavia had been confident of success. But now she found it hard to recognise the wild flowers beneath their covering of grey ash. By mid-afternoon, she and Nubia had found others which might be of use to the doctor: red valerian, dove-weed and blood-blossom.

But no amulet.

So they continued up the mountain, climbing higher and higher. As they ascended, the olive trees gave way to chestnut, beech and pine woods. The air grew cooler.

When they reached the summit, they stopped to catch their breath. Flavia uncorked her water gourd and took a long drink. Then she handed it to Nubia.

When Nubia had finished drinking she wiped her mouth. It left a dark streak across her ash-powdered face.

'You look like a spirit of the dead,' said Flavia.

'Don't say such a thing!' Nubia looked horrified and made the sign against evil. She poured some water into the palms of her hands and rubbed her face. 'Better?' she asked.

Flavia nodded. Up here on the summit the ash was so thick that the puppies were up to their noses in it and had begun to sneeze. Flavia lifted Jonathan's puppy Tigris and absently ruffled the top of his head as she looked around.

Ahead of them, across a level clearing among the pines, was a low wooden fence, made of rough-cut logs. Scuto bounded towards it, sending up puffs of grey ash mixed with pumice. Suddenly he stopped, looked back at Flavia and whined.

The girls reached the rail at the same time. On the other side of it, the mountain fell away in a precipitous drop which made Flavia's stomach contract.

But it was the sight beyond that made her gasp.

From where they stood on the pine-covered ridge, Flavia and Nubia could see the great curving Bay of Neapolis on the left, the water scummy grey under an iron sky. Straight ahead, on the horizon, stood a terrible sight.

Vesuvius.

Its top half had been utterly blown away, leaving an ugly crater where the summit had once been. The edge of this crater glowed red, like a bloody, ragged wound. A plume of black smoke rose into the colourless sky and blurred away towards the south west.

Below the smouldering volcano, a thousand fires burned across the chalky landscape, as if a vast besieging army was encamped at its foot. The smoke from the fires had created a dark, transparent cloud which hung over the plain.

Flavia squinted and tried to find the landmarks she knew must be there: the port of Stabia, her uncle's farm, the town of Pompeii. Finally she found Stabia's harbour almost directly below them. She could make out the curved breakwater and straight piers, and a few minuscule boats.

'Behold,' said Nubia. 'Villa of Clio.'

'Where?' asked Flavia, putting down Tigris and shading her eyes. When the volcano had erupted they had hurried to the Villa Pomponiana, the seaside house of their friend Clio. They had hoped to sail away but had ended up escaping on foot.

'I don't see Clio's villa. Or Uncle Gaius's farm.' Flavia frowned. 'Where *is* the farm? It should be . . .'

'There,' said Nubia, pointing. 'Mound with smoke ascending heavenward.'

Suddenly Flavia saw it all.

Her knees went weak. She gripped the wooden rail at the cliff's edge and held on until her knuckles were white. For a horrible moment she thought she was going to be sick.

'It's gone,' she whispered. 'All of it. Clio's house, Uncle Gaius's farm and . . . the entire town of Pompeii. It's all been buried by the volcano!'

SCROLL II

The girls were halfway down the mountain when Scuto found something. The sun was sinking towards the sea and they needed to get back to the camp before it set, but his steady, urgent barking demanded their attention.

Presently the puppies joined in, echoing Scuto's deep bark with their high yaps. The girls left the path and wove between the gnarled and twisted trunks of ancient olives.

They found the dogs standing near a quince bush by the steep mountain side. Scuto stopped barking when they appeared and took a few steps towards them, tail wagging. Then he trotted back to the bush.

'Scuto! You found the amulet! Good boy!' Flavia knelt to hug Scuto round the neck while Nubia gently brushed ash from the tender blossom of a pink flower. Using a sharp stone Flavia dug it out, careful not to damage the bulb.

'Behold!' cried Nubia, who had been searching for more amulet behind the quince bush.

The shrub hid the entrance to a cave.

'That's what they were barking at,' said Flavia, putting the cyclamen in her shoulder bag and taking a step backwards.

The cliffs and mountains of this region were honeycombed with caves. Flavia's uncle Gaius had warned them never to go in, reminding them that there were all kinds of wild animals in these mountains: foxes, wolves, wildcats, even bears.

Tail wagging, Tigris disappeared into the cave's dark mouth.

'Tigris,' hissed Flavia. 'Come back!'

From inside the cave came a piercing scream.

Flavia and Nubia exchanged horrified glances. Then, with a murmured prayer to her guardian gods, Castor and Pollux, Flavia ducked her head and plunged into the darkness.

The cave smelled of old smoke, musky animal and urine. Before Flavia's eyes could adjust to the dim light, the high scream came again.

'No! Get the wolf away!'

Wolf! Flavia's instinct was to turn and run, but Nubia was close behind her. Then Tigris's bark rang out, unnaturally loud in the confined space.

Now Flavia could see a small figure huddling at the far end of the cave about five feet away, and near it the shape of a small black wolf.

Flavia laughed. 'It's just Tigris. He's a puppy. He won't hurt you.'

She took another step into the cave, crouching because of the low roof. Nubia followed, and as she moved away from the entrance, the orange light of the setting sun poured in, illuminating a little girl who wore a torn tunic and one sandal.

Shivering in terror, the child pressed herself against

the back wall of the cave as the dogs snuffled round her toes.

'Scuto. Tigris. Come here at once!' said Flavia sternly. 'You, too, Nipur.' The cave was low at the back, and Flavia had to approach the girl on hands and knees.

'Don't be afraid. We won't hurt you. What's your name?'

The little girl gazed up at Flavia with large, tear-filled eyes. Her nose was running and she stank. Flavia guessed she had wet herself with fear.

Flavia pulled her handkerchief out of her pouch and put it under the girl's nose.

'Once for Castor,' said Flavia brightly.

The little girl blew obediently.

'And once for Pollux.'

The girl blew again.

'That's better,' said Flavia. She tucked the handkerchief back into her belt and sat cross-legged on the dirt floor of the cave.

'My name's Flavia Gemina. This is Nubia, and these are our dogs. Scuto's the big one. The puppies are Tigris, the brave one, and Nipur, the sensible one. What's your name?'

The little girl sniffed. 'Julia.'

'How old are you, Julia?'

'Five.'

'Where are your mummy and daddy?' Flavia asked.

Julia's chin began to quiver and her eyes welled up with tears again.

'Don't worry,' said Flavia hastily. 'It doesn't matter.

Why don't you come outside with us now? We'll try to find them.'

Julia put her thumb in her mouth and shook her head vigorously.

'Come on! It will be dark soon.'

Julia shook her head again and said in a tiny voice:

'Rufus said for me to wait here.'

'Who's Rufus?'

'My big brother. He told me to wait here when the men were chasing us. He told me not to go away. He promised he would come back.'

'What men?' asked Nubia softly. She had been crouching by the door. Now she moved forward and squatted beside Flavia.

Julia looked at Nubia and her eyes widened.

'You have black skin!' she whispered.

'Nubia's from Africa,' explained Flavia. 'Haven't you ever seen an African before?'

The little girl shook her head again, still staring at Nubia.

'Who were the men chasing you?' asked Flavia patiently.

'The scary men,' whispered Julia, and her lower lip began to quiver. 'Rufus told me to hide here and wait for him. He told me he would come back soon. And then he didn't come and it's been a long time.'

'Did you spend the night here?' asked Flavia.

Julia shook her head and tentatively reached out to stroke Tigris, who was sniffing her big toe.

'Are you thirsty?' asked Flavia, holding out the water gourd.

Julia nodded and took the gourd. She drank in long gulps and then handed it back, gasping.

'Come on, then,' said Flavia brightly. 'It's nearly time for dinner. I'll bet you're getting hungry. We'll leave Rufus a message telling him where you've gone. OK?'

Julia nodded absently. She was busy petting Tigris, who sat beside her with his eyes half closed.

On the way down the mountain, Julia became quite chatty.

She told Flavia that she and her brother Rufus were staying in the refugee camp with their grandparents. They had gone to search for early apples or figs. Then the scary men had come out of the bushes. Two of them. One had grabbed her and one had grabbed Rufus. But Rufus was brave and had kicked one so hard that he had fallen to the ground.

Julia took a breath and continued.

'Then I screamed my loudest scream and bit the other one on the arm and Rufus kicked him between the legs and then we ran and ran up the mountain and I couldn't run any more and then we could hear the men behind us and Rufus saw the cave and said wait here don't move I'll be back, but he never came back.'

'Well,' said Flavia, 'if he does come back he'll find the message I wrote in the ash outside the cave. You're sure he can read?'

Julia nodded. 'He goes to school,' she said in a small voice, and then stopped on the path. 'What if the scary men caught him and he never comes back?' Her brown eyes started to fill with tears again.

Flavia knelt in front of the little girl. 'We'll find him, Julia,' she said. 'Nubia and I are very good at solving mysteries. I promise you we will find your brother and bring him back to you.'

SCROLL III

The sun, enormous and blood-red, began to sink into the sea. Its dying rays lit the ash-covered mountains and cove, so that the whole landscape seemed to be bathed in blood. The sky above it was livid purple, the colour of an angry bruise. There would be no stars that night.

In the camp, people moaned and wailed at the evil omen of a blood-red world. Some believed that Apollo the sun god was dying and that he would never rise again. Others were convinced that the end of the world was days away, or maybe only hours. They called out to their gods, they tore their clothes and they sprinkled ash on their heads.

But among the wails of despair were shouts of joy. An old man and woman were hurrying towards Flavia and Nubia as they came down from the mountain.

'Julia!' cried the woman. 'My baby!' Her hair was streaked with grey, but she lifted her skirts like a girl and ran across the beach.

'Grandma!' Julia threw herself into the woman's arms. Scuto barked and jumped up and down and the puppies raced after him.

The old man ran straight past Julia and her grandmother. He was tall, with a lined, leathery face and thinning grey hair. He looked round wildly, glancing only briefly at the girls and then beyond them.

'Rufus?' he cried. 'Rufus?'

Now Julia's grandmother was on her knees hugging Julia and kissing the girls' hands in tearful gratitude.

The old man looked back at Flavia. 'Where's Rufus?' he cried, 'Where's my grandson?'

He must have seen the answer on her face. Before Flavia could explain, he ran up to the road and cried out in a hoarse voice: 'Rufus! Rufus! RUFUS!'

Nubia's family had always lived in tents so she had been able to help Flavia's household put up one of the best in the camp. It was made of an old ship's sail, several cloaks and a large blanket, purchased from the owner of the baths, a chinless Etruscan named Scraius.

Scraius had consented for Doctor Mordecai to convert the palaestra into a hospital and the solarium into a surgery. He also let the refugees use the toilets and fill their water gourds and jars at the seven pipes which brought mineral water down from the mountains. He could afford to be generous: a steady stream of people passed through baths from dawn till dusk bringing more business than he'd ever had before. The steam room was being repaired, but the hot room and cold plunge were still in use, as were the three mineral pools.

Scraius had also allowed the doctor to pitch his tent against the outer colonnade of the baths, so he could be near his patients. Just inside the entrance of their tent, by one of the columns, Mordecai's daughter Miriam had scraped a depression in the sandy ground.

She had surrounded this hearth with flat stones and filled it with coals. Now she knelt over it, stirring a delicious-smelling stew in an earthenware pot. Nubia recognised the pungent aroma at once: goat.

In the dim interior of the tent, Flavia's tutor Aristo was lighting candles. With his curly, golden-brown hair and smooth, tanned skin, he always reminded Nubia of a bronze statuette of the messenger god Mercury which she had once seen in the market of Ostia. Aristo looked up at the girls and smiled.

The girls smiled back but went straight to Jonathan, who lay on a low couch, the only one in the tent. The girls stood looking down at him and Flavia asked, 'How is he?'

'No better, I'm afraid.' Mordecai sat cross-legged on a rush mat beside his son. 'Did you find the amulet?'

Flavia nodded. 'Only one. Scuto found it. I hope it's enough. And there are some other herbs you might be able to use . . .'

'Thank you, Flavia and Nubia. And Scuto.' Mordecai accepted the cloth shoulder bag with a little bow of his head.

'Would you girls like some stew?' asked Miriam.

'Yes, please,' said Flavia. 'We're famished.'

'It is goat?' asked Nubia.

Miriam nodded. 'Goat and chickpea.'

Rush mats and cloaks had been spread over most of the sandy ground to make the floor of the tent. Flavia sat on one of the cloaks beside a man with hair the same colour as hers.

'How are you, Uncle Gaius?' she asked.

'My ribs hurt like Hades, but Doctor Mordecai says

that means they're healing.' He smiled ruefully, and then winced. The robbers who had cracked his ribs had also bruised his jaw and broken his nose. Beside him an enormous, black, wolf-like creature gnawed a bone.

'How is the Ferox?' asked Nubia, kneeling to stroke the big dog. Once Ferox had been the terror of Stabia. But he had almost died trying to protect his master Gaius from horse thieves, and a knife wound in the chest had rendered him harmless as a lamb.

Ferox wheezed at Nubia, rolling his eyes and thumping his big tail twice on the blanket. Then he returned to his bone.

'He has goat for dinner, too,' observed Nubia.

'Where did you get it?' asked Flavia.

'I bought it with the last of my gold,' sighed Mordecai. 'The vendor was asking a fortune.'

'Father gave half the goat meat to that poor family in the tent next to us,' said Miriam proudly, ladling a spoonful into one of their two bowls.

'Miriam,' chided her father gently, 'we are told not to boast about our giving, or we lose the blessing.'

'Sorry, father.'

Flavia frowned. 'How will we buy food now?' she asked.

'God will provide,' said Mordecai quietly.

There were only two wooden bowls and no spoons, so the girls used pieces of soft, flat bread to spoon the hot stew into their mouths. When the bread grew too soggy, they ate the gravy-soaked morsels.

'Goat was delicious, Miriam,' said Nubia, using a last piece of bread to wipe the bowl clean. She reached for the water gourd and took a long drink. The water was cold and fizzy and smelled of egg. It was so full of iron that it turned their tongues rust red. When Nubia had finished, Flavia took the gourd.

'Mmm,' said Flavia. 'I'm getting used to the taste of this water.'

'It's very good for you,' said Mordecai. 'People come from all over Italia to take the waters here.' He looked down sadly at Jonathan. 'If only you would drink some, my son . . .'

'Behold!' said Nubia suddenly. 'His eyelids butterfly.'

'Yes,' whispered Mordecai. 'I believe there are moments when he is closer to waking than sleeping. Flavia, pass me the water gourd, please.'

Mordecai took the gourd and dribbled a few drops onto Jonathan's cracked and swollen lips.

'Drink, my son,' he said. 'Drink and live.'

But the water merely dribbled down the side of Jonathan's pale cheek and he did not wake.

SCROLL IV

'Lupus!' cried Nubia as the boy came into the tent. 'What is happened to you?' There were red scratch marks on his cheeks.

Lupus shrugged. His eyes were red-rimmed and his face smudged with soot, but Nubia thought his green eyes looked calmer. He went straight to his friend Jonathan, lying as still and pale as a corpse, and looked down at him. After a moment he turned away in silence and sat heavily beside the girls.

Miriam filled a bowl with stew and placed it on the rush mat in front of Lupus.

'We've all eaten,' she said. 'This is yours.' She handed him a piece of bread and a water gourd.

From the corner of her eye, Nubia watched Lupus eat. He had no tongue and they all knew a careless bite could be his last. He chomped with his molars and threw his head back to swallow. If he wanted to chew on the other side of his mouth, he had to tip his whole head to one side. When he drank, he held the gourd at a distance and expertly directed a stream of water to the back of his throat.

Nubia saw the others staring at him openly. Sometimes they forgot that he hated to be watched.

'What is news?' she asked Mordecai, hoping to distract them.

'Two more deaths.' Mordecai was grinding the amulet to a paste using a long, smooth stone and the second wooden bowl. 'When people have no reason to live, they choose to die. One man was not very ill at all.'

'And a boy has gone missing,' said Miriam. 'A boy named Apollo. His mother was looking everywhere for him.'

Nubia gasped and looked at Flavia.

'That's strange,' said Flavia. 'Nubia and I found a little girl named Julia hiding in a cave in the mountains. She said some scary men chased her and her brother. And now her brother is missing, too.'

'Is the little girl all right?' asked Miriam.

Flavia nodded and Nubia explained, 'We take her to grandma and grandpa's tent nearby.'

'Maybe her brother was the same boy. The boy named Apollo,' said Gaius.

'No,' said Flavia. 'Julia's brother is called Rufus.'

'There is no end of men's wickedness.' Mordecai shook his head. 'A terrible disaster occurs and straight away people take advantage of it. The villagers here have been asking huge prices for food and supplies. People strip jewellery from the bodies that wash up on the shore before they can be identified. Now it seems that someone is snatching children, no doubt to sell them into slavery.'

'We're going to find out what's happened to the children,' said Flavia. 'I just need to think how to go about it . . .'

Nubia wondered if Mordecai would object, but he was busy smearing the amulet paste on Jonathan's dry lips.

There was a pause, only broken by Lupus's chomps and smacks. Then a note, the sound of a string being plucked.

Aristo held a tortoiseshell lyre on his lap. He was tuning it by tightening the ivory pegs which held the strings.

'A lyre!' cried Nubia. 'Aristo, where are you finding it?'

'Scraius, the owner of the baths, lent it to me. He says he rarely plays it. It only needed a little tuning.' Aristo strummed the strings. A chord swelled and then died.

'Will you pluck song for us?' asked Nubia.

'I will play if you will play.'

'I will play.' Nubia pulled the lotus-wood flute out from beneath her mustard-yellow tunic. It hung on a silken cord around her neck, always close to her heart, for it was her most treasured possession.

'Good,' smiled Aristo. 'You begin, and I will follow.'

Jonathan was hunting in a green, walled garden which stretched as far as the eye could see. He grasped his bow in his right hand and heard the reassuring rattle of arrows in the quiver slung over his shoulder. In his belt was his sling, and there were seven smooth stones in his pouch. The cicadas in the olive grove zithered a song and the sky above was as blue as turquoise. There was a scent of wild honey in the air.

His puppy Tigris ran ahead, sniffing the sun-dappled trail and looking back every so often to make sure his master was following. Jonathan could not remember what they were hunting, but he trusted Tigris. Presently his puppy left the olive grove and raced down a grassy hill. Now Jonathan could really run, and he almost flew. Something was different, and suddenly he realised what it was. Usually when he ran he had to fight for air. But now it felt as if his sandals were winged, like those of the messenger god Mercury.

There was no tightness in his chest, and he ran as he had never run before.

Presently Tigris led him to a broad river, clear as crystal, with trees on either side. Jonathan stopped and stared. The fruit of the trees glowed with colours he had never seen before.

And on the other side of the river was a city made of jewels, too vast and complicated for his mind to comprehend.

'Jonathan,' said a voice. 'Go back. The children need you.'

The blood-red sun had been extinguished by the sea and black night fell upon the camp. The swelling moon and stars were hidden by ash and cloud, but on the beach yellow fires burned, and hearths glowed red.

The camp was full of restless noise. People still wailed and moaned, only a little less now that their bellies were full. Couples argued, children cried and babies whimpered. But as Nubia began to play her flute all these sounds faded.

She played the Song of the Lost Kid. And as she played, she touched those she loved.

Nubia had named each of the eight polished holes under her fingertips after a member of her family. The deepest note was father-note. Then came mother-note. Her mother's voice had been low and rich, full of warmth and laughter. Then came the Taharqo-note, named after her eldest brother who at sixteen was the best musician in the clan. It was he who had taught her the Song of the Maiden and the Song of the Lost Kid. Then came Kashta-note. Kashta was her cousin. Although he was only thirteen, and had not yet undergone the ceremony, he already seemed to Nubia to be a man. If she still lived in the desert she knew she would soon be betrothed to him.

Then came the higher notes. The Shabaqo and Shebitqo notes. They should have been the same, for Shabaqo and Shebitqo were twins, but Shebitqo had been born second and was a little smaller, so he was the higher of the two notes. Then she fingered the Nipur-note, named after her dog, and finally, the Seyala-note. Seyala had been Nubia's little baby sister, so young she was not out of the sling.

As Nubia played the flute, it was as if her finger tips caressed each one of those she loved, those whom she would never see again. Each note was a voice calling to her from the past begging her not to forget. Tears wet her cheeks, but when she played she touched her family, so she didn't mind.

As Nubia played, she heard Aristo first strum, then pluck the translucent strings of the lyre. Her music was sad, but his was full of hope. It filled her with hope, too, and her sad song became sweeter. Then Lupus found a beat somewhere and pattered it softly on his upturned wooden bowl.

SCROLL V

As the music took wings and bean to soar, a movement caught Flavia's eye. The red cloak, which served as their tent door, had been pulled aside and a small girl stood in its opening.

In the instant before Julia let the flap swing closed, Flavia saw dozens of people standing in the darkness outside the tent, as still as statues.

Julia ran across the tent floor and sat heavily in Flavia's lap. Then she leaned back against Flavia's chest, put her thumb in her mouth and watched Nubia play her lotus-wood flute.

Flavia saw Mordecai give Miriam the merest nod. Jonathan's sister stood and unpinned the red cloak. It slipped to the ground, opening their tent to the west.

A great crowd of refugees stood gazing in at the musicians. They were utterly silent. In the darkness of the night, with the thin ash swirling around them, they looked like ghosts from the underworld.

As Nubia, Aristo and Lupus played on, Flavia saw glints of light and heard tiny thumps. Some of the refugees were tossing coins into the entrance of the tent.

'Remarkable,' Flavia heard Mordecai murmur. 'These people barely have enough money for bread, yet they're willing to spend their precious coins on music.'

The music guided Jonathan back. The notes of the flute were cool and clear: silver, green and blue. The lyre was sweet and warm: honey, damson, and cherry. The drum wove the sounds of the two instruments together, into a carpet of many colours. This musical carpet slipped under him and supported him and lifted him with joy.

Suddenly Jonathan was flying. Flying on the music.

He was flying over silk. Wrinkled, indigo-blue silk. There were tiny dots on the blue fabric. He flew lower and saw that the dots were tiny boats and that the wrinkles on the silk were slowly moving.

He was not flying over cloth.

He was flying over water.

The music helped him stay aloft. It supported and it guided him.

Now he was flying over a ship with a red striped sail. He could see children running back and forth on the deck. He flew over a gold and green island with two peaks, then over the deep blue water again and along a rugged coast.

As he rode upon the musical carpet, the coastline became greyer. Presently he slowed. Below him was a blue cove, a crescent beach, olive trees dusted with what seemed to be dirty snow, a few boats, tents, people, lots of people. People fishing, washing, cooking, talking. And among them . . . among them a thin, bearded man walking through the crowds and pushing aside the flap of a tent. His father.

Inside the tent it was suddenly dark, starred with candle flames and the red glow of a coal fire. There were people here, some playing music, and his father sat beside a dark-haired boy on a low couch. The boy looked thin and pale.

His father's head was bent, the long grey hair pulled back at the neck. His father looked strange and vulnerable without his turban.

Floating above this scene, Jonathan suddenly felt a clutch of horror. The boy he was looking down on was himself!

He must go back into that thin, weak body.

He didn't want to.

He loved flying over the sea and over the islands. He loved the strength and joy he had felt hunting in the garden. His father and the others would be with him soon. Then they would understand. They would not want to leave paradise either.

The music stopped as the musicians put down their instruments for a moment.

His sister's voice in the dim tent: 'Don't stop playing the music. I think I saw him move! I think the music is bringing him back.'

Then Flavia's voice.

'Don't die, Jonathan. We miss you. Tigris misses you. Come back to us . . .'

'Please, Lord, bring him back,' prayed Jonathan's father, and then: 'Play a little more, please, Nubia.'

Nubia raised the flute to her lips.

But already, in his heart, Jonathan had whispered: 'Yes.'

Suddenly he was engulfed in dry pain. He felt

unbearably hot, and his head throbbed. There was a strange taste in his mouth. They were all standing over him and around him. Too close. No space. Tigris's wet tongue was cool on his hot cheek. He could smell doggy breath and he could feel someone's hand gripping his so hard it hurt.

Now the memory of flying and of paradise began to slip away, like water from a cracked cup. No, he cried out silently in his mind, don't let me forget.

Then he shuddered and gasped, and there was only a terrible all-consuming thirst.

'He's awake!' squealed Flavia. 'Jonathan's awake!'

Lupus uttered a whoop, Nubia dropped her flute and clapped her hands. Miriam burst into tears.

'Praise God!' whispered Mordecai, bending close. 'How do you feel, my son?'

Jonathan blinked, as if even the dim candlelight hurt his eyes. He tried to speak but his lips were cracked and swollen.

'Water. He needs some water,' said Mordecai. But Miriam was already at her brother's side with a water gourd.

Miriam wiped the tears from her cheeks and gently held her brother's head. Then she put the gourd to his lips.

Jonathan only drank a little water, then he laid his head back on a scorched silk pillow. He murmured something.

'What?' said Mordecai, 'what did you say?'

'Water. Tastes funny,' croaked Jonathan weakly. 'Tastes like fizzy eggs.'

'This is an Etruscan spa town. Famous for its mineral waters,' said Mordecai. 'Miriam gave you the sulphur water. It's good for you.'

'Sulphur bad,' whispered Jonathan. 'Killed Pliny.'

'Yes,' said Mordecai. 'This region has many under-ground caves full of sulphur gas. Too much of it is deadly, but a little bit is good for you.'

'You should try the iron water,' said Flavia. 'It turns your tongue red!'

'And magnesium-num,' attempted Nubia. 'Tastes like dung of camel.'

Jonathan frowned blearily at the African girl. 'How do you know what – ? No, don't answer that . . .'

They all laughed and Flavia said softly,

'Welcome back, Jonathan.'

Nubia went to sleep happy that night. Somehow Jonathan had woken from his deathlike sleep. The night was hot, but she was used to heat. And there was something comforting about sleeping in a tent on soft sand. It reminded her of home. Nevertheless, or perhaps because of this, she had terrible nightmares.

She dreamt the slave-traders came again, wearing turbans which covered not just their heads but their faces, too, so that only their eyes were visible. In her dream they all had one evil dark eye and one white blind eye, like Venalicius the slave-dealer. The one-eyed men slashed at her tent with sharp dripping swords and then set it on fire.

Nubia woke herself trying to scream.

Stars. She must find the stars.

Hugging her woollen cloak about her, Nubia

rose, slipped out of the tent and lifted her eyes to the sky.

When Venalicius had carried her far across the Land of Blue to the Land of Red, the only familiar thing had been the stars in the sky. At Flavia's house she had slept in the inner garden with Scuto, comforted by his furry warmth and by the familiar constellations overhead. But tonight she could see no stars. Tonight there was nothing to remind her of home and who she had been.

'You play very well.' A low voice in the darkness made her start. 'What clan are you from?'

At first Nubia though she was still dreaming; the voice was speaking her native language!

Then she saw the white gleam of his eyes and teeth.

'I was listening in the shadows,' he whispered. 'Your music brought me down from the cave.'

'Who are you?' whispered Nubia.

'My name is Kuanto of the Jackal Clan, but here they call me Fuscus.'

'I haven't seen you in the camp.'

'Nor will you.' His voice sounded just like her eldest brother's. 'I am the leader of a band of runaway slaves.'

'A slave! But if they find you . . .' She gave an involuntary shudder. Nubia knew that the Romans crucified runaway slaves. She was not sure what 'crucified' meant, only that it was something terrible.

'But they will not find us,' said Fuscus quietly. 'Our masters are dead. Buried under the ash of the volcano, along with our past. This disaster has given us the perfect opportunity to start a new life.'

Then he moved a little closer, so close that the warm

breath from his mouth touched her ear and sent a shiver down the side of her neck.

'I have come to ask you to join us,' he whispered. 'Run away with us, and be free again.'

Years of sleeping in graveyards had taught Lupus to be a light sleeper. His ears were keen as a rabbit's and his vision sharp as an owl's, as if the gods had compensated him for the loss of his tongue.

He crouched at the entrance of the tent and watched as the man gave Nubia something. Then he saw her remove one of her tiger's-eye earrings and give it to him in return. Lupus could hear almost everything they said to one another. Unfortunately, he did not understand one word of the language they were speaking.

When Nubia slipped back into the tent and lay down again beside Flavia, he was already back in his own sleeping place, pretending to be asleep.

But long after Nubia's breathing became low and steady, Lupus remained awake, staring into the darkness with open eyes, and thinking.

SCROLL VI

Flavia was determined to solve the mystery of the missing children, but she and her friends were so relieved to have Jonathan back that for the whole morning they barely moved from the tent. They took it in turns to give him sips of water and chicken soup and tell him what had happened while he had been in the deep sleep which Mordecai called a coma.

The last thing Jonathan remembered was the death of Pliny.

'Well,' said Flavia, 'we left him there on the beach and went up to the road and walked and walked. We made it round the promontory and took shelter in the boathouses with lots of other people. The night seemed to last forever and we thought it was the end of the world.'

'Then sun appears,' said Nubia.

Flavia nodded. 'The next day Pliny's sailors and slave went back to get his body. Tascius and Vulcan went with them. They wanted to go back to Herculaneum to try to find Clio and her sisters and her mother.'

Lupus hung his head. He and Clio had become very close and Flavia knew he feared she was dead, so she hurried on.

'The old cook Frustilla died of breathing sulphur—'

'Like the Pliny,' interrupted Nubia, and added, 'and almost you.'

'The funeral pyre on the beach has been lit every day.' Flavia shuddered.

'Many bodies wash up onto the naked shore,' said Nubia quietly.

Lupus held up both hands, fingers spread.

'And your father?' Jonathan croaked. Flavia's father was a sea captain who had set sail from Pompeii two weeks earlier.

'He should be safe in Alexandria,' she said with forced brightness. 'He wasn't planning to get back until the Ides of September.'

Flavia took a deep breath.

'Jonathan,' she said. 'You must get better quickly, because we have a new mystery to solve. Two boys are missing from the camp: one named Apollo and another named Rufus. Your father thinks someone may be kidnapping them to sell them as slaves. We've got to find out who's doing it and rescue them before it's too late.'

Jonathan frowned.

'Yes,' he whispered. 'While I was asleep I think I dreamed. Something about saving the children. I can't remember exactly. But I know it was important.'

Lupus slipped from tent to tent, listening hard. Jonathan was sleeping and Flavia had asked him to start collecting information while she and Nubia finished their chores. He knew how to make himself look extremely ordinary, so that most people hardly noticed him. To them he was just an eight-year-old boy in a grubby tunic, playing in the sand.

At first there had been over two thousand people in the refugee camp. Most thought they were going to die and spent most of their days praying to the gods to spare them or take them quickly. But gradually as the falling ash began to thin, they realised it might not be the end of the world. Some families set off north to see if they could rebuild their lives. Others headed south to stay with relatives and friends.

In the past two days almost three hundred people had packed up and left.

Lupus sat on the shore near a fishing boat. He pretended to be engaged in a private game of knuckle-bones. On the other side of the boat two fishermen were mending their nets and chatting quietly. He couldn't see them but he could hear them perfectly. And he could see most of the camp. He was watching one family in particular. They had dismantled their makeshift tent of blankets and were preparing to leave.

The father was a stocky, dark-haired man. He carried most of their belongings on his back. The mother was short, with frizzy hair. She was wearing black, as if she'd been in mourning even before the eruption. There were three girls, the youngest of whom was about Lupus's age.

'Melissa!' the father was shouting. 'Melissa!' The girls were calling out, too: 'Melissa, we're going!' They had been calling for some time now, their voices growing louder and more urgent.

'By Jupiter!' scowled the father. 'Where is that girl? I

told her not to go far!' He angrily shrugged his bulky pack of blankets to the sand and stalked off towards the water. The mother wrung her black shawl distractedly and the girls looked miserable.

Then Lupus heard something which puzzled him. One of the fishermen on the other side of the boat said under his breath, 'Looks like Felix just got luckier.'

'Poor little minnow,' replied his friend.

'Best to forget you even heard it,' said the first, and they continued mending their nets.

It was just past noon when Miriam pulled aside the cloak doorway and the dim light in the tent brightened. Nubia put her finger to her lips and Flavia whispered a greeting. Jonathan was still asleep. The girls had been filling water jars and gourds from the water spouts outside the baths. They had just brought the last one in.

Nubia could see that Miriam was exhausted from helping her father in the surgery all morning.

'We just delivered a baby,' whispered Miriam, her violet eyes shining. 'It's so wonderful to see new life after all the death around us.'

She sat on some of the scorched cushions they had taken from Tascius's villa and carefully untied the blue scarf around her head.

On the night of the eruption, a fragment of burning pumice had set Miriam's dark curls on fire. Some of her hair had gone up in flames and part of her scalp had been burnt. As she gingerly uncovered it, Nubia could see that the burn was still ugly and red. The hair over her right ear would probably never grow back.

Miriam reached wearily for a small clay jar of balm and removed the cork with her elegant fingers. Everything about Miriam had seemed perfect to Nubia, especially her beauty. But now that perfect beauty was marred.

Nubia rose from Jonathan's side and went to Miriam.

'Here, let me,' she said, and took the ceramic jar. She dipped her finger in the balm and stroked it very gently onto the ugly red burn.

'Oh, that feels wonderful,' sighed Miriam, and closed her eyes. 'Thank you, Nubia.' After a moment she said, eyes still closed, 'Are you going to try to find the missing children?'

'Yes,' whispered Flavia, 'Lupus was just here. He wrote us a message: a girl named Melissa has gone missing.'

Miriam opened her eyes and frowned.

'Lupus managed to get a piece of her clothing,' continued Flavia. 'He's gone back out with Scuto and the puppies to see if they can track the scent. We're just about to go, too.'

'Poor little creature!' sighed Miriam, and closed her eyes again. She looked as if she were in pain. When Nubia had finished smoothing the ointment onto her burn, Miriam lay back against the cushions. Almost immediately her breathing became slow and steady and the frown on her smooth forehead relaxed.

The girls glanced at each other, then back at the ugly red burn on the side of her head.

'Will her tresses ever be growing back?' whispered Nubia.

'I don't think so,' said Flavia. 'I think she'll always have a scar.'

'So sad,' said Nubia. 'The perfect beauty gone.'

The subdued light around them grew brighter as Flavia's uncle Gaius stepped into the tent, then it dimmed again as he let the cloak fall back.

Both girls put their fingers to their lips and pointed at Miriam.

He nodded, smiling. He'd obviously been to the baths because his light brown hair was damp and he smelled pleasantly of scented oil: balsam and laurel.

Ferox opened both eyes and thumped his tail again. Gaius limped over to his dog and lowered himself carefully onto the soft floor of the tent. He ruffled Ferox's head and scratched behind his ear, but he was gazing at Miriam, asleep on her cushions.

The swelling on Gaius's face was going down, but his nose would be permanently crooked and he still had one black eye. Yet there was such a look of compassion on his battered face that it brought a lump to Nubia's throat. She glanced at Flavia and Flavia smiled back.

Nubia knew they were both thinking the same thing: Miriam's beauty might be marred for others, but for Gaius it would always be perfect.

'Come on, Nubia,' whispered Flavia, 'let's go and see how Lupus is doing.'

'Yes,' said Nubia. 'Let's see how Lupus does.'

Flavia spotted Lupus leaning against a palmetto tree in front of the Inn of Pegasus. The innkeeper must have brought a bowl of water for the dogs because they were lapping thirstily. Lupus saw the girls coming and shook his head to say the dogs hadn't been able to find a scent. He was chomping something and guiltily tried to hide it behind his back as they came up.

'Hey, Lupus! Where'd you get the sausage?' Flavia could smell it.

He looked embarrassed.

'From me,' said a voice from the shadowy doorway. The innkeeper stepped out. He was tall and thin with bony elbows and knees, and moist brown eyes.

'I read your young friend's message,' he said.

Lupus flipped open his wax tablet and showed it to the girls. On it he had written in neat letters:

DO YOU KNOW ABOUT MISSING CHILDREN?

'We're looking, too,' said Flavia.

'You're doing a good thing, trying to find the missing children,' said the innkeeper, who smelled faintly of vinegar. 'But you'd better be careful. You don't want to get captured yourselves.' He reached into a jar on the counter just inside the doorway and brought out two more sausages.

'Thank you,' said Flavia taking them. She handed one to Nubia and took a bite of the other. It was deliciously spicy. 'How do you know about the missing children?' she asked with her mouth full.

The innkeeper shrugged. 'Everyone knows about them.' Then he lowered his voice. 'And some people suspect who is behind it.'

'Who?' said Flavia eagerly.

The innkeeper glanced around. 'I know who you are,' he said. 'Your uncle has paid for three poor widows and their children to lodge here, and the doctor is treating the people of this camp *gratis*. So let me give you some advice. This part of Italia is far from Rome. Things are done differently here. There are some people with great power,' he lowered his voice, 'power almost as great as the Emperor's.'

'Who?' asked Flavia again.

'These men of power are like spiders,' said the innkeeper. 'Their webs are almost invisible and they're everywhere. And like spiders, they are not afraid to bite.'

'But who?' said Flavia for the third time.

'Let's just say there is one particular man and he is . . . fortunate. Very fortunate. Most of the crime in this whole area, from Neapolis to Paestum, can somehow or other be linked back to him. They call him the Patron.' The innkeeper licked his lips nervously and looked over Flavia's shoulder. She glanced back. Some fishermen were making their way up to the inn from the beach.

'Be careful of the spider and his web,' whispered the innkeeper and gripped Flavia's wrist with his bony hand. 'One other thing,' he said. 'There is a rumour that a gang of runaway slaves is on the loose in the area. You know what happens to runaway slaves. If they are recaptured, their lives are not worth living. They will do anything to keep from being caught again. Anything. Do you understand?'

Flavia nodded.

'I must be careful, too.' The innkeeper backed into the shadowy interior of the tavern. 'But I will help you if I can. My name is Petrus.'

SCROLL VII

That evening Nubia noticed the crowds gathering outside their tent even before sunset. As well as coins, some people left gifts at the entrance: loaves of bread, an embroidered belt pouch, a carved wooden beaker, some dried figs wrapped in laurel leaves, a handful of olives.

'What's happening?' said Jonathan, as Flavia came in from the baths. He was propped up against all the cushions. 'Why are all those people outside our tent?'

'Nubia, Aristo and Lupus played music last night,' said Flavia, 'while you were still in a coma.'

'The people are hungry for more than bread and olives,' said Mordecai. 'They long to feed their souls with music.'

He turned to Nubia and Aristo. 'Your music is as important as my medicine. Will you play again tonight?'

'Of course,' said Aristo. He began to unwrap the lyre from its protective piece of linen.

Nubia nodded and pulled the flute from beneath her tunic.

'Hey!' cried Flavia. 'That red cord on your flute is new, isn't it? Where did you get it?'

Nubia's heart skipped a beat. Before she could think of an answer Flavia said:

'Oh, I know! Someone left it as a gift. Don't look so worried! Keep it; you deserve it.'

Miriam rose gracefully to her feet and unpinned not only the red cloak doorway but the dark goat's hair blanket that formed one side of their tent. The interior of the tent was now completely open to the west. A few yards from the new tent opening stood many children and adults. Their backs were turned on the blood-red sun which had terrified them the night before.

As Aristo began to tune his lyre, a hush fell over the crowd.

Nubia noticed Lupus lying on his stomach in the darkest corner of the tent.

'Lupus,' she said, 'Will you drum us?'

Lupus tried not to smile, but Nubia could tell he was pleased. Carrying his wooden soup bowl, he sauntered over and sat between them.

Aristo finished tuning his lyre and Lupus turned his bowl upside down. They both looked at Nubia. She closed her eyes for a moment and then lifted the lotus-wood flute to her lips.

As the sun sank into the sea, she began to play.

Flavia loved the music her friends were making. It made her think of sunnier, happier, greener days. She closed her eyes and let the music guide her to those times.

She didn't know how long she had been listening when a small, hot body landed in her lap.

'Oof!' gasped Flavia, jolted from her reverie. Then she smiled. It was Julia, damp and clean and with her thumb in her mouth. Flavia put her arms round Julia and the girl snuggled tighter, her back against Flavia's front and her hard head under Flavia's chin. Flavia kissed the top of the little girl's head and smelled the sweet, warm fragrance of her silky hair.

Julia was quiet after that and Flavia closed her eyes again and let the silent tears come.

When at last the music died away, it was very dark.

There was a long pause.

'No, don't stop!' someone cried out of the silence.

'One more song,' called out a man.

'Aristo, we love you,' came a girl's voice.

Flavia and Jonathan exchanged surprised looks.

'Wait!' A man in a brown tunic stepped into the dim firelight. 'You've cried with the music, now laugh with our comedy!' he proclaimed dramatically.

Two torch bearers – one short and one tall – appeared on either side of him and the sandy ground was flooded with light. Flavia couldn't see the announcer properly because he had his back to them.

'I am Lucrio,' cried the man in a well-trained voice, 'and I would like to present Actius and Sorex, famous actors of repute and renown. They will present for your enjoyment a short comedy of their own composition: *The Pirates of Pompeii* . . .' Here the announcer stepped aside and made a theatrical gesture.

The torch-bearers fixed their torches in the sand and stepped into the torchlight. They bowed towards the audience. Then they turned to bow to the musicians: Nubia, Aristo and Lupus.

As they lifted their heads, Flavia saw that they wore brightly painted comic masks with huge, leering grins.

In her lap, Julia stiffened. Abruptly the little girl let out a scream so shrill it brought all four dogs to their feet. Everyone in the tent turned towards Flavia and she saw their faces in the torchlight, staring at her wide-eyed. Julia was still screaming but now she had twisted round and buried her face in Flavia's shoulder. As she began to cry, Flavia heard the little girl sob over and over, 'The scary men! The scary men!'

'How was *The Pirates of Pompeii*?' Flavia asked Jonathan the next morning, as they ate breakfast on the beach. She had spent most of the evening helping Julia's grandparents calm the hysterical little girl back at their tent.

Lupus mimed applause.

'It wasn't bad,' Jonathan said. 'It was the usual story of clever slaves, rich but stupid young men and children captured by pirates. Those two actors played all the parts.'

'Oh,' said Flavia, disappointed. 'Sounds good.'

It was Jonathan's first time out of bed since he had woken. The four friends sat by the water's edge, watching the little waves deposit more ash on the sand. They were eating their breakfast: tangy goat's cheese and flat bread. The three dogs sat attentively nearby.

'It was hard to tell because of their masks, but I think the actors were angry that they didn't make as much money as Nubia, Aristo and Lupus,' said Jonathan, gesturing with a piece of bread.

'Probably because it wasn't the best choice for a comedy,' said Flavia. 'Pompeii has been buried and children are going missing.'

Lupus nodded and Flavia tossed a morsel of cheesy bread to Scuto, who caught it in mid-air with a snap of his jaws.

'Jonathan!' she cried suddenly.

'What?'

'Do you think they were trying to tell us something, like the innkeeper was? Only they . . .' she tried to think of the word, '. . . they *disguised* it, so that it wouldn't be obvious?'

'Yes,' he said slowly. 'We never thought of *pirates* taking the children, but that would explain why they completely disappear!'

'And look!' said Flavia, indicating two strong fishermen pulling their boat up onto the beach. 'These boats come and go all the time, but we never take any notice of them.'

'What do you think, Lupus?' asked Jonathan. 'Could it be pirates who are taking the children?'

Lupus pursed his lips and nodded thoughtfully, as if to say he thought it was very possible.

'Nubia?' said Flavia, and glanced at the slave-girl.

But Nubia's amber eyes were directed upwards. For the first time in days the chalky white sky had a tint of blue to it.

'She's miles away,' said Jonathan, feeding his last scrap of bread to Nipur. 'Miles away.'

'OK,' said Flavia, as they strolled back to the tent, 'here's the plan for today. Lupus, you patrol the beach.

Watch all the boats that come and go. Keep an eye out for any unusual behaviour. Jonathan, you go to the baths and see if you can overhear anything.'

'Good idea,' said Jonathan. 'I haven't had a bath in over a week.'

'I know. That's what gave me the idea.' Flavia grinned at him. 'Nubia and I will find those actors from last night and . . . Great Neptune's beard!'

They all stopped a few yards from the red flap of their tent. Two Roman soldiers in dazzling armour stood at the entrance, one on either side. They both held spears and they both stared straight ahead.

Flavia glanced at her friends. Then she set her jaw and took a step forward.

In perfect synchronisation the two spears crossed, blocking the entrance.

'Hey!' cried Flavia. 'That's our tent!'

Keeping his gaze on the horizon, one of the soldiers growled: 'And you would be?'

'Flavia Gemina, daughter of Marcus Flavius Geminus, sea captain!'

'Well, Flavia-Gemina-daughter-of-Marcus-Flavius-Geminus-sea-captain,' said the soldier with the hint of a twinkle in his eye. 'There's a very important person in there at the moment and you'll just have to wait until he comes out.'

A clink of armour sounded from the other side of the tent flap and the two spears pointed up again. Flavia and her friends jumped back as two more soldiers emerged from the tent and stood to attention. Then a bull-necked man with receding sandy hair ducked out through the tent's opening.

He blinked in the light and looked down at Flavia and her friends. Short and stocky, with a pleasant face, he looked strangely familiar to Flavia. He reminded her of Brutus, Ostia's pork butcher. However, the richly embroidered purple toga draped around his shoulders showed he was no butcher.

Flavia's jaw dropped as she looked from the gold laurel wreath on his head, to the heavy gold wrist-guards on his arms and down to his gold-tooled leather sandals. Suddenly she knew why his face seemed so familiar: there was a marble bust of him in her father's study.

'You must be Flavia Gemina,' he said mildly. 'I heard you introducing yourself to my guard. I believe we are distantly related. I am a Flavian, too.'

He extended his ringed hand for her to kiss.

Flavia nearly fainted.

She was standing two feet away from the Emperor Titus!

SCROLL VIII

Scuto wagged his tail as Flavia dutifully pressed her lips to the hand of the most powerful man in the world. The Emperor's thick fingers were laden with gold rings and the back of his hand was soft and freckled.

'Flavia,' said her uncle Gaius, coming out of the tent with a tall, grey-haired man, 'the Emperor has come to our rescue. He has brought food and wine and blankets and medicine. And he wants to see Doctor Mordecai.'

'Um . . . he should be in the infirmary,' Flavia stuttered and the others nodded, wide-eyed.

'Lead on,' said the Emperor, throwing out one arm in a sweep of purple.

Flavia, Jonathan, Nubia and Lupus led the most powerful man in the Roman Empire across the sandy ground, through two columns and into the solarium. The dogs knew from experience that they were not allowed in the baths; they flopped down panting near the entrance.

The solarium was bright and cool. Its outstanding feature was a picture window of tinted green glass, facing north towards the bay.

Miriam, her dark curls bound up in a blue scarf, was talking and laughing with a woman on a massage couch. She looked up as they entered and when she saw the soldiers and the Emperor, her face went pale and she quickly handed the baby back to his mother.

Someone must have told her the Emperor was in the camp, for she immediately went to him, knelt and kissed his hand.

'Beautiful,' breathed the Emperor as he helped her to her feet. And then frowned. 'Have we met before? You look very familiar . . .'

Miriam lowered her eyes and gave her head a slight shake.

'Miriam,' said Gaius, 'the Emperor is looking for your father. He's not in the tent. Is he here?'

'He was here a moment ago,' stammered Miriam. 'I'm not sure where he's gone . . .'

'Shame,' said the Emperor, swivelling majestically on one foot and looking around at the airy room with its frescoed walls and high blue ceiling. 'Reports of his good deeds reached me in Rome even before I set out for the region. I wanted to personally encourage him in his work.'

'I'm sorry,' said Miriam again, and Flavia thought she looked unusually flustered.

'Don't be, my dear.' The Emperor smiled, revealing a row of small white teeth. 'Why don't you take me round the patients? I should like to speak to them.'

'Of course,' said Miriam, and led him towards the new mother, who clutched her baby tightly in a mixture of terror and delight.

'Oh, Flavia,' said Gaius, 'I haven't introduced you to Pollius. He's one of my patrons. He buys more of my wine than anyone else in the region. He lives a few miles south of here, in Surrentum.'

Flavia turned from the Emperor to the man standing beside her uncle. At first she thought he was old, because his hair was mostly grey. Then she noticed his tanned face was as smooth and unlined as Aristo's. He couldn't be much older than her father. But the most striking thing about him was not the contrast of his smooth tanned face and greying hair.

It was his eyes.

Although they were unremarkable – dark and slightly too close together – when he turned them on Flavia she felt a strange thrill.

Her uncle was gesturing for Miriam to come over. With a nervous glance at the Emperor, who was speaking to the young mother, Miriam slipped away to join them.

'And this is my betrothed.' Gaius took Miriam's hand and for a moment they gazed into each other's eyes as if no one else existed. Then Gaius remembered himself.

'Miriam, this is one of my patrons, Publius Pollius Felix. He's a close friend of the Emperor. He's been taking him on a tour of the devastated area.'

'Hello.' Gaius's patron gave Miriam the same direct look he'd given Flavia. He had a light, cultured voice.

Flavia studied the grey-haired man. He was tall and cleanshaven, like her uncle, and very handsome. But there was something else about him. Something she couldn't describe. The thought suddenly occurred to her that he was really the Emperor, and the bull-necked man in the purple robe was an impostor.

She felt a tug on her tunic and turned, irritated. It

was Lupus. He was making bug-eyes at her, as he did whenever he wanted to communicate something important. He tipped his head towards the door.

Jonathan and Nubia were staring at her, too.

'Um, Uncle Gaius,' said Flavia. 'We'll go and find Doctor Mordecai.'

'Good idea,' said her uncle with a smile, and turned back to his patron.

'What is it?' hissed Flavia when they were outside again. They moved along the portico, beyond earshot of the Emperor's guards.

Lupus took out the wax tablet he carried everywhere and opened it with a flick of his wrist.

His notes from the previous days were still etched into the yellow wax on the left-hand leaf.

Flavia took it and frowned as she read it out loud.

GIRL MISSING. MELISSA. "FELIX JUST GOT LUCKIER".

'You told us this yesterday. That's what the fishermen said.'

Lupus nodded urgently.

Jonathan cleared his throat. 'I think what Lupus is trying to tell us is that a man named Felix might be involved in the kidnappings.' Lupus nodded.

'And?'

'Didn't you hear your uncle?' said Jonathan. 'His patron's name is Felix.'

'Great Neptune's . . .' gasped Flavia. 'And *felix* means lucky or . . . fortunate!'

'The innkeeper!' shouted Jonathan, and then clapped

his hand over his mouth. Lupus was nodding vigorously.

Jonathan continued in a whisper: 'You told me the innkeeper said "most of the crime in the area can be linked back to a very *fortunate* man"!'

'Wait!' said Flavia, holding up her hands. 'Wait, wait, wait. Before we get too excited . . . Felix is quite a common name, isn't it?'

'I suppose so . . .' said Jonathan.

'Felix slave name,' offered Nubia.

'She's right,' said Flavia. 'Lots of slaves are called Felix.'

'But that man is no slave,' said Jonathan. 'He has three names. And I don't think he can be a freedman. Did you notice the gold ring on his finger?'

'No. But he must be rich if he can afford to buy lots of my uncle's wine.'

'And he's a close friend of the Emperor,' said Jonathan. 'You can't get much more powerful than that. 'Do you think he's the man they call the Patron?'

Flavia nodded slowly. 'I'll bet he is. The innkeeper said the "fortunate" man had power "almost as great as the Emperor's"! And he is my uncle's patron.'

The four of them looked at each other.

'I have a plan,' said Flavia. 'It probably won't work, but if it does it will be very dangerous. Are you willing to try it?'

Without hesitation, the other three nodded.

'Good. But first, we have to be sure that man is the one the innkeeper thinks is behind the kidnappings. Wait here and make sure he doesn't go anywhere. I'll be right back!'

★

Flavia ran as fast as she could across the ashy beach, dodging children, skirting tents, leaping over smouldering campfires.

The Inn of Pegasus was closed, because it was only mid-morning, but the door was not locked. A serving-girl directed Flavia to a cool, musty storeroom built into the cliff itself. The innkeeper was decanting wine from a large amphora into smaller jugs.

It was dim in the storeroom, but light enough for Flavia to see the innkeeper's expression when she told him breathlessly that the Emperor was in the camp.

Petrus looked surprised and pleased.

'And he's here with my uncle's patron, a man called Felix,' she added.

'Publius Pollius Felix?' said Petrus.

Flavia nodded.

The look on his face told her all she needed to know.

SCROLL IX

Publius Pollius Felix was still in the solarium with her
uncle Gaius, watching as Titus made his circuit of the
sick and injured. The Emperor had just found a veteran
soldier who had served with him in Judaea and the two
of them were deep in conversation.

Aristo and Miriam were changing the bandage on a
burns victim in a far corner of the room.

And Mordecai was nowhere to be seen.

'He's not back yet?' said Flavia breathlessly to her
uncle. 'We couldn't find him anywhere. He must have
gone to someone's tent.'

'That's a pity,' said Felix, 'because the Emperor has
to leave soon. I'm accompanying him to Stabia where
a warship is ready to take him back to Rome.' He
turned to Gaius. 'I'll return this afternoon to help
distribute the blankets and food. It would be useful if
you could tell me which of the refugees are in greatest
need.'

'Of course,' said Gaius, 'I'll make up a list. Jonathan,
are you all right?'

Jonathan had put his hand to his forehead and was
staggering a little.

'Yes,' he said weakly, 'just hard to breathe . . .'

Suddenly he fell back, unconscious.

Flavia and Nubia were standing right behind him. They caught him neatly and lowered him to the floor.

'Is he ill?' said Felix, taking a step forward and looking down at Jonathan with concern.

'He's very asthmatic and the ash in the air is bad for him,' said Flavia. 'He almost died of it. He only came out of his coma yesterday.'

Felix looked sympathetic.

Flavia coughed. 'It's hard for Lupus, too,' she said, 'because when he was younger someone cut out his tongue and all the ash gets down his throat. And Nubia's throat is still sore from the iron collar she had to wear when she was enslaved.' Flavia coughed again and glanced pointedly at Lupus and Nubia, who coughed, too.

'By Jupiter!' exclaimed Felix. 'You children have had a bad time of it.'

Jonathan stirred and groaned. His eyelids fluttered convincingly.

'I told Jonathan he should go where the air is fresher,' said Flavia solemnly, 'but he said he didn't want to take his father away from the important work he is doing here.'

'This boy is the doctor's son?' said Felix.

Flavia looked up at him and nodded. She tried to make her eyes look big and innocent. For a long moment Felix's dark eyes held her gaze and she wondered if he had seen through their ruse.

Then Felix turned to Gaius.

'Flavius Geminus, old friend,' he said. 'Why didn't you say something sooner? I have a huge villa in Surrentum with plenty of spare rooms. Send your niece and her friends to stay with me for a few days while we sort out the refugees.'

'Well,' stammered Gaius. 'It never even occurred to me. Wouldn't it be a terrible imposition? Four children? Not to mention their dogs . . .'

'Not at all,' said Felix with a faint smile. 'I have three daughters, the eldest about the same age as your niece . . . I insist that they come to stay with me at the Villa Limona.'

'I'll have to ask Jonathan's father,' said Gaius, 'but I'm sure he'd be delighted. Thank you, Pollius Felix, thank you very much. I don't know how I shall ever repay you.'

'Don't think of it.' Felix placed his aristocratic hand on Gaius's shoulder. 'That's what patrons are for. Perhaps some day I will call upon you to do me a small service in return.'

Before the Emperor departed, he climbed up onto his imperial carriage and gave a short speech to all those in the camp. He had been an army commander and Jonathan could hear every word perfectly.

Nearly two thousand refugees listened in silence as the Emperor promised to compensate those who had lost property or possessions, to find and return lost children and runaway slaves, to help them rebuild their lives.

'Many of you will be worried about friends and relatives buried in the ash or trapped in buildings which have collapsed,' said the Emperor. 'It may ease your minds to know that even as we speak, an entire legion is combing the affected area, searching for survivors.'

There was a huge cheer, but as it died down Jonathan overheard a man tell his wife that so far they'd found no one alive.

The Emperor continued: 'Those of you who have documents to prove you own property buried by the eruption – be it land, slaves or animals – should present them to the official scribes from tomorrow. If you do not have documentation, two or three witnesses will do. I promise that I will do everything in my power to compensate you. Even if I have to reach into my own purse to do it!'

This statement received the biggest cheer of all. There were shouts of 'Hail Caesar!' and 'May the gods reward you!' Many of the refugees were in tears, but Jonathan noticed a few exchanging sceptical glances.

'My agent for this area,' the Emperor continued, 'is Pollius Felix.' He gestured towards the grey-haired man, who stood nearby. 'He lives a few miles south of here and has assured me that he will visit the camp regularly. If you have any special problems or disputes, take them to Pollius Felix.'

Shortly afterwards, the imperial carriage drove north up the coastal road. The Praetorian Guard followed on horseback.

The plume of grey ash had barely settled when Mordecai appeared at Miriam's side.

'Father!' cried Jonathan. 'Where have you been? They've been looking everywhere for you! The Emperor was here. He wanted to thank you.'

'God forgive me, I could not face the man,' said Mordecai. 'I cannot forget what he did.'

'But Doctor Mordecai,' protested Flavia. 'He promised to help everyone who's been hurt by the volcano.'

'He brought many food and blankets,' said Nubia.

'And he told us,' added Jonathan, 'that you had done the empire a great service. He wants to reward you.'

Mordecai looked at his son from his heavy-lidded eyes. 'That man has the blood of ten thousand Jews on his hands,' he said, 'including that of your mother.'

'How?' said Jonathan. 'How is the Emperor connected with mother's death?' It was noon, and for the first time since the eruption the sun had broken through the ashy cloud cover. They had moved to stand in the thin shade of the colonnade.

'Nine years ago,' said Mordecai heavily, 'he was the commander of the legions which destroyed Jerusalem. It was Titus who gave the command to burn the Temple. Thousands of our people died in the siege of Jerusalem. Among them your mother.'

They all looked at each other in dismay.

'There are even those,' continued Mordecai, 'who say that he is the reason Vesuvius erupted. The rabbis always said God's curse would come upon this land if ever Titus rose to power.'

'And I kissed his hand,' whispered Flavia with a shudder.

'No,' said Mordecai, patting Flavia's shoulder. 'I'm not asking you to hate him. I'm just telling you why I could not face him. I must forgive him.'

'You shouldn't forgive him after what he did!' said Jonathan angrily and Lupus nodded his agreement.

'But I must forgive him.'

'Why?'

'Because we are told to love our enemies. Besides, until I forgive him,' said Mordecai, tapping his black-robed stomach, 'I carry him here, within me. And that is a terrible thing.'

Flavia and Nubia wasted their last afternoon in the camp looking for the comic actors Actius and Sorex. Curiously, although many had either seen the play or heard about it, and some had tossed coins to the actors, not one person knew who they were or where they were from.

Jonathan waited until the tent was empty and then went quickly to his father's spare capsa, the cylindrical leather container for medicines and surgical instruments. Quickly he searched through various twists of papyrus, briefly sniffing each one.

Finally he found the one he wanted, untwisted the papyrus and examined the dark brown powder. Yes. He was almost certain this was the one.

Around his neck Jonathan wore a small pouch full of herbs. He opened this pouch and slipped the papyrus twist inside. Then he closed his father's capsa and put it back exactly as he had found it.

'Don't roll your eyes at me like that,' he muttered to Ferox. 'We're going to an unknown place with a possible criminal mastermind. You never know when you'll need a good sleeping powder!'

Flavia saw Pollius Felix return to the camp in the mid-afternoon. He drove a white carruca with gold trim and two white horses, and was followed by a convoy of five carriages, each one loaded with blankets, fig cakes, flour, olive oil and wine. Each carriage also carried two soldiers who would ensure nothing went missing, two slaves to help with the physical labour of the distribution, and an imperial scribe to record which provisions went to whom.

Within an hour the soldiers had erected a large tent near the eastern side of the baths, ready to distribute aid.

'It's too late to start today,' said Felix, turning to Gaius. 'Will you begin overseeing the operation, Geminus?'

'Of course,' replied Flavia's uncle. 'I'll be glad of the chance to keep myself occupied while my ribs are healing. It won't be strenuous work.'

'Excellent,' said Felix. 'I'll return tomorrow or the next day to see how you're doing and hear any disputes. But now I must return to Surrentum. I believe I am taking your four charges with me.' He turned to Flavia. 'Are you ready to depart?'

Flavia and her friends nodded. They were clean from an afternoon at the baths. Even the three dogs had been washed and brushed.

'Let's go then.' Felix smiled and led the way to his elegant carruca.

They had said their goodbyes earlier, and as the carriage drove away from the camp they turned and looked back at Gaius, Miriam, Mordecai and Aristo. The four figures stood in the road waving, becoming smaller and smaller until the road curved round and they disappeared from sight.

Flavia glanced at her three friends and swallowed. She sensed they were all thinking the same thing.

If Felix was the spider, they were headed straight for his web.

SCROLL X

Flavia was surprised to see Felix at the reins. He had
two slaves with him, dark young men no more than
twenty years old. But he drove the carruca himself.

And he drove fast.

As soon as it left the camp, the road began to climb
the mountainside, twisting and turning. Sometimes they
were only a few feet from stomach-churning drops onto
the rocks and sea far below.

Flavia sensed it was some kind of test, for every now
and then Felix glanced back at them. Each time she
returned his smile brightly, though her knuckles hurt
from gripping the wooden seat.

Lupus was genuinely enjoying every moment. His
eyes blazed with delight at the speed of the carruca.
Jonathan, on the other hand, looked rather green. He
was trying not to look down on the sea as it foamed
against jagged rocks below them.

The dogs lolled on the floor and gave Flavia re-
proachful looks.

Nubia was not even looking at the sheer drop to
their right. She was staring intently at an aqueduct
running along the grey mountainside on their left.
Flavia followed her gaze. Just before the road curved
and the honey-coloured cliff blocked her view, she

thought she saw three men standing on the top of the aqueduct.

And she was sure one of them had been dark-skinned, like Nubia.

They stopped once, after half an hour, so that one of Felix's slaves could relieve himself.

'Stretch your legs,' suggested Felix. Handing the reins to the second slave, he jumped down and helped Flavia and the others out of the carruca. Jonathan and the dogs followed the slave behind some oleanders on the other side of the road. Flavia, Nubia and Lupus walked towards the cliff edge.

Before them, across the bay, smouldered the remains of Vesuvius. Directly below was a dizzying drop to small coves and the shimmering sea.

Flavia suddenly realised her legs were trembling. She tried to stop them by stiffening her knees and clenching her fists. She wasn't going to let Felix see she was afraid.

Suddenly he was standing right next to her. His presence was so intense that for a moment everything else seemed unreal. He smiled down at her and took her right hand.

Flavia stared up at him.

'Hold your hand palm down,' he said. 'That's it. If you curve your forefinger over a little, you have the Bay of Neapolis. See?'

Flavia nodded. His hair smelled faintly of some kind of citron oil.

'The knuckle where your forefinger meets your hand is Vesuvius, or rather what's left of it . . . No, no. Relax your hand, so the thumb points to your heart. We're here.' He touched the web of skin between Flavia's thumb and forefinger. 'And we are going to drive along here . . .' Felix moved his well-manicured finger slowly along the inside of Flavia's thumb '. . . to here, where the pad of your thumb sticks out the most.'

He tapped it. 'That is the Cape of Surrentum, which some people call the Cape of Hercules. My villa is there.'

Felix dropped Flavia's hand and looked with amusement at Lupus, who was hanging his toes over the cliff edge.

'Lupus,' he said, 'would you like to take the reins for a while?'

Lupus turned and stared at him in disbelief. Then, eyes shining, he nodded vigorously.

'Let's go then,' said Pollius Felix.

Lupus drove the carriage the rest of the way to Surrentum. At one point the carruca veered so close to the cliff edge that Flavia screamed and Jonathan began laughing hysterically.

'There's only one thing to do on a road like this,' Felix called back to them. 'To release the tension you must either sing or shout.' He opened his mouth and began to sing a popular song that began *Volare*: 'to fly'.

'*Volare*!' sang Felix, as the carriage wheel sent a shower of pebbles skittering into the void, and they all sang with him at the top of their voices.

'*Volare*: to fly! *Cantare*: To sing! To fly in the painted blue sky, to fly so happy and high . . .'

Even Lupus opened his tongueless mouth and yelled out the notes of the song.

After a while they stopped singing, their cheeks wet with tears of laughter.

The song had brought Flavia a strange release. Suddenly she didn't care if they went hurtling over the edge. She felt immortal, as if she would never die. For the first time since the volcano had erupted she felt totally alive.

As the sun sank lower and lower in the west, Lupus urged the horses along the twisting road through dusty olive groves and orchards. The mountains reared on their left and the cliffs plunged to the sea on their right.

The carriage rattled through Surrentum without stopping and began to climb again. Just as the sun touched the horizon, the horses automatically turned off the main road and trotted down a drive which ran between high stone walls.

Presently the stone wall on their right gave way to columns. Now they were driving beneath a colonnade. The sinking sun painted the white columns orange, and Flavia kept catching glimpses of the shining sea through the twisted, ancient olive groves.

The colonnade went on for nearly half a mile, winding down the mountainside towards the sea. The iron-rimmed wheels of the carriage and the horses' hooves resounded in the half enclosed space.

When at last they emerged into the open, the sudden silence and space around them seemed vast.

The sea blazed like molten copper under the yellow sky of dusk and before them, as if floating on the water, was the most beautiful villa Flavia had ever seen.

Flavia rubbed her eyes and looked harder. It had been built on an island attached to the mainland by two narrow strips of land. As the carruca stopped and one of the slaves wedged its wheels, Flavia stood up to get a better view. There were columns, domes, fountains, palm trees and two covered walkways.

A pool of seawater lay between the villa and the mainland, a secret cove, surrounded on all sides by the honey-coloured rocks. An arch in the rocks led out to sea, making it a small natural harbour.

As Flavia climbed down from the carruca, a girl about her own age came running from the main complex. She had long golden hair and wore a tunic the same dove grey as Felix's tunic.

'Pater,' she cried with delight, and threw herself into his arms. 'Pater! I'm so glad you're home! I was getting terribly worried about you.'

'My little nightingale.' Felix smoothed a strand of pale gold hair and kissed her forehead. Then he turned to the others.

'This is my eldest daughter Polla, whom we call Pulchra. Pulchra, meet Flavia Gemina, Jonathan ben Mordecai, and Lupus. Oh, and these are their dogs.'

'And this is Nubia . . .' began Flavia, but Pulchra had gathered Nipur into her arms and was covering his furry black face with kisses.

'Oh, you are so precious!' she gushed. 'I just want to eat you up!'

SCROLL XI

'Leda, bring me that box,' demanded Polla Pulchra. Then she smiled at Jonathan.

Felix's daughter was showing them her bedroom. It was small, but exquisitely decorated with frescoes of cupids riding dolphins across a dark-blue wall. A window overlooked Vesuvius across the bay, its plume of smoke pink in the evening light.

'Look at that!' said Jonathan, going to the window. 'Look at all the ash the volcano is still sending up.'

'I know,' sighed Pulchra. 'It gets over everything! Leda has to dust twice a day. Leda! My box!'

Pulchra's slave-girl Leda was a thin, pale girl with lank brown hair and dull eyes. She wore a beautiful yellow tunic, but it did not flatter her dingy complexion. She almost stumbled as she held out a small lacquered box to Pulchra.

'Careful!' snapped Pulchra, taking the box impatiently. 'These are my jewels,' she announced, bringing out various necklaces, bracelets and bangles for them to admire.

'Nubia has tiger's-eye earrings,' said Flavia. 'They were given to her by . . . Nubia! One of your earrings is missing!'

'I know,' said Nubia. 'I lose it in the sand by tent.'

433

Polla Pulchra didn't seem to hear. She had found something. She set the lacquered box on her bed and turned to Jonathan.

'Look!' She held out a gold ring. 'This is a real ruby from Arabia.'

'It's . . . um . . . big,' commented Jonathan. He wasn't quite sure what she wanted him to say, so he added, 'It must be worth a lot of money.'

Her pretty face flushed with pleasure. 'At least a thousand sesterces, according to pater,' she said. 'Here. It's yours.'

Jonathan stared at her. He'd only met her ten minutes ago and now she had given him a ring worth a fortune.

There was a sudden clatter as the jewellery box slipped from the edge of the bed. Tails wagging, the dogs sniffed the chains and gems on the floor. Pulchra's slave-girl stared down in horror.

'You stupid girl!' Pulchra said, and slapped Leda hard across the face. 'Pick them up now!'

As the slave-girl got down on her hands and knees, Pulchra smiled prettily at Jonathan and gave a little shrug. Then she scooped up Nipur and kissed his nose. 'Come on,' she said over her shoulder, 'we're late for dinner.'

'Aren't we going to eat with the rest of your family?' asked Flavia, as Pulchra led them into a small sky-blue dining-room with views over the bay.

'No. Pater always has his boring old clients to dinner and mater usually eats in her rooms. My sisters and I have our own private triclinium.'

Pulchra's two younger sisters Pollina and Pollinilla were six and five years old respectively. They had fair hair like Pulchra, though neither was as pretty as their older sister. Each had a slave-girl about her own age. After the slaves had washed their dusty feet and given them linen slippers, they reclined.

Pulchra stretched out on her side on the central dining couch and patted the space next to her.

'Recline by me, Jonathan,' she said, and as her sisters each took one of the other two couches: 'No, you two will have to share a couch so that Fulvia can recline.'

'Flavia,' said Flavia coldly. 'My name is Flavia.'

Pulchra looked horrified as Nubia started to lie down beside Flavia.

'Oh no!' she cried. 'You must never let your slave recline at dinner!'

Flustered, Nubia slipped off the couch and hung her head.

'But where will she sit?' asked Flavia.

'You haven't had a personal slave very long, have you?' Pulchra rolled her eyes. 'She should stand behind your dining couch like Leda here and cut your food for you!'

Flavia was speechless. But she was a guest and could hardly complain. She gave Nubia a small nod.

Nubia slowly went to stand behind Flavia's couch and Lupus, who had been lingering near the doorway, started to recline beside Flavia.

'No, no!' giggled Pulchra to Jonathan. '*Your* slave should stand behind *you*.'

'Lupus isn't a slave, my dear.' Pollius Felix stepped

into the dining room, smiling at them. It was dusk and he held an oil-lamp in one hand.

'Pater! Pater!' The younger girls slipped off their couch and ran to Felix. He put down the lamp, bent to give them each a kiss and then gently directed them back to their couch.

'Oh! But Lupus is so quiet and meek,' said Pulchra with a pout. 'I was sure he must be Jonathan's slave.'

Her father smiled. 'Just because he's quiet doesn't mean he's meek.' Felix turned to Jonathan. 'How is your breathing, now? Are you finding it easier here?'

Jonathan coloured a little and coughed. 'Um. Yes. It's much better here. Sir. Thank you for inviting us.'

'Yes,' said Flavia, smoothing her hair, 'thank you for inviting us.'

Felix turned to Pulchra. 'I've come to ask Lupus to dine with us. Can you spare him?'

'Of course,' said Pulchra, and caught Jonathan's hand. 'But you can't have Jonathan. I want him!'

Pollius Felix led Lupus upstairs to another dining-room.

This triclinium looked inwards, onto a green inner courtyard. It was twice as big as the dining-room Lupus had just left, and the lighting was more subdued. The walls were black, with red panels, and the couches were covered with wine-coloured covers and cushion. All the oil-lamps were bronze, burnished to a deep gold.

A dozen pairs of dark, wary eyes turned to look at Lupus as he stepped into the dining-room. The men were reclining or sitting around the room. Lupus guessed their ages ranged from mid teens to late twenties. Most wore tunics of fashionable sea-green and despite the scented oil they used to slick back their hair they exuded a pungent odour of masculinity.

'This is Lupus,' said Felix, and Lupus felt the Patron's hand rest lightly on his shoulder. 'I sense a rare courage in him. I believe he's one of us.'

'Pssst! Jonathan! Lupus! Wake up!'

Flavia had waited until the entire villa was silent before creeping next door into Jonathan's room.

'Whuzzit?' mumbled Jonathan and then, 'I'm awake. Yes.' He yawned, closed his eyes and snuggled back under the soft woollen cover. It smelled faintly of some disturbingly familiar fragrance.

'Wake up!' hissed Flavia, and shook him again. 'We've got to plan tomorrow.'

'Mmmph! Oh, all right.' Jonathan sat up groggily and pulled the blanket around him. It was after midnight and the air was cool.

Flavia held a small clay oil-lamp. She had trimmed the wick so that it burned dimly. Nubia was beside her and so was Lupus, ready with his wax tablet. Jonathan noticed that Lupus's hair was now long enough to be rumpled by sleep. It had been over two months since the barber had shaved it off at the baths in Ostia.

'Why did Felix ask you to dine with him tonight?' asked Flavia.

Lupus crinkled his chin and gave a little shrug.

'Did you learn anything?' asked Jonathan.

Lupus waggled his head to say 'not really'.

'Who else was there?' said Flavia. 'Any pirates?'

Lupus smiled and then took out his wax tablet and stylus. His spelling wasn't perfect but he could tell them almost anything now, and he relied more and more on writing.

He showed them the tablet:

JUST MEN, XII OR XIII

'Twelve or thirteen men,' read Flavia. 'Friends?'

Lupus shrugged.

'Slaves?' asked Nubia.

Lupus shook his head.

'Clients?' suggested Jonathan.

Lupus looked at him, narrowed his eyes and nodded thoughtfully.

'Anyway,' said Flavia, 'Felix obviously likes you.'

Lupus flushed and looked down.

'Maybe we're mistaken about Felix,' said Flavia, brushing a strand of hair away from her face. 'He seems to be all right: he knows my uncle, he helped the Emperor to bring aid to the camp, and he let Lupus drive the carruca.'

'Which proves he's crazy!' Jonathan grinned.

'Crazy, maybe,' said Flavia with a blush, 'but I like him.'

'This is a bad place,' said Nubia quietly. 'And he is a bad man.'

They all looked at her in surprise. Lupus shook his head in angry disagreement.

'Well,' said Flavia. 'That's what we're here to find out. Lupus, you stick as close to Felix as possible. I think that should be easy. Nubia, you're going to have to stay close to the other slaves and see if you can pick up any gossip from them. I'm sorry Pulchra is treating you so miserably. She's a spoilt, cruel little . . .'

'Hey!' said Jonathan, colouring. 'She's not *that* bad.'

Flavia started to say something and then changed her mind. 'Well, Jonathan, it's obvious that you're the best person to keep an eye on Pulchra. As for me, I'll just generally nose around. We've got to find out as much as we can as quickly as possible, or it may be too late. Any questions?'

They all looked at each other in the dim lamplight.

'I think they divide us,' said Nubia quietly.

'Don't be silly,' said Flavia with a laugh. 'We've been through too much together. But we will have to split up while we're here. We'll learn more that way. We've got to solve this mystery and save the children! Right?'

They all nodded.

SCROLL XII

'Good morning,' breathed a soft voice in Jonathan's ear.

Jonathan snuggled deeper into the covers. The blankets were soft and sweetly fragrant. He never wanted to leave.

'Time to get up,' whispered the voice and something tickled his ear.

Jonathan opened his eyes a crack and then opened them wide.

Pulchra's face was inches from his. Jonathan immediately sat up, wiped the drool from his chin and tried to look alert. At the foot of the bed Tigris stretched and yawned.

Pulchra was holding Nipur in her arms and stroking his silky head.

'Look!' she said. 'I have a puppy, too!'

'That's Nubia's puppy,' he said, and scratched his dark curly hair.

'Don't be silly! Slaves can't own property. They *are* property. Where's Lupus?'

'I don't know.'

'Well, Fulvia told me she isn't feeling well today so you and I can have breakfast all on our own!'

'Oh. Um . . . OK.'

Jonathan looked at Pulchra and waited.

Pulchra looked brightly back at Jonathan.

'I'm . . . I'm not wearing any . . . If you could just . . .'

Pulchra giggled. 'Oh! You want me to turn around. Very well.'

Jonathan quickly got up and slipped on his cream-coloured tunic. He noticed someone had cleaned it during the night. It bore the same smell as the blankets.

He splashed his face with water from the jug, and reached for a small towel. In the middle of drying his face he stopped and sniffed the towel.

'What *is* this smell?' he asked Pulchra. 'It's in all the blankets and cushions, and now even my tunic smells of it.'

'I'll show you!' She caught his hand and pulled him out into the corridor.

It was a still, cool morning just after dawn. A huge moon, almost full and the colour of an apricot, floated just above the milky sea.

Jonathan followed Pulchra up some stairs and into an inner garden surrounded by a peristyle. There were ash-dusted jasmine bushes, pomegranates and quince, but in the middle was a beautiful tree with glossy dark green leaves and heavy yellow fruit. Something about it was different from the other plants around it. Suddenly he realised what it was.

'It's not covered by ash!'

'Pater had the slaves cover it with a linen cloth soon after Vesuvius erupted,' explained Pulchra. 'And they dust it every day. It's one of pater's most precious treasures.'

Something stirred deep in Jonathan's memory as he gazed at the tree.

'What kind of tree is it?'

'Some people call it the Persian apple tree but pater says it's a citron tree. He calls it lemon. He named Villa Limona after this tree. Here.' She carefully twisted one of the yellow fruits from the branch and handed it to Jonathan. It was heavy, with a waxy surface, and it filled the palm of his hand.

'Pierce the skin with your fingernail and smell it,' she said.

Jonathan dug his thumbnail into the yellow skin and then brought the lemon to his nose. Its scent was hauntingly beautiful.

'That lemon alone would cost a hundred sesterces in the markets of Rome,' said Pulchra. 'We use the oil to preserve wood and we make perfume from the little white blossoms that appear in the spring. We use it for everything. Sniff me.' She lifted her golden hair and offered her smooth neck to Jonathan. Tentatively he sniffed the perfumed oil she had dabbed behind her ears.

'Wonderful,' he whispered, and for some reason tears sprang to his eyes.

'Pater's dream,' said Pulchra, caressing one of the glossy green leaves, 'is to cover the hillside with orchards and orchards of these trees.'

'And where is your father now?' Jonathan tried to make his voice sound casual.

'Seeing his boring old clients,' said Pulchra. 'As usual.'

'Oh,' said Jonathan, and sniffed the lemon again.

'Someone mentioned that your father was quite a powerful man and that even his clients were powerful. They must have been wrong.'

Pulchra's blue eyes blazed. 'Pater is powerful! More powerful than the Emperor himself.'

Jonathan shrugged and started to stroll round the garden. 'If you say so . . .'

Pulchra caught his hand. Even though there was no one else in sight she brought her lips close to his ear. 'I have a secret spying place we can watch him from,' she whispered. 'Would you like to see it?'

Jonathan turned and looked at her. He had never seen such blue eyes. He nodded.

Lupus made his way carefully down the steep path to the secret harbour. Although the Villa Limona was over twenty miles from Vesuvius, even here a thin layer of grey ash from the eruption dusted the rocks and wild flowers on either side of the track. Suddenly he stopped as he realised that the path itself was totally clear of ash. That could only mean one thing: it was frequently used.

He shrugged. Perhaps they just came down to swim. But Felix's daughter had mentioned that they had their own baths complex, so why bathe here? Then he noticed a rowing boat pulled up on the shore. It was small, but only a small boat would fit through the arched opening that led to the open sea.

Lupus looked all around. He was alone. Pulling off his tunic, he quickly hid it beneath an oleander bush and then stepped into the water. There was a scum of grey ash and pumice dust at the waterline, but further out the surface of the sea was clean. He slipped naked into the water.

Although its coldness took his breath away, he felt he was home. He had learned to swim before he could walk and now he swam forward with smooth powerful strokes, heading towards the arch in the rocks which led out to sea.

'Shhh! I thought I heard a noise! Is anyone coming?' Flavia was searching Pulchra's bedroom for clues. Nubia stood guard at the door. She peeped out, then turned back and shook her head.

Flavia closed the jewellery box and replaced it on the elegant bronze table. Arranged on the table were the usual things: ivory combs and hairpins, coloured glass perfume bottles, a highly polished bronze mirror.

There was also a long thin rod. Flavia frowned and picked it up. It seemed to be made of willow or birch and it tapered at one end. It was slightly sticky. Flavia shrugged and replaced it exactly where she had found it.

She turned and surveyed the room. There was a bed with dark blue woollen covers, a bronze standing lamp and a small leather and bronze stool. There was also a large cedar chest against the wall by the foot of the bed. Flavia tiptoed over to it, undid the latch and slowly lifted its heavy lid.

Then she screamed.

Curled up inside the chest was Pulchra's slave-girl.

Jonathan squeezed after Pulchra along a narrow space between two walls. They had left the puppies in the garden near the lemon tree and Pulchra had led him through a maze of porticoes and rooms through the kitchen and into a kind of pantry.

'Along here,' she gasped, edging her way along. 'Pretty soon I won't be able to fit any more.'

A week earlier Jonathan wouldn't have been able to fit either, but he had been in a coma for three days with no food and had eaten very little since. He had never been so thin.

Finally they reached a place with tiny gaps in the bricks. Pulchra silently pointed to one. Jonathan brought his eye close and found he was looking into a large room, a tablinum. He could see the backs of two muscular men in sea-green standing beside a column. Beside them stood a short man in a tan tunic. Beyond him Jonathan could see part of a table and a frescoed wall.

After a moment the muscular men shifted to one side and Jonathan saw that Pulchra's father sat behind the table. A scribe in a lemon-yellow tunic stood beside him.

Pollius Felix was leaning back in a bronze and leather chair, listening to the man in the tan tunic. The sun streamed in from the left, illuminating the short man and part of the table, but leaving Felix's face in shadow.

'Please do me this service, Patron,' the man in tan was saying. His voice was muffled but perfectly audible. 'It's a terrible thing that my lovely little Maia has disappeared. For ten years I have brought you the first crop of olives and the first pressing of oil. I have never asked a favour in return, only your protection. But now I ask that you find and return her to me and punish the men who took her!'

Jonathan and Pulchra exchanged wide-eyed looks, then returned to their peepholes. Felix had risen from his chair and moved out from behind the table. He wore a white toga over a pale blue tunic.

'Rusticus.' Felix embraced the man, then held him at arm's length. Jonathan could see the man was a peasant, with sunburnt, leathery skin.

Felix put an arm around Rusticus and walked him away from the desk, towards Jonathan and Pulchra. 'You were right to come to me first, Rusticus. I will find your little Maia and punish the culprits. Tell me what happened.'

'My youngest son Quintus saw everything,' stammered the farmer. 'He and Maia were playing hide-and-seek among the olives when the men appeared.' His voice broke. 'Maia drew the men away from his hiding-place, so that they wouldn't catch him, too.'

The farmer stifled a sob and Jonathan saw Felix signal one of his men. A moment later a slave stepped into Jonathan's field of vision with a wine cup.

'Here,' said Felix. 'Drink this.'

The farmer drained the cup and shuddered. 'I'm sorry, Patron.'

'Don't be ashamed of your tears,' said Felix. 'A real man is never afraid to weep for his family. Tell me. Was there anything else about these men? Anything which might identify them?'

'I'm not sure. My little Quintus has a great imagination, but I don't think he made this up . . .'

'Go on,' said Felix quietly, his arm still around the shorter man's shoulders.

'Quintus said the men who took Maia were wearing masks, like the ones actors wear at the theatre. Horrible, grinning masks.'

SCROLL XIII

Lupus stopped swimming. He rolled over and floated on the gentle swell of the bay, looking back towards the Villa Limona. From most angles it was impossible to see the entrance to the villa's secret harbour.

The villa itself was built on at least four levels. He saw a row of white columns half way down and realised it was the portico outside his bedroom. On the floor above it, the ground floor, was a larger portico. Its columns were fluted and they had red bases.

With all its different levels and domes the Villa Limona looked more like a small village than a villa. Beyond it he could see the long covered colonnade down which he had driven the day before. It was surrounded by silvery-green olives, looking greyer under their covering of ash. Beyond them rose more grey-green slopes, then rugged mountains. The sun was just rising behind them to his left.

Lupus was beginning to get cold, but his short rest had re-energised him so he swam south, away from the villa and its secret harbour.

Some of Felix's slaves were climbing up the rocks on the other side of the villa. He could see their fishing nets full of shining fish thrown over their backs. He stopped to tread water and look.

Near the fishing rocks was a man-made pier. Moored to it was a long sleek ship. It had a mast and sail and holes for ten oars on either side. It was light and narrow, designed more for speed than transport. Beyond it a small headland offered some protection from the winds.

Further south, the shore became rugged. There was a small beach and then sheer cliffs plunging straight into the water. These cliffs were riddled with grottoes at water level, and caves above.

Suddenly a flash of colour caught Lupus's eye. Emerging from one of the grottoes was a boat. At any other time of day it would have been difficult to see, especially at this distance, but the early morning surface of the water was still milky and so the dark blue boat stood out clearly against it.

Flavia and Nubia stared down in horror at the slave-girl curled up in the box, and she gazed back, rolling her eyes in terror. She lay on one side with her knees drawn up almost to her face, which was red and swollen from crying.

Flavia couldn't remember the girl's name, but Nubia did. She held out her hand.

'Come out, Leda,' she whispered.

Leda shook her head. 'I can't,' she whimpered. 'She'll beat me even more if I don't stay here.'

'You mean she knows you're here?' gasped Flavia.

Leda nodded. 'She makes me stay in here when I

misbehave.' The slave-girl's nose was running, so Flavia held out a linen handkerchief. Leda made no move to take it. She stared as if she had never seen one before.

'It's all right,' said Flavia. 'Blow your nose. And you can keep it,' she added.

'No!' whimpered Leda. 'She'd only say I stole it and then she'd beat me.'

Flavia and Nubia looked at each other in dismay.

'Please come out,' Flavia said. 'I'll make sure you aren't punished.'

Leda shook her head. 'You'll be gone in a day or a week and when you're gone she'll just beat me again, even harder.'

Flavia knelt on the floor beside the cedarwood chest so that she wasn't looming over the slave-girl.

'Leda,' she whispered. 'I'll talk to Pulchra. I promise I'll try to make things better for you. Please don't worry.' She patted the girl on the shoulder, and Leda winced.

Flavia suddenly went cold. She stood and leaned further over, trying to see the slave-girl's back. In one or two places, seeping through the fine yellow linen of her tunic, Flavia could see the dark stain of fresh blood where Pulchra had wielded the birch switch with particular vigour.

Jonathan's stomach growled loudly. For over two hours he'd been riveted to his peephole, watching Felix receive his clients. Now at last, his stomach was protesting. He glanced at Pulchra ruefully. She smiled and nodded and motioned for him to go. But just as he began to edge back towards the kitchen, he felt her hand catch his.

He turned and looked back at her.

Pulchra was pointing urgently towards the peephole.

Curious, Jonathan put his eye back to the chink in the bricks. And gasped.

Felix stood in front of his desk facing left, his fine profile lit by the weak morning sun.

Approaching him was the biggest, ugliest man Jonathan had ever seen. The giant wore a sea-green tunic the size of a ship's sail and his thin black hair was plastered over his balding scalp in ridiculous imitation of the younger men around him. His thighs were so huge that they rubbed together as he moved forward, yet they were not fat, but solid muscle. His chest was massive and his arms muscular and oiled. His nose had been broken at least twice and his ears were swollen like cauliflowers.

The big man lumbered up to Felix, dropped to his knees and fervently kissed his patron's hand.

Back in the sky-blue triclinium, when it was safe to talk, Jonathan turned to Pulchra. 'Who was that huge man?'

'I could tell you some stories about him!' Pulchra dipped a piece of bread in liquid honey and took a dainty bite. 'His name is Lucius Brassus and he's one of my father's most loyal soldiers.'

Jonathan frowned. 'What do you mean, soldier?'

'Did I say soldier?' Pulchra giggled. 'I meant client of course . . . Oh, good morning, Fulvia! You're just in time for some breakfast.'

Jonathan looked up to see Flavia and Nubia standing in the doorway with Scuto behind them. Flavia's face was pale.

'Oh, dear,' said Pulchra, 'you don't look at all well, Fulvia. And look at your hair! You must ask Leda to arrange it for you right away.'

'What's wrong with my hair?' Flavia's hand went automatically to her head.

'Nothing's wrong with it,' said Jonathan. 'It looks like it always does.'

'Oh,' said Flavia, and Jonathan was startled by the look of cold fury on her face. Pulchra didn't notice; she was letting Nipur lick honey from her finger.

Jonathan opened his eyes wide at Flavia, as if to say: What's the matter?

She took a deep breath and gave a little shake of her head. Some colour returned to her face.

'Actually, Pulchra,' said Flavia in a sweet voice, 'I'd love Leda to style my hair. You're absolutely right. I can't possibly go out in public with it looking like this. Where is Leda anyway?' Flavia looked round innocently.

Pulchra didn't even bother to look up. 'She's in the big cedar chest in my bedroom. Just tell her to do your hair like mine. And you may as well bring her back here afterwards.'

Lupus had just slipped on his tunic and was pushing his wet hair back from his forehead when he heard voices.

People were coming down the path.

He quickly ducked behind the oleander bushes, glad he was wearing his olive green tunic. He made himself as still and quiet as possible.

'What's her name again?' Lupus heard a man's voice say.

'Maia. Maia Rustica. About nine or ten years old.' The second voice was very deep and Lupus thought he recognised it from dinner the night before.

'I don't see why it's so urgent,' said the first man. Lupus heard a scraping noise and a splash; they were launching the boat. 'Besides, now that she knows where the others are she could ruin everything.'

'It's urgent because her father Rusticus lives just up the hill,' said the man with the deep voice. 'He's one of the Patron's clients. They never should have taken a child from so close to home. My brother and his friends are idiots. I hear they performed a comedy about pirates on their last night at the refugee camp. Imagine. Risking everything for a few coins!' Deep Voice swore. 'Anyway, bring the girl straight back to me.'

'I still don't see what good that will do,' Lupus heard the first man grumble. There was a creak and the soft plop of oars. He must be in the boat now.

'I'll have a word with her,' said Deep Voice. 'She's a local girl; she'll know enough to keep her mouth shut.'

'All right,' said the first man. 'I should be back in about an hour.'

'I'll be here,' said Deep Voice. Suddenly Lupus remembered his name. He was Crispus, a muscular man with black hair, dark stubble on his jaw and eyelashes as long as a girl's. The night before, he'd told a funny joke about two Greek merchants and an olive.

He was also the Patron's right-hand man.

SCROLL XIV

Lupus breathed a sigh of relief as he heard Crispus go back up the path. He counted to one hundred and then slowly rose and peered round the dusty oleander. There was no one in sight, so he strolled casually back up the path, as if returning from a morning walk.

His mind was racing. The actors from the camp must be the kidnappers. But who was Maia? How could she ruin everything? And who was Crispus's brother? He needed to talk to Flavia and the others. He turned and passed between marble columns into the garden. It was only three hours past dawn and already the air was shimmering with heat.

Suddenly he realised he'd taken a wrong turn. This wasn't the same garden he'd come out of.

He knew his bedroom faced west so he walked away from the rising sun. Yes, there was the sea, straight ahead, visible through more columns. But these columns were fluted, and painted deep red to about his shoulder height. He was on the upper portico, one floor above his bedroom.

He stood and looked out at the view for a moment, enjoying the faint offshore breeze which touched his hair.

'Hello,' said a pleasant voice behind him. 'Who are you?'

Lupus turned. Sitting in a chair beside one of the columns was a beautiful woman in pale blue. She had delicate features and golden hair.

Lupus flipped open his wax tablet and wrote

MY NAME IS LUPUS. I CAN'T SPEAK.

'I'm sorry,' said the woman, and then gave him a sweet smile. 'Please sit beside me and keep me company for a while.' She patted the empty chair next to her.

Lupus hesitated, but only for the briefest moment. Flavia wanted them to learn all they could about Felix. This woman might know something. He sat beside her on a comfortable wicker chair with yellow linen cushions.

'I suppose you're one of my husband's new proteges,' the woman said. 'He seems to recruit them younger every year. How old are you? About eight?'

Lupus nodded.

She smiled. 'My name is Polla Argentaria,' she said, 'wife of the most powerful man in the Roman Empire. Or so they say. A man who inspires fear or devotion. Sometimes both.' She glanced at Lupus. 'I can see you are one of those who is devoted to Felix. How does he do that?' she said, almost to herself. 'How does he win people's hearts so easily?'

Lupus glanced at her. She had high cheekbones and arched eyebrows.

'I believe,' said Felix's wife, gazing out towards the

horizon, 'that when he is with you, he focuses all his power and charm and attention on you alone. The rest of the world seems to fade away and he is yours. But,' she said, 'at the very moment you think he is yours, you become his.'

Lupus looked out towards the horizon, waiting for his face to cool and his heart to stop pounding. When he finally glanced back at her, he saw that she was asleep. He rose carefully, so that the wicker chair would not creak.

As he turned to go, something on the water caught his eye. A small rowing boat was moving slowly south, heading for the grottoes.

He must find the others as soon as possible.

Leda climbed out of the cedarwood chest to do Flavia's hair. But before she began, she let the girls smooth balm over the ugly welts on her back.

After that, it only took Pulchra's slave-girl a few minutes to arrange Flavia's hair. She pulled it up in an elegant but comfortable twist, held with just four ivory hairpins.

'You're very good!' said Flavia, gazing into Pulchra's bronze hand mirror and patting her hair.

Leda turned bright pink, and Flavia guessed it was probably the first time in her life the slave-girl had ever been praised.

Lupus found them all in one of the inner gardens. They were staring at a tree. Apart from the yellow fruit it looked like an ordinary bay tree to him.

As soon as Pulchra's back was turned he signalled

Flavia that he had urgent news. Flavia looked pointedly at Pulchra and shrugged, as if to say: What can we do?

'. . . and it's worth over a million sesterces,' Pulchra was saying.

Lupus saw Flavia looking around for inspiration. Suddenly her eye focused on something on the hillside.

'What's that up in the vineyards?' Flavia asked Pulchra. 'It looks like a little temple.'

'Oh, that's an ancient shrine to the wine god Dionysus,' said Pulchra importantly. 'Of course we own all that land up there.'

'Could we go and see it? Dionysus is my favourite god.' Lupus had never heard Flavia mention Dionysus before.

'I don't know,' said Pulchra slowly. 'I don't usually walk anywhere, and it's too steep for a litter . . .'

'I'd love to go for a walk with you,' said Jonathan, with his most charming smile. 'I'll bet the view from there is wonderful.'

'We could take a picnic lunch,' suggested Flavia.

'We want to go! We want to go!' cried Pulchra's little sisters. 'A picnic! A picnic!'

'Don't be silly.' Pulchra tossed her golden hair. 'You're too young. You'd get terribly tired.' She turned to the others. 'You wait here. I'll tell our cook to prepare a picnic. Come on, Leda!'

Pulchra went off towards the kitchen with her two little sisters clamouring at her heels.

When they were gone the four friends turned to each other and Lupus gave Flavia a thumbs up.

'Quickly,' said Flavia, 'Before she gets back. Any clues?'

Lupus began to write on his wax tablet.

'Pulchra took me to spy on her own father!' said Jonathan and his dark eyes gleamed. 'We watched him receiving his clients for nearly two hours. He gives people money or advice and they kiss his hand and call him Patron and he has one client named Lucius Brassus, who's the size of Ostia's lighthouse. And,' Jonathan took a breath and continued before Flavia could comment, 'he promised to find the daughter of one of his clients. She was kidnapped yesterday!'

As Jonathan finished speaking, Lupus held his wax tablet behind Jonathan's shoulder.

'Was she by any chance named . . . Maia?' asked Flavia.

Jonathan's jaw dropped. 'How did you know?'

Flavia nodded towards Lupus. On his tablet he had written:

MAIA. IX OR X. KIDNAPPED.
ARRIVING SOON AT COVE.
I WILL GO AND TRY TO FIND OUT MORE

*

Nubia shifted the picnic basket on her shoulder. She and Leda were both carrying baskets and water gourds. The baskets and gourds weren't particularly heavy but Nubia thought the straps must hurt Leda's tender back. Nubia also noted that Leda was barefoot.

Pulchra, on the other hand, wore pretty leather slippers that were totally unsuitable for climbing. Whenever she slipped she squealed and clutched at

Jonathan. She soon decided it was easier to hold his hand all the time.

By the time they reached the shrine her pretty yellow locks were clinging damply to her forehead.

'Great Juno!' Pulchra gasped, as they finally reached the small marble building. 'Give me that water, Leda.'

The dogs had begun by running up the path ahead of them, sniffing eagerly here and there, tails wagging, but they were soon defeated by the heat and humidity. Now they flopped panting in the cool shade of an ancient yew tree beside the shrine.

Nubia turned and looked around. She could see for miles. She gazed back down the silver, olive-covered slopes towards the Villa Limona. There were the domes of the bathhouse, the covered walkway, and the spot in the garden where they'd stood an hour before. She could also see the secret harbour. As she watched, a small boat appeared through the arched opening and she saw two figures in it.

Then they were blocked from her view.

Behind her she heard Flavia say, 'Can we look inside the shrine?'

Nubia turned.

'I don't think it's locked,' Pulchra said, handing the gourd back to Leda without even looking at her.

The temple was made of pink and cream marble. Up three steps and through four columns was a bronze door leading into the shrine. Pulchra turned the handle and Jonathan applied his shoulder. The door was heavy but swung open smoothly. They all went in, apart from Leda, who waited outside.

It was a very small shrine, dimly lit by small, high

windows. The air inside was cool and musty and smelled of stale incense and wine. On the walls were frescoes of dolphins and in front of them was the image of the god: a painted wooden statue of a young man striding forward with an oddly frozen smile. The young god had red lips and black-rimmed eyes which stared over their heads, out towards the blue sea. Around his neck was a withered garland so old it was brown.

'How strange.' Flavia was studying the walls. 'Why dolphins?'

A movement caught Nubia's eye. A large brown spider moved delicately down the statue's wooden thigh. Nubia shivered and was just turning away when a gleam of gold caught her eye. Something lay on the pedestal near the god's left foot.

While the others were still examining the dolphins on the walls, Nubia quickly reached out and took the tiny object. Her heart was pounding as her fist closed tightly around it.

It was the tiger's-eye earring she had given to Kuanto.

SCROLL XV

As they sat in the shade of the yew tree and unpacked their picnic lunches, Nubia's mind raced.

'What a strange thing to find in a shrine of Dionysus,' said Flavia, uncorking her water gourd.

Nubia looked up, alarmed. Had Flavia seen her take the earring?

'Dolphins have nothing to do with the god of wine,' mused Flavia. 'Satyrs, yes. Or frenzied dancing girls, but dolphins?'

Nubia breathed a sigh of relief and bent her head over her lunch again. The cook had prepared six napkins, each wrapped around a selection of delicacies. There were stuffed vine leaves, cold chicken, glossy purple olives, fig cakes and flat white bread.

As the others were opening their own napkins, Nubia slipped the earring into the leather pouch at her belt. Then she took a bite of chicken and carefully scanned the vines below and the trees above.

Kuanto had told her that when the time was near he would leave her earring where she would see it.

Somehow he had followed and found her. She had only spoken to him once in the refugee camp, was it three nights ago? It had been so dark that she hadn't even been able to see what he looked like. Perhaps he was watching her even now.

Again she studied the trees, looking for the signal. Suddenly she saw it: a scarlet cord tied round a branch of another yew further up the hill. Nubia forced herself to take another bite of chicken even though her stomach was churning with excitement.

'These stuffed vine leaves are delicious,' Flavia was saying to Pulchra. 'What's in them?'

'Chickpeas, pepper and lemon juice,' said Pulchra, nipping one neatly in half with her even, white teeth and then popping the remaining half into Jonathan's mouth.

'Mmmph!' said Jonathan, then chewed and swallowed. 'Tart. But nice.'

Flavia was unwrapping hers to examine its contents.

Nubia slowly got to her feet and Flavia squinted up at her. 'Are you all right, Nubia? You look . . . strange.'

'My stomach is unhappy,' said Nubia. 'I go behind bushes.'

'OK,' said Flavia, and turned back to her stuffed grape leaf.

Nubia glanced back once as she walked up towards the yew tree. The others were all intent on their lunches. All except Nipur, who yawned and stretched and trotted after her up the slope, wagging his little black tail.

Lupus watched from the hillside above the Villa Limona as the girl stepped out of the rowing boat onto the shore of the secret cove.

Crispus was waiting for her, looking around nervously. When she reached him he bent down and spoke to her urgently. The girl was crying, but she nodded her head. Finally Crispus stood and tousled her dark hair.

Then he took the girl's hand and led her up the path. They went into the stables, and a moment later emerged on horseback, with the girl sitting in front of Crispus. Lupus hadn't expected that.

As they trotted past him, he hid behind an ancient olive tree, then slipped off his sandals and ran after them. The white paving stones were smooth on his bare feet, for the covered drive was as superbly made as any Roman road, gently rising in the middle and with drains to carry away rainwater on either side. It occurred to him, as he ran, that it must have taken hundreds of soldiers to build such a road. He wondered how Felix had arranged it and how much it had cost.

By the time he'd reached the main coastal road his heart was pounding and he was gasping for breath. Lupus looked right and left and up the slopes. But the horse and its riders were nowhere to be seen.

Nubia reached up and touched the scarlet cord.

The trunk of the yew screened her from the others and she looked eagerly around for another red cord. There it was! Tied around the lowest branch of a tree further up the slope. She ran to it as lightly and quickly as she could, conscious that the others would soon wonder where she was.

Suddenly Nipur growled at a movement in the shrubbery. Before she could gasp, someone grabbed her round the waist and a hand covered her mouth. She felt hot breath in her ear and heard a voice whisper, 'It's me. Fuscus. Kuanto, I mean. Don't scream.'

He released her slowly and Nubia turned to look at him.

Kuanto of the Jackal Clan stood looking down at her. She guessed he was the age of her eldest brother, about sixteen or seventeen. He was smiling at her with perfect teeth and she felt her face grow hot.

He was very handsome.

Later that afternoon, Nubia stood behind Flavia, combing her mistress's light brown hair, still damp from the baths.

'Do you think you can do my hair the way Leda did it this morning?' asked Flavia. Her grey eyes were sparkling. They'd been invited to dine with Pollius Felix and his wife.

Pulchra's sisters had run to meet them as soon as they got back from their picnic.

'Pater and mater have invited us to dine with them tonight,' they squealed with excitement. 'All of us.'

'Don't be silly,' Pulchra had replied irritably; she was very hot and tired. But it had been true.

'This is a real honour,' Pulchra told Flavia at least half a dozen times while they made the circuit of the Villa Limona's private baths. 'They almost never dine with us any more.' And Nubia had noticed a strange expression on Pulchra's face.

After their bath, Nubia tried to arrange Flavia's hair the way Leda had done it that morning.

'Thank you, Nubia.' Flavia, patted her hair and looked in the bronze mirror. 'You've done it just as nicely as Leda did it. I can't believe Felix is actually going to dine with us . . .' She sighed. 'Now where's my bulla?'

Nubia bent to do the fine clasp of the silver chain around Flavia's neck. Attached to the chain was a bulla – the charm worn by freeborn children until they were considered grown-up. As Nubia tried to open the clasp, she wondered if anyone would ever comb her hair again, as her mother had used to do. Her fingers were still oily from rubbing Flavia down and suddenly the chain slipped and the bulla fell onto the tiled floor.

'Stupid!' muttered Flavia angrily. She bent to retrieve it and thrust it impatiently at Nubia. With shaking hands, Nubia finally managed to do the clasp.

'Do I look all right?' said Flavia, holding up the bronze mirror again.

But Nubia could tell she wasn't expecting an answer.

As Flavia followed Pulchra into the private triclinium of Polla Argentaria, she was handed a garland of ivy, miniature yellow roses, and lemon leaves. Pulchra's younger sisters were already there, reclining on cream linen couches. So were Jonathan and Lupus. They both wore new sea-green tunics. Lupus had slicked his dark hair back from his forehead.

'Very fashionable!' observed Flavia.

Lupus tried to look unconcerned as he adjusted his garland, but Jonathan coloured. 'I think they're a gift from Felix. They were laid out on our beds when we came out of the baths.'

Nubia was already there, standing beside Leda. She wore one of the lemon-yellow tunics worn by all the slaves of the Villa Limona. The colour glowed against her dark skin and Flavia was proud to have such a beautiful slave-girl standing behind her as she reclined.

The walls of the north-facing dining-room were pale yellow, with an elegant black and cream frieze of winged cupids riding chariots. In one corner of the room was a Greek sculpture of Venus; the bronze goddess was shown undressing for her bath. Beneath the statue of Venus sat a young slave strumming melodious chords on a lyre. It was definitely a woman's dining-room, decided Flavia. She could hardly wait to see what Felix's wife looked like.

At last, followed by their slaves, Publius Pollius Felix and his wife Polla Argentaria stepped into the dining-room.

SCROLL XVI

Polla was almost as tall as her husband, and very beautiful. But it was a pale, transparent beauty, and she seemed almost ghostlike beside Felix's intense presence.

After the introductions had been made, Felix and Polla reclined on the central couch. The serving-girls immediately brought in the first tables and set them before the couches.

The first course consisted of hard-boiled quail eggs and button mushrooms glazed with honey and fish sauce. They were delicious, and small enough to be eaten elegantly. Lupus seemed to like them, probably because they slipped down his throat so easily.

As they ate, Felix turned to Flavia, who reclined on the couch to his right. 'Tell me, Flavia Gemina,' he said, 'what did you do today?'

For a moment Flavia was tempted to say, 'We spied on you,' but instead she said, 'We walked up to the shrine of Dionysus and had a picnic lunch there.'

'The wine god loves the hills, the north wind and the cool shade of the yew tree,' quoted Felix.

'Virgil?' asked Flavia.

Felix opened his eyes in surprise and nodded. '*The Georgics*. I'm impressed.'

'Why are dolphins painted on the walls of his shrine?' asked Flavia, not wanting to lose his attention.

Felix raised one of his dark eyebrows and gave her an amused glance. 'I'm surprised a well-educated girl like you doesn't know the connection.' He glanced up and whispered something to the slave who stood behind him. The young man nodded and hurried out of the dining-room.

A moment later the slave was back. He handed Felix a ceramic drinking-cup and resumed his place behind his master's couch.

Felix held the cup out to Flavia. She could tell at once that it was Greek and probably an antique, so she took it carefully with both hands.

'It's an Athenian kylix,' said Felix, 'one of the most valuable antiques I own. Any idea how old it is?'

Flavia thought quickly. Her uncle Gaius had a mixing bowl with red figures on black which was over five hundred years old. This elegant cup had black figures on red, and she knew black-figure was even older than red-figure.

'Over six hundred years old?' she hazarded a guess.

Felix raised both eyebrows this time. 'Again I'm impressed, Flavia Gemina. Very impressed. Now, can you tell me who is painted inside?'

Painted in black glaze on the bottom of the cup's wide flat bowl was an elegant ship with a white sail and a tiny white dolphin on its prow. The potter had painted a man reclining in the ship, completely filling it up. This figure wore a garland on his head and in his hand he held a wine cup.

Flavia studied the kylix for a moment and then held

it up so that Pulchra, Jonathan and Lupus could see, too.

'It's Dionysus, the god of wine, isn't it?' said Pulchra.

'Clever girl,' said Felix with a smile. 'But tell me, what's unusual about the scene?'

'The fact that there's an enormous grapevine growing up the mast?' suggested Jonathan.

'Exactly.'

'And there are six, no – seven dolphins swimming in the water,' said Flavia.

'The Greek poet Homer tells the story in his seventh hymn,' said Felix, as the serving-girls cleared away the tables.

'One day the god Dionysus was standing on the shore of the Tyrrhenian Sea when some pirates came sailing by. Even from a distance they could see he was a noble man so they decided to kidnap him and ask an enormous ransom.'

Flavia, Jonathan and Lupus exchanged glances.

'The pirates dragged the god into their ship and tied him up. But when they were well out to sea, Dionysus caused the ropes which bound him to become grape-vines. The vines curled up the mast and over the rigging and in no time bore huge clusters of blue-black grapes. The pirates gazed at each other in horror. They knew their captive must be a god, one of the immortals.'

Felix was reclining with a garland on his head as he told the story, and Flavia could easily imagine what Dionysus had looked like.

'Suddenly,' said Felix, 'Dionysus turned into a lion and roared in their faces. After all, he is the god of wine, intoxication and madness. The pirates leapt over-board before the beast could devour them.'

Lupus guffawed loudly and Felix gave him an amused glance.

'Then the god became himself again and enjoyed a leisurely cup of wine as the boat carried him back home.'

'But what do the dolphins have to do with the story?' asked Flavia.

'Well,' said Felix, 'the wine put Dionysus in such good spirits that he took pity on the drowning sailors and turned them all into dolphins. And that is how dolphins came to be.'

'What a wonderful story,' sighed Flavia, gazing at the brave and handsome god who vanquished pirates. At last she handed the beautiful cup back to Felix.

He gave a little shake of his head. 'Keep it,' he said. 'It's yours.'

Flavia felt her face go cold and then hot. She swallowed and tried to protest. But no words came.

Felix smiled. 'What good are riches if you can't give them away?' he said. 'Friends are far more important than possessions.'

The serving-girls brought in the second course: white fish, baked fennel and sweet baby onions. The fish was cod, baked in a crust of rock salt and coriander seeds. Beside each piece was a wedge of lemon.

'Finally! Some lemon!' cried Jonathan. He popped the entire wedge into his mouth and began to chew it.

At the look on his face everyone burst out laughing, especially Pollina and Pollinilla, who screamed with laughter and kicked their chubby legs in the air. Polla smiled and made a subtle gesture. Her slave demonstrated how to squeeze the lemon wedge over the fish.

Jonathan squeezed another wedge of lemon over his fish and tentatively took a bite. It was salty and sour at the same time. And absolutely delicious.

'Speaking of Dionysus . . .' said Felix, and nodded at a slave hovering in the doorway. The wine steward moved smoothly forward, a jug in either hand. Expertly he filled each guest's cup, simultaneously pouring out foamy black wine from one jug, and clear water from the other. The mixture ranged from ruby red in Felix's cup to palest pink for the little girls.

Felix took a sip of wine and closed his eyes to savour the taste. Then he raised his cup to Flavia.

'Your uncle's wine,' he said, 'the finest wine in the region. What a pity his vineyards are now buried under the ash of Vesuvius.'

'Did you see the ash when you took the Emperor back to Stabia?' asked Jonathan.

'Indeed I did,' said Felix. 'There were treasure-hunters trying to tunnel their way into rich men's houses.'

'Did they find anything?' asked Jonathan. Lupus, reclining next to him, sat up on his elbow with interest.

'Only their own graves. The ash has hardened on top, but it's only a crust. If you walk on the crust you fall in. Then you sink down and drown in the ash.'

Jonathan shuddered.

'So far,' continued Felix, 'despite what Titus said, we have not found one person alive. I don't think you realise how lucky you were to survive. The gods must surely have favoured you.' He sipped his wine and turned his dark eyes on Flavia.

'Tell us, Flavia Gemina, how did you manage to escape the volcano?'

Flavia told them.

When she started her story, the evening sky was as pink as half-watered wine, and a slave was lighting the bronze lamps. When she finished, night had fallen. One or two of the brighter stars winked dimly above the horizon.

Flavia looked up and realised the lyre player had stopped strumming some time ago; he was staring at her, his mouth wide open. The serving-girls stood transfixed in the doorway, unwilling to take out the main course and miss any of the tale. Polla had a pained look on her face, as if she had experienced the terror of that night with them.

And Flavia knew without looking that Felix's eyes had never left her face. She glanced at him quickly and felt a thrill of pleasure at the admiration in his eyes.

'Remarkable,' he murmured. 'I think we should celebrate your survival with something special. Pulchra? Do you agree?'

'Yes, pater!' She clapped her hands. 'The lemon wine!'

Pollina and Pollinilla had been dozing off. Suddenly they were wide awake, chanting: 'Lemon wine! Lemon wine!'

Felix nodded at the wine steward, who tried to suppress a smile.

The serving-girls took away the empty plates and brought dessert: honey-soaked sesame cakes.

'Mmmm, my favourite,' said Jonathan, licking the honey from his fingers.

The wine steward appeared with a painted wooden tray. On it were a dozen small cups of fine Alexandrian glass. Flavia knew they were of the highest quality because the glass was almost clear. In the centre of the tray was a clear glass decanter full of bright yellow liquid.

The steward filled the little glasses and gave one to each of the guests.

Flavia sipped hers. It was tart and lemony, but at the same time deliciously sweet and sticky. She drained it and boldly extended her empty glass for a refill.

Felix was tuning the strings of a lyre. 'My turn to tell a story,' he said. 'Or rather, to sing a story.'

For a while he played a complicated, bittersweet tune. Then he began to sing. Pollina and Pollinilla had fallen asleep, their faces flushed and damp, their fine hair golden in the lamplight. Pulchra gazed at her father with adoration. Lupus was watching him, too, his eyes as green and still as a cat's. Polla's eyes were closed, but she was not asleep.

Felix sang a song Flavia was not familiar with. It was a song about the Cretan princess Ariadne, and how she found love on the island of Naxos. His voice was slightly husky and he sang as beautifully as he played. When he finished everyone applauded, but softly, so as not to wake the little girls.

Polla opened her eyes. 'My husband is too modest to tell you,' she said quietly, 'but he wrote the song himself and won a prize for it at the festival last year.'

Felix inclined his head graciously. Then he turned to Flavia. 'Do you play?'

Flavia's heart sank. The only instrument she could play was the tambourine, and even that not very well. Then she had an idea.

'I don't play, but Nubia does!' she glanced over her shoulder. 'Nubia, play your flute for us! Come on!' Flavia tugged the hem of Nubia's yellow tunic in order to pull her onto the foot of the dining-couch.

Nubia was not used to standing for so long and she was glad to sit. As she took out her flute she was aware of everyone watching her, so she closed her eyes to concentrate. After a moment a picture came into her mind.

She lifted the flute to her lips and began to play. She played a new song, a song her father had never taught her, a song her brother had never taught her. In her mind Nubia called it Slave Song.

She played the desert at sunset, with slanting purple shadows, and a line of swaying camels, moving on, always on.

Riding one of the camels was a girl whose amber eyes were full of tears. The girl had nothing. Her family was gone. Her tents were burnt. Her dog lay in the dust. The girl's back was raw from the whip, and around her neck was a cold iron collar.

But the tears on her cheek were tears of joy.

A crescent moon hung above the horizon. Beneath it were date palms, silhouetted against a violet sky. An oasis.

She knew there would be water there. And honey-sweet dates. And cool silver sand. And someone who cared for her.

And best of all, freedom.

Flavia woke the next morning with a throbbing headache and a sick feeling in the pit of her stomach. She didn't even remember going to bed.

'Nubia?' she croaked. 'Bring me some water, please. My throat feels as dry as ash. Nubia?' She could tell from the heat and the brightness of the sunlight that it was very late, probably mid-morning.

She groaned, sat up in bed and looked around blearily. The dogs were not there and Nubia was gone, too. Grumpily, Flavia slipped on her tunic and sandals and rose unsteadily to her feet.

Then she sat down again, because she felt dizzy. There was a jug and beaker beside her bed, so she filled the beaker with water and drank it down.

Presently she stood up and took a step forward.

Then she sat down again, this time because she felt sick.

On the floor near Nubia's bed were drops of blood. And next to them lay Nubia's lotus-wood flute, broken in half.

SCROLL XVII

'Where is she?' said Flavia quietly, trying to keep her voice from shaking.

'Oh, good morning, Fulvia,' said Pulchra. 'Or should I say "Good afternoon"?' Pulchra was sitting with Jonathan on her bed. They were playing a board game.

'Where's who?' said Jonathan absently, trying to decide his next move.

'Nubia. She's missing. I've been looking everywhere for her. And her lotus-wood flute is broken.'

'I haven't seen her today.' Jonathan put down his counter and looked at Flavia. 'I thought she was still asleep in your room.'

'No. She isn't.' Flavia folded her arms and stared at Pulchra, who was studying the board.

'Pulchra?' said Flavia at last. 'Where is Nubia?'

'She was insolent,' said Pulchra, without looking up. 'I only wanted to look at her flute and she wouldn't even let me touch it. She ran off and I assumed she went crying back to you. You're far too soft on her, you know. She's terribly spoiled.'

'What did you do to her?'

'I beat her, of course.' Pulchra's blue eyes flickered nervously up at Jonathan.

'And?' Flavia's lips were white with fury.

'And I broke her silly flute.'

'I know Felix will help us,' said Flavia to Jonathan an hour later.

They stood in the garden in the cool shade of the lemon tree. When Jonathan had seen the look on Flavia's face he had scrambled off the bed and hurried her out of Pulchra's room. Pulchra hadn't the nerve to follow them. The two of them had searched the Villa Limona for nearly an hour before they found a slave who claimed he had seen a dark-skinned girl going up the mountainside.

'Felix found that other girl,' Flavia continued feverishly. 'He has lots of men and servants. We don't know the hills around here but his men do. He'll help us find Nubia before something happens to her. I know he will.'

'I'm not sure,' said Jonathan doubtfully.

'Of course he will. Come on. I'll prove it to you.'

It was almost midday and Felix had seen all but a few of his clients. There were only two other men still waiting when they stepped into the atrium.

Felix's secretary raised an eyebrow when they told him they wanted to see the Patron, but Flavia assured him that she was a client, so he noted her name on his wax tablet.

She flopped on the cold marble bench beside Jonathan and looked around the atrium outside Felix's study. It was cool but light, lit by the usual rectangular gap in the high ceiling.

'Oh, Jonathan,' she sighed. 'Why didn't Nubia come straight to me after Pulchra beat her?'

'Well . . .' Jonathan began, and then hesitated.

'What?' Flavia scowled at Jonathan. She was still feeling sick from too much lemon wine.

'You've started treating Nubia the same way Pulchra treats Leda.'

'Don't be ridiculous.'

'Last night at dinner she stood behind your couch all evening and she didn't have a bite to eat and then you commanded her to play her flute, just so you could impress that spider . . .'

'That spider?' Flavia knew he meant Felix.

Jonathan looked at her. 'Remember at the camp, the innkeeper telling us about the spider and the web? Well I think Felix is a big, fat spider.'

The double doors of Felix's study opened and they heard voices from inside.

'Thank you, Patron, thank you. I don't know how I can ever repay you. You are like one of the gods, bringing my little girl back to me from the dead.'

A short peasant in a tan tunic backed out of the tablinum, his arm around a dark-haired girl. As they turned to go, Flavia saw that he was smiling through tears of joy.

'Some spider!' she snorted.

The secretary came out and murmured apologetically to the two men waiting on the other side of the atrium. Then he approached Flavia and Jonathan.

'The Patron will see you now.'

★

479

'Flavia. Jonathan. Come in.'

Behind his table, Felix stood to greet them. Jonathan swallowed. Felix's formal toga made him seem even more impressive than usual.

'Sit and tell me what I can do for you,' said Felix. He gestured to two chairs on the other side of his table. As Jonathan moved to sit, he glanced quickly at the back wall, wondering whether the peepholes were visible.

The plaster-covered wall was pale blue, with rectangular panels of deep red. On the panels were frescoes of comic and tragic masks, skilfully painted so that they seemed to really hang from the wall. The plaster had slight cracks in places, but this gave the frescoes an impressive antique appearance.

Jonathan couldn't see the spyholes anywhere, but he suddenly noticed a dark-haired boy in a sea-green tunic leaning against a column. Flavia saw him at the same moment.

'Lupus!' she cried.

Lupus gave them a small nod, but did not smile. He turned his gaze back towards Felix.

Flavia sat and faced Publius Pollius Felix. 'Patron,' she said, getting straight to the point, 'we need your help.'

Felix had taken a seat on the other side of his desk. 'How can I help you, Flavia Gemina?' His tone was cool.

'Nubia is missing. Please can you find her?'

Felix frowned. 'Who's Nubia?'

'My slave-girl,' said Flavia, and Jonathan could see she was surprised he didn't know.

'Ah, the dark-skinned girl who played last night. A curious tune, neither Greek nor Roman. You say she's missing?'

'She ran away this morning, after . . .' Flavia stopped and began again. 'I think she ran away.'

'Flavia Gemina,' said Felix. 'I do have men who track down runaway slaves, but I must tell you that when we find these slaves we punish them according to Roman law. I suggest you wait until she returns of her own accord. Meanwhile, please feel free to take any female slave you like from my household as a replacement. Just check with Justus here that it's one who is dispensable.' He glanced up at this scribe who nodded and made a note.

'But Nubia might be in danger!'

Felix leaned forward onto his desk and gave Flavia a sympathetic look that Jonathan didn't trust one bit.

'I can see you're very fond of her,' said Felix quietly. 'But the Emperor has just decreed that runaway slaves should be crucified or executed in the amphitheatre. If my men find her . . .'

Jonathan shivered and glanced at Flavia, who had turned as white as Felix's toga.

'I'm sorry,' continued Pollius Felix, 'but we don't want another slave revolt and that's how we maintain control. It's especially important now, after the volcano has caused so much chaos. We've heard many reports of damage and theft caused by runaway slaves.'

'But she's my friend,' said Flavia. 'She saved my life.'

'You love your dog, too, I imagine,' he said. 'But if he were rabid you would have to put him down, wouldn't you?' Felix sat back and opened his hands, palms to the ceiling. 'I'm sorry, Flavia. In this case I'm afraid I must refuse your request.'

SCROLL XVIII

'You were right, Jonathan,' sobbed Flavia. 'He's a big fat spider.'

They had barely left the atrium before Flavia burst in tears. She slumped beneath the shade of the lemon tree. Jonathan sat beside her and patted her shoulder.

'And Nubia was right, too.' She turned her blotched face towards Jonathan, 'He's divided us. He makes you love him and then . . . Lupus is under his spell, too.'

Hot tears splashed onto her knees and tunic, and her whole body shuddered with sobs. Jonathan tried to console her by patting her back. Presently Scuto wandered into the garden and came up to his mistress, wagging his tail.

Flavia threw her arms around his woolly neck and sobbed into his fur. Scuto sat, panting gently and rolling his eyes at Jonathan.

A shadow fell across them and they looked up.

It was Lupus. The sun was behind his head so they couldn't see the expression on his face. But his feelings were made clear by the wax tablet he held out. On it he had written:

WHAT ARE YOU WAITING FOR?
LET'S FIND NUBIA OURSELVES!

*

Flavia took Scuto's big head between her hands and gazed into his brown eyes. 'Find Nubia, Scuto. Nu-bi-a.' She let him sniff the lemon-yellow tunic Nubia had worn the night before. 'Go on, Scuto. You, too, Tigris.' She stood up. 'Go find her!'

As the three friends followed Scuto and Tigris up through the silver olive groves, Flavia cast her mind back over the events of the previous day.

She thought about the beautiful song Nubia had played the night before, of the yearning it had expressed. She remembered how she had muttered 'stupid' while Nubia was helping her dress for dinner and suddenly a terrible thought occurred to her. She'd been thinking about Felix and how wearing a bulla was stupid, because it showed she was still just a little girl. But perhaps Nubia had thought she'd meant it for her.

And later, at dinner, she had been so busy trying to impress Felix that she hadn't even looked at Nubia, standing patiently behind her. She assumed the slaves would eat, too, but of course they hadn't had a chance. They probably fought for scraps in the kitchens afterwards.

Flavia stopped and uncorked her water gourd. She felt sick from the heat and too much lemon wine. After a long drink she continued up the path after the boys.

It was all Pulchra's fault, thought Flavia, grinding her teeth. That stupid, spoilt little harpy with her

484

golden hair and her big blue eyes. She had dared to strike Nubia! And then she had broken Nubia's precious flute!

Flavia's anger gave her strength and before she knew it she was standing at the shrine of Dionysus while the dogs sniffed excitedly round the yew tree.

Flavia's heart sank.

'Oh no,' she said to the boys, and her eyes filled with tears of frustration. 'They haven't followed her scent from today. They followed it from yesterday!'

'Wait!' said Jonathan, 'Tigris is going further up the hill. We didn't go that far yesterday.' Now Scuto had the scent, too, and was following Tigris into a grove of pines and yew trees.

'Nubia had to relieve herself,' said Flavia, not bothering to look.

'Are you sure? All the way up there?'

Flavia turned and peered through the dappled shade up the hill.

Suddenly Lupus grunted and pointed.

'What?' said Flavia, 'Do you see something?'

'A red cord!' cried Jonathan. 'Tied to that branch.'

'Yes, I see it! And there's another further up! They look like markers for a trail. Let's follow them!'

The red cords led them up the hill, across a road and over a low ridge. Now they were out of sight of the Villa Limona. Jonathan was wheezing a little, so they stopped in a clearing and looked out at the new vista which lay before them.

The sea shimmered in a heat haze beneath the noonday sun. Below them a silvery blanket of olive groves rolled down to the shore. On the slopes rising behind them the pines thinned and eventually gave way to rugged cliffs honeycombed with caves.

Scuto stood for a moment, eyes half closed, testing the wind with his nose. Tigris was already moving further up the path, so intent on tracking Nipur's scent that he only wagged his tail occasionally.

'Look, there's an island out there.' Flavia pointed. 'I wonder if that's Caprea.'

Jonathan stood very still.

He knew this place. And yet he had never been here in his life. He stared at the distant island and the sea. From this height, the water looked like dark blue silk. He almost remembered. Then the memory slipped away, like smoke.

Behind him a twig snapped and there was the faint rustle of leaves.

'Flavia! Lupus!' he hissed. 'Someone's following us!'

Flavia heard it the moment Jonathan did: someone was coming up the track behind them. Lupus put his finger to his lips and melted into the shade of the pine trees.

A moment later he was back, tugging a very pink-faced Pulchra by the wrist. Leda trailed behind him.

'You!' cried Flavia, stalking forward and thrusting her face close to Pulchra's. 'Why are you following us? Haven't you caused enough trouble already?'

Pulchra took a small step backwards. 'We weren't following you. We were just going for a walk.'

'Dressed in those old green tunics? You were too following us!'

Pulchra tried to toss her hair but it stuck damply to her neck.

'I thought you might need some help,' she said imperiously, folding her arms.

'What? Help us find Nubia so your father can have her crucified? You . . . you spoilt little patrician!'

'Peasant!' retorted Pulchra, narrowing her eyes.

'Harpy!'

'Gorgon!'

Furiously, Flavia grabbed a handful of Pulchra's yellow hair and tugged as hard as she could. 'You should be whipped yourself!' she yelled.

Pulchra screeched and aimed a few feeble blows at Flavia.

'You fight like a girl!' sneered Flavia, easily fending them off.

'I am . . . a girl . . .' gasped Pulchra, 'unlike YOU!' She punched Flavia hard in the stomach.

Flavia doubled over, trying desperately not to be sick, then furiously tackled Pulchra round the knees and brought her thudding down onto the dusty ground.

'Oof!' cried Pulchra.

Flavia straddled her but Pulchra writhed and twisted furiously.

Lupus, Jonathan and Leda watched in stunned amazement as the two girls rolled on the ground.

'Ow!' yelled Flavia, as Pulchra sunk her perfect white teeth into Flavia's forearm. 'Biting's not fair!' And she raked her fingernails hard across Pulchra's cheek and neck.

Pulchra screamed and thrashed with her legs and arms.

Lupus and Jonathan moved forward to separate them, but the girls weren't holding back now and the boys hesitated over the tumbling pair.

Somewhere up the hill, Scuto barked his warning bark, but they didn't hear him. And they didn't see the masked men come out of the bushes until it was too late.

SCROLL XIX

There were only two of them, but they were strong men, hardened by living rough and scouring the mountains for stray children.

Lupus was the only one who got away.

Jonathan fought back, but was soon gasping for breath. A blow to his head left him stunned and sick on the ground. Leda simply stood there and allowed them to tie her hands. Flavia and Pulchra were still rolling in the dust when the masked men lifted them apart and wrenched their hands behind their backs. When she saw the leering masks, Pulchra screamed.

'Pollux!' cursed Flavia, and kicked out at the little one. But she was exhausted from fighting Pulchra and her foot failed to connect.

Within moments, the four of them stood in the hot sunshine, their hands bound tightly behind their backs. Flavia and Pulchra were still breathing hard, covered with dust and blood.

Scuto stood at the edge of the clearing, half wagging his tail. He was not sure whether it was a game or not.

'Well, Actius,' said the short one from behind his grinning mask, 'this is the best haul we've had so far.'

'It certainly is, Sorex, it certainly is,' said the tall one, who also wore a mask. 'Two lively ones and two not-so-lively ones.'

'One got away.'

'Yes. Pity about that one. But he was smaller. You have to throw the small ones back sometimes. Anyway, four brings the total up to fifty. A nice round number.'

'A very nice round number,' agreed Sorex. 'Lucrio says the Patron promised another ten thousand sesterces if we could get our numbers up to fifty.'

The Patron.

Watching and listening from the bushes, Lupus couldn't believe what he had heard. He felt sick. Could Felix really be behind this?

No, there must be some mistake. They couldn't be Felix's men. It must be another patron they meant. Surely if Felix was their patron they would recognise his daughter, Pulchra.

Besides, Felix used his power to help his clients, not hurt them. He had helped find the farmer's daughter and he had lent the tent-maker money to help him expand his business. Lupus knew that Felix had personally paid for many of the provisions for the refugee camp.

He shifted to get a better viewpoint. The masked men were shoving his friends, prodding them across the clearing. Scuto stood nearby, his tail wagging hesitantly. Suddenly a black puppy raced down the hillside and sunk his teeth into the shorter man's ankle. Unlike Scuto, Tigris knew the men were not playing a game.

The masked man cursed and kicked the puppy hard.

Tigris flew up into the air, then landed in the dust with a thud. He lay motionless.

'Tigris!' Lupus saw Jonathan twist to look back. But the masked men laughed and pushed him roughly towards a rocky path which led down the mountain to the sea.

SCROLL XX

Jonathan needed all his powers of concentration to descend the path, but that was good. Anything which took his mind off the image of Tigris lying so still in the dust was good. So he focused on putting one foot in front of the other. Going downhill was always harder than going uphill, because it was so easy to slip. And with his hands tied behind his back it was almost impossible to keep his balance.

Twice already Pulchra had slipped and skidded on her bottom down the path. The masked men had laughed before yanking her roughly to her feet. She had been sobbing ever since.

Suddenly Jonathan started to slip, too. He only just caught himself, but in doing so he wrenched his ankle and it hurt so much that tears sprang to his eyes.

'Oh dear!' said Sorex, who had an oddly high voice. 'We almost lost Curlytop.'

'Do you think we should untie their hands?' said Actius. He was the tall one with the deeper voice.

'And spoil all our fun?' squeaked Sorex. 'Not on your life. I wager two sesterces that Blondie's going to fall at least once more before we reach the Green Grotto.'

'You're on.'

Lupus knelt beside Tigris and put one ear against the puppy's chest. Tigris was very still, but he was still warm, and Lupus could hear his little heart beating. Scuto whined softly.

Lupus gathered the puppy into his arms and stood.

For a while he and Scuto followed the track down the mountain, but Tigris was a big puppy and Lupus's arms soon grew tired. He stopped. He reckoned the men could only be going to one place. To the grotto from which he'd seen the ship emerging the day before. It must be their hideout.

Lupus didn't need to go any further. He needed to get Tigris back to the Villa Limona. And then he needed to get help.

He would go to Felix. Despite what the masked men had said, he felt sure the Patron had nothing to do with the kidnappings. He knew Felix wouldn't let him down.

At last Flavia and the others reached level ground. They were on the cliffs above the sea. The masked men were prodding them towards a small pomegranate tree between them and the cliff edge. It was only when they were nearly upon it that Flavia saw a depression in the ground with steps leading down. The masked men untied their hands.

'Down you go,' said Sorex, the small one. His eyes behind the grinning mask were cold. 'Don't try anything or you'll go head first.'

Flavia started down the steps, followed by Pulchra, Jonathan, and Leda. Their captors took up the rear.

The stairs descended into darkness. As the weak white light of the overcast sun grew fainter behind her, Flavia moved carefully, feeling her way with her feet, fingertips touching damp rock on either side. Gradually the steps curved to the left and suddenly Flavia stepped out into a huge, cool, blue-green space.

It was a grotto.

'Move along!' Sorex's nasal voice echoed strangely in the vast space. Flavia found herself standing on a broad shelf of rock. Before her, a pool of milky blue water filled the dome of the cave with a bluish-green light. Above Flavia's head, the ceiling was ridged and arched, like the roof of Scuto's mouth when he yawned. Somewhere water dripped, echoing eerily in the vast enclosed space. Bright daylight streamed in to her right. Flavia knew that must be the way out to the sea.

She was just wondering whether she should risk jumping in the water and trying to swim away when the one called Actius tied her hands behind her back again.

The kidnappers had removed their masks before coming down the dangerous steps and now Flavia saw their faces. Sorex had a small red mouth, a snub nose and a cleft chin. Actius had a large head and big smooth features.

Flavia heard footsteps and saw a third man approaching from the left. His face, lit green by the shimmering water, looked familiar. It was the announcer from the refugee camp, the man who had introduced the two actors.

'Hey, Lucrio. Look what we found wandering the

hills.' Sorex's high voice echoed in the vast space of the grotto.

'Well, well, well!' said Lucrio. He had a narrow face and cheeks dark with stubble. 'Just in time for delivery, too. Let's introduce them to the others.'

Leda was nearest him. He shoved her roughly towards the back of the cave. The others stumbled after her.

As they rounded a curve on the shelf of rock, Flavia gasped. The cave extended further back, and the rocky shelf became a sandy beach leading down to the water. Huddled on the damp sand against the dripping cave wall were nearly fifty children, hands bound, dimly lit by the blue-green light reflecting off the water. Flavia scanned their faces hopefully, but Nubia was not among them.

Flavia wasn't sure whether to be disappointed or relieved.

It was two hours after noon when Lupus got back to the Villa Limona with Tigris and Scuto. His arms were aching. Tigris had revived but had been too groggy to walk. Lupus had carried him all the way.

The porter recognised him and let him in with a yawn. Lupus left the dogs in his bedroom, then went to the kitchens to get them some food and drink. Back in his room, he gave them each a marrow bone and filled their water bowls. Then he grunted Stay!

Tigris had curled up on Jonathan's pillow but Scuto whined. Lupus knew he wanted to search for Flavia.

Lupus grunted Stay! again, and this time Scuto gave

a deep sigh and lay down beside Tigris. Lupus patted his head.

Then he went to find the Patron.

'Sit there on the sand,' said Sorex, pushing Flavia roughly forward.

'I need to use the latrine,' whimpered Pulchra. Her voice sounded tiny in the vast cavern.

'As you can probably smell,' said Actius with a shrug, 'everyone just goes in the sand where they're sitting.'

Pulchra looked at him in horror. She opened her mouth to wail and then thought better of it. Instead she turned to Lucrio, who was obviously the leader.

'Do you know who I am?' she said.

The three men exchanged glances.

'I am Polla Pulchra!'

Lucrio, Sorex and Actius looked at Pulchra.

They looked at each other.

Then they burst out laughing. Pulchra's hair was tangled and full of twigs. Her drab green tunic was ripped along the shoulder seam. Her face was grubby and smudged, with four red scratch marks across her left cheek and a smear of dried blood beneath her nose.

'That's a good one, darling,' said Sorex in his high voice. 'Shows real imagination!'

'Besides,' said Lucrio, 'I saw Polla Pulchra once, and you're nothing like her.'

'Nonsense! I'm Pulchra and this is my slave Leda. Tell them, Leda. Tell them who I am.'

But Leda was so terrified that she couldn't even raise her eyes.

'So,' said Lucrio, 'she's your slave, is she? Let's just have a look and see how you've treated her.'

He stepped over to Leda and tugged the back of her tunic neck. The slave-girl winced.

'You freeborn types make me sick,' Lucrio snarled at Pulchra. 'Don't you realise slaves have feelings, too?'

'All of you, turn around!' commanded Sorex. 'Come on, Curlytop. You too, Knobbly-knees. Turn around.'

They stared at him blankly, so he roughly turned them to face the children who sat shivering on the sand.

Flavia tried to smile bravely down at the wretched faces looking up at her. Some of the children lowered their eyes in shame, as if they knew what was coming. One boy with reddish hair stared back at her steadily and she felt he was trying to give her courage.

'Don't worry,' said Actius to Leda, 'you've been beaten quite enough. Stop crying. Maybe your new master will be kinder.' Flavia saw Leda stumble forward onto the sand, as if she'd been pushed.

'Which one first?' came Lucrio's cultured voice from behind them. 'Knobbly-knees, I think. You do the honours, Sorex. And try not to damage the merchandise.'

There was an ominous pause.

Then Flavia felt a searing streak of pain across her back. And then another. And another.

They were beating her.

The Villa Limona seemed strangely empty. There were a few drowsy slaves in yellow, but all the dark-haired young men in fashionable sea-green seemed to have gone. Lupus couldn't find Felix anywhere. The atrium was silent and the double doors of the tablinum locked. The inner gardens and courtyards shimmered in the hot afternoon, and even the baths were deserted.

'The Patron left an hour ago,' said the porter. 'Not sure where he's gone.'

At last Lupus found Polla Argentaria sitting in her shaded portico, gazing out over the blue Bay of Neapolis.

'Hello, again,' she smiled. 'Sit beside me for a while.'

Lupus shook his head vigorously and held out the tablet he'd been showing to anyone who could read:

WHERE IS FELIX? I MUST SEE HIM.

'My husband left for Rome a little while ago.'
Lupus wrote with a trembling hand:

PULCHRA IS IN TROUBLE! KIDNAPPERS.

'Sit beside me for a moment,' smiled Polla, patting the yellow cushion. Lupus was exhausted, so he sank gratefully onto the chair. Polla would know what to do.

'I have a theory about my husband,' she said, 'which I've never told anyone before.'

Lupus looked at her in surprise, but she put an elegant finger to her lips and smiled at him. 'I believe,' she said, 'that my husband is part man, part god. Like Hercules.'

Lupus stared at her.

'For a long time,' Polla continued serenely, 'I

wondered which of the gods was his father. At first I thought it was Jupiter, but now I think it was Dionysus.'

Lupus gave her a look of alarm and held up his wax tablet, pointing urgently at Pulchra's name. Couldn't Polla read?

'No, no.' She touched his arm with fingers as cool and light as a butterfly. 'Don't worry about Pulchra. The son of Dionysus will protect her.'

Polla smiled and closed her eyes.

SCROLL XXI

Jonathan sat miserably on the damp sand, his back on fire with pain.

Flavia sat next to him, shivering and silent. Sorex had beaten her hard, too, though he had taken care not to break the skin.

'Don't damage the merchandise,' Lucrio had growled once or twice.

Poor Pulchra lay in the sand on Jonathan's other side. Lucrio had beaten her himself because she had shrieked with each blow and this had amused them greatly.

'We are the *pirates*, the *pirates* of Pompeii!' Sorex and Actius had sung, and with each 'pirates' Lucrio had struck Pulchra's back. After a while she had fainted, so they dropped her on the sand and went off towards the stairs.

As Jonathan sat trembling with pain and fear and shame, he closed his eyes and prayed.

Almost immediately a thought came into his head. A thought as fully formed and solid as a pebble dropped in a bucket. 'Make them laugh.'

He thought about this for a moment. He didn't really understand what it meant but he knew it was something he could do. When he'd attended school at

Ostia's synagogue he'd always been in trouble for making the others laugh.

Jonathan took a breath, struggled to his feet and looked around. Some of the children looked up at him, terrified of what the pirates might do if they came back and saw him standing. The others kept their eyes averted.

'Hello everyone,' he began, but his voice cracked and he had to clear his throat. 'Hello! My name is Jonathan. Those men captured me, laughed at me and beat me. And that makes me angry. But you know what makes me angriest of all?'

They were all looking at him now.

'What makes me angriest of all is that they called my friend Flavia here, well, they called her Knobbly-knees. And that makes me *really* angry!' Some of the children tittered and the red-haired boy laughed out loud.

Jonathan smiled down at Flavia. Her eyes were red-rimmed and her face smeared with dust. But there was a gleam in her grey eyes and she rose awkwardly to join him. She turned and looked at them all.

'Hi!' she said, as brightly as she could. 'My name's Flavia Gemina, daughter of Marcus Flavius Geminus, sea captain. Do you think I have knobbly knees?'

The red-haired boy called out, 'You have beautiful knees!' More children laughed and Flavia gave him a mock bow.

'Tell me, Flavia,' said Jonathan. 'How many pirates does it take to light an oil-lamp?'

'I don't know, Jonathan,' said Flavia, playing along. 'How many pirates does it take to light an oil-lamp?'

'Three,' said Jonathan. 'One to light the wick and two to sing the pirate song!'

Several more children laughed at the audacity of this. Pulchra lifted her head from the sand and blinked groggily.

'Tell me, Jonathan. How many patrons does it take to light an oil-lamp?'

'I don't know, Flavia.' Jonathan looked at the children and wiggled his eyebrows up and down. 'How many patrons does it take to light an oil-lamp?'

'Only one, but he can't do it unless twenty clients kiss his . . .'

'Flavia!'

More laughter.

'You know, Flavia,' said Jonathan. 'I was in Pompeii last week and a funny thing happened to me on the way to the forum . . .'

'Yes?' said Flavia.

'It wasn't there any more!' Everyone laughed at this dreadful joke, including Jonathan. The laughter made his back hurt less.

'Anyone here from Oplontis?' he said.

A few children nodded.

'Well, we won't hold it against you . . .' The laughing children were looking at him with shining eyes.

'Anyone here named Apollo?' said Jonathan.

'I am,' said a boy with dark brown hair. He sat up straighter.

'I think you'd better go and sit with the kids from Oplontis,' said Jonathan.

'Is there a Rufus here?' said Flavia suddenly.

'That's me,' said the red-haired boy.

'Well your sister Julia and your grandparents miss you, Rufus, so I don't know what you're still hanging around here for.'

'And Melissa . . .' said Jonathan. 'Boy! Are you in a lot of trouble with your father!'

A frizzy-haired girl laughed through her tears.

'My name's Helena Cornelia!' cried another girl. 'Have you seen my parents?'

'I'm Quintus Caedius Curio,' called a boy.

'I'm Thamyris,' said another.

Soon all the children were calling out their names, laughing and crying, asking for news of their parents, relatives or friends.

Abruptly they all fell silent.

Jonathan and Flavia slowly turned to see Lucrio coming towards them. He held a birch switch in one hand and was tapping it against the palm of the other.

'Turn around,' he said coldly. Jonathan turned and faced the children. Every eye was on him, so Jonathan smiled and winked at them.

Lucrio shoved Flavia. 'You, too, Knobbly-knees,' he sneered, and his jaw dropped as all the children burst out laughing.

Jonathan laughed too. But he knew as the first blow landed on his back that he would pay for that laughter.

Lupus paced up and down the lower portico of the Villa Limona, desperately trying to think what to do next.

Felix was gone. Polla was obviously insane. The slaves were useless.

He had two choices. He could try to rescue his

friends himself or he could go back to the refugee camp for help.

He glanced at the sun, already beginning its descent. He reckoned he had about four hours till sunset.

Finally he made his decision. In Jonathan's room he found an extra wax tablet and after a few minutes thought, he composed a careful message to Felix, in case he should by some miracle turn back from Rome.

Then he made certain he had a sharp knife, his sling and stones, his wax tablet and a gourd of water.

He grunted a firm 'Stay!' to the dogs and made his way to Felix's tablinum, where he slipped the wax tablet under the double doors.

Then, looking around to make sure no one was watching him, Lupus made his way through the villa and down the path to the secret cove.

SCROLL XXII

Lupus pulled the rowing boat up onto the crunchy beach, and sprinkled it with ashy sand to make it less noticeable. It had taken him longer than he had hoped to row from the Villa Limona to the crescent beach, but he still had a few hours before sunset.

Crouching behind the rocks, he studied the narrow strip of ashy beach and the cliffs which rose up from it. When he was sure he had not been observed, he slipped back into the water and swam a short distance out to sea.

He stopped to tread water and get his bearings. There were several grottoes along the water line. Which one had the blue boat come from? Not the largest one. At last he struck out for the middle cave.

The water was cool and silky against his skin, and as he swam Lupus thought of his father.

He remembered the time they had sailed together to a neighbouring island, how they had caught fish and grilled them right there on the beach and lay under the stars talking long into the night. And in the morning they had sailed home.

Suddenly Lupus almost swallowed a mouthful of seawater. In his memory, the image of his father had been replaced by that of Felix. Gasping for breath, he clung to some rocks and took several deep breaths.

He must never forget his father's face. He must never forget his father's death. He closed his eyes and forced himself to remember. His father had been shorter than Felix, with straight black hair and green eyes.

After a while his father's image grew clear in his mind and his heartbeat slowed to normal. Lupus released the slippery rock he'd been clinging to and looked around. He was at the entrance to the grotto, and he could see it went a long way back. This must be the one.

He took several breaths and finally pushed all the air out of his lungs before filling them as full as he could.

Then he frog-kicked down and down, feeling the familiar weight of the water above him. Fine ash suspended in the water made it seem thick and green, so that for a moment he imagined he was swimming in a giant liquid emerald. He kept his mouth closed and his eyes open and saw a silver cloud of fish flicker and turn before his eyes. He looked up. Above him rays from the late afternoon sun struck the surface skin of the water like spears, and bled light into the emerald underbelly of the sea.

Lupus rejoiced in the water's beauty and swam on. Gradually the emerald water became turquoise, then sapphire, then lapis lazuli.

Presently he knew he must surface for air. Luckily the rock above formed a kind of shelf. He found a place where the rock projected above the water and slowly surfaced. Quietly he filled his lungs with cool, life-giving oxygen. Then he looked around.

High in the mountains, in one of the cliff-caves overlooking the sea, Nubia sat stroking Nipur's silky fur and gazing out at the sunset. It was evening and though the stones of the cliff still glowed with heat, a cool breeze ruffled her tunic.

Beside her sat Kuanto of the Jackal Clan, whom the other slaves called Fuscus. He and Nubia had been sitting here all afternoon in the cool shade, talking about their desert homeland and learning about each other.

She had not intended to run away, even though Kuanto was handsome and Flavia had called her stupid. Not even when Pulchra beat her. But when Pulchra had snapped the lotus-wood flute across her knee, something inside Nubia had snapped with it.

She had taken Nipur and run out of the Villa Limona and made her way up to the shrine of Dionysus. Then she had followed the red cords on the branches. Even before she reached the cave, Kuanto had seen her and had run to meet her, sure-footed as a mountain goat on the steep path.

The cave was wide-mouthed and bright, with a level sandy floor. A dozen other runaway slaves were there, cooking, weaving, chatting softly. They ranged in age from a newborn baby at his mother's breast to an old Greek with a bushy white beard.

One of the women slaves had smoothed ointment over the wounds on Nubia's back. Then they gave her brown bread and cheese and a cup of hot sage sweetened with fig syrup.

As she sat on a threadbare carpet at the mouth of the cave, Nubia sipped the bittersweet drink and listened to Kuanto speak of his life and his dreams.

He was older than she had first thought: almost twenty. Seven years ago, he told her, Arab slave-traders had captured him and taken him to the slave-markets of Alexandria. A Roman slave-dealer had bought him and taken him to the great port of Puteoli, and there he had been sold again, this time to a rich man who owned many other slaves.

This man put Kuanto to work on his estate of olives and vines. For seven years Kuanto worked well and, as he gained his master's trust, he was given more and more responsibility.

Then, a week ago he had been travelling on business to Pompeii. Suddenly the earth had trembled and the mountain exploded. Immediately he made for the town gates. The city officials were telling people to stay put, but he ignored them. Borrowing a horse, he rode south as fast as he could.

After the days of darkness, Kuanto met other slaves separated from their masters or mistresses. They began to stay together, living in caves in the hills and stealing or buying food where they could.

As he spoke, Nubia turned to look at the twelve slaves further back in the cave. They seemed content, and all of them had hope in their eyes.

Kuanto told her his plan. He knew a ship's captain willing to carry them to the great city of Alexandria in Egypt.

Alexandria was a city of possibilities. One could begin a new life there. From there one could catch a ship to any land. From there one could follow the Nile back to the desert.

'Come with me,' he said to Nubia in their own language. 'Come back to the sea of sand and the tents of my clan. Perhaps some of your family survived or escaped.'

Nubia nodded. 'My brother Taharqo,' she said. 'He fought bravely but they chained him and after the slave-traders came he went with the men and I went with the women. He may still be alive. Perhaps he escaped!'

'It is possible,' said Kuanto.

Nubia frowned. 'But how will you pay the ship's captain?' she asked. She knew that it cost a lot of money to hire a ship. Flavia's father had very rich patrons who paid for each voyage.

'My master entrusted me with a bag of gold. I was to purchase spices and fish sauce, but I never had a chance to spend it. That gold will pay for the voyage with plenty left over.'

He gazed towards the horizon and said quietly, 'Of course, if they should catch me, I will be crucified. But it is a risk worth taking to rescue my fellow slaves!'

Nubia looked sideways at Kuanto. He had a fine nose and a sensitive mouth and his body was lithe and muscular.

'Look,' said Kuanto, and pointed with his chin at the huge red sun just touching the horizon. He spoke softly in their native language: 'To most of them a blood-red sun is a portent of doom. But those of us from the desert know differently.'

He turned his tawny eyes upon her. 'For us,' he whispered, 'the red sky is a sign of fair days ahead.'

Before the pirates left the cave, they gave their fifty captives a drink of water. Then they bound Flavia's and Jonathan's ankles with leather thongs and poured buckets of sea water over the two of them. Flavia gasped as the cold salt water drenched her skin and tunic.

Pulchra was conscious now. Her voice rang out clearly as the three men walked away: 'You'll be sorry one day.'

The pirates did not even turn to look at her.

'Goodnight, children.' Actius's deep voice echoed from the stairs. 'Sweet dreams!'

Flavia heard their echoing footsteps grow fainter and fainter. The sun must have been setting outside, for the diffused light from the entrance was orange now. She struggled to untie the bonds on her ankles but they were too tight. Tighter than they had been a moment ago.

Suddenly Flavia realised why the kidnappers had poured water on her. As the wet leather thongs around her wrists and ankles slowly dried, they tightened. In an hour or so they would begin to cut into her skin.

SCROLL XXIII

Nubia listened to the other runaway slaves tell their stories. They had all eaten from a communal pot, using the soft, flat bread to scoop the stew into their mouths, and now, as the sun set, they spoke of their past.

The young mother, Sperata, was sixteen. She told how, when she was fourteen, she and her mistress had both given birth to baby girls on the same day. Although the master of the household had been father to both children, hers had been taken away and she had been forced to nurse her mistress's child. The baby she held in her arms – a boy – was her second. The volcano's eruption had prevented them from taking this one from her, too.

The Greek with the white beard was named Socrates. He spoke three languages and had taught the children of a rich senator all his life. Now that the children were grown and had left home, he had been put to work in the vineyards, doing backbreaking work under a blazing sun. He was sixty-four years old and suffered from arthritis.

Phoebus, a cleanshaven, dark-haired man of about thirty, was also a well-educated Greek. He had kept his master's accounts until he had been falsely accused of stealing. His master had sold him to the manager of the

Nucerian baths, where he had spent four years cleaning the latrines and scrubbing down walls. His poorly-educated new master resented his knowledge, and often beat him for fun.

Kuanto looked across the fire at Nubia.

'Do you have a story?' he asked in Latin.

Nubia swallowed. She had been well-treated from the moment Flavia had bought her. Already she was beginning to miss her friends.

'No story,' she replied after a moment. 'But I have a song. A song of hope.'

And because she had no flute, Nubia sang the Song of the Traveller, the song her father had sung the night he died.

She sang of the young traveller who sets out to find happiness. He leaves his family in the Land of Gold, where the sun and the sand and the goats are golden. First he travels to the Land of Blue, where everything is water and fish and sky, and people live in boxes which float on the water. Then he travels to the Land of Red, where everything is made of brick and tile and the people do not move from place to place. He travels to the Land of White, full of snow and ice and frost, and so cold that people dress in white animal fur.

Finally he travels to the Land of Grey, a terrible land full of smoke and ashes and drifting spirits. He believes there is still another land, the best land of all, but he cannot find it. The young traveller grows thinner and thinner, greyer and greyer, but he never stops searching.

At last he finds the Land of Green, a garden full of

fruit-bearing trees and shrubs and flowers and lush grass. A land of rivers and fountains and rain and life. He finds his family there, waiting for him. And so they live happily ever after, laughing and feasting, telling stories and playing music.

The light in the grotto had turned from orange to a deep glowing red. The water was as purple as wine. Jonathan was leading the others in a chorus of 'Volare!' and the fifty voices echoing off the walls and dome of the grotto made the jolly song sound ethereal, as if angels were singing with them.

Suddenly a girl screamed.

A dripping figure in a sea-green tunic was rising up from the water.

'Lupus!' Jonathan and Flavia cheered at the same time.

Lupus slicked his hair back with both hands and grinned at them. Then he took out his sharp knife, stepped forward and began to cut their bonds.

As Nubia finished her song, three men appeared in the mouth of the cave.

'What news?' said the first one, looking down at Kuanto. 'Has the ship arrived?'

'Just there,' said Kuanto. 'Coming from Caprea with the evening breeze. She'll be in the cove shortly and we'll go as soon as the moon rises. But that's not for a few hours. Come! Sit! Have a cup of spiced wine and some stew. We've saved you some.'

'Who is this?' said the first man, smiling down at Nubia. He had a narrow face and a jaw dark with stubble. 'I've seen you before, haven't I, in the refugee camp?'

Nubia looked at him and then at the other two, a short man and a tall man.

'This is the girl who plays a flute like a bird and sings like an angel,' said Kuanto. 'Nubia has joined us in our flight to freedom. Nubia, meets the actors Lucrio, Sorex and Actius. They're going to help us escape!'

By the time Lupus had cut their bonds and fifty children had rubbed life back into their wrists the red light in the grotto had deepened to purple and then dark blue.

'The light will be gone soon,' said Jonathan, 'but in a few hours the moon will rise. I saw it last night when we finished dinner: a full moon.'

Lupus nodded to confirm this.

'I don't even remember going back to my room,' said Flavia. 'But if you're right, it should give us enough light to escape and be far away from here by dawn.'

'But where can we go?' said Jonathan. 'We can't go back to the Villa Limona. Felix is behind all this.'

'Of course he's not!' said Pulchra angrily. They were sitting in a circle on a dry patch of sand. 'Pater would never be involved in anything like this!'

Lupus flipped open his wax tablet and wrote:

FELIX ISN'T THERE. HE'S IN ROME.

'Ridiculous,' said Pulchra. 'Pater hasn't been to Rome for years. Who told you that?'

YOUR MOTHER

Pulchra went silent and stared at the sand. Finally she said, 'Mater isn't well. She had a bad fever after Pollinilla was born. Ever since that she's been getting bad headaches. Sometimes she can't tell what's real and what isn't.' After a moment Pulchra added, 'That's why we moved here three years ago. Pater wanted to keep her safe. He hardly ever spends the night away.'

Lupus looked up sharply. If Felix hadn't gone to Rome . . .

'I'm sorry your mother isn't well,' said Jonathan.

Pulchra looked at them. In the deep blue light it was hard for Lupus to see the exact expression on her face. 'Pater thinks she's dying,' she said quietly. 'He's never told me, but I can tell. That's why last night was so special. You don't realise . . . She gets so tired . . .'

Flavia swallowed. 'We're sorry,' she said. Then she took a deep breath. 'I'm sorry, too, Pulchra. I'm sorry I called you names and fought with you. But Nubia is more than my slave. She's my friend.'

In the dark blue gloom which filled the grotto, Lupus saw Pulchra turn her head away.

'You're lucky to have such a friend,' Pulchra said to Flavia.

'Lupus,' said Jonathan. 'I can barely see you or your wax tablet. Is there anything you want to tell us before it's completely black in here?'

Lupus bent his head over his tablet and wrote. Then he showed it to them:

LET'S GO TO VILLA LIMONA
WHEN MOON IS UP

SCROLL XXIV

'. . . and my name is Titus Tadienus Rufus,' called a voice in the darkness. 'I'm from Rome, but we were staying with my grandparents in Nuceria. My favourite colour is red, my favourite food is venison and the person I miss most is my little sister Julia. Even though she can be as annoying as a broken sandal strap.' Jonathan could hear the grin in his voice. 'And this is my favourite joke: A butcher visited a farmer from Oplontis who bred four-legged chickens. My customers would love these, he said to the farmer, but tell me, what do they taste like? I don't know, said the farmer. They run so fast I've never been able to catch one!'

Laughter echoed in the pitch black darkness of the grotto. It had been Jonathan's idea, to help pass the time and give the others courage.

'Thank you, Rufus,' he said. 'Next!'

'I think that's everybody,' came Flavia's voice.

'No, there's one more person,' said Pulchra's voice.

'I know,' said Jonathan, 'but it's too dark for us to read what Lupus writes . . .'

'Not Lupus. Leda. My slave-girl.'

'Oh,' said Jonathan. And then, 'Um . . . sorry, Leda. It's your turn.'

There was a long pause and then a small voice said, 'My name is Leda. I come from Surrentum. My favourite colour is blue, my favourite food is cod with lemon and the person I miss most is our cook, because she gives me food when I'm hungry. And I don't know any jokes . . .'

There was a hurried whisper and then Leda said:

'How many gladiators does it take to light an oil-lamp?'

'I don't know, Leda,' said Jonathan. 'How many gladiators does it take to light an oil-lamp?'

'None. Gladiators aren't afraid of the dark!'

Everyone laughed and then Jonathan said, 'And neither are we! Are we?'

Fifty voices shouted 'No!'

'Look! I think the moon is rising!' It was Flavia's voice.

Jonathan could just make out pale ripples undulating towards him on the black surface of the water. Gradually the ripples grew brighter and a faint, milky pink light began to infuse the cave. Within minutes he could see their faces, pale globes in the darkness.

Flavia stood up, and gave her hand to Jonathan and then Lupus.

'This is it,' she said. 'Let's get out of here and go to the Villa Limona! Come on, everybody, follow me!'

'You really are bossy, aren't you?' said Pulchra, and smiled as Flavia whirled to face her. 'Almost as bossy as I am.'

'Don't be silly.' Flavia lifted her chin. 'I'm far bossier than you!'

Jonathan couldn't help smiling.

★

Because Flavia's only thought was to get the children out of the grotto and away as quickly as possible, she didn't think to check the cliff top first. She led the children up the narrow steps towards the rosy light of a cherry-red moon. As she emerged from the secret entrance and stepped out onto the cliff top an arm roughly circled her shoulders and chest. She felt cold, sharp metal hard against her throat and heard Lucrio's voice snarl out to the others coming after her:

'Get back down, you miserable lot, and if there aren't fifty of you waiting when I come back down, I swear I'll cut her throat. Do you hear me? I said I'll kill Knobbly-knees.'

This time no one laughed.

His teeth chattering and his heart pounding, Lupus clung to a rough, wet stone and bobbed in the dark water just outside the mouth of the grotto. Luckily he had been the last in line. When he had heard the man's voice at the top of the stairs, he had slipped back into the sea. He had surfaced to see a large merchant ship lying at anchor in the moonlit cove and its rowing boat coming straight towards him.

The men on the rowing boat hadn't seen him. Hiding behind his rock, he had watched the boat make several trips from the grotto to the ship and back. Now he saw the boat come out again. By the light of a torch held by the man at the front, he could see a dozen children, Flavia and Jonathan among them. This must be the final load.

Lupus knew the merchant ship would probably set sail with the dawn breeze. And once the ship sailed, his friends would be gone forever.

He must return to the Villa Limona quickly to get help.

As he pushed out through the skin of silver moonlight on the surface of the inky water, Lupus prayed that Pulchra was right and that her father hadn't gone to Rome. There was no one else he could turn to now. He knew Felix would do anything to help his daughter, if only he could be reached.

'Please God,' Lupus prayed. 'Let him be there.'

The moon was high in the sky by the time Nubia followed Kuanto and the other runaway slaves down onto a crescent beach. A fisherman and his rowing boat were waiting to take them to a large merchant ship which floated close to shore.

Kuanto was the last into the rowing boat. He pushed the boat into the water and jumped in, making the small boat rock. As he and the old fisherman pulled at the oars, Nubia shivered and hugged Nipur tightly. She was taking a dangerous step towards freedom. The journey might end in death or punishment.

She thought of all the things she would miss about this country called Italia. She would miss mint tea and stuffed dates and inner gardens and fountains. She would miss Scuto and Tigris. Most of all she would miss Flavia and Jonathan and Lupus. Especially Flavia, who had been so kind to her.

Nubia gazed up at the moon. It seemed to stare back at her coolly. It was smaller now, and more remote, and its silvery light washed the sea and shore and ship, and made everything seem unreal.

She would miss Mordecai and Alma and Flavia's father and uncle. And beautiful Miriam. Nubia had no family to go back to. What if she and Kuanto couldn't find her clan? What if all her relatives had been captured by slave-dealers?

She remembered her father, lying on the blood-soaked sand, and her mother screaming and . . . no. She refused to think about that. She had Kuanto now. He would protect her. He would protect her as her eldest brother Taharqo would have protected her.

Presently they reached the ship. Its wooden side towered over them now, rocking and creaking gently. One by one, the others went up the rope ladder. Kuanto handed Nipur up to a pair of reaching hands and went up himself, as nimbly as a monkey. Then he helped Nubia up the ladder and over the ship's rail. As he lowered her gently onto the deck Nubia turned. And stifled a gasp.

Before her stood fifty children, bound and trembling with fear. Beside them men were binding the hands of Socrates, Phoebus and her other new slave-friends.

It was then that Nubia realised she had made a terrible mistake.

When Flavia saw the dark-skinned young man lift Nubia's puppy over the rail and put him on the deck she almost cried out. But she bit her lip and waited. Then he was helping Nubia over the rail and Flavia heard him say to the others, 'Don't tie this one up. She's with me.' He put his arm around Nubia's shoulder and Flavia heard him say, 'You are with me, aren't you?'

Nubia nodded, her face solemn and composed. She was looking around the ship at the bound children. For a moment her eyes locked with Flavia's but then passed on, betraying no recognition.

With his arm still around Nubia, the dark-skinned young man addressed the prisoners.

'My name is Fuscus,' he said. 'This is Crispus, the Patron's right hand man, and his brother Lucrio from Pompeii. Those are Sorex and Actius. That's Captain Murex at the helm. We are the pirates,' here he laughed, showing straight white teeth, 'and you are the booty! Behave yourselves and we'll treat you well. But I warn you. If you make the least trouble we'll toss you overboard.'

The Kalends of September dawned hazy and bright. The water was as smooth as milk and a gentle breeze filled the red and white striped sail, carrying the pirate ship sweetly towards the island of Caprea.

In the dark hold of the ship, the captive children stirred and groaned. The baby cried insistently, and Sperata tried to soothe him through her own tears.

Nubia came silently up the rough wooden stairs from the hold and stepped onto the deck, shivering a little in the cool morning air. Nipur followed, his claws tapping softly on the wooden deck.

She looked at the pirates, still asleep on their cloaks near the prow: Kuanto hidden under a blanket, Actius snoring on his back, Sorex curled up like a baby, Lucrio next to his brother Crispus. They had let her sleep on the couch in the cabin but it had been one of the worst nights of her life.

How could she have been so wrong about Kuanto? Since coming to this new land her instincts had never failed her. Until now. She had been tricked by someone from her own country.

Perhaps it was because the more words her head understood, the less truth her heart saw.

'And where have you been?' The quiet voice in her ear made her jump. Kuanto was not cocooned in his blankets. He was standing behind her.

'I was looking for the latrine.' She gave him her most solemn gaze.

Kuanto grinned. 'It's at the very front of the ship. There's a place you can sit over the water and do your business. But if you don't want everyone watching, I suggest you find a dark corner in the hold. It stinks down there anyway.'

Nubia nodded. 'I did.'

Kuanto showed his beautiful white teeth again. 'Come, let's celebrate with some spiced wine!'

He took her hand and led her back towards the helm. Captain Murex lay asleep on a folded blanket beside the open cabin. One of the crew held the steering paddle while another heated a pot of wine over a small brazier.

Nubia made herself smile at the sailor stirring the wine. He had a large red birthmark across one cheek.

'Here, let me,' she said, taking the spoon. She stirred the wine and when she thought no one was looking, she did what she had to do. Presently she ladled some of the dark, fragrant liquid into four ceramic beakers near the pot. She handed them to Kuanto and the two sailors and hoped they didn't notice her trembling hand.

'To freedom,' she said, and pretended to sip from the fourth beaker.

'To us!' said Kuanto, and drained his cup.

'Who are you really?' Nubia asked Kuanto in their native language, refilling his cup. 'Are you a slave?'

'Most of what I told you was true. I was a slave at an estate in Pausilypon. What I didn't tell you was that the estate is called Limon and it also belongs to the Patron. He owns several, you know. He's as rich as Crassus.' Kuanto sipped his spiced wine and stared at her.

'So you're one of Felix's slaves?'

'I'm his freedman. The Patron recruited me to be one of his soldiers, so now I work for him. Crispus is his second-in-command. Our job was to keep law and order among his many clients. That mainly meant catching runaway slaves and returning them to their owners, usually to be crucified. But it seemed such a waste that we made a few changes. We started selling some of the slaves we caught to passing slave-dealers. That way we make money, the slaves aren't executed, everybody's happy.' Kuanto drained his cup. Nubia refilled it.

'The Patron knew there would be plenty of run-aways after the volcano. He told us to recruit a few extra boys for the clean-up operation. So we brought in the three actors. Lucrio is Crispus's brother, but until now he lived in Pompeii. The actors are from Pompeii, too. They lost everything in the eruption, and they were out of work anyway, so they were ready for a change of career.'

'But they aren't just taking runaway slaves. They're taking freeborn children.'

'That was Lucrio's idea. In all the confusion, who's going to know? They took the daughter of one of the Patron's clients by mistake but even that worked to his advantage. We returned her, and now the old farmer's forever in his debt. It was my idea to hold the rich ones for ransom. That's where the real money is.'

'So Felix doesn't know about any of this?'

'Not a clue,' said Kuanto. 'He's lost touch of operations since he took up residence at that floating palace. Too busy composing poetry, if you ask me. But he built a good command structure. When Crispus says the Patron has given him an order people tend not to question it.'

Nubia stirred the wine thoughtfully and when little Sorex and big Actius came up, yawning and rubbing their eyes, she ladled some into beakers and handed them each a drink.

'What a nice start to the day.' Sorex slurped his drink noisily. 'Being served spiced wine by a dusky beauty. Lucrio! Wake up! It's time to have your morning cup and take inventory.'

As Nubia served Lucrio and Crispus, Sorex and Actius led the kidnapped children and the runaway slaves up from the hold.

'Over there! Stand by the rail!' squeaked Sorex, and pushed them across the deck. Soon they stood, wrists bound, shivering against the ship's starboard rail.

Captain Murex was awake now, too. He and his crew sipped their wine and watched the show.

Crispus went to the end of the line, wine cup in one hand and a birch switch in the other.

'Name?'

'Jonathan ben Mordecai.'

'Where are you from?' growled Crispus in his deep voice.

'Ostia.'

'Are your parents or relatives rich enough to pay a ransom for you?'

'I think so . . . we own a house . . .'

'Good enough. Stand on the other side.'

Jonathan stared at him blankly. Lucrio shoved him roughly across the deck to stand by the opposite rail.

'Name?' said Crispus, taking another sip of his wine.

'Flavia Gemina, daughter of Marcus Flavius Geminus, sea captain.'

'Sea captain, eh? He should be able to afford your ransom if he charges as much as Captain Murex. Stand over there . . .' He gave her a push towards Jonathan.

'Name?'

'Leda.'

'Where are you from?'

'She's just a slave,' said Lucrio.

'Right. You stay here.' He moved on to the next in line. 'Name?'

'Polla Pulchra, daughter of Publius Pollius Felix, your patron.'

Crispus's dark head jerked up and he peered at the

grubby, blood-smeared girl who stood before him. Then his long-lashed eyes opened wide in horror.

'Lucrio! You blockhead!' he bellowed. 'You've kidnapped the Patron's eldest daughter!'

SCROLL XXV

Nubia heard Kuanto curse under his breath.

'You idiot!' Crispus was saying to his brother. 'How could you have made such a blunder?' His face was pale with fury.

'It can't be her,' said Lucrio. 'I've seen the Patron's daughter. She's a prissy little blonde.'

'And what colour do you call this?' roared Crispus, holding up a lock of Pulchra's hair.

'I call it filthy,' said Lucrio with a smirk.

'It *is* her!' Kuanto went over to them. 'I'm sure of it!'

'Anyway, it wasn't me who took her!' said Lucrio. 'It was Sorex and Actius.'

'She wasn't acting like a noble-born girl,' grumbled Actius.

'Don't blame us!' said Sorex, licking his small red lips. 'You told us to grab as many kids as we could and we did. Those two were rolling in the dust, fighting like a pair of wildcats! How were we to know?'

'You fool!' Crispus ignored the actors and thrust his face close to Lucrio's. 'Do you realise the power the Patron has? Have you seen that thug Lucius Brassus? He'll crack your head like a pistachio shell!'

'So we give her back like you gave back the other one. Earn his undying gratitude.'

'We can't do that,' said Kuanto to Lucrio. 'Pulchra's not some timid farmer's daughter. She's bound to talk. Then Felix will discover what we've been doing all these years.'

'Pollux!' cursed Crispus. 'He'll hunt us all down. And he'll never forgive me. He'll have that giant Lucius Brassus chop me up into tiny pieces and throw me to the fishes!'

In the silence that followed, Nubia could hear the hiss of water against the keel, the creak of the rigging and the persistent cry of Sperata's baby.

'Shut that thing up!' Crispus screamed at Sperata. 'I'm trying to think. Shut him up or I swear I'll throw him overboard.'

Crispus had drawn the others aside for a conference. While they were occupied, Jonathan managed to catch Nubia's eye. He raised his eyebrows. Had she put the sleeping powder in the wine?

Nubia gave the merest nod of her head and looked away in case Kuanto noticed. Earlier that morning when she had gone down to the hold, Jonathan had told her about the powder in his neck-pouch and she had taken away the twist of papyrus.

Now, standing on the gently rocking deck, Jonathan couldn't understand what had gone wrong. The pirates should be snoring like babies by now. He knew because he had helped his father administer the sleeping powder many times before.

Flavia gave him a sideways glance, raising her own eyebrows in question. Jonathan shrugged, then frowned. Something was wrong. Very wrong.

The pirates had come out of their huddle and were moving towards him.

'They looked grim.

Lucrio gestured at Jonathan and Flavia. 'You might as well join the others.' His narrow face wore a sour expression. 'Go on! Back over to the other side!'

'But aren't you going to hold us for ransom?' asked Flavia.

'Not any more,' he muttered.

'What's happening?' Nubia asked Kuanto, as he rejoined her. He folded his arms and scowled at Lucrio.

'It's too risky to ransom them now, even though it means losing hundreds of thousands of sesterces. We're going to have to sell the whole lot cheap to the buyer. On condition that he sells them in the furthest corner of the world, Britannia maybe.' He glanced at her. 'If the Patron finds out what we did he would hunt us down, even in Alexandria.'

'What will you do with his daughter?'

'We can't let her go,' said Kuanto. 'She'd lead Felix straight to us. I voted to cut her throat and throw her overboard but Crispus refuses. So she'll be sold with the rest of them.'

'Where are we going now?' asked Nubia.

'To meet the buyer near the Blue Grotto in Caprea. As soon as we've collected the money we'll pay Captain Murex to take us to Alexandria. If we're lucky . . . if we're lucky . . . By the gods!' His eyes widened in horror.

'What?' asked Nubia, alarmed.

'Don't move!' he whispered. 'Right beside you . . . sand cobra! The biggest one I've ever seen!'

Nubia's heart skipped a beat. Of all desert creatures, the sand cobra was the deadliest.

'Where?' Her voice caught in her throat.

'Right there!' Sweat beaded his forehead and his pointing hand was trembling. 'Don't you see it? It's huge!'

Nubia followed his gaze, but all she could see was a rope coiled on the deck beside the rail.

Suddenly there was a cry from the rigging. Nubia and the others looked up. One of Captain Murex's crew was flapping his arms. It was the one with the birthmark who'd been heating the wine.

'I can fly,' he yelled.

Then he leapt into space and plummeted to the deck below.

At first Nubia thought the flying sailor was dead, but then she heard him groan. He tried to lift himself, then slumped back, unconscious. She noticed he wore a knife in his belt.

'What in Hades . . . ?' said Crispus, looking down at the man.

Suddenly Kuanto clung tightly to Crispus. 'Cobras! Cobras!' he shrieked.

Crispus rubbed his long-lashed eyes, then widened them, as if he, too saw the snakes. 'Great gods!' he cried, 'In the rigging! And there! And there! They're everywhere . . .'

While they gazed up at the sail, Nubia bent and swiftly removed the knife from the unconscious sailor's belt. None of the other sailors noticed; they were also beginning to point and scream. Suddenly there was a splash. One of them had jumped overboard.

Nubia edged over to Jonathan and cut the leather thongs around his wrists.

'I am thinking it was not sleeping powder you gave me to put in the wine,' she whispered, as she cut Flavia's bonds.

'I must have taken father's mushroom powder by mistake,' muttered Jonathan. 'It makes people see things that aren't there.'

Nubia cut Leda free and then moved on to Pulchra. For a brief moment the two girls gazed into each other's eyes; Pulchra looked away first. Nubia cut her bonds without a word and moved on to Rufus and the others.

Suddenly Pulchra screamed. Lucrio was running at them with a knife. 'Vermin!' he yelled. 'Rats and vermin!'

His knife embedded itself in the railing inches from Rufus's shoulder. The red-haired boy bent, grabbed Lucrio round the ankles and flipped him neatly over the ship's side. A moment later they heard a resounding splash. All the children cheered.

'Good work, Rufus!' said Flavia.

'Thanks.' He grinned and pulled the knife out of the railing. 'I work out in the palaestra.' He helped Nubia cut the others free.

Soon the children were running all over the deck, cheering and laughing and roaring at the remaining pirates and Captain Murex.

'Hey!' said Flavia. 'It's just like the picture in the cup. The pirates are jumping overboard! Look, Sorex! I'm a lion! I'm coming to get you!' She charged the little actor, roaring like a lion.

With a high-pitched squeal of fear Sorex leapt overboard, into the wine-dark sea.

Jonathan and Nubia joined Flavia. Their three heads peered over the rail.

'Is Sorex turning into a dolphin?' Jonathan asked.

'Doesn't look like it,' said Flavia.

'Behold!' said Nubia. 'He sinks like a stone!'

SCROLL XXVI

Flavia Gemina was tying Actius's hands together when she heard Jonathan call out: 'Hey, Flavia! Your father's a sea captain. How do you sail one of these things?'

Jonathan was back at the helm, struggling with the steering paddle.

'No idea!' she yelled back. Actius gazed up at her with fear-filled eyes. 'Grrr!' she growled. The big actor whimpered and pressed himself against the ship's rail.

Pulchra and Leda were binding Kuanto and Crispus back to back, winding the huge cobra rope around them.

'I found bread!' cried Rufus, coming up from the hold with a basket. The children yelled with delight and mobbed him. He laughed as they grabbed the flat discs and tore into them. It was ship's bread – brown and hard – but most of the children hadn't eaten in over three days.

Soon the basket was empty. 'There's more down in the hold,' said Rufus. 'I'll bring up another basket.'

'I'll help you,' said Melissa, the frizzy-haired girl. Together they disappeared down the stairs.

'Help!' cried Jonathan, wrestling the steering paddle.

'We keep going in the same direction. We've got to turn around. Otherwise we'll crash into the island.'

'I believe,' said old Socrates, coming up to him, 'that you need a man up in the rigging. Have any of you got experience as sailors?' he called to his fellow slaves. They all shook their heads at him.

'I'm good at climbing trees,' said Flavia. 'I'll go up!'

'I'll come with you,' said Nubia.

Flavia and Nubia started for the mast. Then they stopped and looked at each other. Then they hugged.

'Nubia, I'm so sorry! I was horrible to you! Please forgive me.'

Nubia nodded. 'You are all I have now. Please don't be angry if I am being stupid.' Her golden eyes were full of tears.

'You're not stupid,' said Flavia, holding her friend at arm's length and looking earnestly into her face. 'I meant the bulla was stupid because I was trying to impress that . . . that spider Felix.'

'Felix is not the spider,' said Nubia. 'Kuanto is the spider. And the other one. The Crispus. He pretends orders come from Felix.'

'Then Felix isn't behind all this?' said Flavia.

Nubia shook her head.

Flavia whooped with delight, and Nubia giggled behind her hand.

As they climbed the webbing up the mast, Nubia told Flavia what she had learned from Kuanto. How he and Crispus had been re-selling slaves and kidnapping freeborn children behind Felix's back.

'We must turn ship around soon,' concluded Nubia. 'Because the buyer is waiting behind this island.'

'Yes,' agreed Flavia. 'We have to get back to the Villa Limona. Oh, dear. The sail is too heavy. I don't think we can lift it. Can you pull that rope, Nubia? Nubia! What's wrong?'

There was a look of horror on Nubia's face as she stared towards the island. A ship was emerging from behind a cliff. As they watched, the ship's sail fluttered then ballooned as the wind filled it and pushed the vessel towards them. Both girls knew the sail well. It was a striped sail, yellow and black, like the colouring of a wasp. It was the sail of the slave-ship *Vespa*, and now they knew who the buyer was.

It was Venalicius the slave-dealer.

'The little sail at the front,' cried Jonathan. 'I think you turn the boat with the sail at the front! But you have to take the big one in first I think.'

'I can't!' Flavia sobbed, 'It's too heavy.'

'Come down,' yelled Rufus. 'We'll try to turn the ship anyway but it could be dangerous for you up there.'

Hand over hand, like monkeys, Flavia and Nubia descended loose ropes attached to the ends of the yard. When they were a few feet above the deck they jumped.

'Now!' cried Jonathan.

Rufus undid a rope and pulled at it. The ship shuddered and tipped alarmingly to one side.

'Hey!' some of the children yelled as they tumbled head over heel. The brazier and drugged wine tipped and spilled out over the deck.

'The coals!' cried Jonathan. 'Douse the coals or the ship will catch fire!'

The ship had righted itself with a groan but it had lost all momentum and there was no hope now of out-running the slave-ship.

'Jonathan, what is it?' said Flavia. 'Are you all right?'

Jonathan had been staring into space. Now he turned to her and said slowly, 'I think I've dreamed this.'

'Well, now is no time for dreaming. It's time to do something.'

'You're right,' said Jonathan and began to undo the belt of his tunic.

'What are you doing, Jonathan?' hissed Flavia.

'It's my sling!' said Jonathan proudly. 'It looks like a belt, but it's really a sling! Now what can I use as missiles? Something small but heavy . . .'

Nubia went to Kuanto and reached under the thick ropes binding him to Crispus. Shivering and babbling to themselves, they were oblivious to her. She pulled out a small leather pouch, opened it and tipped out a few heavy gold coins.

'Perfect!' cried Jonathan. 'Now we need a way to catch them off guard . . .' He scratched his curly head and looked around. Suddenly his face lit up.

'Chickpeas!' he shouted.

Flavia and the others looked at him as if he were mad.

'Down in the hold!' he said. 'I spent the night with my back against a sack of dried chickpeas! Listen care-fully. Here's what we'll do . . .'

The slave-ship had drawn up alongside them. From high in the rigging, Nubia watched her hated enemy jump down onto the deck of the ship. Three of his henchmen were with him; the other two remained on the *Vespa*.

Nubia forced herself to look down at his face. Venalicius's blind eye was white and milky and swollen in its socket. The other eye, small and bloodshot, contained enough malevolence for both. His left ear was missing and the wound was still red and weeping.

Venalicius held a razor-sharp dagger in one hand and swivelled his big head. Nubia prayed that Jonathan's plan would work: that he would see what he expected to see.

'What took you so long?' said old Socrates, putting on a good show of being irritable.

'Who are you?' sneered Venalicius.

'I'm Sorex. Actor and pirate. And here they are.' He made a dramatic flourish with one hand towards thirty children, all standing against the opposite rail of the ship with their hands apparently bound behind their backs.

'I thought there'd be more,' Venalicius grumbled. 'Still, they're a fine lot.' He walked along the line of miserable-looking children and Nubia saw him stop in front of Pulchra, who had volunteered to stay on deck. 'High quality,' said Venalicius, and fingered a strand of her hair. 'This one should clean up nicely.' He moved on. 'Well, well, well! The sea captain's daughter. You're a long way from home, my dear.'

Even from her perch high in the rigging Nubia saw Flavia shudder.

Venalicius nodded and looked around. 'Where's Crispus?'

'Right here!' said the younger Greek slave Phoebus, coming up from the hold. He was dark, like Crispus, and about the same height. 'Where's our money?'

'Not so fast,' said Venalicius. 'Who says we're going to pay you?' He nodded at his henchmen, who grinned and pulled out their daggers.

Phoebus saw the knives come out and he yelled the code-word at the top of his lungs: 'Chickpeas!'

'Beg pardon?' Venalicius squinted at him.

At that moment Flavia and Pulchra kicked over the sacks of chickpeas at their feet. As the tiny hard spheres rattled across the deck all the children lifted themselves up onto the rail.

'What the . . . ?' As one of Venalicius' big men took a step forward, his foot flew out in front of him and he crashed to the deck.

Jonathan appeared on the cabin roof and swung his sling. Another henchman fell unconscious. The gold coin which had struck him rolled across the deck.

'Don't move!' screamed Venalicius to his last man. 'Stay still!'

Hoping the man would obey, Nubia took careful aim. From her perch high in the rigging she threw a terracotta wine jug.

It shattered on the man's head and he sank gently to the deck.

Venalicius looked up and for a moment Nubia's blood ran cold as he spotted her. 'You!' he spat out. 'One of the Nubias!'

The first henchman was struggling to his feet. He looked round, saw Phoebus, and charged him again. Again he fell with a crash that shook the whole ship.

'Your guys aren't very bright, are they?' commented Jonathan, and he let fly with his sling.

A gold coin struck Venalicius in the centre of his forehead. He staggered and then fell on his bottom.

'Oof!' he grunted. He sat looking blearily around, half-stunned.

Nubia grabbed the end of a free rope and launched herself into space. She swung out and then down in a perfectly judged arc. Her feet connected with Venalicius' fat stomach and pushed him across the deck and hard up against the cabin wall.

'Burrf!' he gasped, both winded and stunned. Nubia dropped to the deck, one foot on either side of him, and sat hard on his chest. His horrible eyes were closed and a bright string of saliva emerged from the corner of his mouth.

Nubia wrenched the razor-sharp knife from the slave-dealer's hand and pressed it to his neck. If she slit his throat maybe the nightmares would end, not just for her but for others.

But she couldn't do it.

After a long moment, Nubia stood and stabbed the knife into the wall of the cabin and left it thrumming in the wood. Then she turned to find a length of rope with which to tie Venalicius.

The chickpeas had mostly rolled to the port side of the ship. Phoebus and the children were tying up Venalicius' three men. And the slave-ship *Vespa* was sailing away.

'Nubia! Look out!' Flavia screamed.

Nubia whirled to see Venalicius on his feet, staring at her in fury. One hand had closed on the handle of the dagger in the wall behind him. He was about to wrench it from the cabin wall.

Time seemed to move very slowly.

One motion of his arm and she was dead.

Then a figure with tangled hair head-butted Venalicius in his stomach.

He was down.

The knife was still in the cabin wall.

And now the children were swarming over him, tying his hands and legs and stomach until he was more rope than man.

Nubia turned and looked at her rescuer in amazement.

Polla Pulchra stood with her hands on her hips and her foot on the slave-dealer's neck. She grinned back at Nubia. Suddenly Pulchra's blue eyes focused on something behind Nubia and they widened in delight.

'Pater!' she squealed.

SCROLL XXVII

Lupus followed the Patron over the ship's rail.

The boy had swum across the cove and reached the Villa Limona at dawn to discover Felix just emerging from his study with Lupus's wax tablet in his hand. Felix had not gone to Rome the day before, just to the refugee camp. Pulchra had been right.

The only ones to notice the swift approach of Felix's racing yacht had been Venalicius' two crewmen. The slave-ship *Vespa* was now small on the horizon.

Pulchra ran squealing into her father's arms and Lupus allowed Flavia, Jonathan and Nubia to hug him, too. Nipur scampered up from the hold and skittered across the deck, barking and licking everyone.

'Pater!' Pulchra cried. 'They kidnapped us and tied us up and beat us and kept us in a grotto, but I head-butted the ugly one and I saved Nubia's life! Didn't I, Nubia?'

Nubia nodded and Lupus gave Pulchra a thumbs-up.

Jonathan lifted Nipur into his arms and turned to Lupus. 'Is Tigris . . . ?' Lupus gave him the thumbs-up, too. And he gave Flavia the thumbs-up for Scuto.

Pollius Felix looked around the ship in wonder. Behind him stood a dozen of his toughest soldiers, including the ugly giant Brassus.

'Lucius Brassus!' cried Pulchra, and threw her arms around him. 'He's really just a big softie!' she grinned over her shoulder at the others.

'Well,' said Felix, looking around at the happy, grubby children and their bound captives. 'Not much left for us to do! Shall we sail home again, Lupus, and leave them to it? Lupus?'

But Lupus did not hear him. He was standing over Venalicius, looking down at him. The slave-dealer lay on the deck, trussed up like a pig for slaughter. His single malevolent eye opened wide in terror.

Before anyone could move, Lupus wrenched the dagger from the cabin wall and in one savage motion he brought it down towards the slave-dealer's throat.

Flavia screamed as she saw the blood spurt from the slave-dealer's head.

He had writhed away and Lupus had only succeeded in cutting off the tip of his good ear. Now Venalicius screamed as he felt the searing pain.

Lupus screamed too as he lifted the dagger up and brought it down towards the slave-dealer's heart.

'NO!' cried Felix, lunging forward and catching Lupus's wrist. He wrenched the knife from the boy's hand and hurled it into the sea. Then he pulled Lupus away and held him tightly. Lupus thrashed and kicked and cried out incoherently but Felix did not let go. Finally Lupus's howls of rage became sobs which racked his body.

Felix was on his knees now, his arms still around Lupus, whispering soothing words in his ear.

Flavia stared.

She had never seen Lupus cry.

She had never seen anyone cry like that.

'Get him out of sight,' Felix said quietly to Brassus over Lupus's shoulder. Lucius Brassus nodded, lifted Venalicius with one massive hand and took him down to the hold.

That afternoon, fifty-two very grubby children made use of the private baths at the Villa Limona. Afterwards, they were given new yellow tunics to replace their old ones. Then they were fed: roast chicken, salad and white rolls, with dried fig-cakes for dessert.

Before the sun set, most of them were sailing back to the refugee camp on the Patron's yacht. Felix had promised to deploy all his clerks and scribes and his vast network of contacts to reunite these children with their families.

As for the twelve runaway slaves, Felix had promised them their freedom as a reward for helping to save his daughter. If any of their masters still lived, he would pay to redeem them.

Flavia, Jonathan, Nubia, Lupus, Pulchra and Leda were asleep before the first star had appeared in the sky and they slept late into the morning of the following day.

A strange, soft muttering woke Nubia, and she stretched and yawned. She felt Nipur stir at the foot of her bed.

'Nubia?' came Flavia's voice from the other bed. 'Are you awake?'

'Yes.' The light that filled the bedroom was pearly grey, though it must be nearly midday.

'Lupus tried to kill Venalicius, didn't he?' said Flavia quietly.

'Yes,' said Nubia. 'He is hating him more than even me or you.'

'I wonder why?'

They were quiet for a moment and Nubia heard the pattering become a soft wet drumming. The air smelled different.

'Nubia?'

'Yes?'

'What did Venalicius mean when he said you were one of the Nubias?'

'He was naming us all Nubia. All the girls he takes from my clan.'

'You mean your real name isn't Nubia?'

'No.'

Nubia heard Flavia's bed creak as she sat up. 'What is it?'

'My name is Shepenwepet, daughter of Nastasen, of the leopard clan.'

'Wepenshepet?'

'Shepenwepet.'

'Oh,' said Flavia. 'Shall I call you that from now on?'

'No. I am used to wearing Nubia now. It is my new name for my new life.'

The strange wet drumming outside their room had become a chuckling and gurgling in the gutters.

'What is that sound?' Nubia asked Flavia.

'What? Oh. Sounds like rain.'

Nubia sat up in bed and looked at the grey sky between the white pillars of the colonnade. But it was not an ashy grey. It was a wet, fresh, bright grey.

'Rain,' she whispered, almost to herself. Flavia, rumpled and sleepy, looked up from scratching Scuto behind the ear.

'Rain!' said Nubia. Scuto and Nipur lifted their heads to look at her, too.

She jumped up from her bed.

In the peristyles and courtyards of the Villa Limona, the slaves who had been commanded not to make the least noise heard Nubia cry 'Rain!'

She ran out into the colonnade. Flavia and the dogs followed her curiously and the boys came out of their bedroom, rubbing their eyes and yawning. Nubia stretched out her hand to feel the drops, but the colonnade was sheltered so she hurried up the stairs to the inner garden. The others followed.

'Rain,' said Nubia, standing in the garden by the lemon tree and looking around her. A soft, steady downpour was washing the crusted ash from tree and shrub. On the mountain slopes the grey vineyards and olive trees were melting to green before her eyes.

The thirsty soil beneath her bare feet drank the rain with tiny squeaks and exhaled a rich, dark perfume. In the trees the birds began singing. Nubia lifted her face to the heavens and let the cool rain wash over her. She stretched out her arms and twirled and laughed.

She had found her way from the Land of Grey into the Land of Green.

By dusk the fast, low-moving clouds were disappearing over the horizon to the southwest. The rain had washed the hills and scrubbed the sky, which was a vibrant magenta.

They had all gathered for dinner in Polla's yellow triclinium. A slave lit the lamps while Leda handed myrtle garlands to the diners. Her clean hair was pinned up with four new ivory hairpins and her face transformed by a smile.

Beneath the couches Scuto and the puppies were already crunching marrowbones. They had been bathed and brushed and were on their best behaviour.

Felix reclined beside his wife, whose face was not as pale as usual.

'Patron,' said Flavia, adjusting her garland. 'My father told me that if you invite a slave to recline with you at dinner it means you are setting them free. Is that true?'

Felix nodded. 'I believe it is. Technically a slave has to be over thirty before you can free them, but no one can enforce that.'

Flavia raised her eyebrows at him to say: May I?

Felix closed his eyes and gave a small nod.

Flavia looked around the room at old friends and new. They all looked back expectantly.

'Nubia,' she said in a clear voice. 'Nubia. In front of all these witnesses, I invite you to recline with me here on this couch. Will you accept?'

'No,' replied Nubia softly.

Flavia twisted round on the couch. 'What? You won't recline? Don't you want to be free?'

Nubia shook her head. 'I don't want to leave you and Jonathan and Lupus,' she whispered. 'I have no family, no home, nowhere to go . . .'

'But you won't have to leave us!' cried Flavia. 'Whether you decide to be free or not, you will always be part of our family. But don't you think it's better to be free and stay by choice than to be a slave and have no choice?'

'Very well. Then I am choosing to be free and to be in your family.' Nubia walked round the couch and solemnly reclined beside her former mistress.

Flavia took the garland from her head and placed it on Nubia's. Then they ate the dishes set before them and drank the drink of the god Dionysus.

'Nubia,' said Pollius Felix, when the serving-girls had cleared away the dessert course. 'Now that you are a free girl will you consent to sit by me for a moment?'

Nubia glanced at Flavia, who smiled and nodded.

Gracefully Nubia rose and went to the couch on which Felix and Polla reclined. She sat at the end.

Felix beckoned Pulchra, who came to his couch and held something out to Nubia.

'I am sorry I broke your lotus-wood flute, Nubia,' said Pulchra. 'Pater and I have bought you another one. Please accept it as a gift on the day of your freedom.'

Nubia took the flute. It was made of a beautiful cherry-coloured wood. She looked up at Pulchra with glistening eyes. Impulsively Pulchra bent and kissed her dark cheek, then whispered in Nubia's ear, 'Thank you for saving me.'

'Thank you for saving *me*.' Nubia smiled through her tears.

Pulchra returned to her couch and Nubia looked at Felix, who was tuning his lyre.

'Thank you, Patron,' she said.

He looked up at her with his dark eyes and nodded.

'You have taught us quite a lot, Nubia the ex-slave girl.' As he finished tuning his third string he said casually, 'Oh, Lupus, I believe you'll find a goatskin drum under your couch. Will you accompany us?'

Lupus brought forth a small drum. It was copper inlaid with silver, with a pumiced goatskin taut across its surface.

He looked at Felix with shining eyes and nodded.

'Tomorrow at noon,' said Felix, placing the lyre against his left shoulder, 'a warship arrives from Misenum. It will take you to the refugee camp to pick up Flavia's uncle and tutor, as well as Jonathan's father and sister. I will accompany you that far. Then the warship will take you on to Ostia. This is my gift to all of you, for giving me back my precious daughter and for opening my eyes.'

Polla squeezed her husband's hand and he looked at her, surprised. For a long moment they looked at one another with affection. Then Felix bowed his head. When he lifted it again Flavia saw that his eyes were wet with tears.

'That is tomorrow,' he said at last. 'But tonight . . . tonight we have many things to celebrate and to my mind there is only one way to express our feelings. We will play music.'

He looked at Nubia and smiled.

'You begin.'

FINIS

THE LAST SCROLL

Many people who visit the Bay of Naples to explore Pompeii make the town of Sorrento (ancient Surrentum) their base. The pretty harbour town is located on one of the most beautiful peninsulas in the world amid lemon groves and vineyards. From here, the *Circumvesuviana* railway makes it easy to visit the cities of Vesuvius.

South of Sorrento town on the Cape of Sorrento you will find an extremely well-preserved Roman road. Follow it down through ancient olive groves, and you will come to the remains of an opulent Roman villa right on the water. Many historians believe it belonged to a rich and cultured man named Pollius Felix. Their evidence is a poem written by a poet named Statius, a client of Felix. In his poem Statius describes Felix's villa, which is very like the Roman villa on the Cape of Sorrento.

Further up the coast – sheltered from Vesuvius by tall mountains – is a pretty spa town. Vico Equense is mostly built on the slopes but there is a small beach where you can still drink mineral water so full of iron that it turns your tongue red.

ARISTO'S SCROLL

Aeneas (ee-*nee*-uss)
> mythological hero, Trojan son of the goddess Venus, he escaped from Troy to have many adventures and finally settle in what would become Rome

Aeneid (ee-*nee*-id)
> long poem by the famous poet Virgil about the Roman hero Aeneus

Achilles (ack-*ill*-eez)
> mythological hero, Greek son of mortal Peleus and the sea-nymph Thetis

Alexandria (al-ex-*and*-ree-uh)
> port of Egypt and one of the greatest cities of the ancient world

amphitheatre (*am*-pee-theatre)
> an oval-shaped stadium for watching gladiator shows and beast fights

amphora (am-*for*-a)
> large clay storage jar for holding wine, oil or grain

Ariadne (arry-*ad*-nee)
> mythological Cretan princess who helped Theseus overcome the Minotaur; when he abandoned her on the island of Naxos, Dionysus comforted her

atrium (*eh*-tree-um)
>   the reception room in larger Roman homes, often with a rectangular skylight and rainwater pool beneath it

brazier (*braze*-yer)
>   coal-filled metal bowl on legs, used to heat a room

bulla (*bull*-a)
>   amulet of leather or metal worn by many freeborn children in Roman times

Caprea (kap-*ray*-uh)
>   modern Capri, an island off the coast of Italy near Sorrento (also known as Capreae)

capsa (*kap*-suh)
>   cylindrical leather case, usually for medical equipment or scrolls

carruca (ka-*roo*-ka)
>   a four-wheeled travelling coach, often covered

Castor (*kass*-tor)
>   one of the two mythological twins known as the Gemini, his brother is Pollux

Catullus (kuh-*tull*-uss)
>   Latin poet who lived *c.* 84–54 BC, famous for his love poems

centaur (*sen*-tor)
>   mythological creature: half man, half horse

centurion (sent-*yur*-ee-on)
>   soldier in the Roman army in charge of at least a hundred men

ceramic (sir-*am*-ik)
>   clay which has been fired in a kiln, very hard and usually smooth

Cerberus (*sir*-bur-uss)
> mythological three-headed dog who guarded the gates of the underworld

cicada (sick-*ah*-duh)
> an insect like a grasshopper that chirrs during the day

Claudius (*klaw*-dee-uss)
> Roman emperor (ruled AD 41–54) who built the harbour two miles north of Ostia

client
> in ancient Rome a client was someone who received help from a more powerful patron; in return the client performed various services for his patron

colonnade (*kol*-uh-nade)
> a covered walkway lined with columns

Dionysus (dye-oh-*nye*-suss)
> Greek god of vineyards and wine, also known as Bacchus

en (en)
> Latin word which means 'behold!' or 'look!'

finis (*feen*-iss)
> Latin for 'the end'

Flavia (*flay*-vee-uh)
> feminine form of Flavius (which means 'fair-haired'), a common Roman name

forum (*for*-um)
> ancient marketplace and civic centre in Roman towns

freedman (*freed*-man)
> slave who has been granted freedom by his master, who then becomes his patron

fresco (*fress*-ko)
> a painting done on the fresh plaster of a wall, when it is still wet; when the plaster dries the painting becomes part of the wall

garland (gar-land)
    wreath of of flowers and often ivy, worn at dinner parties
Gemina (*jem*-in-uh)
    Roman name meaning 'twin'; Geminus and Gemini are
    other forms
gratis (*grah*-tiss)
    Latin word which means 'for free'
Herculaneum (herk-you-*lane*-ee-um)
    the 'town of Hercules' at the foot of Vesuvius northwest
    of Pompeii; it was buried by mud in the eruption of AD
    79; has now been partially excavated
hours
    the Romans counted the hours of the day from dawn,
    dividing the daylight into twelve hours and the night into
    twelve hours; this meant the 'hours' of daylight were
    'longer' in summer and 'shorter' in winter
Ides (eyedz)
    one of the three key dates in the Roman month; they fell
    on the 13th day of most months, but in March, May, July
    and October they fell on the 15th day of the month.
impluvium (im-*ploo*-vee-um)
    rainwater pool under a rectangular skylight in the atrium
    of a Roman house
Judaea (joo-*dee*-uh)
    ancient province of the Roman Empire, modern Israel
Juno (*joo*-no)
    queen of the Roman gods, wife of the god Jupiter; her
    Greek counterpart is Hera
Kalends (*kal*-ends)
    Latin for the first day of the month in a Roman calendar

kylix (*kie*-liks)
  elegant Greek drinking cup with a shallow, flat bowl, especially for dinner parties
Laurentum (lore-*en*-tum)
  small town on the coast of Italy a few miles south of Ostia
Lupus (*loo*-puss)
  Roman name which means 'wolf'
mantle (*man*-tul)
  a length of cloth which could be draped round the body and used to cover the head; Roman women wore the mantle for modesty as well as protection
Minerva (min-er-vuh)
  Roman goddess of war and wisdom, her Greek counterpart is Athena
Misenum (my-*see*-num)
  modern Capo di Miseno, ancient Rome's chief naval harbour, near the commercial port of Puteoli on the northern shore of the Bay of Naples
Mordecai (*mord*-uk-eye)
  Hebrew man's name
Neapolis (ne-*ah*-po-liss)
  modern Naples, a large city in the south of Italy near Vesuvius
necropolis (neck-*rop*-o-liss)
  'city of the dead' or graveyard, always outside the city walls in Roman times
Nuceria (noo-*kerry*-uh)
  modern Nocera, a small town near Vesuvius, several miles east of Pompeii
Oplontis (oh-*plon*-tiss)
  modern Torre Annunziata, a coastal village near Pompeii

Ostia (*oss*-tee-uh)
   modern Ostia Antica, the port of ancient Rome and
   home town of Flavia Gemina
Paestum (*pie*-stum)
   Greek colony south of Sorrento, site of an impressive
   Doric temple
palaestra (pa-*lice*-tra)
   exercise area of the baths, usually enclosed but open to
   the sky
papyrus (pa-*pie*-russ)
   the cheapest writing material, made of Egyptian reeds
   pounded together
parapet (*pare*-uh-pet)
   a low wall usually at the edge of a ledge or balcony
pater (pah-*tare*)
   the Latin word for 'father'
patrician (pa-*trish*-un)
   person from highest social class of Roman citizens
patron (*pay*-tron)
   a man who gave help, protection and support to people
   less rich or powerful than himself; they were his clients
   and they performed services for him in return
Pausilypon (pow-*sil*-lip-on)
   modern Posillipo, a coastal town near Naples across the
   Bay from Sorrento
pax (paks)
   Latin for 'peace'
peristyle (*perry*-stile)
   a row of columns around a garden or courtyard
Pliny (*plin*-ee)
   (full name Gaius Plinius Secundus) famous Roman who

was a prolific scholar and admiral of the Roman fleet at Misenum; later known as Pliny the Elder

Pollux (*pol*-uks)

one of the two mythological twins known as the Gemini, his brother is Castor

Pompeii (pom-*pay*)

prosperous coastal town south of Rome on the Bay of Naples, buried by eruption of Vesuvius in AD 79; has now been partially excavated

Puteoli (poo-tee-*oh*-lee)

modern Pozzuoli, the main commercial port on the Bay of Naples in Roman times

Roman numerals

the Romans used capital letters to stand for numbers; here are a few Roman numerals and their equivalents.

I = 1	VI = 6	XI = 11	XVI = 16
II = 2	VII = 7	XII = 12	XVII = 17
III = 3	VIII = 8	XIII = 13	XVIII = 18
IV = 4	IX = 9	XIV = 14	XIX = 19
V = 5	X = 10	XV = 15	XX = 20
L = 50	C = 100	D = 500	M = 1000

salve! (*sal*-vay)

Latin for 'hello'

Saturnalia (sat-urn-*ale*-ya)

Roman mid-winter festival in honour of the god Saturn which included feasting and the giving of gifts; the holiday began on 17 December and lasted a week

scroll (skrole)
    a papyrus or parchment 'book', usually unrolled from
    side to side as it was read
sesterces (sess-*tur*-seez)
    more than one sestertius, a brass coin
signet-ring (*sig*-net ring)
    ring with an image carved in it, which could be pressed
    into soft wax as a personal seal
solarium (sole-*air*-ee-um)
    a sunny room, usually in public baths, for resting, read-
    ing, and beauty treatment
Stabia (*stab*-ee-uh)
    modern Castellammare di Stabia, a town to the south of
    Pompeii (also known as Stabiae)
stola (*stol*-uh)
    a woman's dress, usually worn by married women
strigil (*strij*-ill)
    metal instrument like a blunt sickle for scraping oil, dust,
    sweat and dead skin off the body after a workout and
    before proceeding to the warm or cold plunge in the
    baths
stylus (*stile*-us)
    a metal, wood or ivory tool for writing or drawing on
    wax tablets
Surrentum (sir-*wren*-tum)
    modern Sorrento, a pretty harbour town south of
    Vesuvius and the Bay of Naples
tablinum (tab-*lee*-num)
    the study in a Roman house; traditionally where a patron
    received early morning visits from his clients

Thetis (*thet*-iss)
  mythological sea-nymph; she was mother of Achilles and
  foster-mother of Vulcan
Titus (*tie*-tuss)
  (full name Titus Flavius Vespasianus) elder son of
  Vespasian, he became emperor after his father died in
  July AD 79
toga (*toe*-ga)
  a blanket-like outer garment mainly worn by upper-class
  Roman men
toga virilis (*toe*-ga vi-*reel*-iss)
  pure-white toga worn by Roman boys after their 16th
  birthday
Torah (*tor*-ah)
  a Hebrew word which means 'instruction' and can refer
  to either the first five books of the 'Old Testament' or the
  entire Hebrew Bible
triclinium (trick-*leen*-yum)
  the ancient Roman dining room, so called because it
  usually had three dining-couches on which up to three
  adults each could recline to eat
tunic (*tyoo*-nik)
  piece of clothing like a big T-shirt; boys and girls usually
  wore a long-sleeved one
Tyrrhenian (tie-*reen*-ee-an)
  name of the sea off the western coast of Italy
Venalicius (ven-a-*lee*-kee-us)
  Roman name which means 'slave-dealer'
Vespasian (vess-*pay*-zhun)
  (full name Titus Flavius Vespasianus) Roman emperor
  who ruled from AD 69–79

Vesuvius (vuh-*soo*-vee-yus)
>the famous volcano near Naples, which erupted on 24th August AD 79

Vinalia (vee-*nahl*-ya)
>late summer wine festival sacred to Venus held every August 19th

Virgil (*vur*-jill)
>Latin poet who lived *c.* 70–19 BC; *The Aeneid* is his masterpiece

Vulcan (*vul*-kan)
>Roman blacksmith god, he was son of Jupiter and Juno and husband to Venus

Vulcanalia (vul-kan-*ale*-ya)
>two-day Roman festival of Vulcan, held every August 23rd and 24th

wax tablet
>a wax-covered rectangle of wood for writing and note-taking; when the wax was scratched away with a stylus, the wood beneath showed as a mark

——— The Roman Mysteries ———

I THE THIEVES OF OSTIA

In the bustling, cosmopolitan port of Ostia, near Rome, a killer is at large. He is trying to silence the watchdogs. Flavia Gemina and her three new friends – Jonathan, Lupus and Nubia – follow the trail to find out why.

II THE SECRETS OF VESUVIUS

The four friends are staying near Pompeii, and trying to solve a strange riddle, when Mount Vesuvius erupts and they must flee for their lives. A thrilling account of one of the greatest natural disasters of all time.

III THE PIRATES OF POMPEII

The four friends discover that children are being kidnapped from the camps where hundreds of refugees are sheltering after the eruption of Vesuvius, and proceed to solve the mystery of the pirates of Pompeii.

IV THE ASSASSINS OF ROME

Jonathan disappears and his friends trace him to the Golden House of the Emperor Nero in Rome, where they learn the terrible story of what happened to his family in Jerusalem – and face a deadly assassin.

V THE DOLPHINS OF LAURENTUM

Off the coast of Laurentum, near Ostia, is a sunken wreck full of treasure. The friends are determined to retrieve it – but so is someone else. An exciting adventure which reveals the secret of Lupus's past.

VI THE TWELVE TASKS OF FLAVIA GEMINA

It's December AD 79, and time for the Saturnalia festival, when anything goes. There's a lion on the loose in Ostia – and Flavia has reason to suspect the motives of a Roman widow who is interested in her father.

VII THE ENEMIES OF JUPITER

Emperor Titus summons the children to help him find the mysterious enemy who seeks to destroy Rome through plague and fire. Jonathan is distracted by a secret mission of his own, and suddenly everything gets terrifyingly out of control.

VIII THE GLADIATORS FROM CAPUA

One hundred days of games are to be held to celebrate the opening of the new Flavian amphitheatre. Hoping to find Jonathan, the friends organise an invitation to Rome, where they encounter wild beasts, criminals, conspirators and gladiators.

IX THE COLOSSUS OF RHODES

The sailing season has begun. Lupus decides to see if his mother is still alive and to follow his uncle's dying wish. The friends sail to the island of Rhodes, site of one of the seven wonders of the ancient world, and base of a criminal mastermind.

X THE FUGITIVE FROM CORINTH

In Cenchrea, the eastern harbour of Corinth, Aristo, the children's tutor, is found with a knife in his hand crouched over Flavia's father, who has been stabbed. When he escapes, the friends set off for Delphi in pursuit.